"I can't 🕊 P9-ELS-547 with you right now, Grey."

His arms tightened around her, his head lowered, and his lips covered hers in a searing kiss. The room started spinning again; it was not caused by her head this time but by her heart. She stood on her tiptoes and kissed him back, feeling a shiver run through her body. Grace kneaded his shoulders with her fingers, pulling him closer, deepening their kiss. She was floating on air, and it wasn't until she felt a hard surface against her bottom that Grace realized Grey had set her on the counter. He moved her knees apart with his legs and nestled himself firmly against her.

"It's too late, Grace," he said, breaking their kiss to stare down at her with eyes the color of winter spruce. "It's already begun, and there's no going back. Forget what your mind says, and listen to what your body is telling you."

CHARMING
THE
HIGHLANDER

JANET
CHAPMAN

POCKET BOOKS

New York London Toronto Sydney Singapore

An *Original* Publication of POCKET BOOKS

POCKET BOOKS, a division of Simon & Schuster, Inc.
1230 Avenue of the Americas, New York, NY 10020

ISBN: 0-7434-5306-9

First Pocket Books printing February 2003

10 9 8 7 6 5 4 3 2 1

POCKET and colophon are registered trademarks of Simon & Schuster, Inc.

For information regarding special discounts for bulk purchases, please contact Simon & Schuster Special Sales at 1-800-456-6798 or business@simonandschuster.com

Book design by Alyssa Taragano
Front cover illustration by Jung Min Choi
Photo credit: Sime s.a.s./PictureQuest
Back cover illustration by Jon Paul Ferrara

Printed in the U.S.A.

This one is for Robbie,

who stood guard at the gate all these years, refusing to let the world intrude on my dream.

For your patience, support, and strength to shoulder the load, for being a rock through the currents of life—quite simply put, thank you.

It's been twenty-five years, husband, and the journey only gets better.

Prologue

The Highlands of Scotland, A.D. 1200

It was a hellish day to be casting a spell. The relentless glare of the sun nearing its zenith reflected off the parched landscape in waves of stifling heat. Occasional dust devils, pushed into action by an arid breeze, were the only movement in the gleann below. Even the birds refused to stir from the protective shade of the thirsty oak forest.

Leaning heavily on his ancient cherrywood staff for support, Pendaär slowly picked his way to the top of the bluff, silently scolding himself for making the climb in full ceremonial dress. More than once the aging wizard had to stop and free his robe when it snagged on a bush.

God's teeth, but he was tired.

Pendaär stopped and leaned against a boulder to catch his breath, pushing his now damp, long white hair from his face as he searched the road below for any sign of the MacKeages. Thank the stars, he'd soon be leaving this god-forsaken place. He'd had his fill of this harsh time, of the constant struggle for survival, and of the incessant, senseless wars between arrogant men fighting for power and position.

Yes, he was more than ready to discover the comforts of a much more modern world.

Pendaär shook his robes and brushed at the dust gathering near the hem, once again cursing the heavenly bodies for marching into perfect alignment on such a godawful day. But Laird Greylen MacKeage was about to begin a most remarkable journey, and Pendaär was determined to have a good seat for the send-off. Anxious to get into position, the tired wizard pushed away from his resting place and continued up the hill.

Once he finally reached the summit, he settled himself on an outcropping of granite and lifted his face to the sun, letting the warm breeze rustle his hair and cool his neck. When he was finally able to breathe without panting, Pendaär brought his gnarled cherrywood staff to his lap and fingered the burls in the wood, slowly repeating the words of his spell, concentrating on reciting them correctly.

Thirty-one years of painstaking work was culminating today. Thirty-one years of watching over and worrying about the powerful, oftentimes hell-raising laird of the clan MacKeage was finally coming to fruition. The sun had nearly reached its zenith. The celestial bodies were falling into alignment.

And Greylen MacKeage was late.

Pendaär wasn't surprised. The boy had been late for his own birth by a good two weeks. And now he was in danger of missing the very destiny the stars had promised thirty-two years ago, on the night of the young laird's conception.

Greylen MacKeage carried the seed of Pendaär's successor.

Greylen's match, however, had been born in twentieth-century America. And getting the two of them together was causing the aging wizard untold fits of frustration.

It would help, of course, if he knew who the woman was.

And that was the problem. The powers-that-be had a heartless and sometimes warped sense of humor, giving Pendaär the choice of knowing only the man or the woman who would beget his heir, but not both.

Pendaär had chosen the spell that would show him Greylen MacKeage. Then he had spent the first thirty-one years of Greylen's life trying to keep him alive. It had not been an easy task. The MacKeages were a small but mighty clan who seemed to have more enemies than most. They were constantly at war with one tribe or another, and their brash young laird insisted on riding up front into battle.

But it was the woman Pendaär wished to know more about now. Was she beautiful? Intelligent? Did she have the spunk and the courage necessary to match up with a man like Greylen MacKeage? Surely the other half of this magical couple would have what it takes to give birth to a wizard. Wouldn't she?

Pendaär had spent many sleepless nights with such worries. He had even gone so far as to visit the northwestern mountains of Maine, eight hundred years into the future, in hopes of recognizing the woman. But the spell that protected her was sealed, and no magic he possessed would unlock it.

Only the man destined to have her could find her. In his own way and on his own terms, only Greylen MacKeage could claim the woman the ancients had chosen as his mate.

If, that is, he ever showed up.

Nearly an hour passed before Greylen and three of his warriors rounded the bend in the rutted path and finally came into sight. And what a sight they were. The MacKeages rode in silence, single file, on powerful warhorses they controlled with seemingly little effort. The men were dirty, and maybe a bit tired from their long journey, but they appeared to have made the trip without mishap.

Pendaär scrambled to his feet. It was time. He pushed back the sleeves of his gown and pointed his staff at the sky, closing his eyes as he began to chant the spell that would call forth the powers of nature.

A battle cry suddenly pierced the air.

Greylen MacKeage brought his warhorse to a halt and pulled his sword free of its sheath at the sound, seeing the mounted warriors rushing toward him from the cover of the trees. They were masked in war paint, in full battle dress, their swords held high as they descended upon Greylen and his small band of travelers.

It was the MacBains, the ambushing bastards.

Greylen's brother, Morgan, immediately moved to his side, and Grey's other two men quickly flanked them to form an imposing wall of might. Greylen looked first to his right and then to his left before returning his attention to his enemy and, with a grin of anticipation, raised his sword and answered the call to battle with a shout of his own. Spurring their horses forward, the four MacKeage warriors charged the MacBains, their laughter quickly lost in the sounds of battle.

Greylen had not sought out this fight, but, by God, if Michael MacBain wanted to die today, Grey would be kind enough to help the blackheart to hell.

If, that is, he could keep Ian from dispatching the bastard first. A good five years past his prime, Ian MacKeage was fighting like a man possessed, and it was all Greylen could do to guard his old friend's back while protecting his own. The smell of horse sweat rose with the dust kicked up by the battle; the taste of blood, bile, and anger burned at the back of Greylen's throat.

His horse stumbled from the charge of MacBain's horse, and Grey ducked to the right and swung his arm in an arc, striking Michael MacBain square on the back with the flat of his sword. The blow would have unseated a lesser man, but MacBain merely laughed out loud and turned his horse away.

This battle was an exercise in futility, and both men knew it. Six MacBains to four MacKeages was hardly fair. It would take another half dozen MacBains to even the fight, and Greylen wondered again at Michael's intent today.

Was the young man only looking for sport? Maybe pricking Greylen's anger? Or had he grown tired of waiting for Grey's retaliation?

Aye. Michael was weary of watching his back these last three years and was now trying to force a war that Greylen had no intention of declaring. No one woman, no matter how innocent and long dead, was worth an entire clan rising in arms against another. Michael need not die today to feel damnation's fires. Greylen would bet his sword arm that MacBain was already well acquainted with Hades.

A brilliant flash of light high on the hill caught Greylen's attention, and he pivoted his warhorse to get a better view. A lone figure stood on the bluff, full robes billowing in the rising wind, tangled white hair obscuring his face. His arms were outstretched, raised against a darkening sky, one hand holding a stick that glowed like the coals of a long-burning fire.

Grey darted a quick look back at the battle and saw Michael MacBain suddenly pull his own horse to a stop and look toward the bluff. But before Grey could dwell on what he was seeing, he and MacBain were both pulled back into the battle that Grey suddenly had no desire to fight.

Pendaär closed his eyes and loudly chanted the spell of his ancestors. Lightning crackled around him, lifting his hair from his neck as the wind molded his robes to his legs. Light burned from beneath his eyelids, and the old wizard staggered under the assault.

The sounds of the battle below rose louder.

Pendaär slowly opened his eyes and glared at the weathered, burl-knotted staff in his hand. Nothing had happened. He looked back at the gleann. Those lawless MacBains were still plaguing the MacKeages.

He raised his staff again and commanded the clouds to boil, the winds to howl, and the rains to fall. He reached deep within his soul and summoned the power of the ancients, adding their strength to his own fourteen hundred years of wizardry. Greylen MacKeage must not be harmed this day. He had a much more noble destiny, one that would take him on a journey the likes of which few mortal men had known.

With his legs spread wide and his feet planted firmly on the bluff, Pendaär braced himself for the familiar jolt of energy he was about to release. His head raised and his arms outstretched, he spoke his wizard's language more slowly to cast his spell of time over matter. His long white hair became charged with electricity once again, and every muscle in his body trembled with power.

And still nothing happened.

With a mighty roar of frustration, Pendaär hurled the cherrywood rod at the boulder he had been sitting on. The staff bounced once and crackled to life before it was suddenly grabbed by a bolt of lightning. It floated high over the gleann, arcs of energy shooting from it in every direction.

A great darkness descended over the land. The clash of steel, shouts of men, and pounding of giant hooves gave way to deafening booms of thunder. A torrential rain poured down, casting a sheet of confusion over the chaos. Trees bent until they snapped. Boulders split, and rocks tumbled free from the bluff where Pendaär stood.

And Pendaär fell with them, rolling head over feet, his now soaked robes tangling around him as he struggled to find purchase on the rockslide. Rain and mud and rocks and shrubs crashed down the side of the bluff, pulling the wizard with them.

And when the turmoil finally ceased, Pendaär landed with a jarring thud, faceup in a puddle of mud. The sun returned, beating down on his face with enough strength to make him squint.

But it was the silence that finally made him stir. The old wizard slowly sat up and pushed the hair from his face, looking around. Then he rubbed his eyes with his fists and looked again, before burying his head in his hands with a groan of dismay.

What had he done?

Yes, Greylen MacKeage had certainly begun his journey this day, but it seemed the warrior did not travel alone.

Because not one MacKeage remained to continue the fight. Not one of the ambushing MacBains could be seen. Even their horses had disappeared with the storm. Naught was left of the battle but trodden mud, churned grass, and the fading rumble of distant thunder.

Pendaär gaped at the empty gleann.

He hadn't gone with them.

Greylen MacKeage, his men, and those damned MacBains had traveled through time without him. God's teeth! They were in the twenty-first century without direction or purpose, and he was sitting here like a wart on a toad, having no idea where his contrary staff had run off to.

Pendaär scrambled to his feet and began to search for it, wringing his hands and muttering curses as he ran frantically in circles. He needed to be with the warriors. He needed to see that they didn't kill each other, or kill some innocent twenty-first-century person who might unwittingly stumble upon them.

Pendaär searched for half an hour before finding his staff. It was standing upright in a puddle of mud, still quivering with volatile energy. The wizard lifted his robes and stepped into the puddle, grasping the humming staff and tugging, trying to free it. The cherrywood hissed and violently twisted, apparently still angry at being thrown away.

Pendaär ignored its grumbling, giving it a mighty tug that sent him sprawling backward onto the wet ground. He clutched the staff to his chest and muttered a prayer for patience.

It took the wizard another twenty minutes to soothe the disgruntled cherrywood, running his hands gently over the burls as he whispered his apologies.

The staff slowly calmed, and Pendaär finally stood up. He urged the cherrywood to grow again, to draw the powers of the universe back to his hand. The staff lengthened and warmed and hummed, this time with cooperation.

Pendaär closed his eyes and began to chant a new spell as he waved the staff in a reaching arc. A satchel suddenly appeared at his feet, and Pendaär's wet and muddy robe magically disappeared from his body. He opened his eyes, smoothed down the crisp, black wool cassock he was now wearing, and fingered the white collar at his throat.

Pendaär smiled. Aye. That was better. He was once again in command of his magic.

He quickly knelt and opened the satchel to make sure everything he needed for his own journey was there. He pushed aside the rosary beads, toothbrush, and electric clippers he was anxious to try, feeling instead for the bundles of paper money he had asked for. They were sitting just beneath another wool cassock, five pairs of socks, and a heavy red plaid Mackinaw coat.

Everything seemed to be in place.

Pendaär straightened and lifted his staff to the sky, chanting again his spell to move matter through time. Darkness returned to the gleann, lightning flashed through the heavens, and Pendaär clutched his satchel, closed his eyes, and hunched his shoulders against the chaos about to consume him.

Dancing sparks swirled around him with ever increasing speed, charged by electricity that made the air crackle with blinding white light. The old wizard took one last peek at the twelfth-century landscape before it disappeared, his laughter trailing to echoes as he excitedly set out on his own remarkable journey to help Greylen MacKeage find the woman he was destined to claim.

Chapter One

It was sheer stubbornness keeping Mary Sutter alive now. She still had something she needed to say, and she refused to give in to the lure of death until she was done giving her instructions to her sister, Grace.

Grace sat by the hospital bed, her eyes swollen with unshed tears and her heart breaking as she watched Mary struggle to speak. The gentle beeps and soft hums were gone; the countless medical machines monitoring her decline had been removed just an hour ago. A pregnant stillness had settled over the room in their stead. Grace sat in painful silence, willing her sister to live.

The phone call telling Grace of the automobile accident had come at noon yesterday. By the time she had arrived at the hospital, Mary's child had already been born, taken from his mother by emergency surgery. And by six this morning, the doctors had finally conceded that her sister was dying.

Younger by three years, Mary had always been the more practical of the two sisters, the down-to-earth one. She'd also been the bossier of the two girls. By the time she was five, Mary had been ruling the Sutter household by imposing her will on their aging parents, her older half brothers still living at home, and Grace. And when their parents had died nine years ago in a boating accident, it had been eighteen-year-old Mary who had handled the tragedy. Their six half brothers had come home from all four corners of the world, only to be told their only chore was that of pallbearers to their father and stepmother.

After the beautiful but painful ceremony, the six brothers had returned to their families and jobs, Grace had gone back to Boston to finish her doctorate in mathematical physics, and Mary had stayed in Pine Creek, Maine, claiming the aged Sutter homestead as her own.

Which was why, when Mary had shown up on her doorstep in Norfolk, Virginia, four months ago, Grace had been truly surprised. It would take something mighty powerful to roust her sister out of the woods she loved so much. But Mary only had to take off her jacket for Grace to understand.

Her sister was pregnant. Mary was just beginning to show when she had arrived, and it was immediately obvious to Grace that her sister didn't know what to do about the situation.

They'd had several discussions over the last four months, some of them heated. But Mary, being the stubborn woman she was, refused to talk about the problem with Grace. She was there to gather her thoughts and her courage and decide what to do. Yes, she loved the baby's father more than life itself, but no, she wasn't sure she could marry him.

Was he married to someone else? Grace had wanted to know.

No.

Did he live in the city, then? She'd have to move?

No.

Was he a convicted felon?

Of course not.

For the life of her, Grace could not get her sister to tell her why she couldn't go home and set a wedding date—hopefully before the birth date.

Mary wouldn't even tell her the man's name. She was closed-mouthed about everything except for the fact that he was a Scot and that he had arrived in Pine Creek just last year. They had met at a grange supper and had fallen madly in love over the next three months. She'd gotten pregnant the first time they made love.

It was another four months of bliss, and then Mary's world had suddenly careened out of control. In the quiet evening hours during a walk one day, the Scot had told her a fantastical tale (Mary's words), and then he had asked her to marry him.

Two days later Mary had arrived at Grace's home in Virginia.

And for the last four months, Grace had asked Mary to reveal what the Scot had told her, but her sister had remained silent and brooding. Until she had announced yesterday, out of the blue and with a promise to explain everything later, that she was returning to Pine Creek. Only she hadn't been gone an hour when the phone call came. Mary had not even made it out of the city when her car had been pushed into the opposite lane of a six-lane highway by a drunk driver. It had taken the rescue team three hours to free Mary from what was left of her rental car.

And now she was dying.

And her new baby son was just down the hall, surprisingly healthy for having been pulled from the sanctuary of his mother's womb a whole month early.

A nurse entered the room and checked the IV hooked up to Mary, then left just as silently, leaving Grace with only a sympathetic smile and a whisper that Grace should let her know if she needed anything. Grace rushed to follow her out the door.

"Can she see the baby?" Grace asked the nurse. "Can she hold him?"

The nurse contemplated the request for only a second. Her motherly face suddenly brightened. "I think I can arrange it," she said, nodding her approval. "Yes, I think we should get that baby in his mother's arms as soon as possible."

She laid a gentle hand on Grace's shoulder. "I'm sorry, Miss Sutter, for what's happening here. But the accident did a lot of damage to your sister, and the emergency cesarean complicated things. Your sister's spleen was severely ruptured, and now her organs are shutting down one at a time. She just isn't responding to anything we try. It's a wonder she's even conscious."

The nurse leaned in and said in a whisper, as if they were in church, "They're calling him the miracle baby, you know. Not one scratch on his beautiful little body. And he's not even needing an incubator, although they have him in one as a precaution."

Grace smiled back, but it was forced. "Please bring Mary her son," she said. "It's important she sees that he's okay. She's been asking about him."

With that said, Grace returned to the room to find Mary awake. Her sister's sunken blue gaze followed her as she rounded the bed and sat down beside her again.

"I want a promise," Mary said in a labored whisper.

Grace carefully picked up Mary's IV-entangled hand and held it. "Anything," she told her, giving her fingers a gentle squeeze. "Just name it."

Mary smiled weakly. "Now I know I'm dying," she said, trying to squeeze back. "You were eight the last time you promised me anything without knowing the facts first."

Grace made a production of rolling her eyes at her sister, not letting her see how much that one simple word, *dying,* wounded her heart. She didn't want her sister to die. She wanted to go back just two days, to when they were arguing the way sisters did when they loved each other. "And I'll probably regret this promise just as much," Grace told her with false cheerfulness.

Mary's eyes darkened. "Yes, you probably will."

"Tell me," she told her sister.

"I want you to promise to take my baby home to his father."

Grace was stunned. She was expecting Mary to ask her to raise her son, not give him away.

"Take him to his father?" Grace repeated, slowly shaking her head. "The same man you ran away from four months ago?"

Mary weakly tightened her grip on Grace's hand. "I was running back to him yesterday," she reminded her.

"I'm not making any promises until you tell me why you left Pine Creek in the first place. And what made you decide to return," Grace told her. "Tell me what scared you badly enough to leave."

Mary stared blankly at nothing, and for a moment Grace was afraid she had lost consciousness. Mary's breathing came in short, shallow breaths that were slowly growing more labored. Her eyelids were heavy, her pupils glazed and distant. Grace feared her question had fallen on deaf ears. But then Mary quietly began to speak.

"He scared me," she said. "When he told me his story, he scared the daylights out of me."

"What story?" Grace asked, reaching for Mary's hand again. "What did he tell you?"

Mary's eyes suddenly brightened with a spark of mischief. "Lift my bed," she instructed. "I want to see the look on your face, my scientist sister, when you hear what he told me."

Grace pushed the bed's lift button and watched her sister sit up. Mary never called her a scientist unless she had some outrageous idea she wanted to convince her was possible. Grace was the rocket scientist, Mary was the dreamer.

"Okay. Out with it," she demanded, seizing on that one little spark like a lifeline. She settled a pillow behind Mary's head. "What did lover boy tell you that made you run away?"

"His name is Michael."

"Finally. The man has a name. Michael what?"

Mary didn't answer. She was already focused on gathering her words as she stared off into space over Grace's right shoulder.

"He moved to Pine Creek from Nova Scotia," Mary said. "And before that he lived in Scotland." She turned her gaze to Grace, her drug-dilated, blue eyes suddenly looking apprehensive. "He told me he was born in Scotland." And then, in a near whisper, she added, "In the year 1171."

Grace straightened in her chair and stared at Mary. "What?" she whispered back, convinced she had heard wrong. "When?"

"In 1171."

"You're meaning in November of 1971, right?"

Mary slowly shook her head. "No. The year eleven hundred seventy-one. Eight hundred years ago."

Grace thought about that. *Fantastical* was putting it mildly. But then she suddenly laughed softly. "Mary. You ran away from the man because he believes in reincarnation?" She waved her hand in the air. "Heck, half the population of the world believes they've led past lives. There are whole religions based on reincarnation."

"No," Mary insisted, shaking her head. "That's not what Michael meant. He says he spent the first twenty-five years of his life in twelfth-century Scotland and the last four years here in modern-day North America. That a storm carried him through time."

Grace was at a loss for words.

"Actually," Mary continued, "five of his clan and their warhorses came with him."

Grace sucked in her breath at the sorrow in her sister's eyes. "And where are these men now? And their . . . their . . . horses?"

"They're dead," Mary said. "All of them. Michael's the last of his clan." Her features suddenly relaxed. "Except for his son now."

She reached for Grace's hand and gripped it with surprising strength. "That's why I was going back. Family is important to Michael. He's all alone in this world, except for our baby. And that's why you have to take his son to him."

Mary let out a tired breath. "I'm dying." She looked at Grace with sadly resigned eyes. "You have to do this for me, Gracie. And you have to tell Michael I love him." Tears were spilling over her cheeks.

Grace stared down at her sister through tears of her own.

"Will you listen to yourself, Mare? You're asking me to take your son to a madman. If he really believes he's traveled through time, then he's touched in the head. You want him bringing up your child?"

Mary released a shuddering breath and closed her eyes again. A stillness settled over the room once more.

Mary was asking her to take a child—her nephew—to a man who was not sane. Grace covered her face with her hands. How could Mary ask such a thing of her?

And how could she not grant her sister's dying wish?

The door opened again with a muted whoosh, and Grace looked up to see a clear plastic basinet being wheeled into the room. White cotton-covered little arms waved in the air, the sleeves so long there was no sign of the tiny hands that should be sticking out of the ends.

Grace had to wipe the tears from her eyes to see that Mary was awake again, straining to see her baby.

"Oh, God. Look at him, Gracie," Mary whispered, reaching toward him with a shaking hand. "He's so tiny."

The nurse placed the basinet next to the bed. She put a pillow on Mary's lap and carefully placed Mary's cast-covered right arm on top of it. Then she picked up the tiny, squeaking bundle from the basinet and gently settled him on the pillow in Mary's lap.

"He's so pink," Mary said, gently cupping his head. "And so beautiful."

"He's thinking it's dinnertime," the nurse said. "You might as well feed him a bit of sugar water if you feel up to it."

"Oh, yes," Mary said, already tugging at his blanket.

The nurse repositioned him in the crook of Mary's broken arm and handed her a tiny bottle of clear liquid with a nipple on it. The tubes sticking in Mary's left hand tangled in her child's kicking feet. The nurse moved around the bed, handed the bottle to Grace, and carefully removed the IV from Mary's hand, covering it with a bandage she pulled from her smock.

"There. You don't really need this," she said, hanging the tubes on the IV stand. She took the bottle of sugar water back and stuck it in the fretting baby's mouth. Free now, Mary awkwardly but eagerly took over.

The nurse watched for a minute, making sure Mary could handle the chore, then turned to Grace.

"I'm going to leave you in privacy," the nurse said, her eyes betraying her sadness as she smiled at Mary and her son. She looked back at Grace. "Just ring for me if you need anything. I'll come immediately."

Panic immobilized Grace. The nurse was leaving them alone? Neither one of them knew a thing about babies.

"Look, Gracie. Isn't he beautiful?" Mary asked.

Grace stood up and examined her nephew. Beautiful? He was unquestionably the homeliest baby she had ever seen. His puffy cheeks were red with exertion, his eyes were scrunched closed, his chin and neck blended into a series of overlapping wrinkles, and gobs of dark straight hair shot out from under a bright blue knit cap.

"He's gorgeous," she told Mary.

"Pull off his cap," her sister asked. "I want to see his hair."

Grace gently eased off her nephew's cap but was immediately tempted to slip it back on. Two rather large, perfectly formed ears popped out a good inch from his head, pushing his now freed hair into frenzied spikes.

He looked like a troll.

"Isn't he beautiful?" Mary repeated.

"He's gorgeous," Grace reconfirmed, trying with all her might to see her nephew the way her sister did.

Mary was the animal lover in the Sutter household and was forever dragging home scruffy kittens, wounded birds and chipmunks, and mangy dogs. It was no wonder Mary thought her little son was precious.

He was. Homely, but precious.

"Let's undress him," Mary said. "Help me count his fingers and toes."

Startled, Grace looked at her sister. "Count them? Why? Do you think he's missing some?"

Mary gave a weak laugh as she wiped her son's mouth with the edge of his blanket. "Of course not. That's just what new mothers do."

Grace decided to humor her sister. Gingerly, she attempted to undo the strings at the bottom of the tiny nightshirt. It was a difficult task as the baby, now happy with a full belly, kept kicking his legs as he mouthed giant bubbles from his pursed lips.

Finally, with her two good hands and Mary's unsteady uninjured one, they freed his legs. Grace held up first one foot and then the other and counted his toes out loud.

She counted them again.

Twelve.

Six on each tiny foot.

Mary gave a weak shriek of joy. At least, it sounded joyful. Grace stared at her numbly.

"Gifts from his daddy," Mary said in a winded whisper. "Michael has six toes on each foot."

And this was a joyful thing? Grace wanted to ask. Being deformed was good?

"Pull his shirt and diaper off," Mary said then. "I want to see him naked."

Grace was afraid to. What other surprises was the clothing hiding? But she did as her sister asked, even though she feared the tiny baby would break from her handling. She didn't know what she was doing. Heck, she hadn't even played with dolls when she was a kid. She had hiked and fished with her father until she was eight, until one of her older brothers had brought home a biography of Albert Einstein and she had discovered the world of science. From then on it was telescopes, science books, and mathematical formulas written on chalkboards.

Grace took off the baby's nightshirt and peeled off the diaper. She gasped and quickly covered him back up.

Mary pulled the diaper completely off. "You're a prude, Gracie," Mary said, cupping her baby's bottom. "He's supposed to look like that. He'll grow into it." Mary traced the outline of his face, then possessively rubbed her fingers over his entire body. "Get a new diaper before we get sprayed," she said.

Grace quickly complied. And between the two of them and their three hands, they eventually got him changed and back into his nightshirt.

Grace was just retying the strings at his feet when she noticed a tear fall onto her hand. She stopped and looked up to find Mary silently crying as she stared down at her son.

"What's the matter, Mare? Are you in pain?" she asked, holding the baby's feet so they couldn't kick out and hurt her.

Mary slowly shook her head, never taking her eyes off her son as she ran a finger over his cheek again. "I want to see him grow up," she whispered in a voice that was growing more fatigued, more faint, by the minute. She looked at Grace. "I want to be there for him when he falls and skins his knee, catches his first snake, kisses his first girl, and gets his heart broken every other day."

Grace flinched as if she'd been struck. She closed her eyes against the pain that welled up in her throat, forcing herself not to cry.

Mary reached up and rubbed her trembling finger over Grace's cheek, just as she had done to her son's. "So it's up to you, Gracie. You have to be there for him, for me. Take him to his daddy, and be there for both of them. Promise me?"

"He's not sane, Mary. He thinks he traveled through time."

Mary looked back at her son. "Maybe he did."

Grace wanted to scream. Were the drugs in her sister's

body clouding her judgment? Was she so fatigued, so mentally weakened, that she didn't realize what she was asking?

"Mary," she said, taking her sister by the chin and making her look at her. "People can't travel through time."

"I don't care if he came from Mars, Gracie. I love him. And he will love our son more than anyone else can. They need each other, and I need your promise to bring them together."

Grace walked away from the bed to look out the window. She was loath to grant such a promise. She didn't know a thing about babies, but she was intelligent and financially stable. How hard could it be to raise one little boy? She could read books on child-rearing and promise him a good life with lots of love and attention.

She had never met this Michael the Scot, and she sure as heck didn't like what she did know about him.

But then, she was even more reluctant to deny Mary her wish. This was the first time her sister had ever asked anything of her, and she was torn between her love for Mary and her worry for her nephew.

"Come get in bed with us, Gracie," Mary said. "Just like we used to."

Grace turned around to find Mary with her eyes closed and her child clutched tightly to her chest. The infant was sleeping. Grace returned to the bed and quickly lowered it. Without hesitation she kicked off her shoes, lowered the side bar, and climbed up beside her sister. Mary immediately snuggled against her.

"Ummm. This is nice," Mary murmured, not opening her eyes. "When was the last time we shared a bed?"

"Mom and Dad's funeral," Grace reminded her. She laid her hand on the baby's backside which was sticking up in the air. "Don't you think we should give this guy a name?" she asked, rubbing his back.

"No. That's Michael's privilege," Mary said. "Until then, just call him Baby."

"Baby what? You didn't tell me his father's last name."

"It's MacBain. Michael MacBain. He bought the Bigelow Christmas Tree Farm."

That was news to Grace. "What happened to John and Ellen Bigelow?"

"They still live there. Michael moved in with them," Mary said, her voice growing distant. She turned and looked at Grace, her once beautiful, vibrant blue eyes now glazed with lackluster tears. "He's a good man, Gracie. As solid as a rock," she said, closing her eyes again.

Except he believes he's eight hundred years old, Grace thought. She moved her hand from her nephew's bottom to her sister's hair, brushing it away from her forehead.

"I'm still waiting for your promise," Mary said, turning her face into Grace's palm.

Grace took a deep breath and finally spoke the words she had so stubbornly, and maybe selfishly, been avoiding.

"I promise, Mare. I'll take your son to Michael MacBain."

Mary kissed Grace's palm and sighed deeply, settling comfortably closer. "And you'll scatter my ashes on TarStone Mountain," she said then, her voice trailing off to a whisper. "On Summer Solstice morning."

"On . . . on Summer Solstice. I promise."

Grace left one hand cupping Mary's head and the other one cradling Baby as a patient, gentle peace returned to the room. Grace placed herself in the crook of her sister's shoulder, feeling the weakening drum of life beneath her tear-dampened cheek.

In two hours it was over, without the pain of a struggle. Mary's heart simply stopped beating. The only sound that remained was the soft, gentle breathing of a sleeping baby.

Chapter Two

If lies were raindrops, Grace would surely be in danger of drowning. She had told so many untruths and prevarications these last four weeks, she barely remembered half of them. And those she did remember were threatening to come back and bite her on the backside.

Grace closed the last of her suitcases and snapped the lock into place. Then she went hunting for her carry-on bag. Twice she had to push her way past Jonathan, and twice he ignored the fact that she wasn't interested in what he was saying.

Or, rather, what he was demanding.

Jonathan Stanhope III was the owner and CEO of StarShip Spaceline, a high-tech company intent on making space travel for private citizens a reality in the very near future. Employing nearly three hundred people, StarShip was on the cutting edge of scientific discovery, and Jonathan had been Grace's boss for the last eighteen months.

He was also the man she hoped to marry.

Although at the moment she wished he would climb aboard one of their untested shuttles and shoot himself into space.

Jonathan was not pleased that she was leaving. He'd done his boss's duty and given her four weeks to "get over" her sister's death, and he couldn't believe that she'd had the audacity to expect even more time.

"But you're talking about *Maine,* Grace," he said for the fourteenth time, following her out of the bedroom and into the kitchen. "They don't even have telephone lines modern enough for data links up there. It's the middle of nowhere."

"Then I'll make a satellite connection," she countered, opening cupboard doors and taking down bottles of formula and baby paraphernalia. She counted out a three-day supply and began packing it in her carry-on bag. She went to the refrigerator and took down the list she had made. Diapers. She was going to need another bag just for the diapers. She headed back into the bedroom.

Jonathan followed her.

"Will you stop," he said, taking her by the shoulder and forcibly pulling her to a halt. He turned her around to face him.

Grace looked up into his usually affable, handsomely sculpted face. Only Jonathan wasn't looking so very agreeable now. He was angry. Truly angry. His intelligent, hazel-gray eyes were narrowed, and his jaw was clenched tightly enough to break his teeth.

Grace moved her gaze first to one of his hands on her arm and then to the other, noticing how his Rolex glistened beneath his perfectly pressed white cuff link shirt.

"You're hurting me," she said.

Ever a gentleman, even when angry, Jonathan immediately released her. He took a deep breath and stepped back, running his hand through his professionally styled sun-blond hair.

"Dammit, Grace. This is the worst possible time for you

to leave. We'll be receiving data from Podly by the end of the week."

And that was Jonathan's real worry. He wasn't disgruntled because he would miss her in a romantic sense, but because his business might suffer in her absence. The satellite pod they had sent up six weeks ago—it had been Grace's idea to name it Podly, because it reminded her of a long pea pod housing several delicate computers—was finally functioning to full capacity. And she was the only person at StarShip Spaceline who could decipher the data Podly sent back.

It was the race into space all over again, only this time it was not the Russians against the Americans. This new race involved private companies competing for the future market of civilian space travel. StarShip Spaceline was in a heated battle with two other private programs, one based in Europe, the other in Japan. And all three of them were on the verge of perfecting alternative forms of propulsion.

Solid rocket fuel, the propulsion used in the NASA space program, was inefficient. Simply put, it weighed too much. The shuttle had to be strapped to a rocket that was several times its size and weight just to get out of the Earth's atmosphere.

Alternative forms, such as ion propulsion or microwaves or antimatter, however, could make space travel a moneymaking venture and even make possible the colonization of the moon and Mars.

Basically, it all boiled down to mathematical physics.

And that was where Grace fit into the picture. She was StarShip Spaceline's resident mathematician. She crunched the numbers and was the troubleshooter for the theories. She could look at a schematic and tell, using mathematical formulas, if it was viable or not.

In just the eighteen months that she'd worked for

StarShip, Grace had saved Jonathan Stanhope's company millions of dollars by disproving theories before they were put into action.

Podly was orbiting Earth right now, and there was great hope that the data it sent back would end the race for a new form of fuel in StarShip's favor.

"I can receive Podly's data in Maine just as well as I can here, Jonathan," she assured him. "I have the satellite link and my computer already packed."

"But what about your other projects?"

"Carl and Simon have been working on them these past four weeks without any problems. I see no reason why they can't continue."

She walked over to her closet and pulled down another bag to fill with diapers. She turned to find Jonathan blocking her path again. His features had softened, and his eyes were once again the intelligent hazel gray she had been falling in love with these past eighteen months.

"Grace. About the baby," he said softly.

"What about him?"

"Is he going to be with you when you return?"

Well now, that was the sixty-four-thousand-dollar question, wasn't it? Grace tried to remember which half-truths she had told Jonathan, as well as which lies she had told the social workers and her brothers. And what about the half-truths she had told Emma, the kindly nurse from the hospital who had been sympathetic enough to give up her vacation and help Grace with Baby these last four weeks?

"That's what I'm going to Maine to find out," she told Jonathan.

"The boy belongs with his father."

"He belongs with the person who can best care for him," she countered.

"You promised your sister," he reminded her. He took her by the shoulders again, but this time his touch was gentle. His expression, however, was not. "You're not dealing with Mary's death, Grace," he said, "because as long as you continue to hold on to her, you won't have to keep your promise."

"That's not true."

He reached up and pushed an unruly strand of hair from her face, tucking it behind her ear. "She's sitting in the middle of your kitchen table right now. You've put your sister in an Oreo cookie tin, and you talk to her."

Grace stood her ground, refusing to let him see her pain. "She's my baby sister, Jonathan. You want me sticking her in a closet? Or maybe I should just FedEx her to Pine Creek? Mary loved Oreo cookies. I can't think of any place she'd rather be right now, until the Summer Solstice, when I'm supposed to put her to rest on TarStone Mountain."

"The Summer Solstice is four months away," he said, looking angry again. "I told you last week when you asked for this leave of absence that four months is too long. You've had one month already, and that's all I can spare right now."

"I'm taking four more months, Jonathan," she told him succinctly, bracing herself for a fight. "I owe that much to Mary and to Baby."

"You need to let go of her, Grace," he repeated, suddenly pulling her into his arms and hugging her tightly.

Grace sighed into his shoulder. She liked being in Jonathan's arms—usually. Heck, the few dates they'd been on had been showing great promise for a future together. Why, then, was she feeling disappointed? Could it be that this thoroughly modern, success-driven man she so admired didn't have a sensitive bone in his body? Could he really be this selfish, not to understand why she had to make things right with her sister?

"You need to go to Maine, find the kid's father, and move on with your life," he continued over her head. "Your sister has all but pulled you into the grave with her." He leaned back to see her. "Have you looked in the mirror lately? You're in jogging pants and a sweatshirt, for Christ's sake. The same ones you were wearing yesterday."

"They clean easier," she said, pulling away and stuffing the bag full of diapers. "Baby spit and formula do not go well with silk."

"And that's another thing," he continued to her back. "You're a scientist, not a mother. You don't know the first thing about raising a child. Hell, you can't even get the snaps on his suits right. The kid looks as disheveled as you do lately."

He took her by the shoulders again as soon as she turned to face him, making her drop the bag of diapers on the floor. "Grace," he whispered, his expression more desperate than angry. "Don't go. Not now. Wait until Podly lands in August, then go to Maine. It will be safer then."

"Safer?"

"It will be better," he amended. "Once the pod is safely landed and back in our hands, then you can leave."

"That's two months too late, Jonathan. I'll miss the Solstice. And I have to deal with Mary's estate. I can't just leave everything hanging for another six months. People in Pine Creek will wonder what happened to her."

"Call them," he said, squeezing her shoulders. "And call the kid's father and have him come get his son. It's the practical thing to do."

"For you," Grace hissed, pulling out of his grip and picking up the diaper bag. She straightened and glared at him. "You don't announce a person's death over the phone, and you sure as heck don't call a man and tell him the woman he loves is dead and 'oh, by the way, she left you a son.'"

Grace left the room before she brained her boss with the bag of diapers. She all but ran into the living room, only to stop at the sight of Emma feeding Baby.

Emma looked up and glared at a spot behind Grace, and Grace knew that Jonathan was standing behind her.

"I'll put your suitcase in my car," he said through gritted teeth. "Place whatever else you want to take by the door, and I'll get it."

"I'll put them in my car," she said, turning to face him. "Emma is driving Baby and me to the airport."

He ran a hand through his hair. "I guess I have no say in the matter," he said, his eyes still sharp with anger. "You know how much StarShip needs your expertise." His jaw tightened, and he pointed a finger at her. "I'll expect daily reports on Podly from you while you're gone—and it better not be for four months," he finished with a growl, just before he turned and silently walked out the door and headed for his car parked on the street.

"Now, don't you take anything he said to heart," Emma told her, admitting she had overheard their entire fight. "You're going to do just fine with this child, Grace. And as for your sister, I know what it's like to lose a loved one. You don't get over it in four weeks."

"Thank you, Emma. Ah, do you mind that I volunteered you to drive us to the airport? I just couldn't stand the thought of twenty more minutes of lectures from Jonathan."

"No, sweetie. It will be my pleasure. Here, he's ready for burping," she said, holding up Baby for Grace to take.

Gingerly, careful of the way she had been taught to support his head, Grace took Baby and turned him onto her shoulder. She patted his back with gentle, rhythmic strokes.

"Have you been thinking of a name?" Emma asked, packing Baby's clothes into yet another bag.

"I've thought of hundreds," Grace admitted, now pacing and patting and softly jouncing him up and down. "But none of them seems right," she said with averted eyes.

Lord, she hated lying to this nice lady. But she couldn't tell her she hadn't the right to christen Baby, that it was his father's privilege.

She had told the hospital staff and the social workers that she did not know who Baby's father was. It was the hardest lie she had ever told, but it was the most expedient—although it had been touch and go for a while. The hospital had been loath to release him without a Christian name to put on the birth certificate. As it stood, he was officially, temporarily, known as Baby Boy Sutter.

With only a bit of paperwork, and not liking the no-name situation any more than the hospital had, the courts had awarded Grace temporary custody of Baby until they could ask their counterparts in Maine to look into the matter. Upon hearing that news, Grace had even gone so far as to make up a tale that Mary had admitted having a one-night stand with a man who had been passing through Pine Creek. It was a wonder the cookie tin hadn't exploded all over her kitchen for that damning lie, but Grace had not wanted anyone investigating anything.

Her brothers were another matter altogether. Every one of them had promised to book a flight when Grace had called with the terrible news. But she convinced them there was nothing they could do here and that if they wished to express their love for Mary, they would show up at TarStone Mountain on the Summer Solstice.

Her lie to them had been one of omission. She had not told them about Baby.

Although Grace loved each of them dearly, she did not want them coming here and taking charge of a situation they knew nothing about. Not that she knew much more. But how could she explain she knew who the father was but that he thought he was a traveler through time? And how could she omit that little detail without first meeting Michael MacBain and deciding for herself if he was sane or not?

No, it was better this way. She didn't want or need six strong-minded men messing up the promise she had made to her sister.

Grace walked to the living-room window and saw Jonathan's Mercedes pull away from the stop sign at the end of her street. She buried her nose in Baby's hair, drawing in a long, satisfying whiff of shampoo and powder.

She had just had her first fight with Jonathan, and it had been an illuminating event.

He was worried about his company, the competition that was rapidly closing in on them, and Podly's performance. Well, she couldn't do anything about their competitors, but she could take care of Podly, even from Maine. Jonathan would calm down once he realized that he hadn't lost her expertise, only her physical presence. She would do a good job for StarShip these next four months and maybe set a precedent for an annual sabbatical in Maine.

But there had been something else in Jonathan's voice and actions lately that simply didn't add up. If she had to put a name on it, Grace would call it fear. Jonathan had seemed scared just now that he couldn't talk her out of leaving.

Was he afraid she might not come back?

Or was the satellite his only concern?

Just before Podly had been launched six weeks ago, Jonathan had become quiet and withdrawn. He'd canceled a date with her at the last minute and had sequestered himself in the lab with Podly for nearly four days after that, placing the last bolt on the satellite himself, sealing it for its eight-month orbit around Earth.

And since it had been launched, Jonathan had been acting strangely with everyone at work. The first two weeks Podly had been up, before Mary's accident, Jonathan had spent every possible minute looking over Grace's shoulder at the computer bank that was the mission control for the small satellite—when, that is, he wasn't locked in his office with the blinds drawn. More than once Grace had come to work only to realize that Jonathan had never left.

He'd doubled security at the lab and threatened everyone to be on the alert for corporate espionage. Probably the only reason Grace wasn't as paranoid as Jonathan was because she had spent the last four weeks wrapped up in her own grief and Baby's care.

And that was another thing.

Jonathan didn't want Baby. He expected her to make a phone call, hand Baby over to a stranger, then get on with business as usual.

The subject of children had come up once on a date, and Jonathan had casually alluded to the fact that they would make quite a baby together, that their child would have a genetic makeup that could not help but ensure great intelligence.

At the time Grace had been thrilled that Jonathan was even thinking such thoughts about their future together. Now, though, she was beginning to wonder if the man was dating her for who she was or for the genes she was carrying. He might be open to the idea of having his own carefully engineered baby, but he definitely wanted nothing to do with another man's child.

That was something else she would have to think about these next four months.

"He's spit up on you again," Emma said, breaking into Grace's thoughts. "It's running down the back of your shoulder."

Emma tossed a towel over Grace's shoulder and took Baby away from her. "You've got to be more gentle with the tyke, Grace," she said, smiling as she gave her critique. "Handle him the way you handle your laptop computer. Hold him firmly, but don't jostle him too much."

Grace wiped the spit from her shirt and flopped down into a chair. She threw the towel across the room, aiming for the dirty clothes basket. She missed. "I'm never going to make it as a mother, Emma. I can't seem to get the hang of it."

Grace blew the hair from her cheek and reached up and tucked it behind her ear. "I have all the confidence a person could want when it comes to splitting atoms or launching rockets into space." She waved at Baby. "But I can't even dress him without having snaps left over when I get to his neck. And the sticky tape on his diapers defeats me. He comes away naked when I pull off his jumpsuits."

Emma was truly laughing now as she set Baby down and started changing him into his traveling clothes. Grace got up from her chair and moved closer to watch.

"You're sure he's not too young to travel?" she asked over Emma's shoulder, fascinated by the woman's effortless skill.

"Naw. He's as strong as an ox, this one. And the doctor gave you permission." She looked up at Grace. "Believe me, Dr. Brown would not have let him go if he had any doubts. Here. You rock him to sleep, and I'll finish packing his things." She walked to where she'd set down her purse and pulled out a book. "Where's your carry-on?" she asked. "I brought you some reading for the flight."

"What is it?" Grace asked.

"It's a book on babies," Emma said, holding it up for Grace to see. "Written by two women who know what they're doing. Between them, they've got eight children." She tucked the book into the bag by the hall doorway.

"You're sending me off with an owner's manual?" Grace asked, her laugh getting stuck on the lump in her throat.

Emma straightened and looked Grace in the eye. "You go with your instincts first, Grace. If you think something's wrong, get Baby to a doctor. But usually just common sense will see you through each day. And if in doubt, check this book or call me." She pulled a piece of paper from her pocket and tucked it into the bag beside the book. "These are my numbers, for home and work. You call."

Grace tamped down the tears threatening to blur her vision. She had known Emma only four weeks, and already the woman was as much a mother as she'd had in more than nine years.

"Thank you, Emma. For everything," Grace whispered hoarsely.

Emma looked at her watch, ducking her head. But not before Grace saw a flush creep into the woman's face.

"I'll take this out to your car and check the car seat," Emma said, her voice gruff as she picked up the bag. "You'll miss your flight if we don't get going."

Grace rocked her nephew, tempted to close her eyes and fall asleep with him. What was she doing, taking him on such a journey at such a young age? Three flights, each plane decidedly smaller than the previous one. A jet from Virginia to Boston, a turbo-prop from Boston to Bangor,

Maine, and then a six-seat bush plane that probably had skis instead of wheels for the last leg from Bangor to home.

What was she hoping to find in Pine Creek?

And just how many more lies would she have to tell before Mary's ghost rose up from her ashes and bit her on the backside?

Chapter Three

The first thing he noticed was the baby strapped to her chest. The second thing was the fact that she wasn't wearing a wedding band.

That first little detail should have made the second one moot, but Greylen MacKeage had never been one to run from a fight or from babies. Nor was he prone to second-guessing his gut. Not when his reaction to a woman was this strong.

The hair on the back of his neck stirred when she walked toward him in the Bangor airport terminal looking lost and tired and in desperate need of assistance. But it wasn't until she walked up to the pilot holding the "Sutter" sign that his senses sharpened acutely.

They would be sharing the plane to Pine Creek.

Which was a blessing for Grey. He needed the distraction of a beautiful woman to take his mind off the fact that he would soon be three thousand feet up in the sky with nothing but air between him and the ground. He couldn't decide which was worse, the three thousand feet for the next leg of his ride from Bangor to Pine Creek or the thirty thousand feet he had flown at coming from Chicago. Not that it mattered. From either height, the ground was just as hard when you fell.

"You're Grace Sutter?" the impatient pilot asked when she stopped in front of him and carefully set down her bags.

She nodded.

"You related to Mary Sutter?"

She nodded again.

Just as impatient to get this flight over with as the pilot seemed to be, Grey silently folded the newspaper he'd been reading and studied Grace Sutter. He knew Mary, too.

"You don't look like your sister," the pilot said, giving her a skeptical once-over, as if he didn't believe her.

Grey did. This woman looked a bit older than Mary, but then that might just be the state of exhaustion she was obviously in. Her soft-looking, tousled blond hair was longer, lighter, and a tad more wild. The cherub shape of her face and the cant of her chin were identical to her sister's, and she was shorter than Mary by a good three inches. And her eyes? Well, they were a deeper, more liquid blue, set off by flawless skin the color of newly fallen snow. But stand the sisters side by side, and a blind man could see the resemblance.

He hoped like hell their pilot wasn't blind.

Grey knew Mary Sutter as a neighbor. She owned a small herb farm on the west side of his mountain. The same farm he had unsuccessfully been trying to buy for the last two years. The MacKeages owned nearly four hundred thousand acres of prime Maine forest, and the Sutter land sat right in the corner of a very nice piece of it.

For two years Mary had sold him eggs, herbs, even goat cheese, but she would not sell him her home.

Grey hadn't pushed the issue. He didn't really need her sixty-one acres, he just wanted to neaten up his western boundary. But all he had been able to get from Mary, other than food, was the promise that if she ever decided to sell, she'd sell to him.

And so Grey had remained content to be good neighbors. When Mary's roof had needed repair, he'd sent Morgan and Callum over to fix it. Not that she had asked for his help.

Mary Sutter was an independent woman. And that had been fine with Grey, until he had caught her thirty feet up on the roof one day, with one end of a rope tied around her waist and the other end tied to the chimney. He had decided then that independence in a woman was a dangerous thing.

He had made the foolish mistake of telling her so.

Mary had laughed in his face.

But she had accepted his offer to help. Mary Sutter may be independent, but she wasn't stupid. She didn't like heights any more than he did.

Grey had asked her out once. So had Morgan and Callum and even too-old-for-her Ian. She had kindly, gracefully, refused them all. And then the crazy woman had been seen all over town with the bastard MacBain.

Go figure.

"I know Mary," the pilot said. He looked around the terminal and then at a piece of paper he held with his sign. "I don't have her listed for this trip." He looked at Grace Sutter. "She's not home, you know. Been gone about five months."

"I know," Grace Sutter said softly.

The baby that was snuggled deeply in the sack on her chest suddenly stirred. The pilot took a step back, not having realized the woman had a child with her.

Dammit. He *was* blind.

Grey was seriously thinking of renting a car for the last ninety miles of his journey. But the rental company insisted he return the damn thing back here; they had no outlets in the middle of the woods. So that wasn't an option. Neither was calling one of his men to come get him. They were too close to the scheduled opening of the resort, and they were nowhere near ready.

Grey stood up, slung his bag over his shoulder, and stooped to pick up Grace Sutter's two bags by her feet. He was surprised by the weight of one of them. He was even more surprised when she grabbed the lightest one back from him.

He lifted his head to find himself staring over a baby's head into the deep blue eyes of the woman he intended to marry.

Grey straightened as if he'd been punched. What in hell was this all about? He suddenly felt too big for his skin, his knees wanted to buckle, and he couldn't seem to catch his breath.

"Ah . . . I'll hold on to this one, thank you," she said, her voice barely penetrating the haze in his head. He saw her turn to the pilot. "I have three more bags and a car seat waiting at the luggage counter."

Grey turned and walked out the side door of the terminal without looking back. The cold, drizzling February rain hit him full on the face. He stood there, his head lifted to the sky, and let the rain wash all the fog from his brain.

Talk about reactions. The lady was beautiful enough to take any man's breath away, but marriage?

Grey shook his head, disgusted with himself. Granted, he did have marriage on his mind lately, but he was expecting the courtship to last a bit longer than two seconds. Yes, that was what had struck him a moment ago—his body was already looking for a mate even if his brain had not caught up to it yet.

Yeah. That's what happened. A beautiful woman had simply stepped in front of a man on the hunt.

Grey had called a clan meeting just a few weeks ago to discuss this very subject. It was time, he had told his men, that they all got married. They had their land, the resort was due to open next month, and it was time they looked to the future. They needed sons. Lots of sons, with whom they could start building the MacKeage clan back to the greatness it once was.

His men had not embraced the idea. They were still trying to cope with the fact that they were no longer warriors, which was an honorable profession in their minds, but merchants, which was not. They were selling pleasure and sport to hordes of vacationers who traveled from the overcrowded cities of the south.

And wives? Why would they want to go and add to their troubles? Wives would mean separate households, regular haircuts, and going to church.

Getting married would also mean having to mingle with the moderns to find those wives in the first place. Courting meant dating now, going to restaurants, dances, and movie theaters where a bunch of people sat in the dark and were nearly bowled over by noisy stories acted out on a screen.

Courting also meant getting involved with the women's families, and it was the consensus of the men that most families today were downright odd. Half the people in this world were divorced, and the rest were on their second, third, and sometimes fourth marriages. People swapped spouses today more often than they had swapped horses eight hundred years ago.

No. None of his men was in any hurry to get married.

But Grey was adamant. They had the financial power base now, and they needed sons to ensure its continuance. The next generation would be businessmen, utilizing the land, the timber, and the political power that came with both. The future of clan MacKeage lay in their children.

Several pellets of ice struck his face, mixed with the cold, heavily misting rain. Grey shrugged his collar closer to his neck and began walking toward the plane.

It was a six-seat DeHaviland Beaver. He had flown in one like it before. Nine cylinders, all of them exposed to the weather, and an oil filler pipe in the cockpit.

Not a reassuring picture.

Damn, he hated small planes. Flying was an unnatural act. It defied common sense that tons of steel could lift into the air by means of a little stick bolted to the nose, spinning around and around to stir up the wind.

But more than he hated small planes, Grey really hated overconfident pilots. While waiting for Grace Sutter to arrive, the pilot—who had introduced himself as Mark— had bragged about his many near misses as a bush pilot up in Alaska. That a little winter rain was nothing to worry about, compared with the blizzards he'd flown through in that great unending land of snow and ice.

Grey had not been impressed. He opened the door of the Beaver and stowed his bag and Grace Sutter's heavy suitcase in the back. He looked around the cramped quarters, and his stomach churned. Mark had offered him a seat up front, but Grey had declined. He'd take the back, thank you, where he wouldn't feel compelled to watch every gauge on the dash for signs of trouble.

"Ah, Mark?" Grace Sutter said from behind him. "The rain is starting to freeze. You're not worried about icing?"

Well, the lady seemed to know a bit about flying. Grey's spirits rose.

"Nope," Mark said, giving her a look that made it clear he hadn't liked the question. "It's warmer aloft. The cold air's locked in under two thousand feet."

"But the landing strip near Pine Creek is at eight hundred," she said then. "And that two-thousand-foot ceiling is probably at three thousand feet in the mountains. We're going to be descending through twenty-two hundred feet of freezing rain."

"You a pilot?" Mark asked, sounding annoyed.

"No."

"Well, lady, I am. And I've flown in every type of weather on this planet. I'm telling you, it's safe to take off. I've checked the radar, and the rain stops twenty miles short of Pine Creek. It won't be a problem."

He cocked his head and shifted his stance, letting them know his patience was drawing to an end. "They're predicting this storm to settle in for several days. So it's either fly out now or be stuck here. It's your call, lady."

Grey watched Grace Sutter look down at the sleeping child on her chest. She looked around the tarmac and held up her hand, letting the freezing rain fall into her palm. She lifted it, watching it melt, and then she looked at Grey.

"Which seat do you want?" she asked then. "Or are you sitting up front in the copilot seat?"

"I'll take the middle," he told her, thankful that whatever had struck him inside the terminal was over. He still wanted the woman to the very soles of his feet, but his mind was once again in control of his body. "Why don't you sit beside me, and we'll make a bed in the backseat for your child?"

Her eyes widened, and Grey didn't know if he'd just scared her spitless or made her own toes tingle. He hoped it was the latter. And he hoped she would be staying in Pine Creek long enough for him to find out what she was doing running around with a bairn and no husband.

"Unless you want to sit up front," he said.

"Ah . . . no. The middle is fine."

Mark looked relieved. He opened the baggage door in the rear and stowed her three other suitcases and a child-carrier seat. Grey reached to take the bag she was holding. She clutched it to her side for a moment, then reluctantly let it go.

"Please be careful with that. And could you set it on the floor by my seat?" she asked.

"Let's load up, people," Mark said, climbing into the front of the plane.

Grey helped Grace Sutter aboard, then took the seat beside her. He handed her the side of her seat belt closer to him. She snapped it closed over her lap and under her child. Then she carefully pulled off her baby's cap.

A full head of dark, spike-straight hair appeared, with two little ears sticking through it. Grey watched as Grace leaned down and kissed the sleeping baby on the top of his head.

"Is it a boy or a girl?" he asked, only to flinch at the sound of the engine sputtering to life.

"A boy."

"How old is he?"

"Four weeks."

Grey's gaze went from the child to her face. Four weeks? He was lusting after a woman barely out of childbed?

He studied her face. She might be tired and a bit frayed around the edges, but Grace Sutter didn't look like a woman who had spent the last nine months being pregnant. There was a special . . . presence new mothers possessed, and he was not seeing it now as he studied her.

"Is he yours?" he asked without thinking.

She turned and gave him an icy glare.

"I'm sorry. That was rude of me," he quickly amended.

"It's just that you look too good to have a four-week-old son."

He watched a flush creep into her cheeks. Great. Maybe his brain really wasn't in charge of his mouth at the moment.

"Look," he said with a sigh. "Can we start over? I'm Greylen MacKeage," he said, holding out his hand for her to take. "And I know your sister. We're neighbors."

"MacKeage," she repeated, staring at his hand, looking as if she was afraid it would bite her.

After a moment she accepted his peace offering and put her small hand into his. He just as carefully closed his fingers around hers and shook it, instantly aware of a warm, unsettling tingle that traveled up his arm.

"I'm Grace Sutter," she said, pulling back her hand. Grey noticed that she clenched that hand into a fist just before she tucked it under her thigh.

"Mary mentioned the MacKeages," she said then. "Don't you own TarStone Mountain?"

"That's right."

"You're building a ski resort and summer spa," she said, not as a question but as a statement of fact. "Mary mentioned that it's due to open soon."

"In about a month," he told her. Maybe they weren't off to such a bad start.

Her face lit up with a smile. "That should help out the economy of Pine Creek."

"Not everyone thinks we're doing a good thing," he admitted with a sheepish grin. "People are afraid the town will lose its identity."

She thought about that. "Maybe," she said, her hand absently petting down her son's hair. "But it survived the boom and then the decline of the logging era. I think it can survive your resort. I bet you a penny the locals will be the first to open up shops and hang out shingles to sell maple syrup, hand-knit sweaters, and bed-and-breakfast rooms."

"You'd probably double your money," he agreed.

"You all buckled up back there?" Mark asked, moving the plane toward the runway.

Grey turned to Grace. "You want to keep your son in his cocoon? Or would you like me to set up his car seat in the back?"

She patted her baby's bottom affectionately. "No, but thank you. He's sleeping now. I think I'll just let him be."

Grey turned toward his window then, so Grace Sutter couldn't see his face when the plane lifted off the tarmac. He gripped the seat with one hand and the door handle with the other, closed his eyes, and started his usual litany of prayers.

They were the same prayers he used late at night, when he was alone in his bed and felt he had lost his mind. Although he would wake up from the nightmares—where he relived the horror of the great storm, the lightning, and the terror—Grey still found himself in a strange new land where metal machines raced by at unbelievable speeds, where light appeared in a room like magic, and where hordes of people seemed to be everywhere.

At first, Grey and his men and the six bastard MacBains had honestly thought they had died and been condemned to hell. They had survived the storm only to be nearly killed by what they had thought were speeding demons but now knew were automobiles. The sheep and cattle in the pastures they recognized. The people in those automobiles, dressed so strangely, they did not. They had seen the steeple of a large stone church in the distance and had hidden in an abandoned barn until dark before they made their way to it, hoping to find sanctuary there.

They'd found Father Daar instead.

The old priest had been at the altar praying when the ten of them had walked inside, leading their warhorses into the church with them, not caring anymore what God might think of such an act.

Daar had calmly turned around and welcomed them into God's house and just as calmly listened to their story. He hadn't keeled over dead or run away screaming— which was suspect in itself to Grey's thinking. How balanced could a man's mind be, no matter how brittle with age, to stand bravely before ten dangerously scared warriors, smiling and nodding as they all rushed to tell him their insane tale.

But Daar had not only understood their language, he spoke it himself, managing to calm their fears even though he couldn't explain what had happened any more than they could.

Over the next nine months the old priest had patiently and steadfastly given them the tools they needed to survive in this twenty-first century. Daar had taught them the modern language, about money and commerce, as well as manners and the use of eating utensils. He had ruthlessly pushed them to drive vehicles and showed them the wondrous technologies available today. And the displaced warriors had reluctantly but quickly adapted to the new world they found themselves in now.

It had not been easy. In fact, it was still not easy for any of them. They were warriors. They still had a hard time comprehending a world full of so many different people, where courts of law settled disputes and where marriages simply ended and women were left to bring up families by themselves.

But not six months into their painstaking lessons, Daar began to insist that it would be wise for them to leave

Scotland. That moving to a more remote, less populated land—such as the northeastern forests of the United States, maybe—might make their lives easier. But before he could convince them that America was where they should go, Grey made the priest take him to the site of their old keep. There was a schoolhouse there now, and the name MacKeage was scattered to all four corners of modern-day Scotland.

And so Grey had agreed to leave.

Michael MacBain and his five men had kept themselves separate as much as was possible, and when the time came for them to go out on their own, he took his men to Nova Scotia.

Daar had sold a couple of their saddles, now valuable antiques, and presented them with bundles of paper money to finance the trip. But it had been Callum's and Ian's swords and Grey's jeweled dagger that had brought them their present fortune, which they had then used to finance the purchase of four hundred thousand acres of Maine timberland and build their home, which they had named Gu Bràth—which, loosely translated from Gaelic, meant "Forever."

Twelfth-century weapons, apparently, were rare. Grey often wondered if anyone had checked to see if the blood staining them was as old as they were.

The men had been adamant that Grey and Morgan not sell their own swords. The younger men, at least, they had said, needed to be armed if they ever found themselves suddenly hurled through time again.

And that was another worry that had plagued all of them for the last four years. It had happened once, could it happen again? As suddenly as they'd been picked up and tossed across time, could that same unholy power do it again?

The old priest didn't think so. The energies that ruled nature were not that fickle, he assured them. If they were here, there was a reason.

It was discovering that reason that was proving difficult.

Grey slit open one eye and peeked at the woman sitting in the small plane beside him now. He did know one thing for certain. He was never, ever, telling anyone—not even the woman he married—about his journey through time.

All of them had agreed to keep their pasts a secret. People today did not believe in magic, the Scots had quickly discovered. And those who did were usually thought of as strange—or insane.

Grey and his men were considered strange enough as it was for keeping so much to themselves; they didn't need to give the moderns another reason to walk silently past them, whispering behind their hands.

Now, though, Grey's immediate worry was the aging DeHaviland plane he was riding in, as it rose into the air with a whine of protest, the tail sinking as the last wheel pulled free of the ground. Grey fought to keep his stomach out of his boots. Ninety miles as the crow flew. Forty-five minutes of terror, and then, so help him God, he was never sitting his ass in another airplane again.

So, this is where you had to come to find a perfect specimen of manhood—the deep woods. She'd been too young when she had left Maine to appreciate what had been right under her nose. Grace decided that if she were ever going to ignore the intellectual side of her brain and go with her ancient feminine instincts, the man sitting beside her was exactly the type of male she would want to regress with.

Greylen MacKeage was ruggedly handsome, darkly compelling, and uncommonly large. He had to stand nearly six and a half feet tall, his broad shoulders took up most of the cabin space, and his hands looked as if they could have crushed her own hand without the least bit of effort.

She had considered that possibility when she had hesitantly shaken his hand, only to be surprised by the gentleness of his grip. But not nearly as surprised as she'd been by the sudden whisper of electricity she'd felt tingle all the way up her arm into the center of her chest. As a matter of fact, her whole body still tingled with feminine awareness.

Greylen MacKeage was much more than just a good-looking man. Something about him bothered her. Something Grace couldn't explain, for the simple reason that she had never felt anything like it before. It was as if her dormant hormones had suddenly awakened after a long sleep and were now swimming all through her body like heat-charged electrons looking for action. She was beginning to suspect—and beginning to dread—that she was experiencing the first awakenings of desire.

This was not good.

Because this was not the time. Or the place. She didn't want to be this strongly attracted to a man like Greylen MacKeage. It didn't make any sense. He looked like a throwback to a much less civilized era, like a man who would rely on primitive instinct to survive, who would use might, not words, to make his point, and who would bowl over anyone or anything that got in his way. Yet she liked the smell of him, the strength he radiated, the steadfast look in his evergreen eyes. He was a man she would want on her side in a crisis. She especially liked the way he comported himself.

Especially when he was scared to death.

Grace could see the white of his knuckles as he gripped the seat beside her. His eyes were tightly shut, and she would bet her same penny that he was praying.

Greylen MacKeage was afraid of flying.

Grace leaned her head back and closed her eyes. She willed her hormones to settle down and pushed her own worries about the air-worthiness of the plane to the back of her mind.

She was going home for the first time in nine years. It was becoming a bad habit, only returning for funerals. She was glad she was staying awhile this time. She needed the rest, the reconnection with the earth and the trees and the granite of the mountains. She'd been looking out at space too long, instead of earthward. She'd forgotten what snow felt like crunching under her feet, what pine pitch smelled like on her hands.

And she had forgotten that men like Greylen MacKeage still existed.

Was that what Mary had found when she'd fallen in love with Michael MacBain? This thrill of being near a perfectly male human being? Of feeling a strength that emanated from him in the form of sweet-smelling heat?

Was Mary's Michael MacBain a large man like Greylen MacKeage? Had she wanted to feel his arms around her the moment she'd laid eyes on him?

Grace used her feet to pull her carry-on bag closer to her seat. Lord, but she missed her sister. There were so many more chapters in her life she wanted to share with Mary. She had questions she wanted answered—about love, relationships, the contentment her sister had found here in her woods in the shadow of TarStone Mountain.

Grace had left Pine Creek for college at the age of six-teen. She didn't regret the decisions she'd made for the last fourteen years, but she had thought she would have more time to catch up with her sister. Mary was supposed to teach her what college couldn't, how to go out on dates, break men's hearts, and fall in love.

How had so many years passed without her noticing? She should have come back sooner, taken a break between doctorates, and spent time with Mary.

The pull of exhaustion finally won its fight, and Grace fell asleep with her arms wrapped around Baby and her legs wrapped around the bag between her feet.

Chapter Four

Give me the child."

Grace woke with a start at the feel of strong hands pulling at her jacket.

"*Now*, Grace. Give me your baby now."

Greylen MacKeage was tugging at the pack strapped to her chest, trying to undo the zipper and pull Baby out. Grace grabbed at his wrists to stop him, until she was awake enough to realize that it was urgency she had heard in his voice, not anger. Without stopping to question why, she started helping him instead. As she worked to free Baby, she slowly became aware that the whine of the engine was growing precariously high-pitched, as if it were laboring beyond its ability.

Mark, the pilot, was cursing under his breath as he struggled to control the shuddering plane. Grace could see he had the yoke pulled nearly into his chest.

"Dammit, I can't climb!" Mark shouted. "We're going down. Buckle up back there!"

Grey all but ripped Baby away from her. Grace frantically tried to grab him back. "He needs to be strapped in his car seat," she said, turning to grab it instead. "That's the safest place for him in a crash."

"No," Grey said evenly, sounding unnaturally calm. He pulled her back into her seat. "Put your bag in your lap, and bury your face in it. I've got your son."

Grace watched him unzip his heavy leather jacket and tuck Baby inside, before zipping it back up until it completely covered the infant's head. He then reached down and picked up her bag. He felt the hardness of it and threw it back on the floor.

"You've got to climb," Grace told Mark, straining to see the altimeter gauge on the dashboard. "We've got to reach warmer air and turn around."

"What in hell do you think I'm trying to do?" he shouted back. "It's no use. The wings and prop are icing up and losing their lift. The weight is taking us down!"

Grey suddenly pulled Grace against him, wrapping his arm around her back and holding her to him, his other arm covering her head. Baby was not happy with his new situation. She could feel him straining against the confines of Grey's jacket, his feet and bottom pushing against her face. Muffled, angry cries sounded from beneath the thick leather of the jacket, sending a chill down every bone of Grace's spine.

My God. She had killed her nephew. He had survived an automobile accident and being surgically pulled from his mother, but now she would kill him by foolishly choosing to fly in questionable weather.

She squeezed her eyes shut and wrapped her arm over Baby and around Greylen MacKeage. The man was a rock. His embrace was fierce as he held the two of them, and Grace was amazed to discover that he wasn't even shaking. She could actually feel the determination in him to keep them safe.

"Brace yourselves!" Mark shouted. "I see the mountains."

Grace pulled her head free to look out the window. She,

too, could see the dark, rain-shrouded mountains not below them but beside them. The stall buzzer suddenly warned that the plane was no longer able to fly. The whine of the struggling engine, the incessant blare of the buzzer, and Baby's muffled cries of terror combined to produce a deafening cacophony of impending disaster.

"Cut the fuel!" she shouted at Mark. "Let it stall into the treetops!"

"Aw, shit!" was the only answer she heard.

The tail wheel clipped the top of a tree, making the plane shudder violently. Grey pulled Grace's head back against his chest, and this time his grip was unbreakable. The right wing hit another tree, jerking the Beaver around with enough force that her head hit the door beside Grey. She would have been knocked unconscious if not for the strong arms protecting her.

Baby's cry of outrage pierced through the chaos, rising above the screech of metal connecting with bark. The plane violently pitched, first in one direction and then another. Luggage fell forward from the cargo bay, smashing into her right hip. A window shattered, spewing glass everywhere. Several shards tore into Grace's cheek, causing her to cry out.

Grey's arms tightened around her.

The noise was deafening as the forest ripped at the plane with relentless, determined precision. Gasoline fumes filled the air, carried in on sheets of frozen mist. Sparks of blue light suddenly shot through the interior of the plane, casting an ethereal glow over the chaos.

They struck something substantial, and the belt at Grace's waist nearly cut her in half. The plane slowly tumbled then, tail over nose, before finally slamming into a tree that would not break from the blow. The airplane hesitated the merest of seconds, as if balancing on a razor-thin fulcrum, before it slowly began its descent down the length of the tree.

Even though she was braced for the final assault, Grace was still surprised by the force of the impact. But not as surprised as she was by the fact that Greylen MacKeage still had more strength to offer. The arms holding her so securely up until now tightened to rib-crushing proportions.

And he didn't let go, even when everything suddenly stopped.

Their flight from hell had finally ended in a semi-upright position. The engine of the DeHaviland now sat in the copilot's seat, hissing angrily as snow and mist pelted it through the broken windows. The air surrounding them actually hummed, charged with the eerie tint of lingering blue light. Both wings had been torn from the body of the plane. Mark, and his seat, were nowhere to be seen.

It wasn't until the silence penetrated her brain and the cold frozen mist touched her face that Grace realized she was still alive.

Baby was not. He wasn't crying, and his struggles had ceased. Grace scrambled to unfasten her seat belt. It released, and she fell onto the wall of the plane. Grey freed himself more carefully and used his arms to stop his fall.

"Oh, God! He's dead!" she wailed, staring at the motionless lump in his jacket.

"He is not," Grey snapped. He unzipped his jacket, and her lifeless nephew fell into his hands. "He's just had the breath knocked out of him," he assured her in a much calmer voice.

She watched as Grey lifted Baby up and covered his mouth with his own. He blew tiny, shallow breaths into the child, pulled back, then gently turned him from side to side. He repeated the breaths, set Baby on his lap, and began massaging his chest.

Grace could only watch in horror.

The infant suddenly began to gasp. His arms and legs started to windmill, and he let out a bellow that echoed throughout the forest.

Grace scooped him up and hugged him to her chest, tears streaming down both of her cheeks. She kissed every inch of his head and face, ignoring his outraged struggles as he threw up all over her. She laughed and cradled him closer, looking at Grey over his head.

"Thank you," she said. "You saved his life. You saved mine. Thank you."

Grey didn't look at all pleased with himself. Actually, he looked downright livid. She watched him push against the side of the fuselage with amazing force, breaking it open and falling out onto the snow-covered forest floor.

He stood up and looked in the front of the plane where the pilot should have been. Grace watched as he slowly looked around the crash site, then suddenly started walking away.

She scrambled out the hole he had made in the plane, Baby in her arms, and immediately sat down. Her legs would not cooperate with her brain. She couldn't stand up, so she sat in the snow, leaned against the plane, and pulled on the string attached to Baby's shirt. His pacifier appeared at the end of it. She stuck it in his mouth, and he immediately stopped his wails, instead putting his energies into ferociously sucking. Satisfied that he was truly okay, Grace pulled his cap out of her jacket pocket and slipped it on his head, being careful to tuck his ears back against his head. Then she took off her jacket and tented it over them both to shield herself and Baby from the freezing drizzle. She looked up to see Grey plodding through the deep snow in ever increasing circles around the plane.

"What are you looking for?" she asked, her voice carrying in echoes through the old-growth forest.

"The pilot," he said, not looking at her. He stopped, scanned the area, then started off to his right. He rounded a large pine tree and stopped again, about twenty feet away.

"Here he is," he said, just standing and staring down at something on the ground.

"Is he okay?" Grace asked.

"He's dead," Grey said, his voice cold. "Too bad. I wanted to kill him myself."

"What?"

He didn't look at her but continued to stare at the ground. "The bastard's not quite so cocky now, is he?" he growled.

"The poor man is dead, and you're cursing him?" she asked, not able to believe that anyone could be so insensitive.

Grey turned his glare on her. "He had no business taking off in this weather."

"He was doing his job. No one tied you up and threw you into this plane. I distinctly remember you climbed in on your own two feet."

He turned to face her, his hands on his hips. "Yeah, well, so did you."

"So this is my fault?"

He stared at her for a silent minute, then blew out a harsh breath and rubbed his face with both hands. "Dammit. As God is my witness, I am never getting into one of your confounded airplanes again. If man was supposed to fly, he'd be born with feathers."

Her confounded planes? So he *was* blaming her. "Even birds have accidents," she ventured lightly, attempting to diffuse his anger.

It didn't work. His glare was back and meaner than

ever. He looked down at the pilot again, kicked the ground at the base of the tree, then plodded back to her, stepping in his same foot tracks, avoiding several large branches that had crashed to the ground with the plane.

Grace forced herself not to flinch when he knelt down in front of her. She didn't have much experience with angry men, especially angry strangers who admitted they wanted to kill people.

"Where are you hurt?" he asked, his tone warning her to answer truthfully.

"I'm not sure I am hurt," she said honestly. "I think I'm just weak in the knees from the . . . ah . . . landing."

She did flinch then, when he reached up and brushed the hair from her face. "You're bleeding," he told her, lightly rubbing a finger over her cheek. He held up his bloody hand for her to see.

"So are you," she told him, nodding at his forehead.

As he gazed into her eyes, he reached up with the same finger that wore her blood and slowly rubbed his own wound. Then he held his hand up between them and rubbed his fingers together, mixing their blood. And still he stared at her.

For the life of her, Grace could not look away. Nor could she breathe very well at the moment. He moved his finger back to her face and rubbed her cheek again, further combining their blood. Something . . . a feeling she couldn't name . . . like a surge of energy maybe, passed between them.

What was he doing? And why did she suddenly feel that her torn-up, grief-ridden, uncertain world had just tilted on its axis yet another ninety degrees?

"Grace," he said, his hand now cupping her chin so that she couldn't turn away even if she found the strength to. "I will never hurt you."

"I . . . I know," she said, wondering where she found the nerve to lie to him now.

"You're afraid of me."

"You were wanting to kill a man."

"I wouldn't have." The right corner of his mouth lifted. "Not with a witness around, anyway."

She tried to pull her chin free, but he spread his fingers along her jaw and turned her face to him, making eye contact again. "I won't hurt you, Grace."

What did he want from her? A grateful thank-you? Acknowledgment that she believed him?

"I won't hurt you, either," she said.

Her absurd promise caused the other side of his mouth to lift, and he gave her an enigmatic smile. "You'll do, Grace Sutter," he said, finally releasing her and standing up.

Grace pulled her jacket back over her head and watched him as he stood ten feet away, facing her and the plane as he surveyed their surroundings.

He really was a strange man. And big. He had long legs, strong hands—she knew that from personal experience— and shoulders wider than any of her brothers'. His over-long hair was nearly black now that it was wet, and it curled over his collar. But earlier, in the terminal, it had been a beautiful, dark mahogany with lighter streaks running through it, as if he spent a lot of time outdoors without a hat. The two-day growth of beard on his face showed signs of having red in it as well.

But his eyes were what really made Grace's heart beat just a little bit faster. They were a deep, pine-forest green that spoke of intelligence and strong character. Those eyes said Greylen MacKeage was a man who lived life on his own terms and made up his own rules as he went.

"I'm trying to figure out where we are," he said, looking around the dense pine forest.

Grace looked around, too, and discovered a wonderland that would have been beautiful in any other circumstance. The old-growth forest, draped in a freezing mist that made it look otherworldly, presented a very real problem for their continued survival. Ice was building on everything, weighing down the stately old trees, crackling in gentle rhythm with the stirring breeze.

It was late afternoon in February in Maine, which meant that what little daylight was left would soon be fading. Fog shrouded the treetops. Grace couldn't see much more than fifty yards in any direction, and what she did see was sloping quite steeply.

"We're on the side of a mountain," she said lamely. She suddenly sat up straighter. "Hey. I have my computer and satellite link. I can get our coordinates."

"Our what?" he asked, turning to face her.

"I can get a GPS reading on our position."

He gave her a blank look. Grace set her jacket on the ground, then set Baby on it and wrapped him up tightly. "Help me find my computer," she said, turning to climb back into the plane.

Grey tried to open the back cargo door, but it wouldn't budge. He walked around the fuselage, tamping snow as he went, and after several tries and a few grunts, he was able to rip open the door on the opposite side. Her carry-on bag fell into the snow.

"Please, be careful with that," she told him, reaching out and pulling it back inside the plane.

"Be careful?" he said, giving her an incredulous look across the compartment. "The damn thing just fell three thousand feet."

"There. That one has my computer," she told him, pointing to the metal suitcase now sitting in the front compartment, on top of the still hissing engine.

Grey worked the suitcase free and handed it to her across the plane. Grace pulled it out into the snow and packed down a level place to set it. Once satisfied that it was not in danger of tipping, she opened it up.

"Have you ever noticed," he said, walking back around and hunching down beside her, "how we package our possessions better than ourselves? Our luggage fared better than we did."

Grace didn't think he wanted an answer to his observation, so she continued her task in silence. She unpacked the satellite link and handed it to him.

"Here. Set that down away from the plane in as open an area as you can find," she instructed. "There's fifty feet of cable, so find a spot where the tree canopy is fairly open to the sky."

"Will the rain bother it?" he asked as he looked for an open space for the device.

"No. That part is waterproof," she said. "No. It's upside down. Turn it over."

He did, then walked back and picked up Baby, who was beginning to fret.

"He's hungry," he said, unwrapping her jacket and peeking inside.

Grace looked up at him, her brow furrowed. "How do you know that? I still can't discern one of his cries from another."

He shot her a crooked grin. "One baby brother and two sisters," he answered.

Grace ducked her head and turned to find her bag with Baby's formula. Grey beat her to it and started to open it.

"No! I'll get that," she said, taking it from him. "I . . . ah . . . I know where everything is."

He didn't question her overreaction. He simply sat down on the snow with Baby. Grace fished around for the formula and pulled out one of the small bottles. She screwed a nipple onto it and handed it to him.

"It's probably cold," she said. "Won't that cramp his stomach?"

"I'm more worried about it bringing down his temperature," he told her, taking the bottle and holding it up to his cheek. He nodded. "Nope. It's fine. It hasn't chilled yet."

Relieved, Grace returned to her task of booting up her computer and pulling up her GPS program. That took her a good five minutes. The formula might not be chilled yet, but her computer sure wasn't happy with the weather.

"What's a satellite link?" he asked, watching her work while Baby contentedly ate. "And what's a GPS position?"

Grace was pleased, if a little surprised, that Greylen MacKeage was not afraid to admit his ignorance about something.

"There are at least nine satellites orbiting the Earth whose sole function is to send signals back to the ground. I can use three of them and get a fix on exactly where we are." She turned to look at him. "The computer will pick the satellites nearest us, lock onto them, and form a triangulation between them and us. My computer will read the data and calculate our position. Using the numbers it gives me, I can pinpoint us on a map."

She watched Grey look up at the overcast sky, his expression contemplative. "There are machines traveling around the Earth and sending signals back down?" he asked, still looking up.

"Oh, there are dozens of satellites, not just the GPS ones. There are communication satellites, weather and photography satellites, and other things, like the Hubble telescope and the space station."

He slowly lowered his gaze back to her. "Really?" he

murmured. His eyes narrowed slightly. "What is it you do for a living, Grace, that you carry computers and satellite links?"

She broke contact with his gaze and punched several buttons on her computer. "I work for StarShip Spaceline, a civilian space travel company." She looked back at him. "I'm a rocket scientist," she said defensively, expecting . . . what? A look of disbelief? Of awe? Or horror, maybe?

What she got from Grey, though, was another smile.

"I'm a lucky man to have crashed with you, then," he said. "Can your satellite link penetrate these heavy clouds?"

Grace returned her attention to the job at hand, so Grey would not see how startled she was by the warmth of his smile. Did nothing rattle this man? He was sitting in the middle of a plane crash on the side of a mountain, feeding a baby, with a woman who had just admitted that she was probably smarter than he was. And he was *smiling*.

"Well, can it?" he asked.

"Can it what?"

"Can your computer read the numbers through the clouds?"

"Yes, of course. At least, I hope so," she said. "But all sorts of things could interfere with the link. The mountains, these trees, or a combination of both. Oh, damn." She pushed a few more buttons, and a map of northwestern Maine popped up on the screen. But there was no magic little dot saying where they were on that map.

"What?" he asked, leaning closer to look over her shoulder.

"It's not going to work. Either the mountains are blocking our trajectory, or the forest is too dense here." She turned to look at him. "And that means the ELT might not get out, either," she told him truthfully. "It can work on the same system, or if we're lucky an overseas plane will pick up the signal. They are constantly monitoring the channel the ELT emits from."

He leaned closer, squinting at the screen. "What's an ELT?"

"It's the emergency locator transmitter every aircraft has. If you crash, it automatically starts sending out a signal for a search party to follow."

Grace climbed back into the plane and searched through the debris for the ELT, keeping her thoughts to herself that Mark might not have been a very conscientious pilot. The guy had been a cowboy, overconfident and reckless by nature. Most bush pilots kept their equipment in pristine condition, knowing their lives often depended on it.

Mark had not. She found the ELT ten minutes later, but she also found that it wasn't working. She opened it and saw that the battery had leaked and corroded the transmitter beyond use.

Grace had a thought, just a fleeting thought, that she wanted to kill Mark herself. The only hope they had was dead in her hands, a useless piece of smart technology that neglect had ruined.

She backed out of the plane and threw the ELT into the forest as far as she could. She swiped at the tears welling up in her eyes and looked at Grey.

"It's useless," she said. "It's broken."

Grey sat back against the fuselage and busied himself with Baby. Grace used her sleeve to wipe off her computer. She shut it down and closed the cover.

"I'm sorry," she said. "Nothing works. We're even too remote to get a cell phone signal."

"It's not your fault," he told her, looking up. He smiled suddenly. "So I guess it's a good thing *you* crashed with *me*.

I can do what your technology can't, Grace. I can get us out of here."

"Excuse me? I'm not walking off this mountain. They say you're supposed to stay with the plane."

"They?" he asked, his dark forest eyes lighting with humor. "Would these be the same *they* who said Baby should be in his car seat? He would have been bludgeoned to death."

"*They* are the experts," Grace retorted, lifting her chin, refusing to let that smile disarm her. "The people who study these things."

Grey set the empty formula bottle on the ground and gently slung Baby onto his shoulder, pulling the edge of his jacket over him.

"Your experts are wrong this time." He waved a hand at the forest. "This is my world. This is where I'm the expert. I can have us off this mountain and in front of a warm fire by morning."

"That's your male ego talking. And more than one group of crash victims have been found dead from such confidence."

He came over and hunkered down in front of her. "Grace. I'm not boasting. If I thought our chances were better here, then we would stay put," he told her, his tone solemn. "But I'm worried this storm will get worse before it gets better. And I want you and your child off this mountain tonight."

"But you don't even know where we are."

"I will, once I get my bearings. I'll have to leave you for maybe an hour, but then I'll come back and take you out of here."

"We shouldn't separate."

He reached out and touched her cheek. "Trust me, Grace. One hour. And then I'll be back. I promise."

★　★　★

And with that promise echoing through his head, Grey laboriously made his way through the steeply sloping deep snow of the forest, the avowed litany interspersed with curses.

How many more storms, more trials of terror, would he have to survive before he understood why he was here? What kind of power brings men eight hundred years forward in time and then places such obstacles in front of them to test their courage?

He wished he had his sword. His right hand felt naked, lost without the security of its weight. It was at home, though, in his room at Gu Bràth, uselessly out of reach.

He'd wanted it with him in Chicago this past week, just as badly as he wanted it now. The travel convention had been noisy, crowded, and oftentimes frightening. He had seen so many people, different-colored complexions, odd languages, and even odder clothing. Thousands—millions of people—all massed together in the city of Chicago, living unimaginable lives. His business trip had been a trial unto itself, necessary to the success of their resort but unpleasant nonetheless. He had accomplished his goal of making TarStone Mountain Ski Resort known to the world of travel experts, but it had come at a price.

The airplane ride to Chicago had nearly undone him.

And the ride home had very nearly killed him.

Grey turned and started making his way back uphill, taking a more northerly direction. Slowly he relaxed, still not knowing where he was but feeling—sensing, really—that he was walking familiar ground. At least here in these mountains his life force was beginning to rebalance.

Grey snorted to himself. If that were even possible now.

For four years he and his men had struggled to make sense of this journey they found themselves on, forced to make their way in this strange new land.

Learning to adapt in order not to perish.

The old priest, Daar, had been their only means of survival, and that simple fact bothered Grey more than he was willing to let anyone know. There was something strange about the priest, something unnatural.

Such as the fact that Daar had sold their daggers and swords for such an unbelievable sum of money. Grey had studied the market, once he'd learned how; though valuable today as antiques, their weapons could not have brought the fortune the priest had said they did. Gu Bràth had been purchased with money that had appeared almost as if by magic.

And that was another thing. Why had the old priest not acted more surprised to find ten dangerously scared warriors invading his church? It was as if Daar, like the money, had appeared by magic just when they needed him most.

And that bothered Grey more than he was willing to admit, even to his men. He'd been tempted more than once to confront Daar, to ask the priest why he'd so readily believed their tale and why he had so eagerly agreed to help them. But each time Grey had thought to broach the subject, he had decided against it.

The old priest reminded Grey too much of the man—or the wizard or whatever the hell he'd been—he had seen on top of the bluff just before the great storm had descended upon them four years ago. Daar's hair was shorter, his beard neatly trimmed, but beyond age and hair color there was an uncanny resemblance that had made Grey suspicious enough ultimately to back down from a confrontation with him.

If Daar really was the same man he'd seen four years ago, Grey needed to tread carefully around him. Because magic was something even a laird didn't mess with. And wizards were not people you wanted to anger. And so Grey had kept his thoughts to himself and contented himself instead by keeping a careful watch on the priest. If the old man began acting strangely, if his crooked old cane ever started to glow, well . . . Grey would find some way then to deal with the problem.

But so far the priest had been nothing but helpful since their suspiciously convenient meeting four years ago. Because of Daar, Grey and his men were viable members of this community now, naturalized citizens who paid taxes, engaged in commerce, and voted in a government they still didn't fully comprehend. They could read, drive automobiles, and function in society without calling undue attention to themselves—insulated from the world while still being part of it.

They had drawn a mantle of security around themselves, walking a very thin line between the present and their eight-hundred-year-old past.

And because they were forever aware of that fragile boundary in time, all of them had spent the last four years looking over their shoulders—watching for storms. Hell, four of MacBain's men had actually died in lightning storms, when they'd foolishly—or maybe insanely—sought them out in hopes of returning home.

Not Grey. Or any of his men. They were here, for better or worse, and determined to rebuild their clan.

If they survived long enough to father children.

Grey crested the top of the ridge and stopped to study the landscape. The clouds hung low, sagging over the summit and rolling through the forest like heavy smoke from a fire. Crystallized rain winked through the last of the daylight, weighing down branches as it clung to everything it touched.

Grey unzipped his jacket, letting his body cool. He thought about this new trial he found himself in. And he thought about the woman who shared it with him.

Grace Sutter. She'd been remarkably calm through it all—through the crash, her son's near death, the pilot's certain death, and finding herself stranded in the woods with a stranger. And yet Grace had put her trust in him when her technology had failed her.

Grey admired her for that.

Which only made him want her more.

She would make a fine wife for a man who needed a woman of courage, intelligence, and endurance. She would be a strong mate, capable of partnering a warrior such as himself. Her son was proof she could bear him children, and her actions in the face of today's danger spoke of her ability to think on her feet.

Although it seemed she would need a firm hand to guide her. Her son was also proof that Grace might be a wee bit too independent, seeing how she was returning to her childhood home with a child of her own—and without the babe's father.

Grey stood overlooking what he now recognized as North Finger Ridge and decided that he could handle Grace Sutter. Once he claimed her, he would see she abandoned this tendency to wander around without the protection of her man.

Satisfied with the direction of his thoughts and with his resolve to claim both woman and child, Grey started back down the ridge in the direction of the plane. It was time he made good his boast that he would have them all safely in front of a fire by morning.

He had already been gone ninety-eight minutes.

And in that time Grace had changed Baby, putting two T-shirts and two jumpsuits on him, and settled him back inside the carrier on her chest. She had to keep his little body close to hers instead of wrapping him up in her jacket, because she was afraid Baby was too small to produce enough body heat to keep himself warm. He only weighed eight and a half pounds now. So she put several layers of her own clothes on, put Baby back on her chest, and zipped him up tight to give him the benefit of her own body heat. Then she rearranged the supplies she wanted to take with her into one bag.

Dammit. She did trust him. She couldn't explain why, but Grace just knew that if Greylen MacKeage said he would get her and Baby off this mountain tonight, it was a statement of fact, not wishful thinking.

The freezing rain had started again about twenty minutes ago, and the daylight was gone now. Only an eerie blue light remained, a persistent glow that seemed to emanate from the wreckage of the plane in swirling waves of effervescent warmth.

Grace couldn't decide what caused the phenomenon, but her educated guess was that maybe the crash had disturbed the energies of the ice storm, charging the heavy atmosphere with ions of light. Mother Nature was fickle sometimes, and if people lived on Earth another million years, Grace knew that man would never explain all her mysteries.

And like the light glowing softly around her now, Grace welcomed that truth. As a scientist, she did not want to conquer Nature or rule her laws; she wished only to understand her.

And this blue light, which seemed to have grown stronger within minutes of Grey's departure, was just one example of why she had left Pine Creek at the age of sixteen to pursue a career in science. So many mysteries, so much to discover, all those unending questions waiting to be answered; science was the passion of her life. And just as soon as she got off this mountain, she intended to figure out what had caused this blue light engulfing her now. And why it gave her such a feeling of well-being, a sense that things would turn out okay.

Grace sat in contemplative silence inside the fuselage, hugging a sleeping Baby to her chest, and listened for sounds of Grey's return. All she heard was the forest cracking with eerie moans as trees protested their growing skin of ice.

Grace peered into the darkness of the forest, in the direction of Mark's body. He was lying out there in the cold, getting covered with ice. She'd been tempted to walk over and cover him with something, but she hadn't been brave enough to do it.

And that sorry state of affairs bothered her. She was a coward. She couldn't give a dead man the dignity he deserved, she couldn't let go of her sister, and she couldn't keep her promise to give Baby to Michael MacBain. As much as she was afraid of taking on the responsibility of Baby, Grace was more afraid of giving him up. He was all she had left of her sister and the one thing in Grace's life that was real. Her dream to travel into space was just that: a dream.

Baby was a reality. Raising him would make her someone, not just something, not just a brain walking around in an inconsequential body. Men either ran from her intelligence or they used it, but they never saw anything else, not her smile, her heart, or her hopes and dreams.

They never saw *her.*

Grace hugged Baby closer against her body. He would see her. She would be his aunt, and that was the one thing no one, not even his father, could take away from her.

She fully intended to keep her promise to Mary and tell Michael MacBain he had a son. It was the timing she just wasn't sure of. Tomorrow or ten days from now, or maybe ten years from now, she would introduce them. That would depend on Michael MacBain when she met him and on her own questionable courage.

Grace jumped as if she'd been shot when Grey suddenly loomed in front of her. She hadn't heard him approach over the crackle of the forest.

"Grace?" he said, peering down into the plane.

"I'm here. Did you get your bearings?" she asked, scrambling to climb out. It wasn't easy. With Baby strapped to her chest and her legs still not working well, she had to grab onto Grey and let him pull her to her feet.

"We're halfway up North Finger Ridge," he told her.

"That runs up the north side of TarStone Mountain," she said, getting excited. "We're only about six or seven miles from Pine Creek."

"You know this land?" he asked.

Grace couldn't see his face very well, but she heard the surprise in his voice. "I grew up here," she told him. "I used to hike all over this place with my father and brothers."

"It's more like eight miles," he told her. "And they're long, steep, hard miles. The snow's deep, and the forest is raining tree limbs and ice the size of my fist."

"Are you saying we can't make it?"

He took her by the shoulders. For some reason the blue glow had suddenly faded, and she couldn't see Grey well enough to judge his expression. But she could feel the tension in him.

"No, I'm not saying we can't. But I have a better idea. There's a cabin about four miles from here. An old priest named Daar lives there. I'm going to get you and your son that far, and then I'll continue on to Gu Bràth. I'll bring back the snowcat then, and my men."

"What's Gu Bràth?"

"That's our home. It's on the west side of TarStone, just a few hundred yards from the resort. Now, are you gripping my jacket so fiercely because you're glad to see me, or are you having a problem standing?"

She almost missed his question, he changed the subject so quickly. "I . . . ah . . . my knees are still a bit shaky," she admitted. She wasn't stupid enough to ignore the problem. Not with the hike he was planning.

"Damn. Can you walk?"

"I've walked a bit just near the plane. I'm not hurt. Not really. I think I'm just bruised."

He was silent so long she was afraid he was angry again. But if he was, it didn't show in his voice when he next spoke.

"Can you rig . . . what is your kid's name, Grace? I've only heard you call him Baby."

"Ah . . . that's it. Baby. I haven't decided on a name yet."

"But you said he's four weeks old."

"He is. But a name is very important. He's going to have to live with it all his life."

She could just make out Grey shaking his head. "Okay," he conceded, warmth in his voice. "Can you rig Baby's pack to fit my shoulders?"

"It adjusts. Why?" she asked, wondering just how *big* it adjusted.

"Because I'm going to carry him, and he'll be more comfortable and secure in the pack."

"I can carry him."

He was shaking his head again. "You just have to worry about putting one foot in front of the other and staying on my heels."

It was Grace's turn to shake her head. "You're not Superman, you know."

"I'm damn close."

"You certainly are arrogant enough to be Superman," she whispered.

"Grace?"

"Yes?"

"Are you married?"

"No."

"Good," he said then, just before he leaned down and kissed her full on the lips.

Grace was so stunned she simply stood there like an inanimate fool. She didn't kiss him back. She just stilled like a stone, feeling his power and warmth wash over her.

He kissed like he looked. Large. Rather overwhelming.

She didn't dare breathe. Every damn one of her primitive instincts told her to kiss the man back. His tongue swept across her lips, sending a shiver through Grace that was electrical in nature.

The ice storm receded, the plane crash never happened, she was not standing on the side of a mountain with her fate uncertain. All that existed for Grace at that moment was the feel of Greylen MacKeage as he wrapped his arms completely around her.

He smelled like the forest, felt solid as rock, tasted warm and sweet and so very male. Her senses swam in chaotic circles. Nothing in her limited experience with men could have prepared Grace for what she was feeling now. Passion overwhelmed her, and she lifted her hands against his shoulders and shoved him away. "Wh-what did you do that for?" she asked, clinging to the side of the plane, afraid her knees were about to buckle.

"Because I wanted to."

Now, there was an answer that fit Greylen MacKeage very well.

She had to admit it had felt deliciously good to have his mouth on hers.

"What would you have done if I said I was married?"

The corner of his mouth lifted into a half-grin. "I'd have kissed you anyway. Any man who would let his woman get into this mess doesn't deserve her. And that makes you available to my way of thinking." He took her chin in his hand. "It's a moot point, though, isn't it, Grace? Baby's father is not in the picture."

"What makes you so sure?"

"Because women with husbands or lovers don't come running home four weeks after childbirth."

Well, she couldn't very well argue the point, now, could she? She didn't have a husband or lover, but then, she hadn't just given birth to Baby, either.

"Are you ready to leave now?" he asked.

"Yes."

"Then let's see if we can get Baby transferred to my chest without waking him."

It was no longer just her knees shaking; her whole body was trembling, and it wasn't from the cold. The heat, maybe. She was feeling unusually warm. Did raging hormones produce heat?

Grace carefully released her death grip on the plane and unzipped her jacket. She peeled it off and relished the fresh, cold, wet air that struck her. She turned around and presented her back to Grey.

"You've got to undo the buckles on my shoulders," she told him. "If Baby's not in it, I can usually pull it off over my head. But we'll have to adjust them anyway." She lifted Baby up slightly to lessen the tension on the buckles. "Okay. I'm holding him. Undo it."

Grey deftly unfastened the straps, lifted Baby off her chest, and placed him against his own. Grace moved to his back and discovered two problems. One, it was too dark for her to see what she was doing. And two, she couldn't reach the buckles even if she could see. The man stood a good deal taller than her five-foot-four-inch frame.

"Ah, could you maybe get down on your knees?" she asked.

Grey craned his head around to look at her, and she made out the slash of his grin. "Sorry," he said. "I didn't think."

He lowered himself, not to his knees but hunkered down on his haunches instead. "Is this okay?" he asked.

"Your knees would be lower."

"Now, lass. I've learned a man best not get on his knees for a woman the very first day. It doesn't bode well for his future."

"You called me lass. Are you Scottish?" she asked, alarmed. She had thought by his slight accent that he might be Irish. Was he related to Michael MacBain?

"Born and bred a Scot," he admitted.

"How long have you lived in America?"

"Oh, nearly three years."

"But your accent is so . . . so . . . American."

"Because I am an American now."

"You've deliberately worked to change your accent? But why? What's wrong with being a Scot and having a Scottish accent?" she asked as she worked on fastening the buckles.

"I've also learned the phrase 'When in Rome, do as the

Romans.' I live here now. I intend to speak like one of you."

Grace laughed as she pushed at his back to let him know the job was done. "Then you've got to drop your final consonants a bit more if you want to sound like a Mainer."

He stood up and turned to face her. "You don't have a Maine accent."

"I haven't lived here for fourteen years. It was washed out of me in college."

Grace was tempted to ask him if he knew Michael MacBain, but then she thought better of it. She wasn't ready to acknowledge the man, not even in her own mind. Not yet. She would wait until she was back in her old house and had recovered from this little adventure.

"Are you ready to go?" he asked.

"Yes. Just let me get my bag."

"It's not the heavy one, is it?"

"No. I repacked everything. I'm only bringing Baby's food and diapers, my bare computer, and one or two personal things. The computer's not heavy. It was the satellite link and other equipment that weighed so much."

She reached into the plane and pulled out the bag, clutching it to her when he tried to take it. "Ah . . . I can carry this. It's really not that heavy."

He planted his feet wide and put his hands on his hips. "Will you tell me what's so godly important about that bag that you can't let it out of your sight? Since I met you, you've done nothing but guard it the way a drunkard guards his wine."

Grace tightened her hold on the bag and lifted her chin, refusing to give in on this point. She didn't care that the man looked big, even scary, and determined enough to stop a freight train. She was carrying her own bag.

"Personal things," she told him. "Precious things."

"There's nothing precious enough to risk your neck over. So what's in the bag, Grace? Thousands of dollars? Illegal drugs?"

"No."

"Then what?"

"My sister."

Chapter Five

*G*rey could only stare at the trembling woman standing in front of him. Had she just said *her sister?*

"Mary? Your sister, Mary Sutter?" he finally asked in a strangled whisper, hoping like hell he'd heard wrong.

She nodded.

He stared at her in silence. "Mary's dead?" he asked, finally comprehending.

She nodded again.

Grey took a step back and leaned against the side of the plane, bending over until he supported himself with his hands on his knees. "When?" he asked, staring at the ground. He looked up at her, just barely able to make out her stark white face in the growing darkness. "How?"

"An automobile accident," she said.

He lowered his gaze to the bag she was clutching with a fierceness that was heartbreaking. "What do you mean, Mary's in there?"

He saw her chin rise again. "I had her cremated, to bring her home. She's in a tin in this bag."

He straightened and rubbed both his hands over his face, several times, trying to wash away the picture of Mary Sutter, so happy, vibrant, and contented with life, now just a handful of ash. "Damn." He looked at Grace. "I'm sorry. I didn't know."

"You said you knew Mary?"

"Yes. We bought eggs and herbs from her. She was a good neighbor and person."

"Yes, she was."

"I'm sorry," he repeated, unable to think of anything else to say. He walked over to her and held out his hand. "Let me carry the bag, Grace. I'll be careful with it. You just worry about keeping your feet beneath you. The going will be rough."

She hesitated but finally handed him the bag. Grey took it gently, unable to believe that he would be carrying Mary Sutter down off this mountain, so close to the home she lived in just five short months ago.

"Has she been with you these last months?" he asked, not turning to leave. There was one other detail he wanted to discuss with her, but he was not in a hurry to broach the subject. Not now. Not after learning that Grace was grieving her sister's death.

"Yes. She was down visiting me."

"I'm glad you had some time together."

"I am, too."

"Ah . . . did you happen to change your shoes while waiting for me to get back?" he asked then, deftly slipping his question into the conversation.

"My shoes? No. Why?"

"You're wearing sneakers, Grace. You don't have any boots?"

"No," she said, ducking her head. "Tell you the truth, I completely forgot it was the dead of winter here. I never even thought of boots."

Damn. Well, he was about to find out just how gutsy, or how squeamish, Grace Sutter really was.

"Then I'd like for you to wear Mark's boots, Grace."

"What?" she asked on an indrawn breath, turning to look at the pine tree where the dead pilot lay.

"I'm talking about the difference between making it down off this mountain or not being able to walk because your feet are wet and frozen. Can you do that, Grace? If I get them for you, will you put them on?"

She turned back to look at him. He could see white completely surrounding her beautiful blue eyes, and he was sorry for having to put her through this. But it was necessary.

She suddenly straightened to her full meager stature. "I'll wear them," she said, her voice sounding strained.

Grey blew out a relieved breath. He handed the bag back to her and walked over to the pine tree. He bent down, careful of Baby and thankful for the wonderful pack that held him secure, and quickly took off Mark's boots. He held them up and spanned their length with his hand.

Thank God Mark had been one of the small, wiry Frenchman who populated these woods. He didn't have size twelve feet. The boots might be a little big for Grace, but with extra socks they should keep her feet dry and allow her to walk well enough.

He'd give his eye teeth to be able to build a fire to dry her out completely before they started off, but every burnable bit of wood was either buried under three feet of snow or covered with ice. Hell, he couldn't even offer her the security of a flashlight.

He didn't need a light to lead them off this mountain. He had excellent night vision. And his body produced more than enough heat to keep himself and Baby warm.

But he was really worried about Grace. She couldn't weigh much over a hundred and ten pounds. She didn't have his strength or physical endurance. And then there was the fact that she had just given birth four weeks earlier. The trek down the mountain might be too much for her.

She had grit, though, he'd grant her that. He was proud of the way she was taking this all in stride. Not many women would be so calm and cooperative, much less agreeable, after crashing into a mountainside. She was capable, in her own right, of making decisions for her own survival—but she was putting her trust in him.

That impressed him most of all.

Grey used his pocketknife and cut the belt that held Mark to his pilot's seat. He pulled off Mark's jacket next and considered its heft against the one Grace was wearing. It would not offer her any advantage. So he carefully set it over Mark, covering him from the elements.

He still damned the man, but he could not, in good conscience, leave him there unprotected. He shook his head. It had already started. Grace Sutter's goodness was already creeping into his own damned soul.

He carried the boots back to Grace. She was sitting on the ground again and already had her sneakers off. One of her other bags was open beside her, the contents spilled over the snow.

"I found some dry socks," she said. "Is there anything in your bag you want to take with you?"

"No," he told her, dropping down and fitting the boots on her himself. Assured that they weren't too big, he finished lacing up the last one and took hold of her legs just below the knees.

"How are your legs?" he asked, running his hand over both calves. "Do they hurt?"

"It's not my legs," she said quickly, attempting to sidle away. "It's my back. I wrenched it. But it's not that bad." She took hold of his wrists to stop his inspection. "I'd tell you if I were really hurt. I'd let you go on without me."

"I thought about doing just that," he admitted.

"Then why don't you?"

He shook his head, not caring if she could see him or not. "The worry would kill me. I'd rather take it slow and have you and your son right beside me, where I can keep an eye on you both. We can't build a fire that would sustain itself, and the cold might get to you before I got back."

She was silent so long that Grey was afraid she was seriously considering that possibility. Which was why he wasn't surprised by her next comment when it finally came.

"You could take Baby with you," she said. "I could put on every piece of clothes in our bags. And it's really not that cold. There's almost no wind, and the temperature is only a bit below freezing. I would be fine," she finished on a strangled squeak.

"Slow your breathing down, Grace." He grabbed the back of her head and gently pushed it to her knees. "Count to ten between breaths."

"I'm not hysterical," she snapped, pulling free. "I'm being reasonable."

"You're going with me. Now tell me if you're still having your woman's flow," he said, hoping the quick change of subject would distract her.

Silence met his demand.

"Are you?" he repeated.

"My what?"

"Your woman's flow. From childbirth."

All he got was silence again, and then finally, "Are you implying that my hysteria is a woman thing?" she whispered.

Grey pinched the bridge of his nose so she wouldn't see his grin. "Grace, I need to know only because of the hike we're about to take. So I'll ask you again. Are you bleeding?"

"No," she squeaked after several long seconds of silence.

Well, he had accomplished two things. She had forgotten all about protesting her going with him, and he had managed to embarrass her beyond speech.

His grin widened. He'd probably riled her just enough that she could walk off this mountain by herself. He stood up, reached down, and pulled her up beside him.

"Come on. We've delayed long enough," he said. "Can you see to follow me?"

"Yes."

He hesitated. "Try to step in my tracks, and if you get tired, tell me. We'll take it slow."

She left without him. Grey hefted the bag holding her sister over his shoulder and ran to catch up. He moved ahead of her, silently laughing to himself.

Yes, Grace Sutter would do.

They walked for nearly an hour before she asked him to stop. Grey found them a place beneath a heavy-branched spruce tree, the only species of tree that seemed to be weathering this ice storm without damage. It protected them from the now driving rain that was only freezing when it connected with something cold. His hair was soaked, and rain was running down the neck of his jacket.

Baby was sleeping. Grey was actually thankful the child was so young. He was content just to sleep and eat, he weighed almost nothing, and as long as he was dry and warm he wasn't even aware of the peril he was in.

"How are you doing?" he asked, sitting down beside the spot where Grace had dropped like a stone.

"Okay. My muscles have actually limbered up. But I'm sweating to death."

That was not good. Wet clothes pulled heat away from

the body. "Unzip your jacket," he told her. "Maybe you should take off a few layers."

"I'm thirsty."

He thought about that. "You can take some snow and suck the water out of it, but then spit it out. Don't hold it until it all melts."

"Why not?"

"It takes too much of your body heat to melt ice. Just suck what water is immediately available. Then spit out the rest."

"How do you know all this stuff?"

He grinned in her direction through the darkness. "I'm from the Highlands," he said. "The tricks of winter survival are taught from the cradle."

"Why did you move to America? And why Maine?"

What to tell her? Not much, that was for sure.

He shrugged his shoulders. "It seemed like a good idea. The four of us wanted to build a new life for ourselves, and Maine, although slightly more forested than the Highlands, seemed as good a place as any."

He couldn't very well tell her that Daar, the old priest, had convinced the four of them that these mountains were where their destiny lay.

Too bad Daar had saved the MacBains' lives, too. All of them had died from their inability to adapt. All except Michael MacBain. Finding himself suddenly alone in this strange world, the bastard had followed them to Maine. And it had taken all of Grey's power as laird of his shrunken clan to keep his men from dispatching Michael MacBain to hell with the others.

"I'm ready now. How far do you think we've come?" Grace asked.

"About one mile," he told her truthfully, thankful that she didn't pursue her previous line of questioning.

"One mile!"

"The crust of ice on the snow is getting thicker. Soon you should be able to walk on top of it. But then there's the risk of you slipping and falling."

"We're not going to make it, are we?"

"We will," he told her. "I'll have you in front of a fire by daybreak."

But for the first time in his life, he was going to break a sincerely given promise, Grey decided three hours later.

Grace could not walk any farther. The crust had grown thick enough to support her, but, as he had feared, she had fallen more than once down a steep incline or stumbled over an ice-covered rock. This time, however, he could see that the fall had finished her.

He helped her up and brushed the hair from her face. His hand came away wet, and he knew it wasn't rain he was feeling. She was crying, silently, not saying a word.

He had to leave her, and that went against every instinct he possessed. The temperature was only just below freezing, but Grace was soaked to the skin. And she was not sweating or shivering. Her exhausted body was no longer producing heat.

"Sit down and rest," he told her, helping her to a spot under the canopy of a giant spruce tree.

Grey walked around, pushing at the crust with his feet. He found a place that he broke through all the way up to his thigh. He walked back and carefully took Baby out of his nest.

"He's stirring. I think you should feed him. Can you do that?" he asked.

"Yes," she answered, her voice barely audible.

He set Baby in her arms and took out one of the bottles he'd put in the bottom of the pack on his chest to keep warm. "When you're done, I'll change his diaper. It's important he keep dry."

She didn't answer him. She was too busy concentrating on her task. Grey watched for only a minute and then went back to the hole he had made in the crust and started digging. He scooped out the dry snow from the drift buried beneath the ice, forming a cave large enough for a person. Then he broke off several pine and spruce branches, shook the ice from them, and laid them on the floor of the cave.

Satisfied with his job, he returned to Grace to find Baby fussing in her arms. Grey picked him up and laid him on his shoulder. The infant let out a burp that would make a drunkard proud. He took off his jacket, laid it on the ground, and quickly changed Baby's diaper. Then he wrapped Baby up, protecting him from the elements, and turned to Grace.

"How are you feeling?" he asked.

"Fine."

"Grace," he said, slowly peeling her jacket off. "I think it's time we changed your clothes."

"I didn't bring any," she said, trying to slip back into her jacket.

He forcibly pulled it away. "I'm going to give you my T-shirt and sweater."

He saw her eyes widen in alarm. "What will you wear?"

"My jacket is waterproof. Yours isn't. I can put Baby's pack against my bare chest and put my jacket over us."

"But your sweater will just get wet then, if I wear it."

Well, at least some part of her brain was still functioning. That gave him hope. "No, it won't, Grace," he told her. "Because I'm going to tuck you into a waterproof cave. But I can't put you in there wet. Help me take off your shirt."

She merely blinked up at him. She wasn't catching on

to his plan. Hell, she probably wouldn't even realize he was leaving her until he was gone. He hoped like hell she didn't panic then and try to follow him. He was going to have to seal her into the cave securely.

He didn't like the idea of burying her. But it was the only thing he could think of to keep Grace alive long enough for him to get help.

He pulled Baby's pack off his shoulders and pulled off his sweater and T-shirt in one swipe. He grabbed Grace's wet tops by the hem and pulled them off over her head. The skin beneath them shone lily-white in contrast to the darkness.

"The bra, too, sweetheart," he said, reaching around her to undo the clasp. He didn't find one. But he saw her hands go to the front of her breasts. He pushed her cold, shivering fingers out of the way and worked at the intricate snaps for at least a minute, finally admitting defeat and ripping the delicate material with his hands.

Her skin was cold to the touch. Grey realized they were both sitting there naked from the waist up, and he quickly gathered her into his arms, pulling her into an embrace that would transfer some of his heat to her.

Grace immediately snuggled against him. Grey closed his eyes with a groan at how cold she was. He tucked her head under his chin and held her tightly.

"My God, you're so warm," she murmured.

He couldn't respond because she was scaring him to death. She should be slapping his face for such intimate contact. The freezing sickness was slowly claiming her body. She was shutting down, and there wasn't a damn thing he could do about it.

Except leave her.

"Aw, hell," he growled, tugging her head back and lowering his mouth to hers, kissing her with a fierceness that heated his blood to near boiling. He moved one hand from her back to her breasts, covering them completely, willing his heat into her.

Grace opened her mouth and accepted his assault. She made a noise that sounded more desperate than lustful and began squirming until she was straddling his lap. She wrapped her legs around his waist and her arms around his neck, tugging him closer, acting as if she wanted to crawl under his skin.

Grey was ashamed of himself. Grace Sutter was acting instinctively, desperate for the contact, wanting to pull his warmth—the very life energy he possessed—into herself. But he couldn't stop kissing her. She felt like an ice cube and tasted like sunshine. He wanted her. He wanted her to live.

And he wanted to get her down off this mountain and claim her as his.

Grey had to force himself to pull his mouth free, but he still couldn't leave her. He rained kisses over her eyes, her tear-covered cheeks, her nose, chin, and throat. He moved his lips lower, to her breasts, and kissed them when she arched her back against his mouth.

He was shaking with need for her.

She was shaking with need for his warmth.

With great reluctance and no small amount of will-power, Grey straightened and embraced Grace against him again, wrapping his arms around her until she was completely surrounded by his heat. He held her in silence as long as he dared, the cold slowly, quietly creeping into his own naked skin.

He gently pushed her away, gave her a quick kiss on the forehead, and settled first his T-shirt and then his sweater over her head, pulling them down to her wet pants.

"Grace," he said, his voice sounding strained even to

himself. He didn't want that. He wanted to sound confident for her. "I've got to leave you," he told her as she stared up at him, her big blue eyes two stark circles of desolation. "I won't be gone long. Just a few hours."

"Are you leaving Baby?" she asked, clutching his arms, that desolation suddenly turning to desperation. "Please, take him with you."

"I will, Grace." He stroked her wet hair. "He won't hamper my travel. I'll get him to safety, and then I'm coming back for you."

His news seemed to calm her. She settled back down, then turned and began looking for her jacket. He found it before she did and tossed it away from her.

"No. That's soaked. It will only freeze you quicker."

She just stared at the spot where her jacket was. Grey picked her up and carried her to the cave he had dug.

"I'm going to tuck you in here, out of the weather." He took her by the chin and made her look at him. "I'm going to seal it up after you're inside. Do you understand, Grace?"

Her chin moved slightly up and down in his hand. He leaned forward and kissed her on the lips. "That's my lass. Are you afraid of small places, Grace?"

She moved her head from side to side. He kissed her again, first on one of her cold cheeks and then on the other. "Good. Here, now, in you go."

He tucked her, feet first, into the hole.

"It's too small. I don't fit."

"Yes, you do. Curl into a ball, just like your baby when he was inside of you. You'll stay warmer."

She popped her head out of the hole and looked at him. "I'm . . . I'm not brave," she told him, as if she were confessing her greatest sin. "I'm a coward."

"You are not. Courage is nothing more than having a

choice and doing the scary thing anyway. You've shown more courage today than any other person I know, Grace Sutter. And you'll continue to fight because of your baby, and because I'm going to be damn mad if you don't." He leaned down until their noses were nearly touching. "And believe me," he said softly, "this cave will seem like heaven compared with my temper."

He almost fell over when she kissed him. She tilted her head and brushed her cold, soft lips against his. His heart nearly stopped beating. He held her by the back of the head and deepened the kiss. She opened her mouth and accepted his tongue inside her again, gently sucking on it with innocent ardor.

It was Grey wanting to crawl inside her skin this time. The woman was slowly killing him with desperation—and with her unbelievable trust. She was kissing him, not crying or railing that he take her with him. Not even questioning his decision.

Just simply kissing him.

Grey pulled her back out of the hole, just enough so he could wrap his arms around her again. He slid his hands up under his shirts that she wore and once more covered both of her breasts as he swallowed her moan with his mouth.

A large chunk of ice suddenly hit him squarely on the back. Grey broke their kiss and stared at Grace, his hands still holding her intimately.

"Thank you," she whispered, covering his hands with hers, clasping them to her breasts.

"You're welcome," he whispered back, looking at her mouth.

"Don't . . . don't read anything into what just happened," she said, suddenly wiggling back, sounding more like herself. "Your kisses just warm me up."

Grey dropped his hands away from her breasts and smoothed down her sweater.

"Can I keep the bag?" she asked.

He had to mentally shift gears. He shook his head. He was still feeling the effects of her kiss, and she was back to business.

"Yes," he said, inwardly cringing at the thought of putting her dead sister into the tomb-like cave with her.

He stood up and found the bag. He took out some supplies for Baby and then carried it over to her, tucking it in beside her.

"Grace. I don't want you going to sleep, do you understand? You've got to stay awake until I come back."

"I know. I might not wake up."

Satisfied that she understood the consequences, he reached down and ran a finger over her face. "I want you to spend your time thinking of a name for your baby, Grace, while I'm gone. I expect to hear your answer when I get back."

She didn't answer him. She was too busy digging into her confounded bag again. He watched her pull out a thin black box, recognizing it as the computer she had used earlier. She opened it up and pushed a button. The machine started to hum and make funny noises, and suddenly Grace's little cave was awash in light.

She looked up at him. "I'm going to write a letter," she said. "And it won't be dark in here, either." She reached up and ran her finger over his cheek. "Okay. Cover me up." He saw her take a deep breath. "I'm ready."

"Never say you're a coward, Grace. Never use that word for yourself again," he said past the lump of anguish clogging his throat. Damn, he wished she had waited until he was gone to give herself light. Now he couldn't get the picture of her out of his head.

He could see her clearly, and it was not a reassuring sight. There was no color left on her face. She was as starkly white as the snow that surrounded her. Her hair was soaked, and her eyes were sunken into her head. Her lips were the only thing he could see that had any color, and they were blue.

And all his lovemaking had accomplished, as far as he could tell, was to warm her up just enough that she was shivering again.

But how long would it last?

Grey forced himself to turn away. He began carving out a large slab of crust with his fist. He pounded the ice until his hands were raw, taking out his frustration at what he was about to do.

He picked up the slab of crust and held it over Grace, and this time it was his turn to take a steadying breath. She was clutching the computer as if it were a lifeline, its light reflecting off her pale features.

"I'm coming back, Grace. In just a few hours, I'll be pulling you out of here."

"I know."

He started to set the slab over the entrance.

"Grey?"

"Yes?" he said, moving it aside.

"Warmth isn't the only reason I like your kisses," she softly admitted, not looking at him.

"I know," he said. "You like kissing a superman."

"Hmmm," she murmured, still not looking at him. "Something like that."

"Tomorrow, lass, once you're sitting in front of the roaring hearth at Gu Bràth, I'll explain to you why you like them so much," he whispered before setting the slab of crust over the entrance, patting it into place and securing it with more snow.

Grey closed his eyes and began the same litany of prayers he usually reserved for flying. They had worked once already today, allowing him to survive plummeting three thousand feet down to the ground. He hoped they worked again to keep Grace Sutter safe.

That done, he quickly returned to Baby. He put the pack back on over his naked chest and then unwrapped his jacket. Baby, still blissfully unaware that he was in the middle of a treacherous march, was sleeping again. Grey picked him up, kissed his warm little cheek, and settled him into his pack. He slipped back into his jacket, then picked up Grace's shirt and coat. He hung them over an ice-encrusted branch, at eye level, to mark the spot for his return.

He headed down the mountain again, this time setting a pace as if the hounds of hell were dogging his heels.

Grace waited until she was sure he was gone before she broke into loud, gut-wrenching sobs. She had survived the terrifying crash with Grey, argued with him, and helped him. He had listened to her opinions, discussed their choices, and allowed her the dignity to go down fighting. Not once had he tried to brush her aside and take complete control of the situation. And she knew, without compunction, that if she had fought him about staying here now, he would have died trying to take her with him.

Today they had forged a bond that she hadn't known could exist between two people. Together they had struggled for their very survival, and they were winning.

She was burrowed into a snow cave like a hibernating bear, but Grey would return for her. She knew he would.

But she wasn't stupid, either. She also knew that anything could happen on his trip down the mountain, and there was no guarantee he would make it back in time. So she was going to pull up her word-processing program and write her last will and testament.

And she was going to write a letter to Michael MacBain.

She was the only living person in the world who knew who Baby's father was. She could not go to her grave without revealing the truth.

Chapter Six

The old wizard opened the door and stepped out onto the cabin porch, ignoring the sting of sleet on his face as he looked up toward where TarStone Mountain stood in dark, stoic indifference. He couldn't see past the end of the clearing that surrounded his home, but he still felt the mountain's substantial presence.

He also knew all was not right with it.

The storm had arrived on unusually silent feet, creeping down over the east ridge like a predatory beast. The rain had started yesterday morning, beginning as a mist that had clung like hoarfrost to everything it touched. By afternoon it had become steady, relentlessly encasing the world under a sheet of glistening ice. And now, deep into the wee hours of the morning, the heavy, entombing ice was half an inch thick.

Daar pulled the collar of his red plaid wool Mackinaw coat up to meet his trimmed white beard. The kerosene porch lamp he had lit at dusk last night, and had filled three times already, dimmed from lack of fuel yet again. He reached up, took it down from the nail, and carried it inside to refill it, his sense of urgency stronger than ever.

All was not right on the mountain.

He hadn't been able to shake the feeling of gathering menace since the storm had descended. He had not slept or eaten since last night. Instead he had kept vigil, refilling his lamps and pacing the length of his porch until the cold seeping into his tired old bones sent him back to the fire. He was in the seventh hour of the incessant ritual.

He poured the last of his kerosene into the lamp, mentally reminding himself to ask Grey to bring him some more. He still had candles, and the old river-stone hearth produced some light, but he liked the brightness the kerosene lamps offered.

Daar suddenly stilled in the act of replacing the chimney on the lamp, and turned to the front door. The sense of urgency was stronger now. Whatever was out there, on the mountain, was coming closer.

He picked up the lamp and carried it back out to the porch, replacing it on the nail pounded into the side of the cabin. Using his stout, burl-ridden cane to steady himself, he walked to the end of the sturdy-planked deck and looked out in the direction of TarStone. The hair on the back of his neck stirred in apprenhension. Urgency, desperation, and fear were moving toward him at a relentless pace, the energy pushing ahead of it strong enough to make Daar step back.

It broke into the clearing with all the racket of cannons going off. Footsteps, pounding through the crust with powerful blasts, thundered over the sound of crackling branches. Without slowing down, Greylen MacKeage took the porch steps two at a time and rushed right past the priest without seeing him.

"Daar!" he hollered into the empty cabin, stepping inside and throwing off his jacket before Daar could even make his way through the door.

"I'm here," he said calmly, stepping into the warmth behind Grey. "What's happened? What do you need?"

Grey swung around to face him, and Daar took a step back. Something unfathomable was in the warrior's eyes.

Something frightening.

Grey unzipped the pack he had strapped to his heaving, sweating chest and pulled out a squirming, mewling infant no larger than a mite.

"He's soaked," he said between labored breaths. "You've got to get him dry before he chills."

"*I* have to?" Daar asked, alarmed, as he looked at the tiny babe Grey had set on the table. "I don't know anything of infants."

Grey ignored his argument and began stripping the child bare. "Get me a towel then," he ordered. "And a washcloth. He's covered with my sweat."

Daar hurried around to the kitchen area of the one-room cabin, found a towel and cloth, and brought them back to Grey, then watched as the young warrior worked.

"Who is he?" he asked, able to see it was a boy-child.

"He belongs to Grace Sutter," Grey said, working quickly and efficiently to wipe down and dry off the child. He pulled a diaper out of his pack, only to realize it was as wet as the infant had been. He tossed it on the floor and used the towel as a makeshift diaper. He looked up at Daar then.

"She's back on the mountain, about two miles up. I've got her tucked into a snow cave, but she's wet, too."

The desperation Daar saw in Grey's eyes was chilling.

"She's not going to last much longer," Grey continued. "I'm leaving Baby here and going on to Gu Bràth for the snowcat."

"Not until you catch your breath, you're not," Daar

said, going to the bucket on the counter and filling a glass with water. "And you need to replenish the water you've lost and get some stew into you. You won't even make it to the natural bridge if you don't."

He set the glass of water on the now empty table. Grey was pacing the floor with the infant in his arms. He'd taken the pack off his chest, and the child was snuggled under the crook of Grey's chin, sucking his fist.

"I don't have time. Do ya not understand?" Grey said, glaring at him. "She's dying."

"And if you collapse before you reach help? What are her chances then?" Daar countered, pulling out a chair and physically guiding Grey to it.

It was not an easy task. The angered, desperate warrior was a solid mass of tension. The muscles of his back were bunched with coiled, waiting power he would not release. Grey still needed something from them, and he wasn't dropping his guard until he was finished.

"Get his bottle from the pack," Grey ordered, sitting finally but looking ready to spring back up at any moment. He did, just as soon as Daar had the bottle in his hand.

"Here. You sit down and feed him," Grey said, moving to hand him the babe. "I'll drink your water, but I'm not eating. That will only make me sick."

Daar didn't want to hold the babe, but then he wasn't up to taking on Greylen MacKeage. He sat down and let him set the bairn in his arms. Grey screwed open the bottle, put a nipple on it, and handed it to him.

"Aren't you supposed to warm it up or something?" Daar asked, carefully holding the fussing bairn.

"It's probably boiling," Grey said. "From the heat of my body."

Daar placed the nipple in the tiny mouth and smiled

suddenly at the sight of the babe eagerly, greedily sucking. Satisfied that he could handle the chore, he looked up at Grey.

"What happened?"

"I was in a goddamned plane when it decided not to fly anymore. We crashed on North Finger Ridge." He drank down the entire glass of water and went to the counter to refill it. "Grace and the babe were with me. The pilot's dead."

Daar looked out the window beside the door, in the direction of TarStone. "You said Grace Sutter? Is she our Mary's sister?"

Another wave of pain rolled over Grey's face as he stared at Daar. He nodded. "Yes. She's Mary's sister."

The old priest stared at the warrior he'd befriended four years ago, when Grey and nine other men had burst into his church. They had formed a pact of necessary means. The men needed him to show them the way, and he needed Greylen MacKeage to father his heir.

Not that Daar had ever mentioned that little detail to the warrior. He was wise enough to have a care for his own welfare. Laird MacKeage had been dangerously mad four years ago, to find himself in a situation he could not control. And if he could have found a target for his anger, well, Daar knew for a fact he would not be here today. The man had a temper that no sane person—semi-immortal or not—would want directed at him.

The old wizard watched the agitated warrior as he downed another full glass of water. This woman, this Grace Sutter, meant something to Grey.

Daar suddenly became excited. Could it be that he was finally going to meet the mother of his heir?

He looked down at the bairn in his arms and frowned. The babe presented a problem. The woman Grey had traveled so far to claim was not supposed to be a mother already.

"I'm leaving," Grey suddenly said, heading for the door. "Once I have Grace, I'm bringing her here to warm her up. Take care of the babe, and have the fire burning strong. And keep your stew warm."

"Wait. You forgot your jacket."

"I donna need it. It only makes me sweat. I only wore it for the bairn."

Daar stared at him. "You're relishing this challenge," he said.

"I'm not," Grey snapped, swinging toward him. "My woman is dying on the mountain."

Daar held up his hand. "And you'll save her. But you've regressed to your old warrior ways, running through a frozen forest half naked, pushing yourself beyond reasonable endurance. All you're lacking is the war paint."

Grey stared at him.

Daar pointed his age-bent finger directly at Grey. "You're more alive than you've been in four years."

The warrior suddenly let out a Gaelic curse that should have set the cabin on fire.

Daar laughed out loud until his eyes watered. "You're going to hell for cursing a priest, MacKeage!" he shouted at Grey's disappearing back. "Go save your woman. And bring her back here for me to meet."

He was talking to an empty room. Grey was already off the porch and running to Gu Bràth. Daar wiped the moisture from his eyes and looked down at the now sleeping infant. He gently pulled the no longer wanted nipple out of its mouth.

He was a pretty bairn. And young. He weighed less than Daar's cherrywood cane. The old priest smiled at the picture the child presented. Grey had taken the oversized towel and wrapped it around the babe's bottom and then over its chest like a plaid. Only his arms and legs and one shoulder remained uncovered.

And that was when Daar discovered another unsettling fact that disturbed him greatly.

Grace Sutter's babe had twelve toes.

They almost missed her, the visibility was so poor. Grey had the door to the snowcat opened before the track-driven machine came to a stop. He ran to the giant spruce and pulled the stiff, frozen jacket and shirts down as he looked around, getting his bearings. The crust was now thick enough to hold even his considerable weight, and he paced to the north another ten feet.

He looked down and saw nothing but smooth white ice.

"You said you left her in a snow cave?" Morgan asked, coming up behind Grey. "Where?"

"Here," he told him, pointing at where the entrance should have been. "Right in this drift."

"It was dark," Callum reminded him, coming up beside both men. He was carrying an axe.

Grey was glad at least one of them was thinking clearly. He took the axe from Callum and started banging the crust along the drift. Now that it was daylight, but still raining, he could see that the drift was nearly twenty feet wide, running along and below an outcropping of ledge. He ordered his men to be silent and listened to the thump of the axe.

He had never in his life been as scared as he was now. Not even four years ago when the storm had carried them all through hell. Then his only focus had been survival, but if he had died, so be it. This time, however, he feared for the life of another.

And that fear was beginning to turn to panic.

Ian joined the party of three, moving awkwardly as he approached on legs riddled with arthritis. "It's been hours. The lass might not be alive," he suggested softly.

"She damn well better be alive," Grey said, not looking up from his task. And that's when he saw it, a faint, barely visible glow of blue light just beneath the surface of ice. "Here," he said, tossing the axe away and getting down on his knees. "Start digging, but use your fists, not tools."

Morgan and Callum got down on their knees with Grey and began beating the crust with their bare, calloused hands. Ian picked up the axe and used it to pull away the broken pieces they produced.

In less than a minute they broke through the barrier he had used to seal Grace up, and Grey closed his eyes at what he found.

She was dead. There was no color left in her face, save for her blue lips. She was clutching the tin that held Mary's ashes, and when he tried to remove it he couldn't. Her arms were locked in their embrace.

Grey pulled himself back out of the hole. He closed his eyes, raised his face to the unending rain, and roared with the anger of a wounded beast.

"By God, that woke the dead," Ian said, pushing Callum aside to move closer. "She flinched. I tell you, the lass just moved."

Grey jerked as if he'd been punched. He dove back into the cave and took Grace by the shoulders, gently prying her out. He had her in his arms and was already started for the snowcat before the others could scramble out of the way.

"Morgan. Get her things from the cave," he said. "Callum, open this door. Ian, get this goddamned cat started again. You shouldn't have shut it off."

"Ya wanted silence," Ian reminded him as he headed around the snowcat to climb into the driver's seat.

Callum, wisely silent, held the door while Grey climbed inside without loosening his hold on the frighteningly stiff woman curled up in his arms like an unborn baby.

Though Callum and Ian were several years Grey's senior, all of the men had grown up in a time when a laird's words, orders, and temper were to be taken seriously.

Grey was glad that some old habits died hard.

He knew he was being unreasonable, but he couldn't help it. The woman in his arms was lifeless. She had given him the gift of her trust last night, and he'd very nearly broken it.

Grey took up the entire backseat of the cat, which meant that Morgan had to ride in the back cargo area in the open rain. The young warrior didn't complain. He simply tossed Grace's bag in with Grey and slammed the door shut. Two seconds later he pounded on the roof, signaling Ian to go.

The large, surprisingly nimble snowcat roared into action, turning around and starting its careful descent back down the mountain, its sure-footed tracks following the same path it had used to ascend. Tree limbs slapped at the windows and roof, raining ice and broken branches over the loudly protesting forest they were leaving behind. Morgan was scrunched up against the back window, his arms covering his head.

Grey knew nothing of what was happening around him. He wasn't even aware they were moving. He was focused on Grace, his hand over her heart, searching for a heartbeat.

"Good Lord," Callum said, turning around in the front seat to face Grey. "Her hair is frozen solid."

Grey touched it, covering her head with his hand and using his fingers to break the ice free to rain onto the floor like beads of crystal.

"You should thaw her brain out first," Ian offered from the driver's seat, not taking his eyes off their path. "People think it's the heart you want to warm up first, but it's the brain."

Grey wanted to warm up every inch of her, all at the same time. He gently pried the tin from her arms and carefully set it in the bag at his feet. He then fought with the button and zipper of her once soaked, now frozen pants. It was difficult because she was still curled up into a ball.

"Straighten her out," Callum suggested. "Is she stuck that way?"

"You're going to be riding in back with Morgan, Callum, if you don't shut up and turn around," Grey said, his threat evident in his tone.

Dammit. She was breathing, but barely. And he could feel her heartbeat, but it was as faint as her breath.

"Face front," he warned Callum again.

Satisfied the man was obeying, Grey pulled his still dry but cold sweater off Grace. He cut the bindings of Mark's boots to remove them, then he forced the zipper on her pants down and pulled them off with all the difficulty of stripping a snake of its skin.

Her flawless body was stone cold and white all over.

"Toss me the blankets that are by the heater," he told Callum. "Without looking," he added, reaching up to catch them. He covered Grace and then took off his own flannel shirt. He pulled her against him and wrapped them both up in one blanket, tenting the other over her head.

He started running his hand over her entire body, careful not to knead her so strongly as to bruise her delicate skin. He splayed his palms over her back and lifted her against his chest, closing his eyes at the feel of her frozen, unresponsive body touching his. And again, Grey wanted to crawl inside Grace's skin and use the strength of his frantically beating heart to stir her blood.

He kissed her instead.

With a quick look to make sure Callum was still turned facing front, Grey carefully brushed the hair from Grace's face and touched his lips to her cold cheek. He sent his hands roaming over her back again, pressing her breasts against his chest as he continued to kiss her eyes, her nose, her forehead, before finally covering her mouth with his own.

And still she didn't respond.

Grey wanted to shout. He didn't know what else to do, other than hug her tightly and give her his warmth. It was like hugging a granite statue. They rode the two miles to Daar's cabin in silence, the drone of the engine and shattering ice serving as warning to anything in their path.

Daar had heard them coming and was standing on the porch in the same place he had been when they had driven by earlier. Grey stepped out of the snowcat with Grace in his arms, and Daar opened the door and led the way inside the cabin. The blast of hot, dry heat nearly overwhelmed him.

"Put her on the bed," Daar instructed.

Grey did as he was told, then pulled off his boots, stripped off the rest of his clothes, and crawled in beside Grace. The old priest stood on the opposite side of the bed and frowned at him.

"What are you doing?" he asked.

"I'm warming her," Grey snapped. "Did you make some coffee?"

Daar didn't move. He simply raised a brow at Grey. "I'm not a MacKeage," he said. "So stop growling at me."

Grey closed his eyes and willed himself patience. "You're our priest, under my protection, therefore you're under my rule."

The old man walked away, muttering to himself. Grey rearranged the blankets around Grace and drew up the ones on the bed to add to them.

Three hours later he was sweating, and the woman beside him was slowly limbering up. But she still hadn't stirred or even fluttered an eyelash. Oh, he was going to lecture her for falling asleep instead of concentrating on the chore he had given her. She was supposed to have been thinking of names for her son, not dying.

Grey looked over at the wall opposite the bed. Baby was sleeping as soundly as his mother, tucked into a wooden box the old priest had padded with clothes. He heard the baby sigh every so often, and Grey wondered what one so young could dream about.

"Now what in hell are you doing?" he asked when Daar returned to sit beside the bed, beads in hand and murmuring under his breath.

"I'm praying, you pagan fool. That's what priests do."

Grey turned at the sound of the cabin door opening. His three men walked in, soaked to the skin and looking mad as hell.

"We've been to the crash site," Callum said, shaking his head. "I'm never flying again, by God."

"We brought the pilot down," Ian added. "The fool was flying barefoot."

Morgan came to stand beside the bed and peer down at Grace. "She appears to be melting okay," he said, grinning. He looked at Grey. "So are you. You're soaked." He unbuttoned his coat and threw it off. "It's damn hot in here."

"Maybe a walk home would cool you off," Grey told him, his eyes warning his brother to back away.

Morgan stood his ground, broadened his grin, and looked back at Grace. "She's pretty." He lifted one brow at Grey. "Need me to spell you a bit?"

"Out!" he said through gritted teeth, pretending to get up and go after Morgan. Unimpressed, Morgan turned around and sauntered over to the stove to pour himself a cup of coffee.

"We couldn't bring all your stuff down," Ian said, settling himself into a chair with a tired groan. He unbuttoned his coat and threw his soggy hat on the table. "We'll make another trip later today. Once we have your woman off this mountain."

"Do you think we should take her to a hospital or something?" Callum asked. "She's not waking up."

"It's forty miles away," Ian reminded him before Grey could answer.

"There's Doc Betters," Morgan suggested.

"He's a horse doctor, you fool," Ian lamented, rolling his eyes at Morgan.

"Did she sustain any injuries in the crash?" the still praying priest asked Grey.

Grey shook his head. "Nothing serious that I know of. She said she was only bruised. And she walked a good three hours before she fell hard enough that she couldn't go on."

"Maybe she hit her head," Callum suggested, walking over to the bed to examine her himself. He suddenly smiled. "Morgan's right. She is a bonny lass." He looked at Grey. "You're acting very possessive. You intend to keep her?"

Grey looked down at the woman in his arms. "I might," he said softly, as if he were speaking to her. He looked back at his man. "Is it still raining?"

"Yes. And it shows no signs of letting up."

"The weatherman is saying this could last for days," Morgan interjected from the counter he was leaning on, sipping his coffee. "Strange conditions have trapped a lot of cold air near the ground and warm air above it."

"The trees are taking a beating," Ian said. "The birch are already bending under the strain. And weaker limbs are breaking clean off."

"It's nature's way of cleaning out the rotten and the weak," Callum said. "We had ice storms in the Highlands."

"Trees can break and regrow," Ian said with a growl, awkwardly getting up from his chair and pouring his own cup of coffee. "But our ski lift won't grow itself back if it breaks. This ice is adding a lot of weight to it."

Careful to keep Grace covered, Grey sat up in the bed and leaned on the headboard, keeping her tucked protectively against his side. The air was still warm in the cabin, but it was a hell of a lot easier to breathe now, with his chest free of the stifling blankets.

"The lift and cables are made of steel," he told Ian, dismissing his concern. "They're much stronger than any tree. They won't break."

"I still say we should have become loggers instead of pursuing this insane notion to cater to a bunch of spoiled vacationers who have nothing better to do," Ian grumbled.

"We voted," Grey told him for the hundredth time, getting tired of Ian's predictions of doom. But Grey and the others usually forgave the old warrior his flaw. It couldn't be easy suddenly, at fifty-eight years of age, to be uprooted from family the way Ian had been.

Ian was the only one of them who had lost a wife, two daughters, and two fine sons four years ago. Callum had been a widower, Morgan had still not decided to settle down, and Grey had not been in any hurry to find a wife back then, either.

One unfaithful fiancée had been enough.

Still, Ian's black view of everything was wearing thin. If they had become loggers as he often suggested, the man would be worried about forest fires instead.

"You may thank me now, Grey," Daar suddenly interjected into the quiet. "My prayers have worked. Your woman is awake."

Grace was dreaming she was in the sauna at her gym. Only something was wrong. She must have fallen asleep and cooked herself, because she was so hot she couldn't move a muscle in her body.

"Open your eyes, Grace," a deep, demanding voice suddenly whispered.

There was a man in the sauna with her? More out of curiosity than obedience, Grace slowly opened her eyes to see who had dared enter the sauna while she was in it. She was going to give him hell for intruding on her privacy.

She screamed instead.

There were four male giants staring down at her.

"Easy, Grace. You're safe now," the same voice said.

Safe? There were *men* in the sauna with her. She turned in the direction the voice had come from, keeping a watch with the corner of her eye on the other four men. But she suddenly gave her full attention to the one leaning over her. It was Greylen MacKeage, the man from the airplane. And he looked as warm as she was. Sweat glistened off his broad, impressively naked, hairy chest.

"How did you get in here? This is the women's sauna."

"Sauna?" he repeated, looking confused.

"I told you we should have warmed her brain up first," another voice said from above her. "Now she's daft."

Frowning, Grace turned to see who had spoken. "Do you work here?" she asked, trying to sound authoritative, wanting to scare him half as much as all of them were scaring her. By heaven, she would bluster her way out of this.

"Grace. You're not in a sauna," Grey said from beside her.

She turned back to him. "It's hot."

"You're at the cabin I told you about. Do you remember the plane crash?"

She thought about that. Yes, she remembered the plane crash. And she remembered the snow cave. She gasped, looking up into Grey's eyes. "I waited for you," she told him. "But you didn't come."

"I did," he said fiercely. "You went to sleep, Grace."

"I did not."

"Your eyes were shut tight when we found you, lass. We thought you were dead."

She turned to glare at the man making that claim; it was the same man who had said she was daft. His fierce face was smiling, though, as he nodded his head at her. "So if you weren't dead, you must have been sleeping," he added.

"You were supposed to be thinking of a name for Baby," Grey told her, drawing her attention again.

"I'm calling him Baby," she said, lifting her chin. By God, he had taken his good old time returning for her.

Oh, she remembered everything now. The cold. The dark when the battery on her computer died. And the terrible sense of loneliness.

"Who are these people?" she whispered to Grey, her gaze moving to the four men who rudely kept staring at her.

"The old man with the wild white hair and the prayer beads is Father Daar. This is his cabin," he told her, nodding toward a man who looked older than time. Except for his eyes. Father Daar had the brightest, clearest blue eyes she had ever seen. He smiled at her when Grey introduced him.

"And this is Callum," he continued, nodding at the man beside Father Daar.

Grace looked at him. Callum grinned past a bushy beard, his hazel-green eyes echoing his smile, his shaggy, dark auburn hair wet and dripping on his shoulders. He looked to be fortyish, and, like all of them, he was well over six feet tall.

"And Morgan," Grey said, moving along to the next man.

Grace turned her attention to Morgan. He was young and clean-shaven, his wet, blond-red hair sticking out as if he'd been running a hand through it. He shot her a crooked grin and winked at her.

Grace quickly looked at the next man.

"And Ian," Grey finished.

Ian was the one who had told Grace she'd fallen asleep. His hair was a brighter red than the others' with gray highlights beginning to show near his ears. He had a beard, too, peppered with white and in dire need of a set of clippers. He wasn't smiling anymore. He was looking at her as if she were a bug under a microscope. So Grace smiled at him instead.

She knew all of them. At least she knew of them. Mary had told her about the MacKeages and Father Daar, five men who had moved here a little over three years ago when they had bought TarStone Mountain as well as most of the forested land for miles around. They kept to themselves for the most part, Mary had said, and nobody in town could find out much about them.

Grace stared at them, unblinking. They didn't look related, although four of them had the same last name. Except for the youngest one, Morgan. There was something familiar about him, the way he carried himself, maybe. A mannerism. An expression. The way the corner of his mouth lifted in amusement.

Actually, he reminded her of Grey. Yes. Morgan had the same dark, penetrating, evergreen eyes.

Grace turned her head enough to see Father Daar. Her sister had also told her about the priest who lived like a hermit halfway up the mountain. Mary had said he was positively ancient, and she had often worried that he was too old to be living alone.

All of them were strangers to her, and although some of them were larger than her half brothers, they seemed harmless enough and sincerely concerned for her welfare. Grace relaxed back into the softness of the bed—until she discovered a rather alarming fact, given the company she was in.

"I'm naked," she accused, turning to glare at Grey. "How did that happen?"

"Is your modesty worth dying over?" he asked.

She closed her eyes and wondered if she could turn any redder than the lobster she must look like already. She also wondered if she might possibly die after all, but from embarrassment, not cold.

"Are you not wondering about your son?" the man named Ian asked.

"Oh my God! Baby. I forgot all about him. Where is he?" she asked, suddenly frantic as she craned her neck to look around the room.

"He's here," Father Daar said, moving aside for her to see Baby. "He's sleeping. He's fine."

Grace closed her eyes and thanked God for that miracle. She also asked him to get her out of the mess she had just made. These men would all think she was an unfit mother for forgetting her son.

Well, she was. Those should have been the first words out of her mouth when she woke up. Instead, she had been too focused on finding herself naked while sharing a bed with a man, her hormones zinging around like crazy, and an audience—part of which was a priest, no less— watching her.

Grace burst into tears. Huge, gut-wrenching sobs shook her body with painful results. Every square inch of her hurt like the devil. But it was nothing compared with the pain she felt in her heart.

She had forgotten Baby.

"Now look what you've done, Ian," Callum accused. "You've made the lass cry."

"Grace. He's okay," Grey told her, brushing the hair away from her face.

She couldn't even look at him. She couldn't look at any of them. She was scum. Just scum. She didn't deserve the child.

"You do," Grey said, his voice sounding harsh. "Anyone who has been through what you have these last few hours would be disoriented. And you've not been a mother very long."

She must have said her thoughts out loud, and Grey was scolding her for them. She tried to roll over to bury her face in the pillow so she could bawl in private, but she couldn't turn over. Her muscles wouldn't work. The attempt did tell her one thing, though. Greylen MacKeage was as naked as she was.

"Could you . . . could you maybe let me have the bed to myself?" she asked in a strained whisper, hoping her shock didn't show in her voice. "I, ah, would be more comfortable."

He laughed out loud, shaking the bed as he did. Grace stifled a groan. Even that movement hurt.

"I will. Just as soon as you tell me where you hurt."

"I'll tell you just as soon as you leave the bed," she countered, still keeping her eyes closed to the pounding in her head.

Silence was all the answer she got. Finally, she felt the bed dip and heard him scramble up and away. She let out a breath she hadn't known she was holding, and the ache in her head suddenly dulled.

"Ho-oh. It's started now," Ian said. "The MacKeage is already backing down from an argument with her."

Grace heard something hit the wall across the room with a plop, followed by good-natured laughter.

Gingerly, and in great pain, she pulled the blankets tight to her neck and concentrated on each inch of her body, taking stock of just where she ached.

She concluded that she was one massive bruise. The muscles in her legs and back were cramping with a will of their own, and the tips of her toes and fingers tingled with needle-pricking intensity.

She had come very close to getting frostbite. If not for the protection of the cave Grey had made her and the pilot's waterproof boots, they would probably be cutting her toes off in less than a week. She had kept her hands warm with the heat from the battery on her computer. But if Grey hadn't arrived when he had, she would be dead now.

He'd saved her life. And he had saved Baby.

How was she ever supposed to repay that kind of debt?

"Are you hungry?" Father Daar asked her in a whisper, leaning close to the bed. "I have some stew ready."

"No, thank you, Father. I'm just sleepy."

"I wouldn't be going back to sleep if I were you," he said in a co-conspirator's tone. "Grey would have a worried fit. You scared ten years off his pagan life this morning."

She gave the priest a huge smile. "If he's a pagan, Father, then he's redeemed himself. He saved me and Baby."

Father Daar gave her a warm smile back. "That was never a question, girl. Greylen MacKeage is a man who succeeds at whatever he sets his mind to. You were never in any real danger."

"I'm still waiting for your answer," the object of their conversation said from right above her.

Grace turned her head and looked up at Grey. "Nothing's broken or frostbit. My muscles are just so sore and stiff that I don't want to move."

He seemed to think about that, staring down at her with assessing evergreen eyes. Finally, he nodded.

"You may sleep, then, if you need to," he arrogantly told her. "When you wake you'll eat, and then we'll take you down the mountain."

"Where's my bag?" she asked. "Is it still in the cave?"

He walked over to the table and brought it back to her. "Here. Do you want the tin?"

"Yes, please," she said. "Thank you."

He took the tin out of the bag and tucked it under the blankets beside her.

"Thank you," she repeated.

"Are ya hungry now, lass?" Callum asked, eyeing the lump in the bed where the tin sat. "Cookies aren't what you should be having. You need real food."

"The tin's not carrying cookies," Grey answered before she could, his gaze not leaving hers. "It's carrying Mary Sutter."

A silence so loud it was nearly deafening suddenly settled over the one-room cabin.

Chapter Seven

$\mathscr{N}$*o matter that they were* all safe now, it seemed that Greylen MacKeage was still in charge of this adventure. Grace could only watch helplessly from the bed as the man issued orders like a general. Within ten minutes the tiny cabin was cleared of Scots except for Grey.

Even the priest was gone. Grace had protested sending the frail-looking man out in this weather, but Grey had been too focused on his plan to hear her opinion. Father Daar was to accompany the pilot's body back down the mountain and stay with him while Callum and Morgan went into town to notify the authorities and lead them back to the crash site. Ian would return with the snowcat to take Grace and Baby back to Gu Bràth.

And so Grace patiently waited until she had Grey's undivided attention before she explained her own plan to him.

Only it wasn't that easy. It's hard to project authority when you're lying naked in bed with the covers pulled up to your chin. It's even harder when the man you're trying to impress is impressively naked himself from the waist up.

"Do you have some clothes I can put on?" she asked Grey.

He turned from the woodstove to face her, a steaming bowl of stew in his hand and a crooked grin lifting one corner of his mouth. "What's wrong with what you're wearing?" he asked, walking toward her.

Grace tightened the covers at her neck. "I'm not wearing anything."

He sat on the bed beside her, the heat from his thigh sending another round of needles shooting through her quickly overheating body. "You don't need clothes," he said. "You need food and rest, in that order."

"I have to get up," she countered. "I need to get my muscles working again so I can take Baby home."

He was shaking his head. "You just survived a great ordeal, Grace. You're still too weak to look after yourself." He lifted the spoon from the bowl and held it up to her lips. "Eat and rest, and leave everything to me. In a day or two I'll take you home."

Grace refused to open her mouth for the stew. She didn't glare or pout but simply stared at Grey with the patience of a woman determined to regain control of her life. She wasn't angry. Not yet. Grace understood that it was hard to relinquish authority once it was given.

Grey slowly set the spoon back in the bowl and lifted one brow at her in question. "What happened to our partnership?"

"I'm dissolving it," she said, tempering her words with a smile. "I owe you my life, Greylen MacKeage, but I want it back now. You don't have to keep taking care of me."

He looked as if he wanted to protest but seemed to think better of it. He stood up and set the stew on the table, grabbed his shirt from the floor, and shrugged into it. He then picked up a bundle of clothes sitting by the door and set it down on the bed beside her.

"I thought to grab these this morning when I reached

Gu Bràth, just before coming back for you. They'll be too big, but they'll be warm." He reached down and took her by the chin, lifting her face to his. "If you can dress yourself without passing out and prove to me that you can care for your son, then maybe I'll think about taking you home."

That said, he turned on his heel, grabbed his jacket, and headed out onto the porch.

Grace blinked at the door softly closing behind him. That had been *way* too easy. She looked at the bundle of clothes and immediately felt bad. Only a caring man would have thought to grab her something to wear while trying to save her life.

And to thank him, she had hurt his feelings.

Baby stirred in the crate beside her, and Grace quickly shook out the bundle of clothes. Her arms felt heavy, and her muscles protested, but she forced herself to sit up and slide into the flannel shirt Grey had brought her. She had to roll up the sleeves several turns just to find her hands. Then she took the large wool socks and slipped them onto her feet.

She swung her legs over the side of the bed, pulled on the soft jogging pants he had brought her, and stood up to pull them up to her waist. She nearly fell down instead.

Her forehead throbbed, and her knees threatened to buckle. Grace immediately sat down and grabbed her head to make the room stop spinning.

Well, this wasn't working. She needed to move more slowly.

She was on her third attempt to stand without throwing up when the cabin door opened and Grey walked in with an armful of firewood. Grace slowly shuffled her way to Baby. She was smart enough not to pick him up, but maybe she could rub his back and he would stay asleep, giving her brain more time to get her muscles under control. Her head was still throbbing, but at least the room had stopped spinning.

"Are ya truly this stubborn, lass, or has the cold affected your thinking?" Grey asked from right beside her.

Grace swung around and would have fallen if Grey hadn't caught her. She swayed against him, clutching his jacket, and looked up into steeled green eyes. But her rebuke turned into a squeak of surprise when he swept her up in his arms and carried her over to the table. He sat her in a chair and slid the bowl of stew in front of her, then shed his jacket and returned to Baby.

Grace stared at her lunch. This was not going well. The bond they had formed on the mountain last night was fading. Stubbornness—on both sides—had replaced cooperation.

Grace looked up to see Grey holding a now wide-awake Baby in the crook of his arm as he rummaged around in her bag for another bottle. She took a spoonful of stew and all but moaned at the feel of it sliding down her throat, realizing just how hungry she was. Grey settled across the table from her with Baby, who was also happily eating, and Grace decided it was time to try another tack with the man.

"Reverse our positions," she suggested to Grey, who lifted his gaze to her in question. "How adamant would you be right now to get back on your feet and regain control of your life?"

He shook his head. "It's not the same, Grace. You're a woman."

Grace looked down at herself in mock surprise. "I am?" She smoothed down the front of her shirt. "Imagine that. What has being a woman got to do with wanting control?"

He set Baby on his shoulder and began rubbing the

infant's back as he shook his head at her again. "It's a fact of nature, Grace. Women are simply weaker. Physically," he quickly added when she opened her mouth to protest.

Grace snapped her mouth shut and leaned back in her chair, crossing her arms under her breasts. She didn't know if it was the full belly she had now, or the anger growing inside her, but she was feeling much stronger all of a sudden.

"Which is why our positions are exactly as they are now," he continued. "I had the endurance to get us off that mountain." He leaned forward, his brows dropping and his eyes darkening. "And I still have enough strength left to put you in that snowcat, take you to Gu Bràth, and keep you there until you can take care of yourself and your son," he finished in an even-toned whisper.

Grace stood up, either to prove to herself that she could or to get away from his veiled threat, she didn't know which.

"That's archaic!" she sputtered, refusing to be intimidated. "Brute strength is not how you solve a problem."

He leaned back in his chair, rubbing Baby's back again, and shrugged. "It usually works for me," he said softly.

Grace picked up her empty bowl and carried it to the counter on the far wall of the cabin. It amazed her how well her muscles were working now; nothing like a little outrage to get the blood flowing.

She shouldn't be surprised by his attitude. The moment she'd sat beside Greylen MacKeage on the plane, she had guessed the man was a bit of a throwback. What had she thought? That he looked as if he made his own rules and that he pounded problems into place when he couldn't solve them any other way?

Yeah. That was the man she owed her life to.

And his arms suddenly moved gently around her,

pulling her back against his warm and very solid chest. Grace turned within his embrace, looked to see Baby sleeping in his crate again, and closed her eyes, setting her hands on Grey's chest in an attempt to hold him away.

Or was it her own urges she was trying to hold at bay?

She knew what he was doing and didn't like it. His threat hadn't worked, so he'd ply her with kisses instead.

Which is exactly why she couldn't go home with him.

Her emotions were too fragile right now; she was in no condition to spend the night in Greylen MacKeage's bed. And if she went to Gu Bràth, that is exactly where she'd end up.

She lifted her face and gave him a smile. "I can't get involved with you right now, Grey."

His arms tightened around her, his head lowered, and his lips covered hers in a searing kiss. The room started spinning again; it was not caused by her head this time but by her heart. And it was all she could do not to rise on her tiptoes and kiss him back.

His tongue sought hers, sending a shiver through her body. Like up on the mountain yesterday, Grace's body yearned to respond; passion ignited, radiating from her soul into her senses. She kneaded his shoulders with her fingers and tried to push him away.

She might as well be pushing a mountain. She was suddenly floating on air, and it wasn't until she felt a hard surface against her bottom that Grace realized Grey had set her on the counter. He moved her knees apart with his legs and nestled himself firmly against her.

"It's too late, Grace," he said, staring down at her with eyes the color of winter spruce. "It's already begun, and there's no going back. Forget what your mind says, and listen to what your body is telling you."

She stared into his bottomless, deep green eyes, and it

took Grace a moment to remember that she must fight her attraction to Grey, not feed it. "But I can't. I have . . . there are issues I need to deal with."

His right brow lifted. "Baby's father?"

Grace's forehead started to throb again. "Yes. Baby's father," she admitted. It was true, just not in the way Grey thought.

"Do you love him?"

"No." Which was also true.

"Are you running from him? Are you in danger?"

"No."

He blew a sigh over her face that moved her hair. "Then what's the problem?" he asked, his patience obviously wearing thin.

"The problem is I have a four-week-old baby, I just lost my sister, and I'm coming home for the first time in nine years. I need this time to get my life back in order."

"I can help."

"No, you can only complicate things. I have decisions to make about Baby, my job, and Baby's father."

He kissed her again, probably because he didn't care for what she was saying.

And she kissed him back, probably because it was easier than arguing with him. Grace wiggled forward on the counter, pressing herself against Grey like a cat curling up to a stove. He trailed his mouth down over her throat and nuzzled the side of her neck. Grace arched against him, wrapping her legs around his waist, only to moan at the feel of him pushing so intimately against her.

She wondered why they both didn't simply burst into flames.

How could something so not right feel so wonderful? Grace had the overwhelming urge to rip off both their shirts and rub her body all over his. She grabbed his hair and pulled his mouth back to hers, driving her tongue inside and pulling the taste of him back into herself. She decided to start with his shirt and reached for the buttons, popping the top two in an effort to feel his skin under her fingers.

At that moment of contact she did burst into flame; the air around them glowed with white light, time suspended, and Grace's heart pounded with an excitement she'd never experienced before.

Ian came slipping and sliding through the door of the cabin with all the noise and dignity of a moose on ice skates.

And that was when Grace made her escape, her body on fire, her resolve shattered, and Grey's mouth just one second away from changing her mind.

Although she had won several of the salvos and probably the battle by default, Grace still couldn't shake the feeling that she was going to lose the war.

With Baby in her arms, she walked into the living room of the house she'd grown up in and set the thermostat on seventy-five degrees. As she walked back to the kitchen, she wondered how she had become engaged in a war in the first place.

Grey had continued to argue all the way down TarStone Mountain for her and Baby to go to Gu Bràth, where he could keep an eye on them at least overnight. But she had remained adamant.

And Grey had not been a graceful loser.

Not if that last, departing kiss was any indication of his mood. Grace raised her fingers to her lips and grinned. Her mouth still tingled with the awareness of being thoroughly possessed. In fact, even her toes still tingled.

This had to stop. She had to break Grey of the habit of

just pulling her into his arms and kissing her senseless whenever he felt like it. It was the wrong time, Greylen MacKeage was the wrong man, and she didn't know how much longer she could resist him.

And she had to, for Baby's sake as well as her own.

It was just the circumstances, that's all. She'd found herself in the arms of a guardian angel who kissed like the devil. Nothing more than mere infatuation. A strong, manly man with eyes the color of winter spruce and the body of Superman. A romantic notion of being in a hero's arms, being swept into a fantasy world.

Grace was sure there was a scientific explanation for what she had felt on TarStone Mountain and the lingering effects she was still experiencing now. Lord, just the memory of the feel of him surrounding her made her knees weak and her heart beat wildly.

This had to stop. Tomorrow. She would dwell on this phenomenon tomorrow, once she was rested and back in charge of her faculties.

Grace set Baby on the overstuffed chair in the kitchen, padding him with a throw pillow so he wouldn't roll off in his sleep. She took off her jacket as she looked out the window at the retreating snowcat.

She had given Grey her trust up on the mountain because it had been the wisest thing to do at the time. If he had been anyone less competent—or even less arrogant about being Superman—she would have looked for another means of survival.

Now that she was home in a warm, secure, nonthreatening environment, she could think of a hundred things they could have done instead of trying to walk off the mountain on their own.

But that was water under the bridge.

It was now time to move on. She needed a bath, and so

did Baby. Then she would have to see if Mary's old pickup parked in the barn would start, so she could go to town and get baby formula, more diapers, and food for herself.

She picked up the bag Grey had set on the floor by the door and carried it over to the table. She pulled out her computer and plugged it into the outlet on the counter to recharge the battery. She hoped the cold and the freezing rain had not ruined it. All of her work was on that machine, and her backup disks were still on the mountain.

She hoped her disks survived, too, until the MacKeages could go and fetch them. They were in her satellite link suitcase, in a waterproof case of their own. They should be okay.

She took the cookie tin out next and set it in the middle of the table. She smiled at her sister.

"Honest to God, you could have heard a mouse sneeze in that cabin, Mare, when Grey told them you were in the tin," Grace said. "Ian almost fell out of his chair. He kept looking at the bed as if you were going to jump out and bite him."

She turned the tin to face her. "They said they were sorry you died and that they would miss you. I thanked them for both of us for their friendship to you and told them how much you appreciated their helping you with the roof."

She dumped the contents of the bag on the table as she continued to talk. "I like your neighbors. Especially Ian. He's such a grumbling sourpuss he's actually cute."

Grace sat down at the table with a groan, cradling her aching back as she did. "They're all a bit weird, don't you think? And I can barely understand them for their accents. Except Grey. His is mild most of the time." She cocked her head. "And that's the weirdest thing. Why would a person deliberately change his accent?"

Grace closed her eyes and laid her head on the table. If

she didn't get up and get into the shower, she and Baby would be sleeping in the kitchen.

Her nose twitched as the familiar, subtle scents of lavender and spice wafted around her, awakening some long-dormant memory from childhood. Grace lifted her head and slowly looked around the silent kitchen.

Home. She smelled home—years of her mother's cooking, her sister's herbs drying on racks hung from the ceiling, the lingering odor of countless winters of wood burning. All the smells, the scarred table, the grandfather clock standing silent in the corner waiting to be rewound, the huge propane range that had fed a family of ten; all of it made this the loving kitchen she'd grown up in.

Home. It settled over Grace like a bulky wool sweater of warm security.

It was so silently empty, except for the memories that swirled like flames on candles lighting individual moments in time. Timmy holding a six-week-old Mary as he carefully fed her a bottle, Brian convincing Mom he needed her car for a special date that night, Paul and David wrestling on the floor until they cracked the glass in the china hutch, and her dad holding Grace on his knee while he dunked her banana in the sugar bowl to reward her for eating her turnip.

Home. She had waited too long to return. Everyone was gone. Even the memories, the scents, the sounds had begun to fade, becoming ghosts of a past life she could never revisit.

Grace laid her head on her arms on the table again, closing her eyes to keep the tears from escaping. She missed her family, her mom and dad's unconditional love, her brothers' combined strengths, and Mary's no-nonsense command of life. All of them the foundation of her existence today.

And all of them out of her reach now.

All except for Baby.

She had brought her sister's child to this wonderful, sometimes magical, always sheltering home. She could live here with Baby and watch him prosper and grow from the roots her family had already laid down in these densely wooded mountains. It could be that simple; she could walk away from her life in Virginia and devote herself to Baby without question or regret. She already loved him more than life itself.

She already wanted to break her promise to Mary.

The shower helped immensely to revive Grace's spirit, recenter her thinking, and soothe her bruised and aching muscles. Baby liked his bath as well. It was fun bathing him in a sink half full of warm water. She was glad his little belly button had finally healed; she had always been afraid of hurting him there. The house had warmed up nicely, and she allowed him to splash about wildly until he was tired again.

She was finally getting the hang of this mothering thing. Now that she was on her own, with only herself to rely on, it was just as Emma said. Her instincts were kicking in and giving her confidence. That was all she had needed, time alone with Baby to find her own path in dealing with him.

Still, she hoped the book Emma had given her was not lost on the mountain. She wasn't quite ready to go it completely alone.

"Only one more bottle after this one," she told Baby as she fed him. She looked out the window and sighed. "I hate to go back out in that weather, but it doesn't look like we have a choice."

The incessant rain wouldn't let up. The windows on the

north side of the kitchen were glazed with ice, making it impossible to see out. She fed Baby the whole bottle and burped him with the skill of a mother of nine, then laid him back in his overstuffed chair while she tried to decide what to put on him to go out.

She found his pack on the table with the other stuff from her bag. It was still damp. She held it up to her face and breathed deeply, pulling in the familiar scent she had been surrounded by since yesterday afternoon. It smelled like Grey; she remembered the scent from when he had held her under the spruce tree, from the sweater he had put on her just before he tucked her in the cave, from the bed she'd shared with him in Daar's cabin, and from the flannel shirt she had worn home this morning and now had safely folded on the pillow in the downstairs bedroom.

It was a smell that soothed her senses, silently speaking of friendship, security, trust, and even adventure.

She was keeping the shirt. She had washed her body, and she had to wash this pack, but she wasn't washing Grey's shirt, and she wasn't returning it. It was a pretty plaid made up of gray and red, dark green and lavender stripes. She had never seen that combination of colors before, but she'd been immediately drawn to it the moment she had put it on. Yes, she was keeping it, and if he asked for it back, she would say she couldn't find it.

She was going to hell for the lies she'd been telling. But here in Pine Creek, at least, she should be able to keep them straight. After all, there was only one that was important—that Baby was hers.

She washed the pack in the kitchen sink and set it near the furnace register to dry. She bundled Baby up in one of Mary's old T-shirts, used a flannel pillowcase for a blanket, and carried him out to the attached barn.

That was when she discovered yet another problem. Baby's car seat was still on top of North Finger Ridge. She looked around the old barn at the eclectic assortment of junk until she found an apple crate large enough for the four-week-old child. She laid Baby inside it, then strapped it into the passenger seat of the pickup. It probably wouldn't pass *Consumer Reports'* standard safety test, but it passed hers. Baby wasn't going anywhere by the time she was done using the seat belts to secure him.

And Baby, good little uncomplaining infant that he was, was simply watching her as she worked.

"Oh, sweetie. I promise the chaos will stop now that we're home. Just this one trip to the store, and we'll both settle down for a well-deserved rest," she whispered to him, running a finger over his cheek and kissing his forehead.

She softly closed the door and walked around to open the two huge barn doors, rolling each of them back, one at a time. Grace thought about Michael MacBain and her promise to Mary. Mary had said that Michael was all alone and new to the area. Which in Mary's book would make the man somewhat of an exile. Could that have attracted her to him initially?

Grace climbed into the truck, chastising herself for being fanciful. Mary had simply found the man she loved. And Grace was sure Michael MacBain was a nice, normal, lovable man who just happened to suffer from the delusion that he'd traveled through time.

Chapter Eight

He was a brute.

And he was standing in the middle of her kitchen. Grace shot a look at the clock on the living-room wall, realized it was nearly midnight, and quickly turned her attention back to the stranger dripping water on her kitchen floor. The freezing rain only added to his frightening appearance as it beat against the broken door behind him. His hands were balled into fists at his side, and his silhouette from the porch light said he was huge, menacing, and mad.

"Mary!" he hollered again, looking around the vacant room. "Dammit, woman. Show yourself."

It took every ounce of courage she possessed, and the security of the baseball bat in her hand, for Grace to step out from behind the living-room door and face him.

"Mary's not here," she told him softly.

The man was a giant. His dripping hair was black, falling below his turned-up collar. His eyes, narrowed dangerously, were a dark, piercing gray. His mouth was thinned by the defensive set of his jaw that was shadowed by a two-day growth of beard. Grounded to her kitchen floor like a statue of granite, he looked formidable. Predatory.

And unmovable.

Grace raised her bat threateningly.

"May I ask who is calling?" she asked, damning her voice for shaking.

Her question momentarily disarmed him, but he quickly recovered. "Michael MacBain is doing the asking. And I'm only asking one more time. Where's Mary?"

Oh, God. She wasn't ready for this. She thought she had more time to prepare. Grace darted a look at the tin on the table. What could she tell him?

"She's . . . ah . . . she's not here, Michael," she whispered. "I'm her sister, Grace." She took a step closer, lowering her weapon. "She may have mentioned me to you?"

He didn't believe her. He strode right past her into the living room. When he didn't find Mary there, he continued going from one room to the other, even upstairs.

Grace let him search. Her baseball bat wouldn't stop him, even if she dared to use it against him. The man looked as solid and indestructible as a mountain.

He found Baby on his second pass through the living room. He stopped suddenly and stared down at the child. He looked at her, then back at Baby, his eyes narrowed and his stance stiff.

There was no way around it. She was going to have to just come out and say the words.

"I'm sorry, Michael," she said, drawing his attention again. "Mary was in an automobile accident six weeks ago," Grace said, lying about the date of Mary's death. She didn't want Michael even to remotely suspect that four-week-old Baby was his son. Grace looked down at the floor, gathering her courage, then looked back at him. "She died. I'm sorry. There was nothing anyone could do."

He simply stared at her, his face growing deathly pale as he listened silently.

"She was on her way back," she told him, walking fully into the living room. "She was returning to you."

He looked back at Baby. "The child?" he asked, his voice dead-toned.

"He's . . . he's mine."

He was silent so long Grace was afraid he didn't believe her. Suddenly, he walked away from the makeshift crib she'd made out of the apple crate and strode past her, back into the kitchen. He walked to the broken door and shut it as best he could, then quietly walked back to the kitchen table and sat down.

He bent at the waist, his hands clasped hanging over his knees, staring at the floor. He stayed that way for a good five minutes.

Grace leaned the baseball bat against the wall and walked to the stove, putting the teakettle on the burner. She took down two cups from the cupboard and measured out hot cocoa mix in each of them.

"Did she suffer?" he asked, his voice echoing softly throughout the kitchen. "Did she die instantly, or was she alive in a hospital?"

Grace turned to face him. The dangerous mountain of a man was no longer looking quite so dangerous. His hands were still hanging over his knees, and he was upright now, but he remained staring at the floor, all the fight suddenly gone from him.

"She lived a day and a half," she told him truthfully. "And she was conscious. We talked about many things, but Mary talked mostly of you."

She walked over to him and gently, hesitantly, set her hand on his shoulder. He didn't move but still stared at a spot between his feet. His muscles, though, were bunched so tightly his back felt like forged steel.

"She asked me to tell you she loved you, Michael. And

that she hopes you'll forgive her for running away in the first place. She said . . . she said she just needed some time to herself, to think about your marriage proposal."

She moved around in front of him and knelt down, wanting him to look at her. "She told me your story, Michael, and said that she didn't care. She was coming home when she had the accident. She was coming to marry you and love you for the rest of your lives."

His eyes widened suddenly, and his face paled even more. He pulled himself upright, leaning against the back of the chair and away from her. "She told you about me?" he whispered.

"On her deathbed, Michael," she hurried to assure him, standing up and going to shut off the whistling kettle. "The whole time she was with me, she never said a thing. But when she was dying, she wanted me to know. She asked me to come tell you that she loved you and to . . . to help you through this time."

"You said six weeks ago. What took you so long?"

She waved a spoon at the living room. "I was a bit tied up with my son."

He followed her gaze to the living room, then looked back at her with narrowed eyes. "Where's your man?" he asked.

"My man?"

"Your son's father."

"Oh. I . . . I don't have a man."

He stood up so suddenly that Grace poured boiling water all over the counter. He walked into the living room and returned with Baby.

Grace nearly fell to her knees. Michael MacBain was cradling his son in his arms as if he were the most precious jewel on Earth.

"He's acting hungry," he said. "He's chewing his fist." He

looked at her strangely. "You didn't hear him fussing?"

Grace tapped the side of her head with the palm of her hand, as if something was bothering her. "My ears seem to be plugged," she quickly prevaricated. "I think I'm coming down with a cold."

She turned back to the cupboard and took down a bottle of baby formula before he could see the lie in her eyes. But when she turned to take Baby and feed him, Michael was sitting with Baby on his lap and his hand held out for the bottle.

Damn. She didn't want him feeding his son. Or holding him. She especially didn't want him unwrapping Baby and discovering the child had twelve toes. The man might look a bit primitive, but there was intelligence written all over his face. He would know immediately that Baby was his.

"Sit," he said, indicating the chair across from him. "I'll feed him." He looked at her, waiting for the bottle. One corner of his mouth rose, not in a smile but in understanding. "I know new mothers can be protective, but you have nothing to fear from me, Grace," he said, using her name for the first time. "I had six younger brothers and sisters. I can feed your son."

She reluctantly handed him the bottle. If she made a scene, he would get suspicious. She sat down and wondered if those six brothers and sisters were eight hundred years dead.

"What's his name?" he asked, watching Baby eagerly latch onto the nipple.

"Ah . . . it's Baby, for now. I haven't decided on a permanent name yet," she told him, carefully moving the cookie tin to the side of the table so that it wasn't between them. She turned it until the front of the tin was facing Michael MacBain, foolishly thinking her sister would like to see her lover feeding their son.

He looked up from his task. "He's a month old and you haven't named him?" he asked, sounding appalled.

Grace wanted to close her eyes and shake her head at the thought of repeating this particular lie yet again. She did neither. She simply spoke from rote.

"A name is very important. He's going to have to live with it the rest of his life. I'm waiting for the perfect one to come to mind."

"Why is he in clothes that still have the price tag on them?" he asked, lifting the tag on the sleeve with his fingers.

Grace did close her eyes then and covered her face with her hands. She was so tired. After returning from the store, she'd thrown herself on the couch and managed to get only four hours of sleep before this man had broken into her house. She pushed the hair away from her face and looked at him.

"It's the only thing he has to wear," she explained with tired patience. "All of his clothes, and mine, are up on North Finger Ridge getting covered with ice. Our plane crashed there yesterday." She looked at the clock on the wall. It was just past midnight. "Make that two days ago now. We just got here this afternoon. Yesterday afternoon," she amended. "They only had two outfits at the store that fit him. I wasn't thinking about tags when I dressed him."

He looked from her to Baby, clearly surprised. "You survived a plane crash? Both of you?"

"Greylen MacKeage was with us. He saved our lives."

His face immediately hardened. "MacKeage was with you?"

Grace didn't know what to make of the sudden change in him. She recalled that Mary had said there was no love lost between her neighbors and Michael, but looking at him now, Mary's account of the animosity had been understated. Michael MacBain looked like Grey had when he had wanted to kill the pilot all over again.

"We wouldn't be here, either one of us, if it weren't for him," she said, lifting her chin and looking Michael right in the eye so that he would understand that she would defend Greylen MacKeage to him or to anyone else. "He carried Baby down the mountain and then returned for me. He saved our lives," she repeated, just in case he hadn't caught that little fact the first time.

He grinned at her anger. "I'm glad for you," he said. He suddenly sobered, taking a deep breath. "Tell me more about Mary. Where is she buried? And why didn't you bring her home to lie beside her father and mother?"

"I did bring her home," Grace said. "Only not to be buried. Mary wants her ashes spread over TarStone Mountain. But not until Summer Solstice."

Michael MacBain sat up straighter. "Her ashes? You've turned her to ash?"

She could already see the horror building in his expression. He was going to have the same reaction as the MacKeages. Only Michael had been in love with Mary. He would likely want to break something. Grace looked at the wall where the bat was leaning.

"Yes," she told him.

"Where is she?" he asked, craning his head to look toward the living room.

Grace stood and took Baby out of Michael's arms, laying the child on her shoulder. "He needs to be burped," she told him by way of explanation as she inched her way toward the broken kitchen door, appearing to soothe Baby as she looked out through the still intact storm door. "And Mary's . . . well, she's sitting on the table beside you, in the cookie tin."

She closed her eyes and waited for the explosion.

It didn't come. The only sound in the room was the gentle crack of the house settling under the weight of the ice building on its roof.

Grace opened her eyes to see Michael MacBain carefully pick up the cookie tin and hold it, painful sorrow drawing his features into taut, harsh planes of despair. He tried to pry off the cover, but it wouldn't budge.

"I—I sealed it with glue," she said softly.

As if he didn't hear her, he pushed his thumb against the cover, holding pressure until it gave. He took the cover off and dipped his hand inside, lifting out some of the ash and letting it sift through his fingers back into the tin.

Grace wiped at the tears streaming down both of her cheeks. This man was looking at all his hopes and dreams for the future having been turned into ash.

Except for the child she now held in her arms and her heart.

Michael's anguish appeared so raw, so heartbreakingly painful, that Grace very nearly blurted out her secret right then and there. She held the power to take away part of Michael's pain by giving him a son.

Which would keep her promise to Mary.

But break her own heart for the second time this month.

Grace quietly walked out of the kitchen and into the downstairs bedroom, softly closing the door behind her. She lay down on the bed with Baby in her arms and let her tears flow freely. Michael MacBain could say his goodbyes to Mary in peace. He deserved this time.

And she could no longer witness his grief.

Chapter Nine

A terrible racket startled Grace awake at dawn. There was a dog barking in her yard, chasing something that was protesting being chased even more loudly. A man hollered, and if she wasn't mistaken, she could hear a goat bleating.

Grace climbed out of bed and set a pillow where she'd been to block Baby from rolling off the bed. She slipped into the pair of Mary's shoes she had hunted up yesterday and headed out into the kitchen. She didn't have to dress; she had slept in her clothes.

She opened her broken kitchen door just as a chicken went flapping by in a panic, a huge black dog slipping and sliding on the ice right behind it.

"Ben!" the man hollered again. "Leave that bird and get over here!"

He slammed the tailgate of his pickup truck and started toward his still open driver's door. "In the truck, Ben," he said again.

Grace scrambled off the porch toward him, nearly falling as soon as her feet hit the icy driveway. "Wait! What are you doing?" she hollered after the man, who was just getting into his truck.

He got back out and faced her, his stance defensive. Grace slid to a halt in front of him, having to grab the fender to keep from falling. She took a tiny step back.

He smelled like a farm, and from the looks of his clothes, he'd been sleeping in the barn with his animals. His weathered face was scrunched up into such a glower Grace couldn't tell if he was red from the weather or if a cow had stepped on his cheek. The right side of his mouth bulged out as if he had a golf ball stuck in it.

"I'm returning your blasted animals," he told her, spitting a wad of brown tobacco juice on the ground.

Grace took another step back.

He raised his blunt, calloused hand and counted off on his dirty fingers. "Three cats, one goat, and sixteen hens. Two of them died, and I'm not replacing them. They're old hens, and they don't produce enough eggs to keep them in feed."

"But . . . but why are you bringing them here?"

"They're Mary's," he told her succinctly, just before he spit another wad of tobacco juice on the ground. "I saw the porch light on last night. She's home now, she can have them back."

He pointed at the detached barn at the end of the yard. "That damn goat is a menace. She's managed to break every fence in my place. And she ate my best pair of long johns," he finished, signaling to the huge black dog, who had finally obeyed and come running and jumped into the front seat of the truck. The man climbed in behind him and slammed the door shut.

"Wait! Mary's not here. And I don't know anything about taking care of these animals."

He rolled down his window and looked at her. "Just give them food and water. They'll take care of themselves until Mary gets back." He looked up toward the barn.

"And don't turn your back on that Jezebel of a goat. You're liable to find yourself not able to sit down for a week."

That said, he had the truck started and was racing out of the driveway before she could protest. The ice-coated gravel caused his truck to slide first in one direction and then the other. He never stopped, even when he reached the main road, skidded around the corner, and slammed into the opposite snowbank. Grace cringed at the sound of tires spinning for traction. The man swerved his truck back onto the road and roared out of sight.

She stared at the spot where he had disappeared until something pecked at her foot. She looked down to see a plump, mahogany-red chicken interested in eating her shoe. Several more birds quickly joined it, descending on Grace as if someone had suddenly rung the dinner bell.

"Shoo. Get, you birds," she said, backing away. She slowly headed toward the barn and retrieved the two half-empty bags of animal feed she could see sitting just inside the door, being careful not to fall for fear the birds would eat her.

She unrolled the tops of the paper bags and looked at the pictures on them. One had chickens all over the front of it, and the other one had a herd of goats grazing placidly in a pasture.

Well, that was easy enough. She scooped a handful of the chicken feed out and scattered it over the floor of the barn. The entire bunch of chickens immediately started flocking inside, quickly gobbling up the feed. Grace spread a few more handfuls for good measure.

She stood inside the door, out of the rain, and looked back down the driveway. She was stunned. The entire world for as far as she could see was covered in ice. Trees bowed with the weight of the freezing precipitation, some of their tops touching the ground and now frozen into place. The forest crackled around her as if in pain, the sound carried on eerie, moaning echoes through the cold but very humid air. The sky was low, completely masking the mountains that surrounded Pine Creek, so low in places that even the tops of tall trees were hidden. And her house looked as if it was covered in a crystalline skin.

An urgent, angry bleat came from inside the barn behind her. Grace turned to see the head of a goat, with two pointed horns and two huge black eyes staring at her from behind a half-chewed wooden stall door.

The Jezebel. She grabbed the other bag of feed and dragged it over to the impatient animal. She dumped several handfuls in a pail by the stall door and opened the door to set it inside. But she didn't even get the latch sprung before the pail went flying and Grace found herself sitting on the floor. The goat jumped over her, just missing her head with its sharp little hooves, and ran out of the barn before she could scream.

Dammit. She didn't know a thing about handling animals. She stood up and brushed herself off. Let the stupid beast run around in the rain if it wanted. She righted the pail and refilled it with more food, then pulled down a bale of hay that was stacked in the next stall. She spread it out over the barn floor, away from the chickens.

As she was leaving, Grace saw the baby monitor. Mary must have used it to monitor the animals at night. Grace unplugged the transmitter and took it down off the shelf. The receiver would be in the house someplace. She could use this with Baby. She'd put this transmitter in her bedroom and carry the receiver on her belt whenever she had to come outside and tend these blasted animals. She'd have to look for a book on animal care while she was at it. She hoped Mary had an entire library of them.

Grace hurried back to the house to check on Baby,

nearly tripping over three cats who were determined to beat her inside. Damn. She hoped there was cat food in the cupboard.

"There you are, sweetie," she whispered to the just waking baby. "That was a good nap you had." She laughed as she picked him up. "It's the first time in a long time you're actually waking up in the same place where you went to sleep."

She kissed his warm, soft cheek and cuddled him against her, inhaling his unique scent. He was so precious. She hoped for some quiet time for just the two of them, so they could get to know each other on a one-to-one basis.

Wishful thinking. Their peace lasted less than an hour.

Grace looked up from the book on animal husbandry she was reading aloud to Baby when she heard the now familiar sound of the snowcat making its way up her drive. She set the book aside and carefully rearranged Baby in her arms as she stood up.

As she walked into the kitchen, she heard the engine shut off and then the voices of men talking. The murmurs suddenly turned into a shout of surprise. She looked out the only window not covered with ice just in time to see Morgan running for his life from Jezebel.

She didn't need to be a rocket scientist to know the outcome. The man lost the race. Grace heard what sounded like a curse, only in a language she didn't recognize, and then Morgan was sitting on the frozen gravel, shouting at the triumphant, retreating goat.

Grey, carrying Grace's two bags from the plane, simply walked past him, chuckling. He strode onto the porch and suddenly stopped, staring at her kitchen door.

Grace used her foot to pull it open and greeted him with a smile. "My bags. You've brought my stuff."

"What happened to your door?" he asked, not moving, still looking at the broken wood.

Grace walked away so he would come in. Morgan, rubbing his butt, followed him.

"It . . . ah, I had a visitor last night. He broke it."

"Who?" Grey asked with anger in his voice, setting her bags down.

What could she tell him without adding fuel to the apparently old, ongoing battle between the MacKeages and Michael MacBain?

She almost wanted to shake her head at the absurdity of it. They were like modern-day Hatfields and McCoys, with only a name being mentioned to set them off. She had witnessed that firsthand last night, when she had innocently told Michael that Grey had saved her and Baby.

"I'm waiting," he said, his stance telling her he might be waiting but his patience was waning.

"Michael MacBain was looking for Mary," she told him, setting Baby down in the overstuffed chair and securing him with the pillow again. She really was going to have to come up with a more respectable crib. Before Baby was three.

"MacBain," Morgan snarled from behind Grey, turning to examine the door himself. "That bastard broke into your home?"

"Do you own a gun?" Grey asked, still unmoved, still looking at her.

"A gun?" Alarmed, she turned to face him. She shook her head. "No. And I wouldn't use one if I did. I'm not going to shoot anybody. That's barbaric. And it's not legal, either."

"It is if you're defending yourself," he countered.

"From Michael? He was just looking for Mary."

"And what was his reaction when he didn't find her?" he asked, taking a step closer to her.

"What do you think it was?" she asked back, moving closer to him herself. Dammit, she didn't like his posturing. He was acting as if she was an idiot for not being afraid of a grieving man. "He was devastated," she told him. "Thank you for bringing my things," she added.

Her change of subject did not deter him. He moved even closer, taking her by the shoulders with his huge, warm hands. "Stay away from him, Grace. Michael MacBain is trouble."

She pulled away from him immediately. His simple touch sent shivers coursing up and down her spine. And those shivers had nothing to do with fear.

It was lust. Pure, stupid lust.

She hadn't seen him for nearly twenty-four hours, and here she was acting like a silly schoolgirl with a crush on the giant. Maybe she was the one experiencing separation withdrawal.

Grace walked to her bags, mentally telling herself—and her hormones—to give it a rest. Grey was acting as if he wanted to kill Michael MacBain, and she was busy fantasizing about his touching her again.

Morgan beat her to the suitcases, lifting them up and setting them on the table for her. She smiled her thank-you and busied herself opening one of them while she spoke.

"Michael was the man my sister was coming home to marry when she died," she informed Grey, who now had his arms crossed over his chest and his eyes narrowed. "And that makes him almost family to me." She turned and looked at Morgan, so he would know she was talking to him as well. "Michael's hurting," she said. "And I'm not going to ignore him or his pain just because you don't like him."

Grey didn't like *her* very much right now, if his expression was any indication. Grace suddenly gave into her urge and laughed out loud.

"I wish you could see yourself. You're like a pouting little boy whose mother won't take him seriously. This . . . this feud between you and Michael is childish."

"You have no idea what you're talking about," he said through gritted teeth. His evergreen eyes drilled into her. "And you are not my mother."

She held up her hands in supplication. "Fine. Feel the way you want. But I'm having no part of it."

She walked up to him and looked him in the eye, staring at him just as fiercely as he was staring at her. "I owe you for saving my life, but I'm remaining neutral in this. Those are my terms. Take them or leave them."

He stared down at her for so long Grace was afraid she had just lost her new friend. She didn't want that. She liked Greylen MacKeage. Heck, who was she kidding? She was strongly attracted to the man and felt they shared a special understanding. They'd had quite an adventure together and had beaten the odds. The bond that had formed between them up on the mountain was sacred to her, and she was loath to let her principles destroy it.

But she would. Because if she backed down now, she was in danger of losing more than just the principles that had always guided her through the major decisions in her life.

She was in danger of losing her heart.

And she couldn't do that, either. She was here for four months, until Summer Solstice, and then she and Baby were going back to Virginia to begin their new lives together.

"Very well," he said finally. "You may speak with MacBain. But you're to be careful around him. He's not to be trusted."

She wanted to ask him what had happened to make him hate Michael so much, but Grace kept her questions to herself. She doubted he'd tell her anyway. Michael hadn't told Mary, and that little fact was revealing enough, considering what he *had* told her. Whatever it was between these men, it wasn't pleasant.

Grace returned to the task of sorting out her things on the table. Grey walked over to Baby and picked him up.

"You shouldn't bother him when he's sleeping," she admonished. "The poor kid needs the rest."

Grey lifted a brow at her. "He's resting. See, he hasn't wakened," he said, tilting Baby so she could see his face.

The infant sighed in his sleep and cuddled comfortably against Grey's chest.

"He likes the heartbeat," Grey told her, smiling at her frown. "Babies need to feel the closeness of another life."

Grace wondered where the man got his information. He said he had younger siblings, but was that enough to explain his ease with Baby? She knew he wasn't married, but he had to be older than thirty. Maybe he had an ex-wife and six kids out there somewhere.

"We brought you some food," Morgan said, coming back through the door with two bags of groceries in his hands.

She hadn't even realized he'd left. "Thank you." She indicated that he should set them on the counter. "But that wasn't necessary. I went out yesterday and got some."

"You went out?" Grey asked. "In this storm? The driving's abominable."

Grace threw the suitcase she'd just emptied onto the floor. "I couldn't very well feed Baby canned soup," she informed him. "And my truck has four-wheel drive."

"It's not the going that's dangerous," Morgan added into the discussion. "It's the stopping that's impossible."

"I discovered that," she admitted. "I'm going to put the chains on the truck this afternoon."

"You know how?" the younger man asked, looking not only surprised but skeptical.

"I grew up here," she reminded him. "I know how to handle bad weather."

Morgan looked at Grey. Grace saw Grey nod his head in the direction of the attached barn. She unzipped the next suitcase. If it made the men feel better to put the chains on for her, she wasn't about to complain. She sorted through her things in the second suitcase, adding items to the pile of ruined clothes. Her silk blouses had not weathered the freezing rain well at all. She found what she had been searching for and hit the switch on her PDA. Nothing happened.

"Darn. This didn't make it."

"What is it?" Grey asked, coming to stand beside her, Baby cuddled contentedly in his arms. "Another computer?"

"It's my PDA. And either the batteries are cold or it's ruined."

"PDA?"

She pulled it out of its leather case and opened the back. "It's a personal data assistant," she explained. "It's my calendar book, task list, and all my contacts. Without it, I'm screwed."

"Wouldn't it just be easier to keep this information in a book?" he asked, leaning over her shoulder as she replaced the batteries with spares she had bought yesterday at the store, having anticipated this possibility as well as the likelihood that they'd eventually lose the electricity.

"Maybe," she said, shrugging. "But paper would be just as ruined, too." She looked at her computer sitting on the counter, charging. She opened it and turned it on.

"Well, at least this works."

Grace decided she needed a cup of cocoa. She grabbed the kettle, filled it with water, and put it on the burner. "I'm lucky the computer is okay and that only the battery got ruined." She patted her computer affectionately. "I don't blame the battery for dying," she said. "Leaving my computer running in the snow cave finished it. Electronics don't like the cold, and they don't like getting wet. But it did a marvelous job keeping me alive." She looked at Grey. "I hugged it to me, using its warmth."

He gave her a strange look. "You were hugging the cookie tin when I found you, Grace. Not the computer."

She shook her head at him. "No. That's impossible. I distinctly remember feeling a great warmth against my chest and my hands. That's the only reason my fingers didn't get frostbite. It had to be the computer. There's no way a tin full of ashes could generate heat."

"Maybe it was your sister's spirit protecting you," he suggested softly. "It's possible that Mary was with you in that cave in more ways than just her ashes. You were hugging her tin, Grace. I know what I found."

She looked at the table, at Mary.

Only she wasn't there. Grace rushed to the table and moved the pile of clothes out of the way. Then she moved the suitcase. The table was empty. She looked around the kitchen but couldn't find the tin. It was nowhere to be seen.

"He took it," she whispered to herself, still scanning the kitchen counter and shelves.

"Who? Took what?" Grey asked, moving up behind her. "What are you looking for?"

She swung around to face him. "Mary. He took Mary."

"Who took Mary?" Morgan asked, walking into the kitchen. He had a hammer and some nails in his hand. He pounded the broken door casing into place.

"MacBain took the tin holding Mary's ashes," Grey answered for her. He handed her Baby. "Come on," he said to Morgan.

"Wait! You are not going over there," she said quickly, running to block his path. She looked Grey squarely in the eye. "This is between him and me. I don't want you going there and starting a fight."

"He's got your sister, lass," Morgan said, sounding appalled. "He stole her right out from under your roof."

Grace looked at Morgan. "But it's not *Mary* he stole. Not really. It's just a tin full of carbon and minerals and potash. Mary left her body behind the moment she died."

"You've been looking after those ashes for days now," Grey reminded her. "I know what that tin means to you."

"I was just being foolish." She shook her head as she looked down at Baby in her arms. She looked up again. "It's not worth causing a scene over. Mary's death is new to Michael. In his mind, he just lost her last night. I know what he's going through, and if he needs her ashes for a while, then I can understand that."

"What about your plan for Summer Solstice?" Grey asked.

"That will still happen. He'll give the tin back before then. I know he will."

Neither man wanted to believe her. And they both looked frustrated that they couldn't act. She quickly handed Baby back to Grey to ensure that he didn't suddenly go after Michael despite her wishes.

"The kettle's boiling. Do you gentlemen want cocoa?"

"No," Grey said, laying Baby back in his chair. "The ice is building on our ski lift, and we need to keep an eye on it." He turned from Baby to face her. "Don't go out. The roads are treacherous, with broken trees blocking them in places."

"You got here okay," she reminded him, disgruntled by his order but relieved that the subject of Michael and Mary seemed laid to rest.

"We're traveling in the snowcat." He took her by the chin and lifted her face to his. "Call us if you need anything."

Grace shot him an overbright smile. "I will," she said so sweetly it was a wonder her teeth didn't hurt.

"Lord, woman, you're reckless with my good intentions," he muttered, scooping her up in his arms and kissing her.

Her head was spinning by the time he let her go.

It took Grace a while to gather her wits. She barely made it to the door before Grey could climb into the snowcat.

"MacKeage!"

He stopped and looked back at her.

"I want your promise you'll stay away from Michael."

She could see his face darken with guilt. Dammit. He'd been planning to go there. "Your promise, Grey. Or don't bother coming back here again."

She wasn't sure if he would heed her words. He probably didn't even care. She touched her lips. Maybe . . . maybe he did.

She saw him standing in the icy rain, getting soaked, staring back at her. He finally nodded and climbed into the snowcat. It roared to life and growled down her driveway, spitting up chunks of ice in its wake.

Grace closed the door softly and leaned against it. Well, that was something to ponder. It appeared Greylen MacKeage wanted to see her again.

Chapter Ten

Grace stopped in the act of folding Baby's clothes and turned up the volume on the television. Scenes of devastation in four states and the province of Quebec were being played out on the newscast. She couldn't believe what she was seeing.

There was footage of an entire high-tension power corridor falling like stacked dominoes, the metal towers crumbling from the weight of the ice and the loss of support as the power lines snapped. Trees, completely covered in sleeves of ice, broke under the stress, blocking roads, taking down cables, and crushing cars and buildings. Everything was covered in white, frozen into place like marble statues. It looked like scenes from Antarctica or the top of Mount Washington.

And still the rain continued to fall, freezing on everything it touched. The weatherman was saying it had to end soon, but he couldn't say when. Mother Nature was being stubborn.

Hundreds of thousands of people were without electricity now, and they were predicting the number would rise into the millions. Northern New England, northern New York, and Quebec were under a state of emergency.

Grace looked away from the television and out the living-room windows. It had been raining for four days, and the ice continued to build. She couldn't see out the windows facing north or west, and out the south windows she saw only ice. Her childhood home was constantly settling, shifting to bear the weight it already carried, groaning occasionally, and snapping every so often.

It was time, she decided, for a trip into the attic to check on the roof supports. She looked in on Baby and saw that he was sleeping off his lunch like a contented cat. As a matter of fact, the three cats she'd inherited from Mary were also sleeping, curled up in front of the fireplace, dreaming cat dreams. She smiled at the picture of them, then picked up the baby monitor and clipped it to the waist of her jogging pants.

She found a flashlight in the kitchen and started her climb to the attic. As soon as she opened the door, a swirling draft of cold air engulfed her, and Grace closed the top button on Grey's flannel shirt, which she was wearing.

She had pulled the shirt out of its hiding place under her pillow this morning, feeling like a ninth-grade schoolgirl with a crush. She missed him already, even though he had been here just yesterday, kissing her senseless again.

Would he come back to check on her and Baby today? And kiss her again?

Well, heck. She needed to get a grip here. She had to keep repeating her mantra; *Wrong man, wrong time.* She couldn't fall in love with one man while she held the child of another in her heart. Not if those two men hated each other.

There was simply no way that Grace and Baby and Grey and Michael could ever share their lives together.

And if she fell in love with Greylen MacKeage, there was no way she could avoid it. Besides, she had to return to her normal life in Virginia after the Summer Solstice.

Grace turned on the flashlight and closed the attic door behind her to keep the warm air below from escaping. As she shone her light around the expanse of the cold room, she was amazed at the accumulation of junk scattered over the entire attic. Years' worth of it, broken chairs waiting for repair, boxes of clothes, lamps, pictures, Christmas decorations, and even an old eight-track tape player the size of a couch.

But what really caught her eye was the baby furniture. There was a crib, a cradle, a changing table, and a high chair, all oak, all covered with years of dust.

She had hit pay dirt. Everything she needed for Baby was up there. There were probably even some of her and Mary's old clothes in some of the boxes.

Grace decided to check the roof first, before hauling her find downstairs. She shone her flashlight onto the ridge pole that ran the length of the attic. Except for the hundred years' accumulation of dust, it looked as solid and new as the day it had been positioned. She let the light beam trail down the rafters to where they ended at the eaves. They, too, looked fine and as straight as arrows.

A large snap suddenly sent a shiver throughout the house, the force of it powerful enough that articles in the attic rattled around her. Grace flinched but quickly shone her light back up at the rafters.

Nothing had changed.

It was the ice, she realized. The ice on the roof was cracking, not the roof itself. She recognized the sound, now that she thought about it. It was the same sound Pine Lake made on cold winter nights, as its frozen mantle shifted under the building pressure, the ice expanding and contracting as it thickened.

She breathed a sigh of relief. The house was certainly straining under the weight, but it was far from being in any danger of breaking. Satisfied that the roof wouldn't fall in on her head, Grace grabbed the cradle and changing table and lowered them into the house. The rest could wait until either Grey or Michael returned to visit.

She carried the cradle into the kitchen and washed away the dirt. Then she used a dry cloth to polish it. That done, she carried the now shining clean cradle into the living room and set it near the fireplace to warm up.

"There you go, Baby. You're going to sleep in a real bed for a change," she told the dreaming child. He was making sucking motions with his mouth against his fist, his long eyelashes resting on his warm, pink cheeks. His hair was still a wild mess, but the haphazard style was growing on Grace.

She pulled his blanket back up to his shoulders and looked at her watch to see that it was one in the afternoon. She heard a knock on her kitchen door. Her heart jumped into overdrive at the thought that Grey had returned. She rushed to the door and opened it, only to find two familiar faces that she couldn't immediately place.

"Oh, Grace," the woman said, reaching out and enveloping her in a gigantic hug. "We're so sorry. We just heard about Mary."

The man, his arms laden with dishes covered in foil, walked past them and set his load on the kitchen table. The woman wouldn't let her go. She just kept hugging her, rocking Grace back and forth.

"I told Peter we weren't going to let a little storm stop us from coming," the woman continued. "We're here for whatever you need."

"Ah . . . thank you," Grace murmured against a wet, woolly shoulder. She pulled herself out of the embrace and stared at the woman. "I know you," she said.

The woman laughed. "Of course you do, Gracie. I'm Mavis. And that's Peter. We're the Pottses. I used to baby-sit you and your sister when you were just barely toddlers."

"Oh, yes," Grace said, taking the woman by both hands and squeezing them affectionately, ashamed of herself for not recognizing them both immediately. "I haven't set eyes on you in years. It's good to see you both again."

Mavis Potts gave her an apologetic smile. "We were in California visiting our son when your parents died, and we couldn't get back in time for the funeral."

The woman hugged her again, quickly this time. "We just heard about Mary, honey. What can we do for you? I brought you something to eat," she said, going over to the table and unwrapping the dishes. Mavis suddenly looked awed, if somewhat abashed, by all the food she found herself unwrapping. "I probably overdid it, but that's what I do when I hear bad news. I cook."

"How did you find out about Mary?" Grace asked, walking up to Peter Potts and giving him a warm hug.

"Ellen Bigelow phoned us this morning," Peter said. "Told us Michael had been out all night and came home this morning with the news."

"He's devastated," Mavis added, holding a heaping, still steaming apple pie in her hand. "He's not handling it well. He's locked himself in his room, and Ellen said he hasn't eaten all day."

"They were going to get married, you know," Mavis added in a saddened whisper. She set the apple pie back on the table, pulled out a chair, and sat down.

Grace could see the seventyish woman's eyes begin to

water. "I just can't believe it," she said, shaking her head. "Mary's dead. When did it happen?"

Grace blew out a tired breath, pulled out another chair, and sat down across from her. The lies were about to begin yet again.

"Six weeks ago," Grace told her. "She was in an automobile accident."

"She was down visiting you? Where? Virginia, isn't it?"

"Yes. She came down because I asked her to. I was pregnant, and I wanted her company."

Mavis's eyes widened to saucers. "Pregnant?" she squeaked, looking toward Grace's stomach.

Grace nodded in the direction of the living room. "I had a son four weeks ago," she told her.

"Oh, you poor child," Mavis lamented, getting up and pulling Grace out of her chair so she could hug her again. "Losing your sister now," she commiserated. "At what should be the happiest time of your life."

Grace hugged her back, her eyes watering with unshed tears. She was glad the woman had come calling today, even if she did make her cry. Mavis let her go and headed into the living room.

"Grace Sutter, you have this child in an apple crate," she chided, appalled. "Why isn't he in his cradle?"

"I just got it down from the attic," she told her, walking into the living room with Peter trailing behind her. "I forgot it even existed. The changing table and some clothes are still up there. I'm going to bring them down later. I just got this cleaned up, but I didn't want to disturb him yet."

"It's a boy? What's his name?" Mavis asked in a hushed tone as she peeked at the sleeping child.

Grace closed her stinging eyes. She liked these people, and she hated to lie to them.

"I'm calling him Baby for now," she told Mavis. "I

haven't been able to decide on a name yet. What with Mary and everything, I've just wanted to wait. I want it to be the right name."

Grace opened her eyes just in time to see Mavis descending on her again. She was hugged so tightly this time she squeaked.

"That's okay, honey. Nothing says you have to name him right off the bat." She pulled back and smiled at her. "I think you're smart to consider the baby's name carefully. Within two months of naming our first son, I was sorry. Preston Potts never did fit the boy." She headed toward the stairs, still smiling. "He finally did grow into it, but it wasn't a pleasant childhood for him. The kids kept calling him Prissy Potts. Where's your husband, Grace? I can't wait to meet him."

"I don't have a husband," she told her, her words nearly getting stuck in her throat.

Mavis flushed. "Oh. I . . . ah . . . I'm sorry." She waved her hand in the air, as if brushing her words away. "That's fine, honey. Does this mean Baby's father is no longer in the picture?"

"Yeah. Something like that," Grace mumbled, turning to smooth out the wrinkles in Baby's blanket. She turned back to Mavis and shot her a forced smile. "But I'm okay with it. Baby and I will be just fine."

Mavis nodded. "Then if you're okay, we're okay, too. Come on, Peter. Let's get the stuff downstairs for Grace."

Grace ran after Mavis, who was surprisingly nimble for a woman her age. "That's not necessary. I can do that."

"Nonsense. You just had a baby. You shouldn't be lifting anything heavier than your child," Mavis said, disappearing up the stairs.

Peter walked to the stairs with an understanding smile on his face and stopped in front of her. "Better not argue with her," he said. "Not once she decides on something. Don't worry. We won't be here long, Grace. We've got to go check on the Merricks and the Colburns, to make sure they're weathering the storm okay."

"You're always welcome here, Peter," she said, not wanting him to think she was ungrateful.

He set an aging but still strong hand on her shoulder. "I know, honey. When my mother died, we appreciated the concern of our friends, but we also wanted some time to ourselves to come to terms with our loss. We're here if you need us, Grace, but we'll be careful not to intrude."

"Thank you," she told him, giving him a big hug.

Mavis returned down the stairs with a box in her hand, and Peter went up and got the changing table and carried it into the kitchen.

It was another three hugs later before the Pottses left as quickly as they had arrived, with instructions that Grace call them immediately if she needed anything.

It was while she was cleaning the changing table that Grace realized what Mavis had said. Michael was home, and he had locked himself in his room. Ellen and John Bigelow were nearing eighty themselves, and they were probably worried about the new owner of their farm, who was also their boarder.

Grace also remembered that Michael MacBain was part of the reason she was here. Not only was she supposed to get to know him, but she was supposed to do for him what the Pottses had automatically done for her without waiting for an invitation.

Instead, she was hiding out in her home like a coward. She was afraid of letting Michael be around Baby too much, afraid he would see the child's twelve toes. But mostly Grace knew that she was afraid she might actually come to like Michael MacBain.

And that was her greatest act of cowardice to date.

It was time for her and Baby to go over to the Bigelow Christmas Tree Farm. Somehow she would pull Michael out of his room, and out of his profound sadness, even if only for a little while. He was not closing himself off from the rest of the world or locking himself away with Mary's ashes.

Grace didn't even get to knock on the door before it opened and Ellen Bigelow waved her out of the rain and into the kitchen of the old but recently remodeled house.

"Land sakes, Grace Sutter, what are you doing running about in this storm?" Ellen asked, her welcoming smile contradicting her scolding. "And with a child in tow to boot."

"Ah, Ellen. It's so good to see you," Grace returned, leaning over Baby and giving Ellen a peck on the cheek. She had no problem recognizing Ellen, having worked for the Bigelows every Christmas season until she left for college. "You're looking very chipper."

The small, elderly, but still spry woman motioned for Grace to sit in one of the chairs at the kitchen table while she put the kettle on the stove to boil. "I'm not as chipper as I used to be," she said, getting down two cups from the cupboard. She gave Grace a wink. "But I've got some years in me yet."

"You haven't aged a day since I last saw you," Grace told her as she shed her jacket and let it fall over the back of her chair. She unzipped Baby from his carrier and pulled him into her lap.

Ellen immediately stopped what she was doing and came over to admire the infant.

"Ellen, I would like you to meet Baby Sutter, my son," Grace said, setting his little butt on the table while she held him up to face her. "He's four weeks old, and you are having the privilege of seeing him awake for a change. Mostly he eats and sleeps."

"Baby Sutter?" the woman asked, raising her left brow. She patted Grace's shoulder. "Having a problem with names, are you?"

"Finally, someone who understands," Grace said gratefully. "I'll name him eventually, when I find the right one."

"Can I hold him?" Ellen asked. "It's been ages since I've held anything this young," she said, carefully taking Baby as Grace handed him to her.

Ellen made cooing noises and tickled his chin. She looked at Grace with sad longing showing in every wrinkle on her face. "I have four grandchildren, but they live halfway around the world. I haven't even met two of them."

And that was why the Bigelows had sold their farm to a stranger. They had raised three sons, but two of them were dead, and the other one lived in Hawaii.

"You should get a computer, Ellen, and get online. You could send E-mail and pictures to your grandchildren."

Ellen's eyes rounded, and she suddenly laughed. "Imagine, me an Internet granny," she said. "I don't know the first thing about computers."

"It's not as complicated as it seems," Grace assured her. "Why, I could have you up and running in a day and teach you all you need to know about E-mail in an hour."

Ellen thought about that, looking down at Baby. She looked back at Grace, a sudden, determined glint in her eyes lifting her expression. "I just might take you up on your offer. I'd love to find out what all the hoopla is about when it comes to this Internet thing. Everywhere you look today, it's dot-com this and dot-com that. Would I be able to go to these dot-coms and buy things?"

"You could. They'll deliver anything you want right to your door."

"It's a deal, then. I've been saving a nest egg for something special for myself, and I can't think of a better use for it than getting in touch with my grandkids and the rest of the world."

"Then as soon as this storm is over, I'll get online with you, and we'll pick out the equipment you need. You can have it here in a week, and I'll set you up."

"Thank you," she said. "I might even let John give it a try, after I learn it," she added.

Grace looked around. "Where is John? And Michael? Is he still in his room?"

Ellen shook her head and sat down at the table across from her, still holding Baby. "No. John got him out of there an hour ago, thank God." Her sadness returned. "He's hurting, the poor man. I'm sorry for your loss, Grace."

"Thank you. I'm going to miss her."

"We all are. Mary was like a daughter to me this last year. But I understand now why she left all of a sudden," she said, looking down at Baby. "She went to be with you during your pregnancy, didn't she? Michael said . . . well, he told us you don't have a husband."

It amazed Grace how modern-minded the women were here in Pine Creek. They were not judging her for showing up with a child and no husband. They were, however, feeling sorry for her, and Grace didn't want that.

"Sometimes a woman is better off without one, instead of living a lifetime with her mistakes," she said as way of explanation.

Ellen nodded. The kettle started to boil, and Grace welcomed the excuse to jump up and fix the tea. "Where did John and Michael go?" she asked.

"They're up in the twelve-acre field, checking on the

new trees Michael set in last spring. This ice is raising havoc with them. The older, established trees can handle it, if it doesn't get much worse, but the young ones aren't strong enough yet. Michael could lose the entire crop."

"What can they do about it? They can't very well shake the ice off every tree on twelve acres."

"John mentioned maybe setting up a system of smudge pots to keep the temperature just above freezing around them. Like they do with the orange trees in Florida when they get a freeze."

Grace set the tea on the stove to steep and looked back at Ellen. "Will that work?"

The worried woman shrugged her shoulders. "I don't know. And neither does John. And we don't even know if we can scrape together enough equipment to try."

Grace pictured the young trees in her mind and what it would take to save them. They needed support to carry them through the ice storm. She knew the twelve-acre field. The west winds often blew the snow right off it most winters.

She suddenly had an idea.

"How tall are the trees, Ellen? One foot? Two feet?"

"They're about a foot and a half, I would say," she told her, her eyes narrowed on Grace's excited expression. "Why?"

"Instead of heating the air to protect them, what if we . . ."

Loud footsteps suddenly sounded on the porch, and the door opened. John Bigelow and Michael MacBain came into the kitchen, stamping their feet on the rug.

When they saw Grace, both men stopped and stared at her. John smiled, and Michael gave her first a surprised look and then a guilty frown. Grace smiled back at both of them.

"John," Ellen said, obviously having caught some of Grace's excitement. "Grace has an idea to save the trees."

Both John and Michael looked from Ellen to Grace.

Grace flushed slightly. "I . . . it's just an idea. And I'm not even sure it will work," she admitted to them.

"What?" John asked, sighing deeply and rubbing his forehead. "At this point, I'll entertain anything."

"Well," she said, still formulating her thoughts from before. "What if, instead of trying to thaw the trees, you bury them?"

"Bury them?" Michael asked. "With what?"

"Snow," she said succinctly. "The snow would surround the young trees and support their weight, and if the snow was deep enough, it would protect them from being damaged by any more ice."

Michael turned and looked out the window, frowning when he looked back at her. "It's raining, not snowing."

"But we can make snow. Maybe. It would be wet snow, but it still might be possible in these temperatures."

Michael was looking at her as if she'd lost her mind. John was shaking his head. "That takes specialized equipment, Grace," John said. "And there's nothing like that around here."

"Yes, there is," she countered. "On TarStone Mountain. I saw it two days ago, when I came down the mountain in the snowcat. There was enough piping and guns to do your twelve-acre field."

A very colorful, very blue curse suddenly scorched the air in the kitchen. Grace looked at Michael and saw his entire face redden and his eyes narrow to pinpricks.

"We're better off with the smudge pots," he said through his teeth, his jaw clenched so tightly Grace thought he was in danger of hurting himself. "That equipment on TarStone will never lie in my fields."

Grace set her hands on her hips. "And why not?"

"MacKeage will never agree, and if he does, I won't allow it. I have no wish to be beholden to the bastard."

Grace ignored Michael's anger and spoke to John. "Will it work?" she asked. "If we can make snow and cover the trees, will it protect them?"

John was scratching his two-day growth of peppered white whiskers. "It might," he said, nodding his head. "It really might work. The snow would support them."

"Dammit. MacKeage won't do it," Michael said, pulling off his jacket and boots, stomping, sock-footed out of the kitchen, and disappearing up the stairs. All three of the adults and even Baby flinched when a door suddenly slammed shut over their heads with enough force to rattle the windows.

Grace looked at Ellen. "Can you keep Baby for me for a few hours?" she asked. "I want to go to TarStone."

But it wasn't until she was halfway to the ski resort that Grace remembered she'd just left a twelve-toed child in the same house as his father.

Chapter Eleven

Grace turned onto the well-marked road that led to TarStone Mountain Resort and drove down it a mile before she came to a stop at the far corner of the massive parking lot. She had seen a bit of the resort on her ride back to her home two days ago, but that was nothing compared with what was in front of her now.

The resort was huge. There was one massive structure just to the left that was obviously the ski lodge. Its three-story-high floor-to-ceiling windows faced the mountain. There were several more outbuildings and a long, two-story hotel on the right. And everything, right down to the ski-lift shed, was built from granite and black stone and large hand-hewn logs.

If she had to describe it, Grace would say that the lodge and hotel looked like a cross between a Scottish castle and a Swiss chalet. The roofs were bulged out like medieval barns and covered with cedar shingles that had been left to weather to a natural gray. Eaves overshot the buildings by a good three feet and swept into a graceful arch just at the ends, further amplifying the architecture of the roofline.

The MacKeages hadn't skimped on the glass. Windows

running from floor to ceiling marked every room of the hotel, and a large carport had been added to the front, held up by massive pillars that looked to be whole trees.

Black stone formed the foundations and lower walls of both the lodge and the hotel, topped by rows of rough-hewed horizontal logs. Only the trim had been painted a deep forest green, while the logs had been left to weather naturally.

It was beautiful. A fairy-tale world. And every square inch of it was covered with ice, which added to its magical aura.

She was very impressed. When the MacKeages did things, they obviously did them well.

She couldn't see their home, though, which Grey had called Gu Bràth. She remembered he had mentioned that it was several hundred yards away, probably tucked up the mountain a bit, back in the woods. She looked around for a driveway leading out of the parking lot but saw none. She did see a light coming from the ski-lift shed. She drove her truck up to it and shut off the ignition.

Morgan popped his head out the door of the shed. Grace got out of her truck and slipped and slid her way toward him.

"Take a care, lass, before you break your beautiful neck," Morgan said, holding the door open for her and grabbing her arm as she stumbled inside.

"Thank you. I've got to find Dad's old ice creepers."

"Grace," Grey said, surprise in his voice. She looked up to see him smiling as he came toward her. His hair was soaked, with little icicles hanging from the ends of it.

"Didn't you get enough weather two nights ago?" she asked, reaching up and brushing some of the melting ice off his shoulder.

"What are you doing here?" He looked out the door

toward her truck, then took her by the shoulders. "And where's Baby? Is everything okay? Is he sick?"

"No," she told him quickly. "He's fine. I left him with Ellen Bigelow."

Grey suddenly stiffened and took a step back from her, dropping his hands to his sides. "Why?" he asked curtly.

Grace shrugged. "It seemed like a good idea at the time."

His expression said he didn't like her answer. Grace wiped the dripping rain from her own hair and sighed. What was it with this man, his mood blowing back and forth like a wind-whipped sheet on the line? "Look, I left him there so that I could come check on you. I wanted to see how your ski lift is standing the strain of the ice. When you left yesterday, you said you were worried about it."

"You're here to check on us?" Morgan asked, sounding as if he couldn't believe what he'd heard. "You've got it backward, lass. We're supposed to be looking after you."

Grace couldn't help but smile at the absurdity of his thinking. "I'm not the one with the imperiled ski lift. I live in a sturdy old house that will still be standing long after we're dead." She looked out the open mountain side of the shed, at the sagging cables that appeared to be stressed to their limits. She nodded in the lift's direction. "That doesn't look good."

"And what would you know about it looking good or bad?" Ian asked, walking out from behind a gondola, rolling up sheets of paper.

Grace spun around to face him. She wasn't insulted by the man's skepticism. She'd run into his kind often enough.

"I know that if those cables break, the arms on every one of your towers will snap like matchsticks. Not to mention the damage it will do to both this shed and the one at the summit. Your last couple of towers will probably be compromised beyond redemption if they don't break off completely, and whatever gondolas you have out there," she added for good measure, "will be destroyed as well."

Ian's eyes widened in alarm as he looked up the mountain to where the towers disappeared into the rain. He looked back at her, his expression darkened with suspicion.

"You're a woman," he said, only to scowl suddenly at his own words.

"Thank you for noticing," she drawled. "Are those the schematics for the lift?" she asked, nodding at the roll of papers in his hands.

Ian looked at Grey, silently asking for help out of the hole he'd dug for himself.

With a chuckle, Grey walked over and took the papers from him. "You're right, Ian," he said. "She is a woman. And she's a damn sight smarter than you. Try to remember that in the future, okay?"

Ian was now flushed to the roots of his graying red hair. He looked at her out of the corner of his eye, then nodded slightly. "Sorry," he murmured. "That was uncalled for."

Grace waved his apology away. "It's okay. I get it all the time."

"Ya do? From who?" Ian wanted to know, appearing ready to run out and defend her.

"From most males," she told him truthfully, walking over to Grey and taking the drawings out of his hands. "But that's the fun part. I always get the last laugh."

Ian nodded. "Good," he said. "Now, lass. Do you think you can read those damnable papers? I've been trying, but I can't make heads or tails of what they mean."

Grace took the papers—which looked as if they'd been rolled up and squeezed quite a bit lately—over to a bench under a light and laid them out to read.

"The specs on the ski lift," she told Ian and Grey, moving aside so Morgan could also look, "give the stress loads for every square inch of the ski lift."

"Where do they say that?" Ian asked, pushing against her to see better. "And what in hell are all those numbers written all over the damn thing?"

"They're weight loads," Grace told him. "Like here. This says this particular beam will withstand the pressure of one thousand pounds of weight sitting on it."

"A thousand pounds?" Ian asked. "Hell, my horse weighs more than that. You're saying this piece of steel wouldn't even hold up my horse?"

"Not by itself, it wouldn't," she explained to him, smiling at his analogy. "But place it in a carefully planned structure, and you can multiply that weight several times. Like here," she said, pointing to a drawing of one of the towers. "This is designed to bear the weight of a cable full of gondolas even if the tower above or below it fails or the arm snaps off one of them. The towers are not your worry; they won't break because of their design. The cable is what can cause the most damage."

Ian looked up from the papers and squinted at her. "How do you know all this?" he asked.

"It's what I do for a living. I work out mathematical equations that prove or disprove whether something like this ski lift system will work. It's basic physics."

"Are ya saying that you can read this and tell us how much weight the cable can bear? If we could find out how much the ice weighed, we could tell if it will break."

He'd finished the last part of his question with a theory of his own. Grace smiled to let him know she liked his logic.

"That's right. But I already know how much ice weighs."

"Ya do? Why would ya know something like that?" he asked.

"When you shoot a rocket into space, Ian, ice sometimes builds up on it as it moves through the atmosphere. Any third-year physics major learns how to calculate lift loss for ice weight and what it will take to shatter it off."

Ian lifted a brow and looked at Grey. "She's pulling my leg, ain't she?" he asked him. "This woman you hauled off the mountain has a daft sense of humor. Nobody can hold that much knowledge in their brain."

Grey simply shook his head as he stared down at her, his evergreen eyes gleaming in the dim light of the shed. He was quite a handsome fellow when he wasn't scowling at her, Grace thought.

"She has no sense of humor," he told Ian, still staring at her. "She thinks flying is a good thing."

"How long would it have taken you to drive from Bangor to TarStone the other day?" she asked him, matching his mischievous look with one of her own. "Ninety minutes? Two hours?"

"Two."

"But you made it here in less than forty minutes because of the plane."

That changed his expression. The man's eyes suddenly narrowed to slits. "We landed ten miles short and one thousand feet high of our mark, woman. And it ended up taking me half the day and the whole night to get home."

Grace reached up to tap his chest and gave him a huge grin. "Details, MacKeage. Minor details. It usually goes much more smoothly."

He appeared to be one second short of throttling her, but Grace wasn't worried. No sense of humor, indeed. She looked back at the papers.

"How thick's the ice now, do you think?" she asked Ian.

He held up his plump and calloused little finger. "This thick," he said. "And it's growing all the time."

"Your finger?"

"Nay, lass," he said with a pained groan. "The ice!"

"We were just deciding to start up the ski lift," Morgan interjected.

Grace turned to the younger man, who had been quiet up until now. "Don't," she said. She turned to Grey. "It might put too much stress on the system."

"But we're thinking to break up the ice so it will fall off," Ian added. "To take off the weight."

"It's too late. You would have had to do that two days ago," she told him.

"Too late? You mean we're going to have to just stand here and watch it collapse?" Morgan asked.

Grace shook her head. "Maybe not. There's always a great safety margin factored into these structures. It may hold until the rain stops."

"If it stops," Ian muttered, turning away from the bench and staring out at the lift. He looked back at her over his shoulder, his brows knitted into a frown. "Is there nothing we can do?"

Grace thought about that. There was, but it was only a theory in her mind. One that could backfire on them with disastrous results. Either the ice would melt off the cable like a spring thaw, or TarStone's ski lift would shatter like glass and probably take them with it.

"Good God," Ian exclaimed. "I swear I can see her brain working," he said, walking back to her and looking quizzically into her eyes. He waved a hand in front of her face. "What's going on in there, lass?" he asked. "Have ya an idea?"

Grace turned her gaze to each of the three men, one at a time. She might have an idea. But she also might just have a very powerful bargaining chip that could save the Bigelow Christmas Tree Farm as well.

"That depends," she started carefully, still undecided about how she wanted to approach this subject.

"On what?" Morgan asked, walking up beside Ian so he could stare into her face as well.

She needed to buy herself some time. She couldn't very well bargain for them to give her their snow-making equipment and not be able to deliver on her promise to save their lift. And truth be told, she preferred to present her offer to Grey, not all three of them, to better her odds of succeeding. It was much easier to sway just one person than it was to convince a united front that helping Michael MacBain would be the decent, neighborly thing for them to do. These men all seemed to respect Grey's opinion, and that made him the person she needed to talk to.

And she needed to talk to him alone.

Ian was waving his hand in front of her face again. "Has your brain cramped, lass?" he asked. "Have ya overworked it?"

Grace blinked, then shot him a smile. "No. But before I get your hopes up, I need to see the top part of the lift." She looked at Grey. "Will you take me up there in the snowcat?"

Grey, who had remained unusually silent except to tell her she had no sense of humor, suddenly lifted the corner of his mouth in a wry grin. "You're actually wanting to go back up that mountain? Didn't you get enough of it the other day?" he asked, repeating her earlier question to him.

"Where's your phone?" she demanded, not taking her eyes off his as she held out her hand. "I'm going to call and ask Ellen if she can watch Baby for a few more hours."

"It's over on the wall," Morgan said.

Already lost in the depths of Grey's unfathomable green

eyes, it took Grace a moment to realize that someone had spoken. She forced herself to break eye contact with Grey and look where Morgan was pointing.

There was the phone, right by the door. She made her legs move next, willing them to carry her over to it. It was a nearly impossible task, what with her knees being so weak and her heart pounding so erratically. It really wasn't fair that Grey was so handsome. Or that not seeing him for twenty-four hours could affect her this way.

Silence, and the feel of evergreen eyes piercing her back, followed Grace across the room as she walked over to the phone.

She didn't make it to the wall before Grey spoke.

"Morgan, go to the house and have Callum make a thermos of hot chocolate," she heard him instruct. "Ian, warm up the snowcat."

"I'm going with you," Ian said, heading for the door.

"No," Grey said, his voice sounding as if he was still looking at her, not at the man he was speaking to. "Grace and I will go alone."

She let out the breath she'd been unconsciously holding and picked up the phone, only to realize she didn't know Ellen Bigelow's number.

"The phone book is right beneath it," Grey said suddenly from right behind her.

Grace knew she just had to sway back on her heels and she would be leaning against him. She suddenly had second thoughts about her plan to travel up TarStone Mountain with Greylen MacKeage. Something deep in the pit of her stomach said this was going to be either the most promising thing she'd ever done or the dumbest.

She didn't need to be a rocket scientist to know that the energy filling this shed now had nothing to do with mere friendship. Feminine instinct was all but screaming at

Grace that if she didn't run out the door and head for the safety of home, the consequences might be more than she bargained for.

"Change your mind?" came his deep voice from behind her.

She stared at the phone receiver in her hand. "No," she said, closing her eyes, feeling the heat of him wrapping around her senses until it feathered itself over her cheeks, making her flush with warmth.

"Good," he said softly, his breath gently wafting past her right ear. "You won't be sorry."

She was sorry already.

Grace stared past the hypnotic wipers, not really seeing the ski slope passing slowly under the tracks of the snow-cat. Her mind's eye was focused on the man sitting silently beside her, who was confidently steering the machine up the winding trails, taking her ever closer to . . .

"Do you remember my promise to you up on the mountain three days ago, Grace?" he asked, his voice soft but still reaching her over the drone of the working engine. "Right after I had found the pilot, and you were afraid of me?"

She turned her head to look at him. "You said you would never hurt me."

He nodded, his attention still on his driving. "That's right. But you still don't believe me, do you?"

"That depends," she said, scooting around in her seat to face him. "I didn't know you then, and I admit you did frighten me. I was alone with a man who wanted to lash out at something."

She smiled at him when he looked at her from the corner of his eye. "But now that I know you, I know you would never hurt me physically."

"Ahh," he said, nodding his head again as he watched the trail in front of them. "What is it, then, that you're guarding from me? Are you afraid I'll hurt your heart maybe?"

"That worry did cross my mind," she admitted.

"Then that tells me you feel the attraction, too." He turned his head and gave her his full attention. "And that's what really scares you. Your own awareness of what is happening between us. That, and the fact that you don't want to be attracted to someone like me, do you, Grace?"

"Someone like what?" she asked, taken aback not only by the realization that he could read her feelings so well but also by his belief that she thought he was somehow lacking.

He seemed to think about her question as he watched the trail again, guiding the snowcat over a particularly rough stretch and up the final climb to the top. She could just make out the shape of the summit house up ahead.

"By my primitiveness, I guess we could call it for lack of a better word," he finally said. He looked back at her, his green eyes unreadable. "You work with modern, civilized males whose minds look into space and see the future, don't you? That's the world you've lived in since you left Pine Creek. The men you know dress in suits and dine in restaurants that serve thousand-dollar bottles of wine."

"The point being?" she asked, getting defensive. He was making her world sound as if it was nothing more than a pretense of life, not the real thing.

"You go out on dates with these men," he continued as if she hadn't spoken. "Probably wearing a silk dress, pearls, and sensible two-inch heels. And at the end of the evening, they walk you to your door and give you a very civilized kiss good night." He darted a glance at her, then looked back at the trail. "They send flowers the next day, don't they, Grace? And ask you out again the next week."

"The point being?" she repeated through clenched teeth.

"Except Baby's father," he said, looking back at her, his eyes now two distinct pools of unreflected light. "He got past your defenses and into your bed. And then he left you with a child to bring up by yourself. Tell me, does he intend to send a check in the mail once a month to compensate for his cowardice?"

"That's enough," she said, turning back in her seat to face forward, her arms crossed under her chest. Oh, she'd made a mistake, all right, coming up here with him today.

He *was* primitive.

"It's none of your business," she told him. "Who and where Baby's father is, it's none of your damn business."

The snowcat came to such a sudden halt Grace had to brace her hands against the dash. She didn't even wait to see where they were, she just opened her door and jumped out. She started plodding over the crusted snow, driving her feet into it until it broke.

Damn him. He was a jerk. And to imagine she thought she liked him.

He was suddenly right beside her, walking on top of the crust, exerting one-tenth the energy she was. Grace stopped and turned, cupping her hand to her forehead to block out the rain so she could glare at him better.

"I'm going to save your damn ski lift, MacKeage, but only under one condition."

"And that would be?" he asked calmly, in stark contradiction to her anger.

It only made her angrier. "That you give me your snow-making equipment and help me set it up at the Bigelow Christmas Tree Farm tonight."

The taunting calmness left his face so suddenly Grace took a step back.

"Not in your lifetime, lady. MacBain's trees can rot in the ground for all I care."

"Fine. Then the same thing can happen to your damn ski lift," she countered, turning around and walking away.

She started walking back down the ski trail, only not breaking through the crust this time and being careful of her footing. She found the tracks the cat had made and began following them—until she was suddenly grabbed from behind and spun around so quickly she screamed.

"You can't walk down this mountain," he said, his evergreen eyes glaring at her.

"I didn't just fall three thousand feet, MacKeage, like the last time."

Although her heart certainly felt as if it had—and that it had broken on impact. She was so disappointed she wanted to sit down and cry. Why was this truly gorgeous, rugged, capable man such a jerk? And worst of all, why was she so attracted to him in the first place?

That was the saddest part. He couldn't see past his hatred for Michael MacBain, and he couldn't see how much, or guess why, that hurt her. The man she had formed a remarkable bond with on the mountain three days ago hated her nephew's father. He didn't know it, but she and Baby would become a link between him and Michael if she let herself get involved with Grey.

She was astute enough to realize that she had already let herself become much too involved with him emotionally. It had started when he had taken Baby to safety and then come back for her. And this afternoon, in the lift shed, she had felt it—the strength of their bond—enveloping her in the warmth of sharing something special with a special man.

But that bond was being smothered by a soulless sleeve of ice, just as surely as the trees around her were being entombed at this very moment.

"Grace," he said, shaking her slightly.

"I don't like you anymore, Grey. I can't."

"You damn well will," he growled, wrapping her up in a fierce embrace that took the wind right out of her. And she never did catch her breath before his mouth descended on hers with demanding possession.

Her head swam with mixed emotions. Being in his arms, feeling his lips on hers, tasting him; it all felt so wonderfully right, no matter how wrong it was. This was the energy, the passion of life, the very soul of her existence that she hadn't even realized she'd been searching for.

This, Grace decided as he ruthlessly awakened her emotions, was about as real as it got. She was in the arms of the man she wanted to belong to for the rest of her life.

Passion rose inside her. She had fallen in lust with Greylen MacKeage the moment she'd met him. She'd fallen in love when she had trusted him enough to let him seal her into an ice cave.

"I love you," she whispered into his mouth. "I love you."

Grace's world tilted on its axis before she had finished her declaration. She found herself being carried up the mountain, the summit house suddenly appearing out of the mist. Grey turned with her still in his arms and tried the knob. When it wouldn't open, he simply used his foot and kicked in the door.

He carried her inside and suddenly stopped, looking around and frowning. He finally lowered her feet to the floor and left her standing in the middle of the large summit house. He walked to the huge granite fireplace and struck a match to the already prepared kindling and logs.

He then walked around the room, pulled cushions off several of the chairs, and threw them on the floor in front of the hearth.

He looked back at her once, as if checking to see if she was still there, then continued his work, pulling a blanket from a shelf near the hearth and tossing it down on the pillows. Grace took off her jacket and silently, albeit shakily, walked over and began arranging the pillows into a bed.

No regrets. No second thoughts. Grey obviously wanted this to happen, but Grace decided she wanted it more. She had known it was inevitable the moment she'd felt him behind her in the lift shed, waiting for her to place the call that would give them this time alone together.

She sat in the middle of her newly made bed and watched him prop the broken door closed to keep out the weather. The dry kindling in the hearth suddenly popped with exploding sap, and Grace jumped.

She didn't have any more clue about what she was doing than Grey had a clue about her history with men. All she knew was that Greylen MacKeage was about to discover she couldn't possibly be Baby's mother.

Chapter Twelve

The poor woman was sitting in the middle of the cozy nest of pillows she'd put together, not a drop of color in her face. Her blue eyes were as wide as saucers, and she looked as if the touch of a feather might shatter her composure.

If he were a gentleman, he would sit beside her and talk to her a bit, gentling her fears and giving her time to come to terms with what was about to happen. Yes, if he were even a little bit civilized, he would at least explain that once they made love there was no going back. That she would be his, and no one, not even God himself, could alter that truth.

Grey took off his jacket as he silently walked toward her. He would undress Grace with all the care a queen deserved, and then he would make love to her until she understood what he couldn't put into words.

And then he'd make love to her again.

Grey took a seat beside her on the cushions, ignoring the fact that she flinched when he did. He wrapped an arm around her stiff shoulders and placed his other hand under her chin to lift her mouth to his.

She was warm and sweet and tasted like the cocoa she

had drunk from the thermos before they had climbed into the snowcat. Grey had been amused when she had swilled the hot drink down as if it was Scotch, as if it would settle her nerves.

It hadn't helped her then and it wasn't helping her now, if her trembling was any indication. Grey lay back on the pillows and turned to settle Grace beneath him.

God, she was precious. Warm, vibrant, filled with a passion he knew was churning just below the surface. He never stopped kissing her as he untucked her shirt and pushed it up to her chest. She was gripping his hair now and finally kissing him back. Grey found the clasp at the front of her bra and opened it, pushing it aside and covering her breast with his hand.

She moaned deep in her throat, arching her breast into his palm. Her nipple sprang to life as he teased it gently, and the woman beneath him squirmed until her hips were directly against his erection.

She let go of his hair and began caressing his shoulders, then ran her fingers down the length of his arms. A surge of energy spiked through his body. She pulled her mouth free and started kissing his jaw as she tugged at his shirt, trying to pull it out of his pants. Grey brushed the hair from her face and began kissing her cheeks, her nose, her closed eyes.

She wasn't having much luck undressing him, probably because his shirttail was caught on the bulge in his trousers. Grey leaned away and quickly pulled off his sweater and undershirt. He took her back in his arms and began kissing her again. Her hands immediately went to his chest, and she moaned into his neck.

"Yes," she said on an excited, breathless whisper. "Take off your pants."

He pulled back and looked at her. He couldn't have

spoken if he wanted to. This beautiful, precious woman wanted him with a fierceness that was nearly overwhelming. She was no longer pale but flushed all the way to her hairline. Her eyes were open, staring at him with such intensity that Grey had to close his own eyes and take a deep breath before he stripped them both naked and drove himself into her.

So he left his pants on for now. He unfastened her belt instead, teasing the tender skin of her belly as he did, fighting his urgency as she continued to run her hands through the hair on his chest. Then her tongue darted out and licked one of his nipples.

His groan echoed off the high ceiling. He throbbed with a heaviness that was almost impossible to hold in check. Grey clenched his jaw as he felt himself break into a sweat.

With dogged determination, and a few prayers for control, Grey slid her pants down to her boots. The flush of her skin traveled the length of her. Her beautiful body slowly emerged, glistening with life in the glow of the firelight.

She was flawless. Her skin felt like silk under his fingers. Her own fingers continued to explore the parts of his body she could reach, tugging to pull him closer.

He couldn't untie her wet boots. Grey cursed under his breath. With a violent tug, he finally got them off and threw them away, hearing them land someplace across the room. He stripped her pants completely off, and she immediately wrapped one silky leg around him.

That simple action was his undoing. Grey unfastened his own pants and pushed them down to his knees. He settled between her thighs and held himself over her.

"Grace. Look at me, lass."

She did, and Grey was stunned by the fire he saw in her

eyes. "N-now," she said with trembling urgency, lifting her hips as she wrapped both her legs around his waist. "Please, Grey. I want you."

He bent down and took one of her nipples in his mouth. Grace arched against him with a shout of pleasure. His whole body shook with barely leashed power. He touched her between the womanly folds that guarded her from him now, his fingers moving through her wetness as he made her ready to take him.

He had been ready for more than eight centuries to claim Grace, the one woman in the world meant for him.

Grey centered himself over her and gently pushed against the wet, hot core of her womanhood. She offered only minor resistance as he moved deeper within her.

Until he suddenly came to her maidenhead.

"Grace," he repeated, his voice a whisper as he strained to hold himself still. It was not an easy task. Grace Sutter was a virgin, and every instinct, every primitive male cell in his body, was screaming to claim her.

"Don't stop," she said, pushing herself lower and lifting her hips higher as her nails dug into his skin. "I want this, Grey. I want to feel all of you inside me."

Their eyes locked together, Grey thrust himself through her virgin's barrier and captured her scream in his mouth. He didn't stop until he was deeply, completely inside her. Only then did he give her a chance to adjust to him.

He waited until she moved first.

And then Grey began a gentle rhythm that only served to harden him more, as he sank deeper into her welcoming softness. Light slowly filled the summit house, blinding him to everything but this act of possession. Time was suspended. Energy sparked around them. Wave after wave of emotion coursed through his body as they rocked together, igniting a fire that touched the very center of his

soul. Grey threw back his head with the force of his pleasure as he finally released his seed deep inside her.

He relaxed on top of her with a sigh, grateful that his
brain still functioned enough to remember not to crush
her completely. He gently kissed her forehead, then slowly
rolled off their comfortable nest of pillows, onto the cold,
hard surface of the concrete floor.

He closed his eyes while he caught his breath, one arm
slung over his face to shield the light of the hearth, the
cold floor cooling his trembling, overheated body.

Grace Sutter now belonged to him.

And Baby, he knew for a fact, did not belong to her.

She wasn't regretful. A bit disappointed, maybe, that what
had started out so nicely had ended so painfully. But Grace
had no regrets.

She had always expected they'd both find satisfaction
the first time, making it a romantic, magical experience.
Now, though, she was only sore and mightily worried
because Grey was unnaturally silent.

He was lying beside her, breathing hard, his eyes closed
and an arm thrown over his face. The set of his jaw didn't
bode well, either. It was clenched so tightly that the cords
bulged in his neck.

Grace became embarrassingly aware of her nakedness
as a draft of air seeped down from the balcony of the summit house. As quietly as she could, she pulled her jacket
out from under her and covered her body from her chin to
her thighs. She lay on her back on the blanket, unmoving,
and watched the intricate play of the firelight reflecting on
the log beams two stories up.

What in hell was he thinking?

She stole a peek at him, then quickly looked back at the
ceiling. He hadn't moved. His pants were still down

around his ankles, his boots were still on, and sweat glistened off every inch of exposed skin. She had noticed also, in that fraction of a second, that there was a smudge of her blood on his thigh.

Grace took stock of her situation.

She hurt like the devil between her legs. That was what she got for keeping her hymen intact for so many years. She knew how unnatural it was to be thirty years old and still a virgin.

And then there was the problem of the silent man beside her. How was she going to get up gracefully, get dressed, and get back down the mountain without making an absolute fool of herself? She had no experience with the aftermath of lovemaking. She didn't know the protocol.

Grey should. He hadn't been a virgin. Heck. He'd probably found himself in this situation hundreds of times. Possibly thousands.

That thought made her mad. Why was he lying there like a half-naked mountain of granite? And what was he thinking?

"I saved MacBain's son three days ago, didn't I?" he suddenly said without moving, his arm still covering his face and his body still rigid.

"Yes, you did. Three times, as a matter of fact." Grace spoke to the ceiling above them. "Once inside your jacket as the plane was going down, once when you covered his mouth with yours and breathed life back into him, and again when you carried him down the mountain."

"Damn."

"You weren't damning him then." She turned to look at him. "You didn't even give a thought to his heritage. You simply saw an innocent child who needed your strength to live."

"Damn."

Grace finally got up, holding her jacket in front of her, and reached down to pick up her clothes. She walked behind one of the couches and started dressing, watching Grey out of the corner of her eye. He still hadn't moved.

"He's still that same innocent baby," she said into the silence. "And he is also my nephew. I will protect him with my dying breath."

He stood up so suddenly Grace nearly tripped trying to pull up her pants and take a step back at the same time. Grey pulled up his own pants but stilled, seeing the blood on his thigh.

Grace hid her blush in the folds of her turtleneck as she pulled it over her head.

He finished his task as he looked at her, fastening his belt around his waist. His evergreen stare bored into her soul.

"You belong to me now, Grace Sutter. Your allegiance is to me," he said with a fierceness she felt all the way down to her bare toes.

Grace looked away and pulled her sweater over her head. Holy Mother Mary. He was even more primitive than she had imagined. He was suddenly acting as if he owned her.

"That's old-fashioned," she told him, waving her socks in the air as she looked for her boots. "Women don't belong to men anymore. That practice stopped nearly two hundred years ago." She pointed her socks at him. "I belong to myself, Greylen MacKeage. And my only allegiance is to my nephew and my dead sister."

He picked up his shirt and put it on, appearing not the least bit put off by her declaration. "Why were you still a virgin?" he asked.

She stopped hunting for her boots and looked at him, feeling a flush climb into her cheeks again. Damn.

She lifted her chin. "I was saving myself for marriage."

The left corner of his mouth kicked up. "That's a bit old-fashioned, don't you think, for a lass as modern as you consider yourself to be?" he asked, throwing her words back at her.

"It is not. A woman keeping herself intact until she marries is a very hip, very modern concept."

He looked down at the pillows on the floor and then back at her. "Then I guess this means I'm the man you intend to marry," he said, his voice washing over Grace with a resonance that made her skin prickle with shivers.

"Marriage means one of us would have to move, and I doubt you'd last a month in Virginia," she told him, walking to a chair to put on her socks, careful to keep the couch between them.

"The question is, Grace, how long will you last here?"

She looked up, alarmed. "My life is in Virginia. I have work to do there."

He stared at her another long minute and then turned and walked over to the opposite wall. He picked up both her boots and carried them to her, holding them out for her to take.

She couldn't move. He had her pinned into place with his gaze again.

"You aren't going back to Virginia, Grace. The moment you decided to bring Baby back here, the decision was also made that you would be staying with him."

How could he possibly know such a thing? She hadn't even come to terms with her own reasoning yet. She had taken four months from work to come here and sort out her feelings. And now he was telling her just what those feelings were?

She took her boots from him, put them on her feet, and stood up. "I'm ready to go home now," she said, walking to the door.

He walked over to the hearth and poked the fire down until it was safely banked, then he moved to the door and pulled the heavy prop away and opened it. Grace stepped out into the late-morning light and tilted her head back, letting the mist wash over her face. Grey stood beside her, looking around at the gently crackling, frozen landscape.

"I will grant you permission to ask my men to use our equipment at the tree farm," he said, drawing her attention. "But I am only allowing this for Baby, not for MacBain. Eventually the farm will belong to your nephew, if you ever tell MacBain that Baby is his son."

He took her by the shoulders and turned her to face him. "I'm thinking you won't do it until the boy reaches his late teens or thereabouts. That's fine with me. I'm willing to raise him as my own son."

He was assuming she was going to marry him. And that they would live happily ever after as a family, with Baby believing she was his mom and Grey was his dad.

And Michael MacBain none the wiser for their deception.

Well, that was far more than Jonathan Stanhope had offered her. He wanted her to dump Baby in his father's lap and come running back to Virginia, maybe bear him his own carefully engineered child, and help him win his space race.

"I made a promise to my sister on her deathbed," she told the man in front of her. "She wants Baby to be with his father."

"Then you made a promise you never intended to keep, Grace. Otherwise MacBain would have him now."

"He still might get him. I haven't decided yet. Mary's wishes are still stronger than my own selfishness."

He was shaking his head. "You don't hold on to a child for just a little while and then give him up. It isn't possible. You already love him like a son."

"Sometimes love can be painful," she said, knowing personally just how truthful her words were.

Her heart was feeling so wounded at the moment she wasn't sure it would ever mend properly. How could she love a man who was asking her to keep a secret that affected so many people? What would Baby think of them both then, when he reached an age where they could tell him he'd been living a lie? How could you explain that his real father was just a mile down the road and had been there his entire life? How do you rob a child of his true heritage and his right to know who he really is?

"Justify your actions by thinking you're doing it for Baby if you want," she told Grey. "And I'll say I'm saving your ski lift because my own conscience won't allow me to walk away from a neighbor in trouble. And let's just leave it at that."

"You're a damn difficult woman to deal with, Grace Sutter. You're far too independent for my liking."

She gave him a sad smile and shrugged her shoulders, which broke her free of his touch.

"That's probably the greatest thing Mary and I had in common. Welcome to the Sutter family, Mr. MacKeage."

Daar paced the length of his porch and stopped to look up at TarStone Mountain. The clouds had lifted just enough that he could see the summit.

He was feeling the energy again. Only this time it was not menacing. The air enveloping TarStone was charged with the white light of life.

This was good. He had heard the snowcat laboring up the mountain on a distant trail two hours ago, and that was when the first wave of energy had assaulted his senses. He had seen a halo of pure white light wreath the summit within minutes of the snowcat's ascent, and he hadn't needed a crystal ball to know that Greylen and Grace were up there.

Daar rubbed his hands together and cackled in glee. It was about time those two stubborn people got down to the business of making babies. He had maybe one or two centuries left in his tired old bones, and that was barely enough time to train a new wizard properly.

Daar counted forward on his fingers nine months from now, and his glee disappeared. The first of December. Close, but not near enough to the Winter Solstice. He suddenly smiled again. MacKeage had been late, content to stay in his mother's womb an extra two weeks. The child conceived today would probably wish to do the same.

Yes, the MacKeage baby would be born on the Winter Solstice, and her birth would begin the quiet shift of power. It was a human misconception that winter was associated with males and summer with females. The strength, the patient power of life, was in the Winter Solstice.

All seven MacKeage girls would be born on that day, over the next eight years.

And the seventh child would be named Winter.

She was the one Daar intended to gift with the new cherrywood cane he was carving.

He buttoned up his Mackinaw coat and picked up his satchel of clothes, stepping off the porch and using his cane for support as he walked over the frozen crust toward the ski trail.

He intended to ride back down the mountain with the warrior and his woman. It was time he spent a few days a bit closer to civilization, getting to know Grace Sutter.

Chapter Thirteen

The snowcat stopped in front of what Grace could only describe as a castle. It was built completely of stone, four stories high, and it was the darkest, ugliest structure she had ever laid eyes on.

It had to cover nearly four acres in footprint, with towers marking each of the four corners and slits for windows rising up each rounded turret in a diagonal procession, as if following the rise of stairs. The stones that made up the walls were black and gray speckled granite. But arched over the doorway and each window the stones were pure black, only slightly less rough than the walls.

The architect they'd hired must have thought he'd died and gone to heaven, being able to design such a huge, modern-day castle. He also must have been drunk.

There was even a moat. Sort of. Grace stared at the bridge that ran over a wild, frothing brook roaring past the castle's foundation.

So this was Gu Bràth.

Grace wondered if Grey thought she would marry him and actually live here. Talk about regressing. The man she'd fallen in love with lived in a castle, for crying out loud.

Ian came out the front door and across the bridge, hurrying over to help Father Daar out of the snowcat. He handed the old priest over to Callum, who had followed him outside, and then Ian descended on Grace.

"Well? Did ya find what you needed up there?" he asked.

She stared at him blankly. No, she had found heartache, and she hadn't needed that at all. She suddenly blushed as his words sank in. She hadn't even seen the ski-lift shed on the summit.

"Ah . . . I . . ." She darted a look at Grey, who had walked up beside her.

"She'll fix the lift," he told Ian, taking her by the arm and leading her toward his home. "After we do a small chore first, she'll save the damn ski lift for us."

Grace let him lead her away without protest. Truth be told, she wanted his support to walk across the narrow, high, slippery-looking bridge that ran over the churning brook.

She walked ahead of him the minute she saw the inside of the castle. Having expected the worst—a dank, dark, chilling interior to match the outside—Grace was amazed at what she found inside.

It was magnificent. Beautiful. The foyer was larger than her house and ran the full four stories up to an oak-beamed ceiling. A stairway as wide as a train ran up the right wall, curving onto an open balcony railed with hand-hewn timber. She walked to the center of the room and turned around, trying to take it all in.

It was so bright inside it hurt her eyes. Lights—tens of dozens of bulbs—shone into every nook and cranny, glistening off the black stone that shined like the ebony keys of a piano. Grace recognized the rock. It was from the mountain. TarStone got its name from fissures of black rock that ran like rivers through the granite. Instead of absorbing the light, the rock had been polished to reflect it.

The effect was so magical it made her dizzy.

She closed her eyes and lowered her head to get her bearings, only to open them up to see five men watching her with grins on their faces.

"You're not the first to have such a reaction," Morgan told her. "Stunning, isn't it?"

"It's beautiful. I never would have guessed, looking at it from the out-" Grace snapped her mouth shut before she finished insulting their home and quickly walked through the archway opposite the entrance. She found herself in a very large, tastefully and comfortably furnished living room. There was a big-screened television in the corner, three leather couches arranged into a sitting area facing it, and a desk in the other corner that held a computer.

She breathed a sigh of relief. She had been entertaining visions of Greylen MacKeage walking up and telling her, "Oh, by the way, I came through time with MacBain." Grey certainly seemed medieval to her sometimes, what with his talk of women being weaker, her belonging to him now, and his general alpha-male attitude. And he did live in a castle.

"Well," she said to the men staring at her. "This is a very nice home you have."

They just kept staring. Grace looked at Grey, her eyes pleading with him to do something. With a laconic smile contradicting the harsh planes of his face, he stepped forward to move beside her. "Father Daar," he said. "Why don't you take a seat?"

The old priest hadn't really waited for the invitation. He was already making his way to a big chair by the fireplace that stood in the center of the far wall. He shut off the television on his way by, shaking his head and muttering something under his breath.

Seeing that he was settled, Grey turned back to the three remaining men. Grace thought about running for the door before the fireworks began, but then she remembered the bridge. She started to inch her way toward Father Daar instead. Grey stopped her, taking her by the hand and pulling her beside him.

"Grace has a favor she wants from us before she gets the ice off the gondola lift," he said, ignoring her nails biting into his palm.

"What would that be, lass?" Ian asked, squinting at her. "It won't take long, will it? The weather's lifted a bit, but it could start raining again soon."

Grace stared at the three men all staring back at her and dug her nails deeper into the hand imprisoning hers.

Grey sighed in resignation. "We're to set up our snow-making equipment," he answered for her, "at the Bigelow Christmas Tree Farm."

The fireworks went off right on schedule, and they were just as loud and far more colorful than she expected. Ian was the worst of the lot, turning as red as his hair and waving his fist in the air.

"That bastard's not getting any help from us!" he shouted, glaring at her while he did.

"Ya canna mean it, man!" Callum said, taking a step forward, his fists clenched at his sides.

Morgan stared in open-mouthed shock, then spit on the floor. "He'll rot in hell before we help him!" he said, his face contorted with rage.

The blast of hatred made Grace take a step back. Grey stood tall and calm beside her, weathering the human storm. She stared up at him, wondering what he was thinking.

She wasn't afraid of the three men still ranting and raving and scorching the air with their curses. She knew to the soles of her feet that Grey would never let them hurt her.

"Grey!" Ian hissed. "What has gotten into ya?" Ian pointed a finger at Grace. "It's her, isn't it? She's softened ya to where you're willing to help an enemy."

"That's enough," Grey said, his expression still calm, his voice whisper soft.

The litany of curses suddenly stopped. The rage, however, continued to emanate from the three men in icy-cold waves. A silence more deafening than the storm that had preceded it settled like lead over the room.

"That's the deal, if you want to save our ski lift. We set up our equipment at MacBain's, and Grace gets the ice off the cable. Or both of our businesses can go to hell along with this accursed storm. Which will it be?"

Ian shook his head in disbelief. "That's blackmail, is what it is." He looked at her, the loathing clear in his eyes. "How do we know she can do as she claims?"

"She can," Grey said succinctly.

"Do you even understand what you're asking of us?" Callum asked her.

"No, actually, I don't," she returned, lifting her chin as she tried to move closer to them. Grey checked her step, keeping her beside him. "Why don't you explain it to me?" she said to Callum.

Clearly surprised to get an answer to his obviously rhetorical question, Callum looked at Grey. So did Grace. She saw him nod curtly.

"Michael MacBain," Callum said, sounding as if just saying the name was painful, "fancied himself in love with the MacKeage's betrothed," he told her. "And he lured her to his bed. Maura was only a naive lass at the time, and she had a romantic notion that they were star-crossed lovers.

She lay with MacBain and soon discovered she was carrying his child," he explained, the distaste for his story obvious in every harsh line on his face.

"Who is Maura?"

"She was Ian's daughter."

"Was?" Grace asked, darting a look at Ian.

"She killed herself when she realized she'd disgraced her family and that the bastard MacBain would not have her," Callum continued, drawing her attention again.

Grace snapped her gaze back to Ian. He was standing stone still, his features harsh, his muted-green eyes glazed with pain. She looked back at Callum. "If Michael loved Maura, why wouldn't he have her?" she asked him.

It was Morgan who snorted. "You're as naive as she was. MacBain didn't love her. He just wanted to ruin her for the MacKeage."

"Who is 'the MacKeage' you keep talking about?" Grace asked. "And where is he now?"

Morgan looked at her with a nasty smirk lifting one side of his angered face. "He's standing beside you," he said, nodding at Grey. "Holding your hand."

Grace pulled her hand away as if it were scorched. She turned and stared up at Grey. "You were engaged to this Maura? Ian's daughter?" She looked at Ian, trying to judge his age. "How old was she?"

"My girl was sixteen at the time," Ian told her. "She was supposed to be wed on her seventeenth birthday. Only she never reached it."

Grace closed her eyes and covered her face with her hands. No wonder these men wanted Michael's head on a platter. If, that is, what they were saying was true, that Michael had rejected Maura when he found out she was pregnant. A thought crossed her mind, and she turned to Grey.

"How old were you?"

He finally looked at her, and, unlike Ian's, his eyes were completely devoid of emotion. "I was twenty-eight."

Grace walked out of the room. There wasn't a damn thing she had to say to any of them. She crossed the foyer and opened the front door, only to be confronted by the treacherous bridge. She grabbed both sides of the rails and closed her eyes and walked across it.

Damn Grey. The man had been engaged to a child!

Damn every one of them. They were all such . . . such . . . *men,* including Michael MacBain. They deserved to hate each other all the way to hell and back, for all she cared. She was going to the Bigelows' and getting Baby, then she was going home, locking her door, and not letting any of them on her property again. And just as soon as this ice storm was over, she was getting into Mary's old beatup truck and driving herself and Baby back to Virginia.

"Are ya not going after her?" Callum asked, looking at the still humming door that Grace had slammed on her way out.

"So I can bring her back to face your anger again?" Grey asked all three of them. "So you can further berate her for being a woman, with a woman's heart that only wants to help *all* of her neighbors?"

He turned to the silent priest sitting by the hearth. "What do you think, old man? Should I go after her?"

Daar shook his head, looking tired from the battle he had just witnessed. "Not if you're not ready to let go of your hatred for MacBain," he said. "The girl feels a powerful duty to her sister, and your little tale has finally made her realize that she can't be loyal to you without being disloyal to Mary."

Grey stared at him for another minute, then turned to look at his men. How was he supposed to put into words what he wasn't sure of himself? How could he tell a father that they were all to blame for Maura's death, and not just MacBain, but Grey, Ian himself, and the very society they had lived in back then?

"Your daughter had no desire to marry your laird, Ian," he began, picking his words carefully but putting the power of his title behind them. "I was twelve years older than she, and I scared her to death. Maura had been in love with MacBain since the summer festival the year before."

"That's not true," Ian protested. "I would have known of such a thing."

Grey shook his head at the suddenly desperate-looking man. "She was too afraid to tell you or her mother because she didn't want to disappoint you. She knew how proud you were that your daughter was chosen to marry your laird," he told him gently.

"That still doesn't justify what he done, going behind my back like a jackal and seeing Maura without her father's permission," Ian said, his expression pained. "She killed herself because she was pregnant and MacBain tossed her away like rubbish."

"Did he?" Grey asked. "Do we know that as fact, or has that been a convenient excuse all these years, to justify our own arrogance and neglect? Were we all not guilty back then, as men, for forgetting to ask our daughters what they wanted? How many marriages were arranged without their consent?"

"Dammit. That was how it was done then," Callum said. "It was our duty to guide them and to protect them from their own soft hearts."

"Why?" Grey asked all three of them. "When you see

women like Mary and Grace Sutter, do you consider them inferior? Unable to think for themselves? Can you see any man today arranging a marriage for either one of them that she had no say in?"

"Of course not," Callum said, frowning. "But that's different. This is now, not eight hundred years ago."

"Were our mothers and wives and daughters any less intelligent than Mary and Grace Sutter? Less capable? Less strong?" Grey asked.

"Dammit. MacBain ruined my little girl, and now she's dead!" Ian shouted hoarsely, wiping at his eyes with the palms of his hands. He wasn't liking what he was hearing, and Grey hated to see the old warrior in such a state. But this had needed saying for seven years now.

Grey wished he could go back, now that he saw things differently. The MacKeage clan would have been the most powerful in all the Highlands, because they would have had the strength of hundreds of strong, intelligent women behind them.

Ian looked up and glared at Grey. "I've kept from killing MacBain myself because that was your duty," he said, pointing at Grey, obviously still not willing to let go of his old beliefs. "One you refused to honor."

"Ian's right," Callum interjected. "It doesn't matter who is to blame, MacBain is still the most responsible for Maura's death. It was his seed she was carrying that caused her to walk onto the rotten ice of Loc Firth. And now you're asking us to help the man."

"I'm not asking," Grey told them softly. "I'm telling you that I am setting up that equipment tonight, and the choice is yours to help me or not."

"Ya cannot mean to do it," Morgan said.

Grey looked around the room. "I don't see anyone with the authority to stop me. I'm still the laird of what's left of this clan, and my word still carries the weight it used to."

"But it's wrong, what you're asking of us. No warrior worth his salt aids his enemy," Ian insisted.

"No, it's you who are wrong. You're wanting to continue a war that's eight hundred years dead. None of it matters anymore. We live here now, the four of us and MacBain. We live in a world where disputes are settled by courts of law. We must adapt to this change in our circumstances and live like the Americans we've become. And that means helping out a neighbor, no matter who he is, when we can."

"It's Grace Sutter putting these thoughts in your head," Ian complained, still refusing to let go of his anger. "Ya want her, and she's twisted your thinking into a knot."

Grey shook his head at his disheartened warrior. "Have you not wondered why I never retaliated for MacBain's role in this?" he asked him. "Not the three years we were still living at home?"

"I thought ya were waiting for a better means of revenge than merely killing him," Ian said. "I thought ya were waiting for him to take a wife."

Grey took a step back, appalled at the insult just given him. "You thought I would use a woman for revenge?" he asked in a hushed tone. "Some innocent like Mary Sutter, maybe? Should I have caused her such terror to get even with MacBain? Taken her by force? Or should I have killed her with my bare hands to rob MacBain of her love?" he ended harshly.

Ian actually flinched.

"Dammit, Grey," Callum interjected. "None of us would have allowed any harm to come to Mary."

Grey looked at each of his men in turn, letting them see his anger. "Four years ago none of you would have given a thought to the woman, whoever she was. So tell me, what's changed?"

"Dammit to hell, we have!" Ian shouted. "We've softened like porridge."

"No," Grey told him softly. "We haven't softened. We've had our eyes opened. Society has changed in eight hundred years, and if we don't adapt to it now, we will perish."

"We have adapted," Morgan said. "Hell, we fly in planes, drive automobiles, and are running a ski resort."

Grey shook his head. "It's not enough simply to embrace the material things. It's here," he said, thumping his chest, "that we have to change. And I intend to begin tonight, for Grace."

The three men simply stared at him, unmoving, not believing what they were hearing.

"You'll be helping MacBain," Ian insisted. "You're forgetting that he stole your woman and caused her death."

"I'm not," Grey growled with waning patience. "Michael MacBain has nothing to do with this." He ran his hands over his face, hoping to wipe away his frustration with his clansmen—and with himself. He hadn't softened. He was simply looking at things through Grace's eyes this once.

"I hate the bastard as much as any of you," he assured them. "But are you willing to let that hatred stand in the way of saving your ski lift?"

"You said it yourself, man," Ian said. "She'll not let it come to that. Her heart's too soft. She'll help us."

"And just where does that leave us with Grace, when this is over and MacBain's future is ruined and ours is not?" Grey asked.

Three sets of frowns faced the floor as the men pictured that problem. "She'll come around once she realizes what a bastard MacBain truly is," Callum said. "She'll eventually see things our way. If not, do ya truly want the woman if she's determined to be nice to our enemies?"

"She's mine," Grey told them, a growl in his voice. "It's already done," he said, walking away, having decided he'd had enough of the company of his men.

He made his way up to his room on tired feet, thinking they could all give lessons in stubbornness to Grace. They'd been through a lot these last four years, and Grey admired his men's stamina and their spirit to survive. But they still had some changing to do. Himself included.

He undressed slowly, thinking about Grace and the horrified look on her face when she had learned he had planned to marry a girl almost twelve years his junior. Or maybe it was the fact that the tug-of-war between him and MacBain, with her and Baby in the middle, had simply been too much.

Whatever had been in her head, he would have to fix it somehow—and quickly.

Naked now, he walked into the bathroom and turned on the shower. He stopped at the sight of himself in the mirror. His gaze was drawn to the blood on his thigh.

Grace's blood. The gift of her virginity that she had been saving for her husband but had given to him instead.

Why? Why had she asked him to make love to her?

From the moment he saw her in the airport, Grey had known he would have Grace Sutter. He just hadn't realized at the time exactly what having her meant.

He had thought it was lust; only it wasn't, and it never had been. He thought he'd at least be dealing with an experienced woman, but Grace had been a virgin. And he had always thought he could take a wife to build back his clan yet not touch his heart when he did. He knew now that was impossible.

More than a simple mating had occurred on TarStone today.

Something. A feeling. An awareness had come to him when he had possessed Grace completely. The room had filled with a brightness so sharp the very air in the summit house had appeared white, like a new-fallen winter snow reflecting full sunshine.

This journey they were on, was somehow tied to Grace Sutter. Grey had felt her strength after the plane crash, when she had fought beside him to survive. He had felt it standing in the freezing rain outside her kitchen door, when she had stood there telling him not to return if he went to Michael MacBain. And this afternoon, in the summit house, the feeling of rightness had been nearly overwhelming.

The swirl of fog filled the bathroom, blocking out Grey's view of himself in the mirror. He stepped into the shower and let the hot water run over his head and face and down his body. He was sorry to be washing away the essence of Grace, but he had to get changed for the night's work ahead. He might find himself laying the pipe in the field by himself next to MacBain, but, by God, he intended to save the man's crop of trees.

Then he would get the ice off his damn ski lift.

And then he would get down to the business of explaining to Grace Sutter that she was never returning to Virginia.

Chapter Fourteen

Her eyes burning with angry tears, Grace completely misjudged the curve in the road and drove straight into a snowbank. The force of the impact threw her against the seat belt, pushing an involuntary scream from her lungs. Ice chunks the size of dinner plates shot into the air and crashed over the hood and windshield of the truck, sending cracks spidering through the glass and making Grace instinctively raise her arms to cover her face.

The rear tires of the suddenly halted truck continued to spin on the slippery road, causing the entire vehicle to strain against the snowbank. Grace slowly lowered her arms and reached a shaking hand out to shut off the engine. The old pickup turned silent but for the angry hiss of steam from the hot engine now packed with snow.

Trembling from her nose to her knees, Grace brushed the hair from her face and took a calming breath while she assessed the damage. She seemed to be relatively intact; she wasn't bleeding anywhere, and nothing felt broken. Her truck had not fared quite so well. It was wedged into the snowbank all the way past her door, the nose stuck up in the air and covered with debris.

Well, her body still worked. Would the truck?

Grace pushed on the brake and clutch peddles, restarted the engine, and wrestled the gear shift into reverse. She slowly let out the clutch and pushed on the gas. The rear tires spun; the truck bucked in place, then jerked sideways instead of backward. Grace crammed the clutch down, shifted into first, and gave the engine more gas. The engine revved, the tires spun, and the truck shot forward several inches. She repeated the process, in reverse this time, but only felt the vehicle settle deeper into the snow just before it coughed and chugged to a stall.

Grace slapped the steering wheel with an angry curse, buried her face in her hands, and broke into tears. Dammit. She should have stayed in bed this morning, watching Baby sleep. She sure as hell had no business trying to help her neighbors. All she'd received for her efforts was heartache.

Michael MacBain was mad at her for even suggesting the MacKeages could help save his trees. Morgan and Callum and Ian were beyond angry for the same reason. And Grey?

Well, on what should have been the most glorious day of her life, the day she had finally decided to make love with a man, she had made a monumental mess of the entire affair.

Grey was also mad at her, and Grace worried that his anger might be based on the fact that she had foolishly preceded their lovemaking with an ultimatum that he help Michael. Even from her own point of view, she looked like a woman willing to bargain with her body.

Hell. What a mess she'd made of this day, with her arrogant intentions and reckless actions. Every damn male she knew was mad at her.

Except Baby.

Grace angrily wiped away her tears, unfastened her seat belt, and started to get out of the truck. Only the door wouldn't budge. She peered out the window to find that the snowbank had trapped her inside, so she rolled down the window, crawled out of the truck, and waded onto the road.

She bent at the waist and looked under the bumper. The frame of the truck was perched high and dry on the snowbank, the front tires suspended in the air and the back tires sunk in a hole the spinning tires had burned in the ice.

Grace straightened and looked in both directions. She had just turned down the road to the Christmas tree farm, but she was still closer to the ski resort than to the Bigelows'. But was she willing to hike back to the resort and ask for the MacKeages's help?

Grace snorted to herself. Not after storming out and slamming the door on their collective rage. She pivoted on her heel and started walking to the Bigelow Christmas farm.

She fell twice and nearly pulled a back muscle trying to stay upright on the slippery road. It took her nearly an hour to travel about two miles, and in that time Grace wondered what she could do to get her life back under control. How could she have gone from an intelligent, dedicated scientist with a sharply focused future to a love-sick, addlebrained puddle of mush in only four days?

When she walked into the Bigelows' yard, Grace was able to answer her own question. She stopped in the middle of the driveway and stared at Michael MacBain chopping wood as if the demons of hell possessed his body.

Michael. Baby. And Mary.

Grace's heart dropped to her knees. Michael's pain, his

anger, his very obvious hurt, emanated toward her in nearly palpable waves. She had lost her sister and been given a nephew to love; Michael had nothing but emptiness.

He turned suddenly to face her, the axe hanging loosely in his large hand at his side. Grace continued into the yard, and Michael walked up to meet her.

His eyes roamed over her body, his expression concerned. "Where's your truck?" he asked, darting a look behind her as if he expected it to be following her. He reached out and took hold of her arm. "Were you in an accident? Are ya hurt?"

Grace shrugged. "I just slid off the road," she told him, and smiled to assure him that she was okay. "But the truck is stuck in a snowbank. I need help to pull it out."

Michael let the axe fall to the ground and put both hands on her shoulders, giving her another, more critical inspection, as if he didn't believe she was okay. He turned, took her by the hand, and began leading her toward the house.

"Come inside and get warm," he said before she could protest. "Tell me where the truck is, and I'll go get it."

Grace planted her feet to stop them both but skidded a good three yards on the ice before Michael realized she wasn't following meekly. He turned and frowned at her.

Grace smiled back. "I want to go with you," she told him. "It's a two-person job, and I don't want John to know about the accident. He'll feel obliged to help, and he might fall and break a hip or something."

"I'll just tow the truck back," Michael countered, tugging on her sleeve to urge her toward the house.

Grace wiggled her arm free of his grasp and shook her head. "No. I want to go with you."

Michael gave her a good glare before he blew out a resigned sigh. "Okay. But you're sitting in the truck and staying out of my way," he said, leading her toward the barn where she could see his truck was parked.

As concessions went, he could have been more gracious, but Grace decided to believe his dictate was from concern for her welfare, not from condescension. She was just thankful he hadn't gotten stubborn himself and that she was able to go with him.

Now was her chance to get to know the man her sister loved.

Grace climbed into the passenger seat of the shiny new truck, folded her hands on her lap, and thought of how to broach the subject of time travel to a person who claimed he had firsthand knowledge of the phenomenon.

"You've been crying," Michael said as soon as he climbed in beside her.

"Not from the accident," she assured him as they backed out of the barn.

He stopped the truck and looked at her. "MacKeage made ya cry?" he asked in a growl.

This time Grace's smile was sad. "Not directly. I made myself cry." She brushed the hair from her face and tucked it behind her ear. "I'm tired, I think. A lot's happened in the last week. The last six weeks," she softly amended.

"I've heard new mothers get weepy sometimes," he said gently, finally heading the truck out the driveway.

"Yeah. I've heard that, too. Michael, why did you tell my sister you traveled through time?" Grace asked, deciding that she really was too tired to beat around the bush.

Silence answered her. Grace turned in her seat to face the man who was such a contradiction to her perception of sanity. He acted more normal than most males she'd met, yet he didn't rush to deny her accusation.

She studied his profile. Michael was a large man, handsome in a rugged sort of way, and as solid-looking as the mountains surrounding Pine Creek. His usually weather-tanned complexion had paled suddenly, except for the flag of red on the cheekbone facing her. Small beads of sweat still lingered near his hairline from his wood-chopping frenzy, his jaw was clenched, and his knuckles gripping the steering wheel were white with tension.

"I want you to talk to me, Michael. I want to under-stand."

He looked at her, his eyes two swirling pools of deep, molten gray. "Why? What's the point?" he asked softly. "Mary's dead, lass. It doesn't matter anymore. Nothing does."

"That's not true, Michael," Grace whispered. "You're the man my sister loved. For all but the lack of a ceremony, you and I are related now. And it was Mary's dying wish that we become friends."

He looked back at the road, silent again. Grace decided to approach the problem more directly. "Mary told me that you didn't travel through time alone. That some of your . . . clansmen came with you. Is that true?"

His complexion darkened, and he nodded curtly. Well, he wasn't talking, but he was responding.

"Where are they now?"

"Dead."

"How . . . how did they die, Michael?"

"In lightning storms, mostly."

"Is that how you got here? In a storm?"

He nodded again, then brought the truck to a stop. Before Grace realized they'd arrived at her pickup, Michael was out the door and headed to her truck.

With a curse of frustration, Grace climbed out and fol-lowed him. Talking to Michael was like pulling teeth. She caught up with him just as he knelt down to look at the underside of her truck.

Grace got down on her own knees and looked at him instead. "Is that what killed your friends?" she asked. "The storm that brought you here?"

He turned only his head to look at her, staring for an overlong minute before he stood up, grabbed her by the shoulders, and lifted her to her own feet in front of him. And it was a good thing he kept holding onto her, because his glare would have knocked her over.

"We will talk about this now, Grace, on the condition that ya never bring it up again." His hands tightened on her shoulders. "And I'll have yar promise that ya won't tell anyone else this story."

Grace could only nod mutely. Michael released her, sighed deep from his chest, and ran a hand through his damp, dark brown hair. He paced several steps away, pivoted, and paced back toward her, stopping only a few feet away.

"Four years ago my men and I were in the middle of a battle when a great storm suddenly swept over our heads," he softly began, not looking at her but staring into the woods, obviously picturing the scene in his mind's eye.

"I looked up and saw a man standing on the bluff. He was holding a staff as thick as my arm and longer than I am tall. It glowed like a shaft of lightning in his hand."

He looked at Grace, his eyes large but his pupils narrowed to pinpricks. Sweat had broken out on his brow again.

"The man suddenly threw the stick, and it bounced off a rock and then began floating over the gleann we were in. A great rain broke from the heavens, and lightning flashed—not from the clouds but from that stick."

Facing her but with his vision turned inward again, Michael slowly shook his head. "As God is my witness, I can't describe what happened next. Light so bright it was blinding consumed us. I could hear the shouts of my men over the howl of the wind. My horse reared in terror, and I was thrown, but my body never reached the ground. It was as if the wind carried me, lifting me further into the sky."

"A tornado, Michael?" Grace whispered, drawing his full attention. "You were caught in a tornado?"

He slowly shook his head. "Nay, lass. This was an unnatural storm. Tornados are dark, littered with debris. This was blinding white light. And once I was lifted, there was no wind. No sound. It was as if . . . I felt . . ."

He stopped speaking, staring at the ground, slowly shaking his head back and forth.

"As if what, Michael? What did you feel?"

He looked back at her. "As if I ceased to exist. For one suspended moment, I was not me." He held his hands up, looking at them. "I had no body. I remember thinking I am here, but I had nothing to show of myself. There was just me . . . my mind . . . and the accursed light."

Grace fought to keep her frown to herself as her own mind frantically worked to understand what had happened. Had Michael been struck by lightning? Had he lived through a near-death experience?

"What happened then?" she asked. "You're obviously here right now. How did you get here?"

"I simply existed again. The light disappeared as suddenly as it appeared, and I was lying on the ground, along with nine other men and our horses."

"Nine men? But Mary said only five men were with you."

Michael averted his gaze. "Others were caught in the storm with us."

"Others? The men you were fighting when the storm came? Where are they now?"

His glare returned as he stared directly at her. "I have a wish they're rotting in hell," he growled, suddenly pivoting on his heel and heading back to his own truck.

Grace started after him, only to have to grab the tailgate of her truck to keep from falling. The rain had started again and was making the ice as slippery as buttered Teflon. Michael returned carrying a tow strap, which he looped over the trailer ball on the rear bumper of her truck.

"Drive my truck up here and point the back toward yours," he instructed.

Grace took the tow strap off her bumper and tossed it on the ground. "Just as soon as we're done with our discussion," she told him. "I promised not to speak of this again, so, by God, we're going to speak of it now. Where did you wake up after the storm?"

Eyes narrowed against the rain, he stared at her in fuming silence. Grace didn't care if they both drowned, she wasn't leaving until he gave her the whole story.

"Did these other men experience the same thing you did?" she asked. "Did they all see this bright light?"

"Yes."

"And everybody lived? Including the horses?"

"Yes."

"If you were in Scotland—what was it—eight hundred years ago when the storm came, where did you wake up?"

"In Scotland. In the same gleann. But everything was different."

"Different how?"

"There were buildings there that hadn't been there before," he said. "And roads, covered with hardened black tar. And automobiles and large trucks. We were nearly killed by the speeding demons."

It was Grace's turn to shake her head, and she couldn't

seem to stop. Michael's story seemed outlandish and would make sense to her only if she believed in time travel.

"Michael? Do you remember how you were dressed when you woke up from this storm? What you looked like?"

"I was wearing the same clothing I'd had on the day of the battle: my hunting plaid, which is a darker, more muted version of the MacBain tartan."

"Anything else? Were you wearing pants that had a zipper, boots with a buckle, a knit jersey? Or a watch, maybe?"

He frowned at her question. "I wore leggings, a shirt, and my sporran. And we knew nothing of watches back then."

"Did the shirt have buttons?"

His frown turned into a scowl. "Nay. It pulled over my head and tied at the neck."

Grace sighed. "Everyone was dressed the same, I take it."

"Nay," Michael said again, one corner of his mouth suddenly lifting into a half grin. "Two of my men were naked."

"Naked?"

"It wasn't uncommon for warriors to fight naked," he elaborated. "So there was nothing for an enemy to grab onto."

Grace snapped her mouth shut. Warriors? Having a battle in the middle of a storm, then waking up in modern time?

It didn't make sense. None of it did.

But the sad part was, it was obvious Michael believed— he sincerely believed—it had really happened to him.

"What year were you born?" she asked.

"It was the year 1171, if you go by the calendar ya use today."

Good Lord. His delusion was based in fact. Michael even knew that today's calendar was not the one in use eight hundred years ago.

But what he believed was impossible.

Which meant that Michael really wasn't of sound mind.

There was no way she could turn Baby over to him. Not her precious, innocent nephew. Who knew where Michael's delusions might lead him—looking for another thunderstorm to take him back home? With Baby?

"Were ya telling me the truth, Grace?" Michael asked, taking her by the shoulders, making her face him squarely as he peered down into her eyes. "Was Mary really coming back to me, to get married?"

Tears suddenly mingled with the rain washing down her face. "Yes, Michael. She was coming home to marry you," Grace said hoarsely, barely getting the words past the lump in her throat.

She was suddenly pulled forward into a fierce embrace. Grace buried her face in the opening of Michael's jacket, feeling his pounding heart beneath her cheek, and she burst into uncontrollable sobs.

The arms holding her tightened. "I'm sorry ya lost your sister," Michael whispered into her hair, the warmth of his breath sending confusing emotions through her saddened heart.

Grace wrapped her arms around his waist and clung to him. "I'm sorry for both of us, Michael. You have no idea how sorry I am," she whispered. "So very, very sorry."

God might consider the two miracles he'd given her today insignificant, but Grace thought they were wonderful. The first miracle was that the socks Baby had worn to Ellen Bigelow's were the same socks on his feet now. Ellen hadn't changed them, and she hadn't discovered Baby's twelve toes.

The second miracle was the smile Baby had given Grace when she returned to pick him up. He had not only recognized her but had been happy to see her.

Grace took her attention away from her slow, careful drive down the icy road long enough to peek at Baby. He was awake, very busy waving his arms wildly in front of his face, blowing bubbles out of his mouth. And he was smiling again.

Her spirits had lifted the moment she had taken him into her arms after returning to the Bigelows' with her rescued truck. She had kissed Baby all over his face, only to be stunned speechless when he had looked up at her with wide gray-blue eyes and smiled.

"We're going home to stay," she told him, reaching over and pulling the left side of his cap back over his ear. "No more running around in this weather to *any* of our neighbors. I'm finishing that book I started reading you this morning, and we'll find another good one to follow it with."

She grinned sadly at the road ahead of her. "It's you and me now, kid. Just the two of us. We'll give you another month of growing and time for us to be alone together, then I'm taking you home to Virginia."

She looked at Baby to make sure he was listening, then turned her attention back to the road. "We don't need anyone, especially not any man. Not Grey, or Michael, or even Jonathan."

Grace carefully slowed the truck to make the turn into her driveway, remembering from her trip out that there was a large branch that had fallen halfway across it.

"And I'm making you this promise now, sweetie. You're going to make some woman a perfect husband, and she'll have me to thank for that."

She stopped talking when she realized the branch was

no longer there. Someone had cut it up into short sections and had stacked it on the side of the driveway in a neat little pile.

Remembering Mavis and Peter's visit yesterday, Grace didn't wonder who had done the chore for her. There was probably more food in her fridge, and her animals had been looked after as well. This is what had happened nine years ago, during the days after her mother and father's accident. Enough food had arrived at the house to feed eight grieving children who might not otherwise have eaten.

Grace suddenly pushed on the brakes a little harder than she intended when her now wet, blurry eyes discovered a car parked next to the back porch, blocking her way into the garage.

She wiped at the tears streaming down her cheeks and shut off the engine. The sound of sleet pelting the windshield drummed through the cab of the truck as she stared in dismay at the dark windows of her house. She distinctly remembered leaving the lights on, both on the porch and over the kitchen table.

The power must have gone out. Ellen had said it had been flickering all afternoon. The lines had finally lost their valiant battle with the ice.

It would probably be days, if not weeks, before the electricity returned. Pine Creek would not be at the top of the power company's priority list. The town had no hospitals, no nursing homes, not even anything that would pass as a real firehouse. At best they had two stores, one gas station, a church, and a grange hall.

Grace unfastened the blissfully unaware Baby from his car seat. "My God, sweetie, you've had the worst kind of luck dogging you since birth, and you don't even know it. It's back to sleeping in the living room for us, next to the fire. And it will be lukewarm formula and sponge baths for another few days."

If the smile he gave her was any indication, he didn't seem to mind one bit. He was proud of his new trick and the response it got him, and he was playing it up for all it was worth.

She kissed his cheek to reward him for being such a steadfast little trooper, then tucked him under her jacket for the walk to the house.

She went in through the garage doors she had left open earlier but stopped before entering the house. A stack of wood, nearly half a cord's worth, was neatly piled next to the entrance. She sent up a prayer of thanks to whichever thoughtful person had done this for her. She needed it now more than ever.

The house was unusually quiet, no sounds of fridge or furnace working. There was no sign of the owner of the car parked outside. The person was probably in the upper barn, tending the animals. Grace hoped he knew his way around goats.

She walked straight through the kitchen to the downstairs bedroom. Without putting Baby down, she grabbed the cradle and dragged it into the living room. She set Baby in it, stuck his pacifier in his mouth, took off her jacket, and threw it on the couch.

Grace was on her knees building the fire back up in the hearth when she heard the sound of footsteps coming down the stairs. She spun around just as Jonathan took the last step into the living room.

"Grace."

"Jonathan," she said, scrambling to her feet to face him. "What are you doing here? You're supposed to be in Virginia, monitoring Podly."

"I was. But something's gone wrong. I grabbed the first

available flight here but was only able to get as far as Boston." He shook his head in disgust. "It took me all night and most of today to get from Boston to here. There weren't any flights to Bangor, so I rented a car. I nearly killed myself trying to keep it on the icy roads."

"But why?"

He walked up and took her by the shoulders, as if to brace her against something unpleasant. "It's Podly, Grace. She's malfunctioning."

"What's wrong with her?"

"I don't know," he said, his hands tightening on her shoulders. "That's why I'm here. The data Podly's sending back are scrambled. And our computers can't sort it out."

She gaped at him. "That's impossible. I ran several tests on that program before Podly even went up. Everything was working fine."

Jonathan let her go and paced across the room, running a hand through his hair before he turned back to her. "I know. It was the damnedest thing. We discovered the problem two days ago, and I've spent hours trying to straighten the mess out myself."

He paced back to her, his expression desperate. "You're the only chance we've got, Grace. You designed that software. You're the only one who can unscramble the data."

"But you didn't have to come up here, Jonathan. I can link up with Podly, fix the glitch from here, and then you can start downloading to the computers back at the lab. I have the program in my laptop."

"There's something you don't know, Grace, about Podly," he said, suddenly pacing back across the room. He stopped and stood facing the window, his hands shoved into his pockets. He kept his back to her when he finally spoke.

"Do you remember six months ago, when Collins pulled his money out of our project?" he asked softly.

"I remember. But you said you found a new money-man."

He turned toward her, still keeping his distance. "I did. But the new money came with a condition."

"What kind of condition?" she asked, hugging herself against the sudden chill of the quiet house.

"A transmitter, Grace. Placed in Podly before she went up."

The hair on the back of her neck stirred, and Grace felt something churn in the pit of her stomach. "Transmitting what?" she whispered.

"Our data," Jonathan said succinctly. He pulled his hands from his pockets and started toward her. Grace took a step back.

Jonathan stopped. "Our competition gave me eighty million dollars for the data, Grace. And now they can't get it."

"You sold out StarShip Spaceline? To who?"

"AeroSaqii. But I didn't sell out. I kept StarShip alive." He shook his head. "Without Collins's money, I would have been bankrupt in twelve months."

"You will be anyway," Grace snapped, her stomach now churning with the violence of a thousand angry bees. "They'll win the race, and we'll be left with nothing."

He moved closer, holding one hand out beseechingly. "We've still got the shuttles, Grace. We can concentrate on those. AeroSaqii will contract with us to build them."

Angry beyond words, Grace turned her back on Jonathan and returned to building the fire in the hearth. The ion propulsion experiment was hers; she'd designed it, laid down the groundwork, and put the processor into Podly herself.

And Jonathan had sold it without telling her.

"That still doesn't explain why you had to come all the

way up here," she said, her back to the room. "I could have just unscrambled the data and sent the results to you."

"There's something else, Grace," Jonathan said from right behind her. He took her shoulders and lifted her up, turning her to face him. "I have reason to believe my deal with AeroSaqii is not exactly . . . well, it appears there's more involved in this deal than I thought there was."

"What do you mean?"

Jonathan shook his head. "AeroSaqii also intends to sell our experiment, once they've perfected it. But to a private consortium that hopes to turn it into a weapon instead of a propulsion agent."

Grace felt the blood drain from her face. "How do you know this?" she whispered.

"I've had a mole planted in AeroSaqii for several months now," he told her. "And he told me that when the transmission came back garbled, people at AeroSaqii became very upset. Paul—that's my mole—thought their reaction was way out of proportion to the problem, and he started digging deeper. It seems that several of the men there were from this consortium and not really AeroSaqii scientists."

"A weapon?" Grace whispered, shrinking away from Jonathan. "They plan to use my experiment to build a weapon?"

His grip tightened. "Of mass proportions," he confirmed. "Can you imagine what an ion-based weapon would be capable of? It would make a nuclear detonation look like a firecracker going off in comparison."

"Jonathan," Grace hissed on an indrawn breath, reversing their positions and grabbing his arms. "We've got to stop it. You need to give AeroSaqii their money back, and we've got to block the transmission they're receiving, garbled or not. Now, before they find a way to unscramble it."

"I tried to reason with them, Grace. I told them the deal was off, but they're having none of it. It's too late. And now I'm afraid they have sent someone here to make sure they get what they paid for."

Grace pushed away from Jonathan and moved to the opposite side of the room, alarmed by what he was implying. Hugging herself against the sudden chill in the room, she turned back to face Jonathan.

"What do you mean, they'll make sure they get what they paid for?"

"Just that, Grace. According to Paul, they've sent men to bring you back to their lab to straighten out the transmission and process the data."

"That's kidnapping, Jonathan."

He nodded. "Yes, it is. But to the devils AeroSaqii crawled into bed with, it's worth the risk. And that's why you've got to come back with me, Grace. Today, before they get here. We have the security in Virginia to protect you."

Hugging herself again, Grace looked at the cradle where Baby was sleeping. "I . . . I can't just up and leave, Jonathan," she said softly. "I'm right in the middle of my own obligations."

Baby started fussing, and Jonathan snapped his head around in surprise. He turned back to her and frowned. "You've still got that kid?"

"Yes. And his name's Baby."

Jonathan snorted. "That's not a name, either. Why haven't you given him to his father?"

"I haven't decided if he deserves him yet," she said, picking Baby up and sticking his pacifier back in his mouth. She headed for the kitchen.

Jonathan followed her.

"Who is he, Grace? Have you even met him?"

"I'm not saying." She reached into the cupboard and took down a bottle of formula. She turned to Jonathan, only to discover that he hadn't liked her answer. He looked . . . well, he looked stunned that she wouldn't confide in him.

His eyes suddenly narrowed. "You have no intention of giving him up, do you? Dammit, Grace, you're in no position to raise a kid on your own. You're a scientist, not a woman who spends her days changing diapers and wiping up baby spit."

"I can do both."

"No, you can't. Your work is too demanding."

"No, Jonathan. *Your* work is too demanding. I hear there's a semiconductor company in California looking for a person with my degrees, and they let their mothers bring their babies to work."

Jonathan snapped his mouth shut so hard Grace heard his teeth click. He didn't even want to entertain the idea that she might leave StarShip Spaceline.

She returned to sit by the fire in the living room and feed Baby. Her boss stayed in the kitchen. Grace knew he was silenced but not defeated. Jonathan was not a man easily thwarted; no five-week-old child, stubborn employee, or angry competition was going to get in the way of his company putting private citizens into space.

Jonathan Stanhope was a survivor.

He would simply change tack to get what he wanted.

While Grace fed Baby, she thought again about Jonathan's startling confession and the problem it created for her. She shook her head, unable to believe that men might be on their way here now with the intention of kidnapping her.

Her first thought was not to run back to Virginia as Jonathan wanted but to run instead to the safety of Gu Bràth and Grey's strong arms.

Would she be welcome at Gu Bràth after that memorable scene in the living room? Grey wouldn't turn his back on her if he knew she was in trouble, but would Callum and Ian and Morgan?

And what about Michael? Could she, in good conscience, ask for help from a man she now had every intention of deceiving?

But then again, could she simply run away from her problems here and hide from her promise to Mary by cowering in Jonathan's lab?

The one answer to all of her questions was no. And Grace's scientist mind finally kicked in. She'd start with Podly and AeroSaqii's threat. She had a computer, a satellite link, and the ability to make her problem with Jonathan simply go away. Then she would deal with the MacKeages. She would fix their damn ski lift without demanding they help Michael, and then she would save Michael's trees if she had to shake the ice off every damn seedling in the twelve-acre field.

And then she would sit Greylen MacKeage down and have a little talk with him about commitment and belonging and neighborly obligations and explain to him exactly how this . . . this . . . thing between them was going to proceed.

Grace tucked a full-bellied and sleeping Baby back into his crib and headed into the kitchen to solve problem number one. She ignored Jonathan standing by the wall talking in a low voice on the phone and took her computer off the counter. She set it on the kitchen table and turned it on. While it booted up, she went into her bedroom, grabbed the suitcase that held the satellite link, and headed out onto the porch.

"What are you doing?" Jonathan asked, standing in the door, watching her.

"I want to see for myself what's happening with Podly's transmission," she said, climbing on a bench and hanging the antenna over a hook sticking out of the icy eave of the porch. Satisfied that it would work this time since there weren't any mountains or trees to block the signal, she climbed down, rubbing her cold hands together, and faced Jonathan.

"I might be able simply to make this entire problem go away." She gave her boss a good glare. "I'm dumping the data, Jonathan. Instead of unscrambling the transmission, I'm going to erase the entire experiment. And you can contact AeroSaqii and tell them to call off their men." She pointed her finger at him. "Then you can go back to Virginia—alone—and build your damn shuttles," she finished, sweeping past him into the kitchen.

"Grace," he said, following her to the table. "I didn't know what they were planning. I did what I had to in order for us to survive."

Grace sat down in front of her computer and clicked open the program she needed to receive Podly's data, then attached the link antenna to the back of the laptop. Jonathan leaned over her shoulder to watch and continued his plea that she understand his actions.

"I know how you feel about this pod, Grace," he said, his voice subdued and beseeching. "And I know I had no right to sell your experiment without telling you. But you have to understand my position. We couldn't have launched Podly without AeroSaqii's help."

Grace tapped several keys and started her program running, then waited for the data to begin downloading. "You could have told me, Jonathan," she said, looking up at him and glaring again. "And you damn well could have looked into the deal more closely before you made it. But what I don't understand, if you truly thought everything was above-board, why the secrecy? You could have come to me and told me about your financial problem. I would have understood."

His hand squeezed her shoulder. "Would you, Grace? Do you now?"

"I understand two businesses merging." She turned and looked up at him. "But I don't understand the secrecy. Why not just announce your partnership with AeroSaqii?"

Jonathan sighed over her head, and his hand dropped away as he straightened. He moved to the other side of the table and sat down facing her, his hands clasped in front of him.

"It's a business problem, Grace," he explained in a tired and somewhat defeated voice as he stared at her. "StarShip is a publicly held company. AeroSaqii isn't. And neither is our European competition. If I'd announced to the world that I was in trouble, there could have been a hostile takeover from Europe. We'd have been swallowed up, with no chance of survival."

"AeroSaqii didn't want to merge?"

"No," he said, shaking his head. "They just wanted the experiment and only gave me a promise to contract the shuttles from me." His smile was sad. "It was the lesser of two evils. And the only option available if I want to stay in business."

"That still doesn't explain why you couldn't confide in me. I thought . . . I thought we had something between us."

"We did. We do, Grace," he whispered, reaching his hand across the table and grasping hers. "But I was scared. I was afraid you might walk. And without you, I had nothing to sell."

Grace pulled her hand back and balled it into a fist on her lap. "Trust means putting yourself at risk, Jonathan," she said. "And I trusted you." She waved an angry hand in the air. "All I receive in return are some men trying to kidnap me."

"I can fix this, Grace. Just come back to Virginia, and I'll keep you safe."

"No. I'll fix it," she snapped, turning her glare to the screen. "And you'll go back to Virginia by yourself."

He stood, opened his mouth to protest, but snapped it shut when Grace gasped at what she was seeing on her computer screen. Jonathan walked around the table and looked over her shoulder again.

"That's it," he said. "That's the mess we were getting back at the lab."

Grace hit several keys on the laptop, and still all she saw was the jumble of codes that would run in sequence for maybe six lines, only to suddenly be interrupted by ten lines of garble. And just that quickly, Grace found herself caught up in the familiar and very comfortable world of mathematical physics and infinite numbers, probabilities and unimaginable possibilities.

Jonathan, her home, the ice storm, and even her own body slowly slipped out of existence as Grace stared at the computer screen and looked into the future.

Chapter Fifteen

It was another three hours before Grace could bring herself to give up. She angrily shut down her computer and stood, stretching her back to get out the kinks. She jumped when Jonathan spoke.

"Were you able to make any headway?" he asked, walking in from the living room, only to frown at the closed computer.

"No. The battery is dying, so I shut it down. But even if we had power, I wouldn't be able to fix it." She looked out the window at the freezing rain that refused to let up. "And I can't even recharge the battery."

"Don't you have a spare?"

"No. That one fried up on the mountain." She turned and frowned at the computer. "And when it did, I think it compromised my program. There are glitches in it that have nothing to do with Podly's transmissions." She looked over at Jonathan. "Did you bring your computer with you?"

"Yes. But it doesn't have your program installed."

"I have backup disks," she said, walking to the kitchen door and picking up the satellite link suitcase. She spoke over her shoulder. "Is Baby still sleeping?"

"Yes," Jonathan said, going into the living room.

Grace set the suitcase on the counter and opened it, rummaging around to find her case of backup disks. Jonathan returned to the kitchen, set his own computer on the table beside hers, and turned it on.

Grace continued looking for her disks. They weren't in the briefcase. She went to her bedroom and looked through the empty luggage Grey and Morgan had brought down from the mountain. She checked every pocket and nook and cranny in both bags, and then she straightened and stared at nothing while she thought.

Jonathan stood in the door of the bedroom. "What? Do you have the disks?" he asked.

Grace shook her head. "No. They must have gotten misplaced on the mountain," she said, more to herself than to him.

He came into the room and stood facing her. "What do you mean, 'on the mountain?'"

She looked up. "My plane crashed. The pilot died. Baby and I and a neighbor who was traveling with us were able to make it down off the mountain okay. But some of my stuff is obviously still up there."

Jonathan's eyes grew wide with shock, and he took hold of her shoulders. "You were in a plane crash? Just a few days ago?"

"Yes. But miraculously, neither Baby nor I was hurt."

She was suddenly pulled into a crushing embrace. "My God, Grace. Why didn't you call and tell me?"

"I forgot," she said into his shoulder. She leaned back and smiled at his stricken expression. "I would have called you today, Jonathan," she quickly assured him. "But you showed up before I got the chance."

"I could have lost you," he whispered, pulling her back against him, hugging her tightly.

Just as Michael had done only a few hours ago. But where Michael's body had been warm and desperate and filled with emotion, Jonathan's embrace stirred nothing inside her.

"Lost me or my brain?" she asked.

He suddenly set her away with a scowl. "You," he snapped.

Grace sighed and shook her head. "Let's be honest now, Jonathan. We have a mutual respect for each other's talents, and there's friendship between us, but there's never been any romance."

"There could be," he growled, his posture defensive. "If you come home to Virginia and give us a chance."

"I am home, Jonathan," she softly told him. "And . . . and I think I'm staying this time."

He reached out to pull her back into his arms, but Grace sidestepped him and walked out of the bedroom.

"You can't mean to give it all up," he entreated, following her. "Grace. We're right on the verge of making a breakthrough that will have people living on the moon in less than ten years."

She shut down Jonathan's computer and slid it back into his briefcase. "No, we're not," she said, looking up. "Because just as soon as I get my computer rebooted, I'm dumping the experiment. You'll be back to square one then, and I have no intention of continuing this work. Not if it can be used as a weapon."

"Dammit, Grace. You can't mean to just walk away from your life's work." He waved an angry hand in the air. "You can't expect science to come to a screeching halt simply because you have a conscience. If every scientist did that, we'd still be living in caves. You can't stop progress, Grace."

"No," she agreed, nodding. "But I can stop this. I will not be a party to building a weapon of mass destruction."

He ran a frustrated hand through his hair, staring at her for several seconds before he let out a tired sigh. "Not if you can't unscramble Podly's signal," he said, sounding defeated.

He walked to the one clear window in the room. "Do you know these mountains, Grace?" he asked, looking toward TarStone Mountain. "Can you find where you crashed, and is there a chance your disks survived this weather?"

"Yes, I can find it. And yes, they're in a waterproof case. But it could take forever to reach the crash site, Jonathan. The weather's bad, and the terrain is rugged."

He turned to her. "Does this town have any equipment we could use? Snowmobiles, maybe? Something that can travel in these conditions?"

Grey's snowcat immediately came to mind, but Grace would not even consider asking his assistance. Not after the scenes she'd just endured, first at his house and then at the Bigelows'. Ellen had actually had tears in her eyes when Grace had told her that she hadn't been able to get any help for their trees.

"Well?" Jonathan asked, walking back to her.

"Nothing that I can think of. Most of the people have snowmobiles, I guess, but the power's gone out," she said, waving at the darkened, silent room around them. "They're not going to want to head into the mountains. They have to stay close to home to keep watch over their fires, their neighbors, and their property."

He gave her a laconic grin. "Not even for twenty thousand dollars? You don't think somebody in this rundown town could use that kind of money?"

She could only stare at Jonathan. "You could buy several snowmobiles with twenty thousand dollars," she said finally. "Why not just do that?"

"We don't have that kind of time. Don't you understand? Our entire future is sitting up on that mountain."

"Where it will have to stay until this storm is over."

"But we need those disks now. AeroSaqii's men are
probably already here in Pine Creek."

"I'm just as frustrated as you are, Jonathan, that the
transmission won't download properly. But those men are
having to deal with the same weather we are. And I doubt
they're here. Ellen Bigelow told me that the main road
coming up from Greenville will likely close soon, and
that's the only way into Pine Creek. Several trees have
fallen, pulling miles of power lines with them. That should
buy us some time."

Jonathan slapped the table in frustration, then picked
up his briefcase and stormed into the living room.

Grace fed Baby, burped him, changed him, and set
him back down to sleep in his cradle by the fire. He was
tuckered out, sound asleep before his head even hit the
mattress. Ellen and John must have spent the entire time
playing with him.

After making sure Baby was covered up warmly, Grace
went about preparing her home for the long winter siege
ahead. While she worked, Jonathan sat in the overstuffed
chair in the living room and alternated between talking on
the phone—which had somehow escaped the wrath of the
ice—and working on his computer.

Grace was glad he was occupied elsewhere and no
longer bothering her. She drained what water was left in
the holding tank into several jugs and set them on the
counter to reserve for drinking. She filled pots with broken
icicles she chopped from the eaves and put them on the
stove to melt. She dug out the kerosene lamps that had
been around since before she was born, and it was just
as she placed them on the sideboard that she found Mary.

The Oreo cookie tin was sitting in the middle of the sideboard. Grace picked it up. There were two small dents in the front of the can, and she slowly spanned her fingers over them. They were placed exactly where two large, strong thumbs would have gripped the tin tightly in grief.

Michael must have slipped out of the house after following her to the Bigelows' in his truck and brought Mary back here. Michael had left the house while Grace had a quick lunch with Ellen and John before she returned home with Baby.

Grace hugged the tin to her chest, glad to have her sister back and sad beyond words for Michael. It must have been hard for him to have spent the last five months wondering where Mary was and if she would return and the last twenty-four hours coming to terms with the fact that he would never see her again.

Grace wiped at the tears that kept leaking from her eyes. It seemed she cried at the drop of a hat these days.

"Oh, Mare. What am I supposed to do?" she asked. "I love Baby. I can't just give him away."

She didn't get an answer. Nor did she wonder about the sudden sensation of warmth pushing against her chest. She simply hugged the tin more fiercely against her aching heart.

"The fire's going out," Jonathan said, walking into the kitchen. He stopped suddenly, a look of annoyance hardening his features.

"You're still talking to her, I see," he said, nodding at the tin in her arms. He took a step closer. "Are you crying?"

She set the tin back on the table and wiped her tears completely away with the palms of her hands. "I do that sometimes, Jonathan. When people lose someone they love, they grieve."

His face flushed to a dull red, and he seemed at a loss for words. He walked out of the kitchen, then turned around and came back. "The fire. It's going out, and I don't see any more wood in the box. Do you have some?"

"It's in the attached barn, just outside the door."

He stood there looking at her. "Should I get it?" he asked, finally realizing that she had no intention of doing it herself.

"You'll probably want to fill the woodbox," she told him, returning to her chores. "It burns better if it's warm."

She began going through the refrigerator to make room for a pot of icicles to keep cold all of the food that had magically multiplied while she was gone. The modern machine was being demoted to an old-fashioned icebox.

While she worked, she thought about her promise to Mary, Michael's remarkable story, Grey's offer to raise Baby, and the monumental step she had taken this afternoon in the summit house. She didn't know if it had been a step backward or forward, but it had certainly changed the direction of her life.

No matter how mad she was at him now, Grace knew in her heart that she would never leave Greylen MacKeage. Not after what had happened this afternoon on the top of TarStone Mountain. Pine Creek was her home now, and she was standing firmly in the center between two warring men. Possibly three, if she counted Jonathan, who would keep pulling with all his might to get her back to Virginia.

Grace felt a twinge between her legs when she knelt down to move the food on the bottom shelf of the fridge. She was still tender from their lovemaking, but it was a warm, welcome kind of tenderness. It reminded her of their time together. The nice time, anyway.

The only thing that nagged at her conscience was the

fact that they hadn't used protection. A sixteen-year-old knew enough to carry a condom in her purse, but Grace had never even purchased such a thing. She hadn't needed to. She was waiting for marriage.

So why hadn't she waited?

It was simple, really, once she thought about it. She hadn't been saving herself for marriage; she'd been waiting to meet a man she could love for the rest of her life.

And she had, if he ever crawled out of his cave—or, rather, his castle—long enough to see the problem from her point of view.

She couldn't commit herself to a man who wanted her to live a lie by the next twenty years. Grey had sorely disappointed her by even suggesting such a thing.

Grace conveniently dismissed the fact that she had been seriously considering that very same lie herself. Because, in all fairness to her principles, even though it would be so easy simply to run away with Baby and never see any of them again, her promise to Mary was still firmly in place in her heart.

It was such a mess. She was damned if she did and damned if she didn't. How would she feel if, say in three years from now, Michael MacBain took a wife and began a new life for himself? And they had children? Where would that leave Baby? How could she walk up to Michael ten or fifteen years from now and say, "Oh, by the way, I'd like to introduce you to your son"?

And how could she give Baby up now, after what Michael had told her today? Although Grace was starting to suspect that a lightning strike was more the culprit than insanity. Michael seemed perfectly normal to her in every other way, if she overlooked this little war he was waging with the MacKeages.

Grace stopped what she was doing and stared at the

inside of the fridge. There was something nagging at her. Something she should realize. Something about the story Callum had told her concerning Maura.

Grace sat down on the floor with a large plate of brownies in her lap. That was it. The story. His engagement to Maura had taken place when Grey was only twenty-eight years old. That had to be at least six or seven years ago. And Michael claimed he had been living in this time only four years.

Which meant the MacKeages had known Michael before his supposed journey.

And that meant that the key to this whole problem lay with them. They could tell her about Michael's past and would know if he was sane or not. If Michael had been fine seven years ago, the MacKeages would be able to tell her that.

Did she want to know? If there was a perfectly logical explanation for why Michael thought he had traveled through time, a near-death experience or something, did she really want to know he was sane?

Because then she would have to keep her promise to Mary.

She would have to give up Baby.

Grace unwrapped the brownies and stuffed one into her mouth. Her damn principles suddenly reared their ugly heads again. She would have to ask the MacKeages. Or the priest. Father Daar wouldn't dare lie to her about something so important. And because he was a priest, if she told him Baby belonged to Michael MacBain, he'd have to keep her confidence, wouldn't he? If it turned out there had never been a terrible storm, Father Daar still couldn't tell her secret.

Grace stuffed the second brownie into her mouth and took another one before she stood and set the plate on the table. It was decided, then. She would speak to Father Daar the first chance she got him alone.

"Grace," Jonathan said, walking through the door with an armful of wood.

"What?" she asked around a mouth full of brownie.

He frowned at her. She wiped her mouth, realized she was covered in crumbs, and wiped the front of her sweat-shirt. "What?" she repeated.

"Someone's here." He walked to the porch door and looked out. "There are lights coming up your driveway."

She looked out the window over the sink and groaned. Speak of the devil. The snowcat was slowly growling its way over the ice, grinding it up like Parmesan cheese. It stopped right behind her truck, and Grey and Morgan climbed out.

Jonathan's eyes widened in surprise. "Well, hell. That's a snowcat. That can easily take us into the mountains."

"Now, Jonathan," she said, walking over to him.

She didn't get a chance to finish. Firewood still in his arms, he was out the door and standing on the porch. And before she could warn him not to even try, he had stuck out his hand to introduce himself.

"Jonathan Stanhope," he said. "That your snowcat?"

"It is," Grey answered, looking first at Jonathan's out-stretched hand and then over to her.

Grace decided to use Grey's trick and attempted to give him an unreadable look. He merely lifted a brow at her, took Jonathan's hand, and shook it.

"Greylen MacKeage," he said.

"MacKeage." Jonathan shifted the wood in his arms. "I want to rent you and your snowcat for a job I need done."

"It's not for hire. And neither am I," Grey said, dismiss-ing the request. He walked past Jonathan and into the house. Grace stepped out of the way so she wouldn't be run over. She moved again when Morgan followed. She looked back out to the porch and saw Jonathan just standing there, stunned into stillness.

She moved once more when Jonathan suddenly dropped the wood on the porch and went running past her after Grey.

"I don't think you understand," Jonathan said. "I'm willing to pay you whatever you want. I need that machine."

"Who the hell are you?" Grey asked.

Jonathan stopped his approach and straightened himself to his full height. "I'm Jonathan Stanhope," he repeated. He nodded at Grace. "I'm Grace's boss."

Grey looked at her. And damn, he was playing that trick with his eyes again. For the life of her, she could not tell what he was thinking.

Morgan struck a match and lit the kerosene lamp on the table, flooding the room with soft yellow light. He stole a brownie off the plate and leaned against the table, crossed his legs at the ankles, and stared at Jonathan as he chewed.

"I'll give you twenty thousand dollars for the use of that machine for one day. That should put a good chunk of its cost back in your pocket," her boss said.

Grace wanted to shake her head in dismay. Jonathan had no idea what he was doing.

Grey never even looked at him. He just kept staring at her.

"Thirty thousand," Jonathan said then.

"It's not for hire," Grey repeated, still not looking at him. "Pack some things, Grace. You're coming to Gu Bràth until the power comes back on."

"She can't," Jonathan said. He moved to stand between them so that Grey would have to look at him. "I need her for work." He waved his hand to encompass the house. "And she seems quite comfortable here."

"What work would that be?" Grey asked, finally giving the man his attention.

Jonathan squared his shoulders. She couldn't see his face because his back was to her, but Grace would bet a penny he was trying to use his winning, businessman-to-businessman smile on Grey. She darted a peek at Morgan. He was eating another brownie, amusement lighting his face. He stopped chewing, looked over, and winked at her.

Grace blinked. Wasn't he supposed to be mad at her?

"It seems Grace was in a plane crash a few days ago, up in the mountains," Jonathan told Grey. "There's important equipment still up there, and I need to get it back as soon as possible. I'll give you forty thousand dollars to help me find it."

"We gathered everything we saw, lass," Morgan said around a mouthful of brownie, frowning. "What is it you're missing?"

"A small black case containing computer disks," she told Morgan. "I remember taking a blank disk out of it to pack in my bag, but I must have set the case on the snow instead of back in the suitcase. It might have slipped under the fuselage."

Apparently not caring one whit about her disks, Grey turned and walked into the living room. Stunned yet again, Jonathan pivoted and looked at her. Grace shrugged her shoulders. Morgan grabbed another brownie and followed Grey.

"Dammit, Grace. Do something," Jonathan hissed. "We need that snowcat."

Grey returned from the living room with Baby in his arms. Morgan was carrying Baby's cradle. Grace moved around Jonathan to intercept them.

"I'm not going to Gu Bràth," she told Grey in a whisper, standing on her toes and grabbing his arm. "I don't want to."

"Ah, lass," Morgan said from right behind her. "We're sorry we frightened you earlier. We promise to be civil this time."

"You can't stay here," Grey said, reaching out and running a finger over her cheek, the act so privately familiar to her yet so outwardly possessive—for Jonathan's sake, she supposed. "You don't have water without electricity to run the well pump," he continued, his eyes flaring with awareness. "And the hearth isn't big enough to heat the downstairs."

"You don't have water, either."

"We do. We have generators enough to run the entire resort if need be," he told her. He shifted Baby in his arms, tucking the sleeping child's head under his chin. "And you have a ski lift to save."

She let go of his arm, walked to the sink, and turned to face him. By God, she would stand her ground on this issue. "No, I don't. Not unless you set up your snow-making equipment in Michael's field."

"That damn equipment will get set up," he said.

She darted a look at Morgan, then back at Grey. "By whom?"

"I'll do it myself if I have to," he told her. "Now, are you content to live in what you're wearing, or do you want to pack some things?

"But . . ."

"Believe me, lass," Morgan interjected. "You're going to Gu Bràth, and it's a lot easier if you just come along peacefully."

"Now, wait a minute," Jonathan suddenly said. "You can't force Grace out of her home."

Grey gave her boss a look that clearly said Jonathan was welcome to try and stop him. Jonathan, being the intelligent man that he was, turned to Grace for help.

"My boss comes with me," Grace said, conceding defeat. Besides, Father Daar was at Gu Bràth, and she wanted to talk to him.

"He can stay in the resort hotel," Grey said.

"I need to be with Grace," Jonathan foolishly said, pushing the issue. "If you've got electricity, then we can use our computers. But we need to find those disks before they're ruined."

"I'll get your damn disks," Grey told him. "Just as soon as I'm free to."

"But it can't wait. There might be other people already here, trying to steal them from us. We need to go now."

Grace tensed when she saw Grey's eyes suddenly narrow to sharp slits of green ice. "Are you saying there are men here wanting something from Grace?" Grey asked in a whisper-soft voice.

Apparently reading the threat in Grey's eyes, Jonathan nodded hesitantly. "There's a problem with the satellite we sent up, and Grace is the only one here who can retrieve the data without destroying them."

"Then those disks will be no good to these other men."

Grace saw Jonathan swallow hard, obviously hoping to push his heart back down in his chest. She was getting a bit alarmed herself, seeing Grey standing so still, hearing the steel in his voice.

"They'll . . . ah, they want the disks, but they also want Grace," Jonathan whispered, swallowing again, just before taking a quick step back from the look that came into Grey's eyes.

Grey turned that look on her. It was all Grace could do to keep from backing up herself. But then, she had the counter to hold her up. Never in her life had she witnessed such fierce foreboding.

And it dawned on her then that the raging scene at Gu Bràth had been nothing close to what Greylen MacKeage was capable of. Even his anger after the plane crash was nothing compared with the lethal rage she could feel radiating out of every pore of his body, filling the room with enough tension that even the air seemed to withdraw.

And then Grace remembered to breathe.

"Pack up," Grey snapped. "I'm putting you in that snowcat in five minutes."

Baby stirred in his arms, and Grey looked down at the child. Grace watched with fascination as Grey forced himself back under control. When he looked at her his eyes were still hard as flint, and his complexion had dulled only slightly, but his voice, when he spoke, was clearly controlled.

"This is important to you?" he asked, again running his finger possessively over her cheek. "These data?"

She nodded. "It could alter the future for mankind. Those data could mean putting people on the moon or on Mars to live," she said, deciding she didn't quite dare mention the possibility if it being used as a weapon. Grey was mad enough as it was.

"Really, lass?" Morgan asked. "You're thinking men can travel to the moon?"

"And women," she said, just to tease him.

His face reddened with embarrassment. "I meant that."

"I know," Grace said, patting his arm on the way to her bedroom. "I'll just be a minute. I need to get some things together." She stopped and looked around the kitchen. "Will you put Mary in Baby's crib, Morgan?" she asked, again enjoying first his surprise at seeing the tin, then his obvious reluctance to touch it. But bless the man, he gingerly picked up Mary and carefully set her in the crib. Now it was the crib he didn't want to pick up.

Grace looked around the silent house. "I hate to leave this place unattended during this storm."

"We'll keep an eye on it for you," Grey assured her, his voice nearly back to normal, his smile tight.

"Oh, the animals. I can't leave them."

"Ya can leave that damn goat," Morgan said, rubbing his backside.

"I'll have Callum fetch them," Grey told her. "We can put them in our barn with the horses."

"You have horses?" Grace asked, getting excited, remembering Ian's claim that his horse weighed more than a thousand pounds. They must be draft animals. "For sleigh rides?"

"They are not plow horses!" Morgan all but shouted, getting red in the face again. "What is it with you people around here? You think just because they're big, they must pull?"

"Well, what else would a ski lodge want with horses?" she asked, wondering at his reaction.

"They're noble beasts, and they're pets now," he told her, picking up the cradle and walking out the door.

Morgan was like the Maine weather; wait five minutes, and he changed. He was either scolding her or winking at her, and she still didn't know which one amused her more. Grace chuckled out loud as she walked into her room but sobered the second she was out of sight of the men.

Whew. Her insides were still shaking from Grey's not-so-subtle display of alpha-male possession. And the sad part was, Jonathan didn't seem to realize just how close he'd come to being flattened. It was as if all of Jonathan's manly instincts had gotten swallowed up by the sophisti-cated civilization he'd been living in all his life.

Somewhere along the line, Jonathan's male traits had been tamed, if not completely repressed, by society. How else could two men—Jonathan and Grey—be so different, being about the same age, living on the same planet, but becoming such contradictions to each other?

Jonathan had been only worried about her safety.

Grey had turned lethally dangerous at the thought of men wanting to kidnap her.

Which was why Grace's own instincts told her that Gu Bràth was a much better choice than Virginia right now. Grey would protect her and Baby with his life if need be. And what woman wouldn't want that kind of commitment from the man she loved?

It was exactly how things should be when two people intended to spend the rest of their lives together.

$\mathcal{D}$*aar paced the length of* the north tower of Gu Bràth, stopping to look toward where TarStone Mountain stood behind low-cast, drizzle-soaked clouds. The rain would start again soon; he could all but smell it coming. This storm, it seemed, was not through raising its havoc yet.

He was on vigil again, trying to read the energy coming from the mountain tonight in waves, first with white potent authority, then with black, menacing acrimony. He could not figure out what it meant. He knew only that the two souls now loving and arguing and feeling their way cautiously toward each other were in the path of what was humming through the forest.

Daar sighed and returned to his pacing, the thump of his cane adding to the sounds of a forest straining under the weight of building ice. He had been wracking his tired old brain since he'd met her, trying to discover who Grace's guardian had been for the first thirty years of her life. Grey would be taking over that task now, but somebody had had that charge before him.

Daar suspected it was Mary. And he also suspected that even though dead, she had not yet relinquished her duty to Grey.

Grey had already appointed himself Grace's guardian. After he'd dropped Grace and Baby and that Stanhope guy off at Gu Bràth, the warrior had pulled Daar aside for a few words, just before he'd left for MacBain's Christmas tree farm. Grey had quietly but firmly warned Daar to stay away from Grace Sutter.

Daar had been amused by Grey's sudden forthrightness. It confirmed what he'd always suspected: Greylen Mac-Keage was aware that the priest he'd been supporting these last four years was also the person responsible for the storm that had carried him forward in time.

Well, Grey's intelligence was never in question. But gaining the warrior's trust would be near impossible now that Grey felt protective of Grace.

Not that Grey ever did trust him, Daar thought with a self-pitying sigh. Wasn't that the very reason he lived in a cabin two miles away instead of at Gu Bràth? The warrior wished to keep Daar close in order to keep an eye on him, but he had no intention of living under the same roof with someone he suspected had caused such a great upset to the natural world.

Daar knew MacBain was suspicious of him also. That was the reason the young warrior had taken his men to Nova Scotia just nine months after arriving in the twenty-first century. But when all his men had died, MacBain had found himself drawn to Pine Creek. Though he didn't visit his old priest and mentor and only nodded his head whenever Daar met him in town, Michael was at least attempting to walk the precarious line between the two distinct worlds of his life.

Daar was actually proud of Michael and had been mightily happy when MacBain had taken up with Mary Sutter—and mightily disappointed to learn she had died.

And Daar couldn't figure out why that was. Why did Mary have to die at such a trying time in Grace's life?

Could it be that Mary Sutter wasn't a wizard at all but merely possessed the soul of a guardian? It wasn't unheard of for angels to walk this earth for only a short time, to look after a charge and then suddenly disappear as mysteriously as they'd arrived.

But Grace herself, it seemed, was not willing to let her sister's spirit completely depart. The poor grieving woman had been clinging to Mary's ashes in an Oreo cookie tin. Grace carried that tin of ashes wherever she went. Daar had seen her place Mary on the mantel in the living room downstairs just this afternoon.

It was past time he had a little talk with Grace Sutter. More worried about the menace clouding the air tonight than Grey's warning to stay away from Grace, Daar turned back toward the stairs that led down the north tower.

He took one last look at the stormy, unsettled sky and headed to the warm fire below. He was confident that the warrior would meet whatever challenge the stormy sky hinted at. After all, that's why Daar had searched through all of time to find such a match for the woman who would have seven daughters.

Tomorrow, Greylen MacKeage would come face to face with his destiny—and then have to prove he was worthy of it.

Grace had not been successful in her plan to speak with Father Daar. She'd tried to talk with him twice, and each time he said he hadn't the time. He was in the middle of a novena. She'd actually gone to the dictionary to look that up. And what she found was that a novena lasted *nine* days.

Which left her with Baby and the MacKeages. And

Jonathan. And the damn ski lift that she still wasn't sure she wouldn't blow up.

She didn't even have any of them at the moment, except Baby, and he was busy sleeping the sleep of the innocent. Grey and Morgan were at Michael MacBain's Christmas tree farm, setting up the equipment and hoping the temperature dropped low enough tonight to make snow. Callum had traveled back to her house to gather the hens, the goat, and the cats. She'd wished him luck when he left, and he had scowled the whole way to his truck. Ian was holed up in the ski lift shed, apparently not willing to share the house with her. Both Ian and Callum had refused to help Grey save Michael's trees, and Grace suspected the only reason Morgan went was that he was worried that even Grey's bitter determination would not be enough to get the job done.

Grace had caused a terrible upset in the MacKeage house by demanding they help Michael if they wanted her to help them. Ian had given her a black look when she and Baby had walked in three hours ago, and he had ignored Jonathan altogether.

And with Ian sulking in the ski lift shed, Grace couldn't work on the lift until Grey returned. Not for all the sun in Florida would she face that angry old man alone.

Jonathan was in the dining room, back on his computer, probably trying to figure out what this little mess was going to cost him if they didn't successfully retrieve Podly's data. Grace couldn't care less at the moment, and that lack of emotion toward something she'd worked so hard for surprised her. Several of the data collectors on Podly were hers. It was her chance to prove what she'd been saying all along, that ion propulsion was viable and at a reasonable cost.

But for some reason, she no longer cared if there were

colonies on Mars within the decade. Sometime over the last several weeks, she'd stopped looking outward to space and turned her attention to what she had discovered to be the real challenge: living and loving and being content here on Earth.

And then there was Grey. He had taught her that there was something much more important than living on the cutting edge of exploration, technology, and modern-minded men. Grey had made her realize that for all of society's evolution, mankind still needed the ancient values to survive. Men and women still needed to belong to each other. A commitment, a bond, and trust of another were still more important than mere coexistence.

Grace had always known these truths, but she had forgotten them sometime in the last fourteen years, living with people who looked only up and outward, not inside themselves.

"This MacKeage guy," Jonathan said, walking into the great room of Gu Bràth. "Do you trust him to do as he said? Will he take us to the crash site tomorrow?" He looked at his watch and frowned. "I mean today. Dammit. It's after midnight. We've wasted thirty-six hours already."

"He will," she assured him.

He walked to the hearth and held his hands to the warmth of the fire while he looked around the room. "This is a hell of a place MacKeage owns." He looked back at her. "I think my last offer of forty thousand was an insult. Where'd he make this kind of money? I've never heard the MacKeage name mentioned in the business world. He sure as hell didn't make this kind of cash living in Pine Creek."

Grace shrugged and closed the old book she had been looking through. She hadn't been able to read it; it was written in a language she didn't recognize.

"You don't seem very worried about our satellite," he observed, taking a chair across from her. He leaned forward, his elbows on his knees as he stared at her. "What's gotten into you? The Grace Sutter I know would be pounding the computer keys now, not reading some ancient tome."

"Why are we doing it, Jonathan? Why are we trying so hard to travel into space? We haven't even finished exploring Earth yet. Why aren't we focused on that?"

Her questions seemed to surprise him. "Because it's where the future is," he told her. "A hundred years from now, Earth will be a wasteland. If we don't travel up and out and explore new worlds, we won't survive."

"But it wouldn't become a wasteland if we put all of our energies into saving it."

He leaned back in his chair, waving that concept away. "That's environmental bunk," he scoffed. "And there's no money in it. The profit is in space, because that's where people want to go." He leaned forward again. "And that's where you and I can take them, Grace. Don't get all introspective on me just because you're visiting your childhood home."

He got down on his knees in front of her and gripped the arms of her chair. "You're just feeling something every scientist feels when he's on the brink of a new discovery that could alter the future of the world. You're worried about the ramifications."

He brushed a strand of hair behind her ear. "Don't be. What we're doing is a good thing, Grace. Future generations will thank us the same way we now thank Galileo, Newton, Einstein, and the Wright brothers."

He cupped her cheek and lifted her face up to his. "You're one of them, Grace," he whispered.

And then he kissed her.

She didn't kiss him back. She couldn't.

He didn't smell right.

And he tasted like bitter coffee.

Her toes didn't tingle, and her breath didn't catch.

It wasn't the same. Heck, it wasn't even close.

"I wouldn't be doing that, girl, if I were you," Father Daar suddenly said from the doorway of the living room.

Grace pulled back and flushed crimson. Great. She'd just been caught kissing—by an old-fashioned priest, of all people.

Jonathan stood up and faced Daar. "It's okay, Father," he said. "Grace and I . . . well, we have a history together."

"You'll not have a future if the MacKeage realizes this," Daar said, walking into the room and settling into Jonathan's seat. He dismissed Jonathan in much the same way Grey had dismissed him at her home earlier that afternoon. And, like before, Jonathan didn't seem to realize the insult or even the threat the priest had alluded to. He simply walked out of the room, back to his computer.

Daar lifted a brow at her, looking at the book in her lap. "Been doing some reading?"

Grace laid the book on the floor by her chair. "No. I thought it might be Scottish, though, and I was looking for the meaning of *Gu Bràth.*"

"It's Gaelic, girl," he said, leaning back in his chair as he grinned at her. "And *Gu Bràth* means "forever." Until eternity." He leaned closer and said, his crystal-clear blue eyes sparkling, "Or until Judgment Day. The old Gaelic language is hard to pin down exactly," he continued, settling back in his chair again. "Words can have many meanings."

"What do the words mean for Grey and the others?"

He looked back at the fire, absently watching the flames. "The MacKeage gave this place the name Gu Bràth and said this mountain was their home now, forever, and that nothing short of God himself would ever uproot them again."

Grace wondered what had happened back in Scotland that had forced the four men to build a new life here. Whatever it was, it had been a painful experience for the priest to use words like *uproot* and for Grey to declare to God that it would never happen again.

"Why do people refer to him as 'the MacKeage'?" she asked, drawing Father Daar's attention again. "What does that mean?"

"The laird of a clan is always referred to by the clan's name. The laird of the Campbells would be the Campbell," he said as example.

"Grey's a laird? A real one?"

"It's an old title." Daar set his cane across his knees and fingered the wood. "It's not used much anymore today. But the title still exists."

Grace was fascinated. So that was why the others listened to Grey, even though Ian and Callum were older. But she hadn't thought people still put stock in rank. Not the way the three men seemed to do, anyway.

She wanted to ask the priest more about it, but he suddenly nodded at the cookie tin sitting on top of the mantel. "She's not in there, you know," he told her softly. "She's here," he said, pointing at her and then tapping his own chest. He waved a hand in the air. "Mary has moved into the energies of our life forces now and is part of the people whose lives she touched."

"I know," Grace admitted rather sheepishly, feeling a bit silly for carrying her sister's ashes everywhere. "But they're all I have left of her. And in less than four months, I won't even have that."

"Ah, the Summer Solstice," he said, nodding. "Your birthdays."

"How do you know that?"

"Mary would walk up the mountain to visit me at least once a week. She told me that you both had the same birthday. Summer Solstice."

Grace felt her insides get all mushy, and she smiled. "It doesn't always fall on the same date every year, you know. Mary was born on June twentieth, and I was born on the twenty-first. But both days were the Summer Solstice on those years, and so Mom decided that we should celebrate that event instead."

"Mary told me you were each born at the exact moment of the Solstice," Daar said. "Is that true, or was she pulling an old man's leg? She had that kind of sense of humor."

"She wasn't lying. It's the weirdest thing. All of my half brothers were born on the same day, too. Mom always made a huge celebration of it, and even after they'd left home, my brothers always came back for our birthdays on Summer Solstice. What are the odds of that happening in one family?"

"You consider it a mere coincidence? Maybe not something a bit more magical?" he asked, his clear, steady blue eyes watching her with an intensity that grew unsettling.

Grace laughed to break the tension she was suddenly feeling. "Of course not, Father. There is no such thing as magic."

He looked aghast. "You don't believe in magic, girl?"

"I'm a scientist. I believe what is based in fact."

"Then explain eight children being born to one father, all on the day of the same celestial event," he demanded gently.

"It's a simple mathematical occurrence. It's no different from what the odds might be that a comet will hit Earth or that a tornado will drive a piece of hay straight through a tree trunk. The probability is not likely, but it still happens occasionally."

"So math explains what magic can't."

"Yes. I'm sure we aren't the first family to have each child born on the same date," she said. "Not when you consider the number of births since the beginning of mankind."

The priest turned and frowned at the fire. Grace hoped she hadn't insulted him. She was enjoying this philosophical discussion.

"Do you believe in time travel, Father?" she asked, deciding to continue with it and maybe bridge the subject of Michael.

He looked back at her, his eyes narrowed. "I doubt you do. Am I right?"

"In theory, it is possible. Einstein may have already proved that for us. But nobody knows. So my answer is no, I don't believe in time travel."

"Then why would you be asking me such a question?"

"Because you and I know somebody who says he's traveled eight hundred years from the past. And I'm wondering if he's insane, or if there's a good explanation for his . . . confusion."

As she spoke, the old priest's eyes grew wide, and his complexion grew paler and paler.

"Who told you this?" he asked in a whisper-soft voice. "Who said he's traveled through time?"

"Michael MacBain," she told him in her own whisper, leaning closer so that only he could hear her. "He told Mary he was born in the year A.D. 1171."

She saw the priest take a deep, almost painful breath as he leaned back in his chair and closed his eyes. Grace waited a good two minutes for him to answer her, but he just sat there, his eyes closed as he fingered the polished burls of his cane.

Grace decided to try another tack.

"Can you keep a secret, Father?" she asked, leaning

closer again. "Baby's not my son. He's Mary's. And Michael's."

He snapped his eyes open and looked at her. You would have thought she had baked him a cake, he looked so suddenly pleased with her. "The bairn's not yours?"

"No," she confirmed for him, nodding her head. "But I'm not sure I should tell Michael he has a son. I don't know if the man is sane or not."

"Of course he's sane, girl. Your sister loved him, didn't she? He's as right in the head as you and I."

"But he thinks he traveled through time."

A look of consternation crossed the old priest's expression. He opened his mouth, then suddenly snapped it shut and glared at her. Grace was getting a little frustrated herself.

"Well? Did you know Michael seven years ago?" she finally asked. "When the incident with Maura happened?"

"Why?" he asked back, sounding defensive.

She wanted to strangle him. Wasn't he listening to her? "Because," she said with as much patience as she could muster, "if you've known Michael that long, you can tell me if anything happened to him that would explain why he believes what he does?"

"I have to finish my Novena," he suddenly said, standing up.

Grace stood up also. "Why won't you tell me?"

"I'm a priest," he said, walking away from her. He stopped and looked back. "I've taken a vow not to repeat what I hear. If you're wanting to know anything about MacBain, you'd best be asking the MacKeage. He's not under any such restriction."

That said, Father Daar left as silently as he had arrived, the thump of his cane swallowed up by the rug.

Grace stared at the door where he disappeared. Well,

that had been productive. She was no closer to finding the answers she needed about Michael than when she had arrived in Pine Creek.

She didn't want to ask Grey. Or the others, either. But what other choice was there? She had to justify her actions if she intended to keep Baby. Grace walked over to his cradle and watched him sleep.

What was she going to do?

Grey helped the last of the older women out of the snowcat and took her arm as they walked into the resort hotel. That meant sixteen of the twenty rooms that were finished were already full. And people from town were still coming in, now that the word seemed to be out.

It had been Morgan's idea that they offer up their hotel to anyone needing a warm, comfortable place to weather the storm now that the power had failed. Morgan had gone into the Bigelow house for a drink of water and discovered an aging Ellen Bigelow dressed in layers of clothes, filling pots with ice to melt on the woodstove in her living room.

Morgan had approached Grey with his idea to fire up their hotel generator and make the older people and women with young children in town more comfortable at TarStone Mountain Resort.

It had been a good idea, but implementing it was easier said than done. The people of Pine Creek were an independent lot, *especially* the older ones. They didn't want to leave their homes. Grey was blue in the face from talking before he was able to convince John and Ellen Bigelow that it was the practical thing to do. And that was all it took, it seemed, for someone to make the first move. If the Bigelows thought it was a smart decision, the others quickly followed suit.

It had taken both snowcats to transport everyone. As soon as Grey or Morgan brought someone to the hotel, someone else thought of others who needed rescuing. Callum and Morgan and Grey had spent all evening shuttling women, children, and old people from all over town.

The storm had taken a turn for the worse, and it was now sleeting at a rate of an inch an hour. If it kept up, Grey wouldn't even need the snow-making equipment to cover MacBain's trees.

Grey might not care for the man they had helped tonight, but he had to admire Grace's ingenious yet very simple plan to save MacBain from ruin. Instead of trying to fight Mother Nature, they were using snow to protect the young trees by burying them. It was working beautifully.

But what surprised him even more was the fact that Morgan and eventually Callum had helped. He didn't fault Ian for wanting to remain stubborn; given a choice, he would have also.

Grey was not about to face Grace Sutter, however, when this was over and MacBain was ruined and he was not. Giving into her ultimatum may not be the wisest way to begin their relationship, with Grace thinking she had that kind of control over him, but it was better than having no relationship at all.

Besides, something good was coming from their efforts. The townspeople were responding to their offer of help. For the last four years, the four men and the priest, Daar, had kept to themselves, isolated from the rest of the world, seeking the sanctuary of their mountain forest while they came to terms with the new life they had been so violently thrown into.

The isolation was over now, and it seemed they had inherited themselves a community. The fact that half the town was suddenly living in their resort now was probably the best example of just how far Grey and his men had come. Community was still the best means of survival.

They had simply forgotten that truth—until today.

Word had gotten out within an hour of their starting to set up their equipment at the Christmas tree farm. Eight able-bodied men had arrived to work beside them, and they had completed the job in half the time.

All without the help of the bastard MacBain. He had disappeared before Grey and Morgan had arrived. According to John Bigelow, MacBain was in the habit of heading off into the mountains every so often, whenever he took to brooding and wanted to be alone. John felt that MacBain was probably trying to come to terms with Mary's death.

Which was fine with Grey, although it was ironic that they were trying to save MacBain's future and the man wasn't even present. But Grey had found himself looking up toward the mountains, wondering how he would feel, how he would react, if something happened to Grace. He, too, would probably head into the wilderness. He just wasn't sure he would return. Not without Grace to come back to.

"I never imagined I'd ever see the inside of this place," the woman he was helping said, gawking around at the two-story lobby. "And now I'm staying here."

"We've been planning an open house for the people of Pine Creek," Grey lied, suddenly deciding he'd make it a truth.

"A real party, with dancing?" she asked, looking up at him with sparkling, excited brown eyes.

"And gondola rides to the top," he added, smiling at her, hoping they still had a gondola lift come spring.

The woman stopped and grabbed her chest with a gasp that nearly knocked her over, her eyes widening to the size of dinner plates. "I've always wanted to ride on one of those lifts. But I don't ski," the eightyish woman said. "You're going to run it in the summer?"

"Yes. You can see the whole of Pine Lake from the top," he told her. "And there will be a restaurant at the summit."

"How do you get the food up there?" she wanted to know, eyeing him suspiciously.

"We use the snowcat you just rode in."

"Oh, of course. Thank you, young man," she said, patting his arm. "I see Mavis over there. I want to tell her I'm here. She's probably worried sick about me." She attempted to straighten her time-bent frame as she smoothed the front of her coat. "Mavis thinks I need looking after like a child, just because I'm old," she told Grey in a co-conspirator's voice. "I don't, but I haven't the heart tell her. She needs to be helpful."

And you do need looking after, Grey said to himself. He didn't even know her name, but he did know about pride and independence.

He was in love with a woman who had buckets of both.

He watched as the old lady made her way over to the woman who must be Mavis and smiled when Mavis immediately began mothering her.

Grey headed back out into the sleet, pulling up the collar of his coat as he let his tired feet carry him up the path to Gu Bràth. He was nearly finished. All that was left to do before he found his bed was ensure that he had a gondola come spring.

Grey let himself in quietly and stood in the doorway to the living room, watching Grace and Baby sleeping together in the chair by the fire. Baby was snuggled under her chin, and Grace had her arms wrapped securely around him as they both slept. An empty bottle of formula lay on the floor beside the chair, and a discarded diaper was rolled up beside it.

Grey took a deep, almost painful breath. This is what he wanted, to come home to a woman and child and to know that he was needed by them.

He wasn't sure when he had fallen in love with both of them. It was possible it had happened on the mountain, on their desperate descent to safety. Or when he had used his body to warm Grace. His heart may have warmed up with her then. But if he had to choose one single moment, Grey would guess it was when they had been standing outside the summit house, when Grace was bargaining to save his lift for the use of his equipment to save his enemy.

That was when he knew he'd found the woman of his heart. He'd pricked her temper, and she had given him an ultimatum. He knew she hadn't intended to ask him that way, but when Grace Sutter got mad and she felt she had the power of right on her side, she was a force to be reckoned with.

Yes, it was then, as she'd stood facing him, the rain driving her long, curly hair against her face and the fire of anger driving her words, that Grey had felt the sledgehammer blow to his chest.

That was when he decided he wasn't letting her back off that mountain without claiming her first. Finding out he was *her* first had only strengthened the bond that was now sealed. The marriage was only a matter of legalities now, as far as he was concerned. She was his, and though she probably didn't realize it yet, he was hers for the rest of their lives.

And Baby, too, he hoped.

He had fallen in love with the bairn long before he'd known Baby's heritage. Not that it would have mattered. There was something about the innocent and unquestioning trust Baby had given him that had tugged at Grey's heart strings.

He didn't want Grace to give Baby to MacBain.

And that ate at his insides. He couldn't imagine having fathered a child and not even knowing it existed. There would be hell to pay for anyone who dared keep such a secret from him. Yet that was the very sin he was willing to commit against Michael MacBain if it kept Grace's heart from breaking.

Only time would tell. It was Grace's decision, not his and not anyone else's. She would have to come to terms with her sister's wish and with her own desire to keep the child.

Grey finally entered the living room and gently picked Baby up from Grace's arms, careful not to wake either one of them. He settled the child into his cradle. The boy was growing like a weed on fertile ground. He looked as if he had gained at least a pound this week. His baby cheeks were plumper, his features seemed less wrinkled, and even his terrible mess of hair looked longer.

Grey covered Baby with a blanket, smiling at the sucking motions he made with his mouth in his sleep. Such an adventurous beginning in such a short life, and still Baby prospered. That, Grey decided, was a miracle. He was grateful the child was young. An older babe might not have fared as well, considering what he'd been through. He leaned down and kissed the relaxed, tiny fist on the blanket and slowly straightened.

He wanted a dozen more just like him. Strong, healthy sons that would be the foundation of the future.

And the woman who would give him that future was in desperate need of some rest herself. Grey checked the baby monitor sitting on the table beside the cradle and picked up the small receiver that Grace had explained to him earlier would allow them to hear Baby from another room. He tucked the small box into his belt, then turned and carefully picked Grace up, holding her against his chest. She instinctively settled her head in the crook of his neck, and a shiver of warmth ran through Grey at the feel of her breath on his skin.

Damn the ski lift, he decided. It had waited this long, it could wait until daybreak. He was taking his woman upstairs and lying beside her while they both caught up on their sleep.

He carried her through the foyer and started up the stairs, smiling at the thought of Grace's reaction when she woke up and found herself in his bed.

"Are we leaving now?" Jonathan Stanhope asked from the foyer below, looking as if he had just woken up. He yawned and ran a hand through his hair. His other hand held a map.

Grey stopped and turned. "No," he said softly, not wanting to disturb Grace. "We'll leave at noon."

Jonathan came fully awake and rushed to the bottom step, grabbing the newel post. "But that will be too late!" he said. He stared at the woman in Grey's arms, and his eyes widened with surprise. "Where are you going with Grace?"

"To bed," Grey told him, turning and heading back up the stairs.

"Wait! Grace!" Jonathan shouted.

Grey felt the warm, pliant woman in his arms stir against him, and he stopped again and turned to look at Jonathan. "You're beginning to annoy me, Stanhope," he growled. "Now, get the hell out of my house."

Chapter Seventeen

Grace didn't know what to think. She was somewhat disconcerted to find herself waking up in bed with a man beside her. Or, rather, with a man sprawled on top of her.

She couldn't move. Grey had thrown his leg over her thighs and his arm across her chest, pinning her down as if he were afraid she might disappear while he slept.

So while Grace lay there contented and in no hurry to move, she studied Grey's bedroom.

She was back in a castle.

And she was the most modern thing in the room. The ceiling above her was at least twelve feet high and made of darkened wood. Two of the walls were of black stone like below, polished to brilliance. The other two walls were of honey oak paneling. And nowhere did she see an electrical fixture or switch. There were candles in wall sconces, and on a table beside the bed was an entire candelabra of half-burned tapers and a box of matches.

There was a giant hearth on the far wall, flanked on both sides by narrow windows high enough up the wall that she wouldn't be able to see out them if she were standing on her tiptoes. The bed beneath her was the size of her kitchen at home, and it was a good three feet above the floor.

And those were the more normal things she could see. The rest of the room looked as if it had come directly out of a picture book of medieval castles. A long, narrow length of cloth was draped over the mantel, its colors the same as the shirt she had stolen from Grey. There was an odd-looking saddle with a thick leather bridle hanging down the front of it on a wooden rack standing in the corner of the room.

And then there was a sword lying across the arms of a chair, as if it had been absentmindedly placed there after slaying a dragon.

A sword. She didn't know much about antiques, but Grace would bet a penny it was worth a fortune. It looked just as tall and heavy as she was. The blade wasn't shined to a mirror finish like other swords she'd seen in museums but had the patina of age and use. The handle was not ornate by any means. It had a worn, comfortable look, perfectly designed for a large, masculine hand. The sword was obviously a service weapon, not a ceremonial decoration.

A sword. An antique saddle. Candles. And a castle.

Grace frowned at the hearth as she tried to assimilate what she was seeing, remembering Michael's story of his supposed journey through time. Ten men, he had said, were caught in the storm. Six MacBains and four others he had refused to talk about, much less name.

A battle. Enemies. And seven years of hatred.

Naw. It couldn't be. Not one of the four MacKeages had shown even the smallest sign of being delusional.

They were Scots, so why shouldn't they want to live in a castle? It probably reminded them of home. Castles were part of their culture, after all.

And besides, would Michael have moved here a year ago if Grey and the others were the enemies he'd been fighting during that storm?

But it was the MacKeages themselves who had told her about Maura. Seven years ago. Before Michael's . . . mishap.

Grace turned her head and looked at the man beside her. His eyes were open, watching her.

"You live in a castle, Greylen MacKeage."

"Aye. I do."

"Why?"

"I like castles."

She waited for him to elaborate, but apparently that was all he had to say on the subject. Grace wiggled to see if he was ready to let her up. He wasn't.

"This is your bedroom," she said lamely.

"It is."

"And this is your bed I'm in."

"I so admire your mind," he drawled, the corners of his eyes crinkling with amusement.

Dammit. She couldn't seem to find the willpower to move.

"How did I get in your bed?"

"I brought you here."

"Why?"

"Because it's where you belong."

She had to look away from him then, so she could remember to breathe. She stared up at the ceiling.

"You don't have a shirt on," she thought to tell him, moving her free hand to the top button on her blouse. At least she was still dressed. Why did that disappoint her?

"I was hot."

She was getting a little hot herself. Why was he just lying there staring at her? She didn't have to look at him to know those evergreen eyes were watching her with the intensity and the patience of a cat preparing to pounce.

She should probably pounce first.

Grace suddenly pulled herself out from beneath his leg and rolled on top of him, bracing her hands on his chest as she straddled his waist. That got his attention.

"I want to register a complaint about your resort," she told him, swatting his hands away when he tried to take hold of her hips. "It seems your guests go to sleep in one place and wake up in another. Are you in the habit of carrying women up to your bed, Mr. MacKeage?"

Realizing she was going to keep swatting him if he kept trying to grab her, Grey conceded and folded his hands behind his head, giving her a negligent shrug.

"Not usually," he returned. "Only the beautiful ones."

Grace dug her fingers into his bare chest, determined not to be swayed by his compliment.

Or by that gleam of pure male lust sparking in his eyes.

Nor would she let herself be distracted by the growing evidence of his arousal she felt beneath her.

Dammit. She'd known that if she came to Gu Bràth she'd end up in his bed. But that didn't mean she had to fall all over him like a love-sick schoolgirl.

But she did fall, when Grey moved so quickly that Grace only had time to squeak before she found herself flat on her back again, once more pinned down by a half-naked body of forged steel. And those evergreen eyes she'd been getting lost in? They were now fire-laced spruce, full of intent.

Grey brushed the hair from her face and smiled at her with all the warmth of a preying cat who'd just caught supper. "I'll consider your complaint registered, lass. And I'll give ya one of my own. You're taking way too long to kiss me."

"I'm not in the habit of rewarding arrogance."

He leaned back. "Arrogance? For giving you a comfortable bed to sleep in?"

"For it being *your* bed," she countered. "And for being in it with me."

He lowered his mouth to within inches of hers, smiled, and whispered, "Ah, lass. That's not arrogance. That's belonging." He lowered his head and covered her mouth with his.

Grace stopped blustering and kissed him back, cupping his face with her hands, splaying her fingers through his silky hair. She liked the way its wavy auburn length made her fingertips tingle. He had the softest hair.

And the hardest body. He was like hot steel, rigid with an escalating tension brought on by her teasing.

A tension that started to echo inside her own body.

"We . . . we should stop," she whispered in blatant contradiction to her action, sliding her mouth over his jaw and tightening her arms around him.

"The hell we will," he said through gritted teeth, pulling her lips back to his. Grace almost laughed at his anything but subtle desire for her. Loving Greylen MacKeage was such a natural thing, warm and fun and so very thrilling.

She opened her mouth and eagerly took his tongue inside. Her senses reeled as his scent assaulted her. He smelled of nature, of the weather, and of himself. His chest radiated heat, and her breasts ached with longing to be naked against him. She wanted to feel the hair on his chest tickle her bare skin.

"We're going to make love again," she said, pulling away and staring up at him. It wasn't a question.

He nodded. Curtly.

He was so unbelievably handsome. His eyes burned with the fire of passion, and his broad shoulders and marvelous chest radiated unimaginable strength. Grace shivered. She wanted him again with a fierceness that consumed her.

And he wanted her. She could feel his desire straining

against his pants, pulsing at the very heart of her womanhood. Grace shifted to feel more of him push against her as she began unbuttoning her blouse, her eyes never leaving his, her whole body trembling with urgency.

As soon as she got her blouse open and her bra unsnapped, Grey lowered himself down until his chest covered hers. She moaned with pleasure.

He groaned in triumph.

He kissed her again, and Grace clung to him, opened her mouth to his, and wrapped her legs around his waist, lifting her hips against his erection. His groan became louder, more urgent, and as arrogantly male as he was.

He turned onto his back, taking her with him, and Grace found herself straddling his hips again. She didn't swat his hands away this time when he captured her breasts and sent a bolt of sensuous heat coursing through her.

Callum came bursting through the bedroom door, Morgan one step behind him.

"If you're not wanting your carpets bloodied," Callum said, "you'll get yourself downstairs and shut up Stanhope."

"Dammit. Get the hell out of here," Grey shouted, the power of his voice jouncing Grace like an earthquake.

Callum came to a sudden stop. Morgan ran into his back. Both men turned as red as their hair and immediately faced the hearth. But they didn't leave.

Grace certainly wanted to. Preferably by seeping through a crack in the floor. She didn't need a mirror to know her cheeks were flaming red. She hastily buttoned her blouse back up and tried to slide off Grey. He took hold of her hips and held her in place.

She glared at him.

He grinned at her.

"We're sorry, Grey," Callum said, still facing the hearth. "But Ian's threatening to toss Stanhope off the north tower. He caught him trying to steal one of the snowcats."

"Out," Grey repeated, with less volume this time.

Callum and Morgan headed for the door. Morgan darted a quick look over his shoulder at Grace and shot her a wink. He turned back and all but ran over Father Daar, who came walking into the room next.

Grace closed her eyes and groaned, throwing herself forward and burying her face in Grey's chest. She felt his sigh lift her a foot toward the ceiling and blow against her hair.

But it wasn't until she heard Jonathan calling her name as he walked into the room that Grey finally moved. He tossed her off him and stood up, leaving Grace to tumble about wildly on the bed for balance. She ended up rolling to the other side of the bed and slipping down onto the floor.

"Goddammit! Can a man not have privacy in his own house?" Grey shouted at them.

"Grace!" Jonathan said with a gasp, staring at her with an appalled expression distorting his face. His features suddenly darkened, and his eyes turned hard. "What are you doing?" he asked in a tone that said he already knew and that he didn't like it.

"Anyone still in this room in two seconds is dead," Grey said. "And that includes you, old man," he added, glaring at the grinning priest.

Grace looked down to see if she could crawl under the bed and disappear. First, Father Daar had caught her kissing Jonathan, and now, he'd found her in bed with Grey. The man was going to make her kneel in a corner for nine days straight.

Apparently, Callum and Morgan believed Grey's threat.

They grabbed the old priest by his arms and all but carried him out of the room. Jonathan, still standing across the bed staring at her, didn't move. It was as if he couldn't come to terms with what he had found.

Grace watched as Grey strode to the chair by the hearth and picked up the sword. Her embarrassment forgotten, she jumped on the bed, crossed its great width, and pushed Jonathan with all her might.

"Get out," she said, stepping down to the floor, still pushing him. "If you want to save Podly, you'll get out now."

The name of his precious satellite roused him into action. He turned and walked to the door but stopped and stared first at Grace and then at the half-naked, dangerously serious man holding a sword in his hand, looking as if he knew how to use it.

"I'll . . . ah . . . wait downstairs," Jonathan said then, eyeing the sword as he shrugged his shoulders to straighten his shirt, smoothing down the front of it with an unsteady hand.

Grey advanced on him. Jonathan pivoted and ran out. Grace heard him bump into the end of the hall and then stumble down the stairs. And she flinched when Grey slammed the door shut with enough force to rattle the windows.

Grace could only gape as he turned and stood facing her. The man looked like a medieval warlord from the same picture book as his castle. He was impressively naked from the waist up, his broad shoulders and muscled arms rippling with tension that also shone in the taut planes of his chiseled face. His bare feet were planted wide for balance, and his sword was gripped with the surety of one who was comfortable handling it.

If he replaced his pants with the plaid hanging over the

hearth and added a sporran like the one Michael had mentioned, Grey would actually look like a Scots warrior ready for battle.

Grace took a step back. He started toward her, and she turned and jumped on the bed, moving to the middle before she faced him again. He didn't stop his advance until his thighs were touching the blankets.

"You've buttoned your blouse crooked," he said, his soft voice in stark contrast to his posture.

"I . . . I'm not falling for that trick, MacKeage. The minute I look down, you're going to jump me."

The left corner of his mouth kicked up. "You aren't afraid of me, are you, Grace?"

"N-no."

"Then what seems to be the problem?"

"You are. You should see yourself," she said, waving at him. "You look like a . . . like a . . ."

"A what?"

"Like a warrior."

He puffed out his already broad chest, running a hand over it as if to smooth down a shirt he wasn't wearing. "You think so?" he asked. "Does the look appeal to you?"

"Appeal to me?" she whispered. Was he teasing her now? "Like an *ancient* warrior," she clarified, more to test his reaction than to insult him.

He didn't bat an eyelash. "I'm thirty-five. That's not old."

He was toying with her, the way a cat toyed with a mouse just before he ate it. Grace slowly inched her way further across the bed and caught her lip between her teeth to keep it from trembling. If she didn't know better, she would think she was the one who had traveled eight hundred years through time—backward.

Grace couldn't get Michael's story out of her head. Her

stomach churned, and she felt dizzy in an Alice-in-Wonderland sort of way.

"Where . . . where did you get that sword?" she asked, slowly heading for the opposite side of the bed.

Her feet got caught up in the blankets, and she lost her balance. Grey was on her before she finished falling, covering her with his body, his sword now resting beside her head.

"It's been in my family for generations," he told her, continuing their conversation as if nothing had changed. "Would you like for me to straighten your blouse for you?"

She blinked at him. "N-no," she said in a whisper, unable to look away from his amused eyes. He was laughing at her, enjoying her state of confusion.

She didn't know which confused her more, what she was seeing or what she was feeling. He was acting like a throwback to an era long dead, yet she loved the feel of his body covering hers.

It felt natural. Right. And so very confusing.

He brushed the hair back from her forehead and kissed her there. "If you don't get up now, I'm going to finish what we started," he said, ignoring the fact that he had to move first, since he was on top of her.

Not that Grace wanted to move. She wanted to lose herself with this man, until all her problems ceased to exist and the old priest died so she wouldn't have to face him ever again. She wanted to stay in bed with Greylen MacKeage until the rain stopped falling, the ice melted, and Jonathan Stanhope went home.

She also wanted to ask Grey a very important question.

But she just didn't have the nerve, or the courage, to deal with his answer if that answer was yes—yes, he had been one of the men in Michael's storm four years ago.

He suddenly sighed and laid his forehead on hers.

"Now what's the matter, lass? You're looking as if the weight of the world just dropped on your shoulders. Are ya embarrassed?"

Grace quickly grabbed the excuse he gave her. "Yes," she blatantly lied. "Father Daar's going to have me kneeling in a corner for nine days."

"Nay," he growled through a chuckle. "I have some influence with the old priest. I'll not let him set a nine-day penance for ya." He leaned back and grinned at her. "Two days should be enough to make ya change your ways."

"Change my ways?"

"Aye," he said with a nod, his eyes twinkling with mischief. "You're a passionate woman, Grace Sutter, and I'm thinking ya need taming."

"By a priest?"

"Nay," he whispered, lowering his head. "By me, lass," he breathed into her mouth, covering her lips with his.

And quietly, slowly, the storm of passion returned. Grey trailed kisses down the column of her throat, and Grace tilted her head back to give him better access. One by one, he undid the buttons on her blouse, then slowly pushed back the cloth to expose her.

The warmth of his breath caressed her naked skin, followed closely by the heat of his mouth. Grace cupped his head and guided his exploration, whimpering when he found just the right spot and mewling when he moved to another.

"Yar skin is like cream," he said with appreciation, his tongue coaxing a shuddering response from her. "So soft. So supple," he continued between lavishing, savoring licks that slowly trailed down from her chest to her stomach. "And so very responsive," he finished, nipping her lightly where her skin stopped and her pants began.

Her head thrown back on a pleasured moan, Grace felt

her pants being unsnapped just before Grey's mouth continued its journey. As his head moved lower, her hips were exposed, and then she felt her pants slide off and heard them fall to the floor.

Warm fingers, feeling like fairy kisses, trailed up her legs and came to rest on the downy-soft hair at the juncture of her thighs. Grace sat up, reaching to cup his face, and Grey moved back to her, sealing their lips in a searing kiss.

His hand, however, remained behind and continued to drive her to distraction with incredibly gentle but maddening caresses.

Grace lifted her hips as she pushed at the waistband of his pants. But he would not be distracted. Or hurried. In fact, it was as if time stood still for them. The world receded. Colors faded, blending into a glow of brilliant white.

Only Grey remained in focus for her. The look of his eyes filled with passion was forever burned in her brain. With her own eyes closed, she could see him perfectly, feel what he was doing to her, and she prayed that he didn't stop.

His mouth started its journey down her body again, and Grace could only helplessly, and eagerly, anticipate where he would touch her next.

And then it came—that hot, wet, and most intimate kiss. Grace bucked against him, and he held her hips and used his tongue to send her over the edge.

She tightened, spiraling upward, keening her pleasure aloud. And then Grey was there, kissing her face, her neck, and finally settling back over her mouth. His hands cupped her breasts, his thumbs brushing across her sensitive nipples. He entered her slowly, pulling back and then pushing just a little bit deeper in an unhurried rhythm that sent her spiraling again.

His tongue made love to her mouth, and Grace could only cling to him as brilliant flashes went off in her head. She reached down and grabbed his hips, pulling him even more deeply inside her.

His hard, overheated body drove against her again and again, and Grace gloried in the strength of his response to her own pleasure. He reared up suddenly, deeply sheathed inside her, threw back his head, and let out a growl that echoed off the high ceiling.

Grace stroked his arms and shoulders and ran her hands over his chest. And when he lowered himself to his elbows and kissed her, she ran her fingers through his damp hair and savored the taste of their lingering passion.

"I'm thinking I can talk Daar into only one day," he whispered past a lazy smile, moving to lie beside her. "And if I find ya in my bed tonight, I might even talk him into letting me work out your penance."

Grace was too spent to rally a response. She was more inclined to cuddle against him and go to sleep. She yawned, rather loudly, wrapped her arm around his waist, and settled her head on his shoulder.

He shrugged, disturbing her contentment. "Hey. You have a ski lift to save," he reminded her. "And a boss to get rid of."

Grace lifted her head and tried to work up enough energy to glare at him. "They've both lasted this long, they can last a few more minutes. Or didn't you know that a woman needs cuddle time after, just as much as she needs foreplay?"

"Cuddle time?" He choked on a chuckle, relaxing back against the bed and gathering her tightly against him.

The sound of a child fussing came from the baby monitor by the side of the bed. Grace let out a groan and tried to sit up.

"I have to go to him," she said when Grey wouldn't let her.

He merely cocked his ear to the sounds of Baby demanding attention. "Wait," he said. "Somebody will get him."

It was Ian they heard coming into the room, talking to the child in a voice that was barely recognizable.

"Ah, wee one," Ian said with a sing-song lilt. "Are ya feeling abandoned? Come to your new uncle, little bairn," he continued.

Grace listened to the rustle of Baby being picked up.

"There now," Ian said. "You come with me. I'll fill that tiny belly of yours. And I'll change that uncomfortable nappy while we're at it."

Grace turned a horrified look on Grey as a thought struck her. What would Ian think of Baby if he knew who his father was?

As if he could read her mind, Grey slowly shook his head. "He'll never know, Grace. Unless you tell him, he will not know."

"What . . . what would he do?"

"To the babe?" he asked, leaning back in surprise. "Nothing. Ian's not a cruel man. But I would just as soon he not have that kind of weapon against MacBain."

"As you do? It was Ian's daughter who died, and your . . . your fiancée," she said, almost choking on the word. *Child-bride* would be more appropriate. She met his penetrating stare with a defiant lift of her chin.

"Ah, Grace," he finally said. "You're going to make me pay for that supposed sin for a long time, aren't you?"

She wiggled to see if he would let her up.

Surprisingly, he did. He climbed off the bed, leaving his sword lying beside her. Grace stood up, pulling the sheet with her, wrapping it around her like a cloak. She then took hold of the sword. She couldn't lift it, so she dragged it across the bed. And as she had guessed, once she stood it on the floor, her hands were even with her chin. It was as tall as she was.

"Well, you don't ever have to worry I'll use this on you," she said, using both hands to try to hold it up like a weapon.

"Wee blessings," he agreed, taking it from her just as she was about to drop it on her bare toes.

He hefted it with his right hand and held it up without the least bit of effort, saluting her by bringing it to his forehead and bowing.

"Your full accent is back," she said.

He placed the sword over the arms of the chair. "I'm comfortable with you, I guess." He shrugged his shoulders. "I need not guard my words."

Grace went weak in the knees. There wasn't another thing this man could have said that would have tugged at her heart strings more profoundly.

Grey was comfortable with her, like warm slippers on a cold winter night, like hot cocoa in front of a fire, like loafing in bed all day on Sunday reading the papers. She liked the thought of everyday life with Grey. If she overlooked the fact that the man had no electricity in his bedroom and that he acted more like a medieval warrior than a ski resort owner, she just might like to spend the rest of her days here at Gu Bràth.

Grace sat at the end of a large table loaded with enough food for ten men. At the moment, there were only five of them eating. Father Daar, bless her good luck, was off someplace, she hoped on only day two of his novena. She was still embarrassed about being discovered in bed with Grey and was in no hurry to face the man of the cloth any time soon.

Jonathan was conspicuously missing as well, and Grace guessed he had finally come to his senses and stopped beating his head against the brick wall the four MacKeages presented. Either that, or he had walked into the mountains on his own to look for her disks.

Baby was present, however. He was on his second trip around the table, being passed from man to man, entertaining them all with his new trick. It was becoming a contest to see who could get him to smile the most.

Ian was winning. The grumpy old sourpuss was making a complete fool of himself, rubbing Baby's chin with his beard and making funny cooing sounds.

As each man got Baby in turn, he gave his opinion on a name for the child. Each MacKeage had lectured her already, saying it was indecent to let the boy go so long without a proper name.

Callum wanted to call him Duncan, saying it was a noble, strong name for such a hearty lad.

Morgan thought Douglas was a finer name and that they could call him Dougie while he was young.

Ian thought she should call him Malcolm.

And Grey? Well, he had given her a cheeky grin and said he thought Satchel fit the boy pretty well.

Their little game reminded her that it was Mary's wish that Michael name his son. Yet Grace still did not know if the man was sane or not. And she was sitting at a table with the only people she could ask.

She was loath to bring up the subject, though. Her head ached from too little sleep, and she was in no hurry for the shouting to start again.

But the men all looked tired and weather-worn. It was possible they might not even be up to causing a scene. And their bellies were full. Grace remembered from having six older half brothers that a man with a full belly was usually more mellow. More pliable. And less inclined to argue.

"I was wondering," she started, reaching out to take Baby and settle him onto her lap, "if you gentlemen would answer a question that's been bothering me for some time."

"What would that be, lass?" Callum asked, just before he put a fork full of eggs in his mouth.

"I was wondering if you could set aside your prejudices just for a moment. I need your honest and *unbiased*," she emphasized for good measure, "opinion. I have a worry that Michael MacBain isn't quite . . . well, that he's not quite sane."

She ducked her head after her statement, prepared to weather another gale of shouting for mentioning Michael's name.

But it did not come. Several eyebrows rose in surprise, and then all of them, Grey included, frowned at her.

"What do you mean, not quite sane?" Ian asked, curious despite his darkening expression.

"You know. Not right in the head. Given to delusions. Has he ever had an accident that you know of? Or been caught in a thunderstorm? Did something happen to Michael four years ago that would make him think he traveled through time?"

Every fork in every hand fell to the table, clattering with a loudness that echoed like gunfire in the sudden silence of the room. Every face looking at her suddenly paled.

Grace was beginning to suspect the worst. Father Daar had said he couldn't confide in her because he was bound by his position not to tell what he knew. And now every MacKeage at the table looked guilty as hell.

"You beat him up, didn't you?" she accused, pointing

her fork at them. "Four years ago, you had a confrontation and put Michael in a coma."

"What are you blathering about, woman?" Callum asked, his voice hoarse with disbelief. "You're accusing *us* of assaulting MacBain?"

"Well, something happened four years ago. Michael told Mary and then me that he'd traveled here eight hundred years from the past. That he'd been in a fight when a terrible storm appeared. And he'd been consumed by a bright light and woke up in modern time."

"He said that?" Morgan whispered, his face turning slightly green. "To Mary? And you?"

Why were they all acting as if she had just told them ghosts were sitting on their shoulders? Grace looked up the length of the table at Grey. He was sitting stone still, his features drawn, his evergreen eyes unreadable.

She looked down and picked up Baby's pacifier and stuck it in his mouth. Great. Another dead end. And that left only Michael MacBain himself. She was going to have to confront him again and not let up until she understood what had happened.

"You will not," Grey said from the head of the table. "You stay the hell away from him."

She hadn't realized she'd spoken her decision aloud. Grace looked up, making sure he could read in *her* eyes everything she was thinking.

"I want to know the truth."

Callum, Morgan, and Ian turned and looked at Grey.

"It's unimportant," he said. "MacBain's sanity is not the issue."

"Tell me, lass," Ian interjected, looking back at her. "Was this why Mary went to Virginia?"

"Yes."

"But she was coming back?" he asked.

"Yes."

"Does that not answer your question, then?" Ian said. "Your sister must have thought him right in the head. And may I ask what difference it makes? Mary's dead, lass," he reminded her in a gentle voice, his eyes suddenly softening. "It's over."

"But it's still important to me," she argued. "I want to know the truth. Mary loved him, and I want to understand why he told her such a story."

"He's as sane as we are," Grey said then, standing up and walking to her end of the table. He took Baby from her and settled him against his chest. He reached down and turned her chin with his fingers, forcing her to meet his gaze.

"I'm sorry if that only makes things harder for you, Grace, but we will not lie to you. Michael MacBain is no more crazy than I am."

Chapter Eighteen

$\mathscr{G}$rey, Jonathan, and the MacKeages were standing in the ski-lift shed waiting for Grace to perform her magic on the heavy, ice-burdened gondola cable. And it looked to Grey as if it was about to snap at any minute.

Jonathan stood next to Grace, discussing stress loads, amps, volts, and dead shorts. Jonathan shook his head steadily, saying it didn't sound feasible. Grace nodded her head and said it should work. Her beautiful features were set in determined lines.

Ian stood between Grace and Jonathan, his head moving back and forth like a child's swing. He scratched his beard and frowned every time Jonathan said no and mimicked Grace when she nodded.

Callum was fueling up the two snowcats and keeping the generators fueled as well, and Morgan had taken Baby over to the hotel for Ellen Bigelow to watch. Ellen and half the town of Pine Creek, more likely. The kid was going to come back to them spoiled as hell and probably smiled to death.

Grey realized he'd barely dodged the swing of the sword back there in the dining room. He couldn't believe MacBain had been stupid enough to tell Mary Sutter what had happened four years ago.

And then the idiot had repeated the story to Grace.

Grey had decided that he'd go to his grave with his secret, and Mary's and Grace's reactions were exactly the reason why. Mary had fled to her sister in horror, and Grace had labeled Michael MacBain insane.

What other conclusion could anyone draw from such an outrageous story? If he hadn't actually lived it himself, he would have the same reaction as the Sutter women.

"I'm not an electrician or a lineman," he heard Grace say to Ian. "I'm only speculating here. If we create a dead short in that lift cable, then send enough amps through it, the ice should simply melt off."

"Or?" Ian said, giving her a crooked look.

Grace shrugged, tossing her hands up and letting them fall back against her sides. "Or it might blow up," she said, darting a look at Grey, then back at Ian. "I don't know."

"How do we put power to it?" Ian asked.

"An arc welder would be good, but I don't know if the one you have is powerful enough. There's almost two miles of thick cable. It could take days to build up the kind of energy we're talking about."

"Our generator is powerful," Ian suggested. "Would that work?"

"It would," Grace said, her brows knitted into a frown again. "Is it portable?"

"No. It's permanently wired into its own shed. There," Ian said, pointing toward the hotel.

"But there are wires running from it to here," she observed, looking at the lightbulb glaring over their heads. She frowned again. "We could convert it to two-twenty, but that might create another problem."

If the sigh he sent through the building was any indication, Ian was getting mighty tired of problems.

"And what would that be, lass?" he asked tiredly.

"We could burn down the shed."

The old warrior tore off his hat and threw it on the floor. "God's teeth! It might as well all burn if the cable snaps," he shouted in frustration. "Just quit talking about it and do the thing, lass."

Grey walked over to Grace, who was obviously reluctant to blow his business to hell. He took her by the shoulders from behind and whispered into her ear. "If it doesn't work, Grace, it doesn't matter. It's about to collapse on its own."

She leaned back against his chest and looked up into his eyes. "I made you a promise."

"Nay. You said only that you would try, and that's all I'm asking now."

"The generator might blow up, too, and take half the hotel with it if a fire breaks out."

She looked so worried he wanted to kiss her. Didn't she realize that none of it mattered?

"They're only things, Grace. We'll make sure no one is in harm's way, and the rest can take care of itself."

"It'll take all day and half the night to make this thing work," Jonathan said. "What about my disks?"

"Callum can take you into the mountains in the snowcat," Grey told him. "He knows where the crash site is."

Jonathan turned his attention to Grace, apparently having learned she was easier to deal with. "You have to come back with me to Virginia the moment I get the disks," he said. "It's the only place I can keep you safe."

Grey waited, his hands still firm and steady on her shoulders, for Grace to decide which was more important to her, him or a satellite that held the key to future space exploration.

What he was asking of her was unfair, but it was also important. What she chose now would tell Grey if her heart was someplace out of this world or with him.

"I'm not going back, Jonathan," she said. "And Gu Bràth is the safest place I can be right now. Callum can get the disks, I'll work with Podly from here, and then you can hand-deliver it to AeroSaqii yourself."

Ian gave a shout of relief, clapped his hands, and rubbed them together. "That's a good lass."

"Grace," Jonathan said, staring at her, then darting a look over her shoulder at Grey. "Dammit, MacKeage. I'll rebuild your damn ski lift if it's destroyed. Grace's project is worth millions of dollars."

Grey heard only half of what Jonathan said. He was still reeling with relief that Grace had chosen him over her life's work. He spun her around and embraced her so fiercely he heard her squeak.

It was only then that the guilt set in.

What was he doing?

Eight hundred years ago this is how it would have been; the woman he'd chosen for his mate would suppress her dreams, her wishes, and her hopes—all for him.

Grey was ashamed of himself, considering the heated lecture he had given his men yesterday. He was being selfish, demanding that his hopes for the future take precedence over hers.

"Grace," he said, leaning back to see her face. "I—"

Morgan suddenly burst into the shed, nearly falling on the path of melting ice. "The Grange Hall is on fire," he said, out of breath. "And they're needing every able-bodied man they can get hold of to help put it out before it spreads to Hellman's store."

Grey let go of Grace and started giving orders. "Morgan, tell Callum to hook the large sled to the snowcat, bring it over to the hotel, and load it up with whatever men are available. Ian," he said, turning to him. "Find us some tools. Shovels, axes, whatever will help."

"But the lift," Ian said lamely, already moving to do as he was told.

"It will be here when we get back," he said, taking Grace by the hand and leading her toward the door. He stopped and looked back at Jonathan. "You're staying here, Stanhope. But know this. Just as soon as we get back, we're going to the crash site. Then you and your disks are getting the hell off my mountain. And you're leaving alone."

Once outside, Grey turned Grace to face him. "I want your promise to stay here," he said. "Ian will stay with you, and the two of you can work on the lift if you want."

He waited for her to nod before he continued. "Promise me you'll be watchful, Grace," he demanded, gripping her tightly to show he was deadly serious. "You'll be safe here as long as you keep close to Ian. I've already warned him about the men who may be after you."

She nodded again, and Grey pulled her into his embrace, rocking her back and forth like a child. "Did you mean it, lass? That you're really staying?"

"I meant it."

He leaned back. "What about your work?"

"This is the age of technology, MacKeage. With my computer and a good link-up, I can be thousands of miles away from anywhere and still be able to work. I'll free-lance." She glanced toward Gu Bràth, an impish spark lighting her eyes. "Do you think it will spoil the look of your castle if I put an antenna on the roof?"

With a laugh born of pure joy, Grey lifted Grace off her feet and set his mouth firmly over hers. She wrapped her arms around his neck and kissed him back, her own laughter sending a surge through his body that felt more like contentment than passion.

And Grey knew then why he was here.

Grace Sutter was the other half of his soul, and it had taken a storm and eight hundred years to find her.

And the real journey was only just beginning.

Chapter Nineteen

Working with Ian MacKeage was like being in a fourth-grade science class. The man had more questions than a ten-year-old. All he knew about electricity was that when he flipped a switch, a light came on or a motor started. Grace was careful to hide her amusement while she patiently answered Ian's questions.

"Electricity runs through a wire the same way a truck travels down a road," she told him as she stripped a foot of casing off the end of the wire she was holding. "The energy we're using runs only in one direction, then returns back to the circuit through another wire."

"It makes a loop?" Ian asked, squinting to see what she was doing.

"Yes. But the switch is what interrupts the electricity's journey, shutting it off. When you flip a switch, it allows the energy to travel, making the lightbulb glow."

"That makes sense," he said, nodding while he scratched at his beard. "So we're going to run electricity through this lift cable?"

Grace smiled at his quick reasoning. "Sort of. Remember that truck traveling down the road I spoke of?"

"I do."

"Well, if a bunch of trucks are traveling in only one direction and the first truck suddenly sees that the bridge is out and has to come to a screeching halt, what will happen?"

"An accident," he said, giving her a narrow-eyed look. "All the trucks will pile up behind the first truck and not be able to move anywhere."

"That's right. And that's what we're going to do with the lift cable. We're going to cause an energy accident by creating a dead short."

Grace bent the wire to make sure it didn't touch anything, then she began stripping the casing off the other strand of wire that was its twin.

"The energy will be diverted into the ground, where it will hit a dead end," she continued. "Only, instead of dented fenders, this accident will produce heat that will melt the ice."

Furiously scratching his beard now, Ian looked over at the ski-lift cable where it entered and exited the shed. Still narrow-eyed, he looked back at her.

"That cable isn't covered with plastic like this one is," he said, nodding toward the wire in her hand. "Does that mean if I touch it I'll get burned?"

Grace shook her head. "No. We're going to put low volts into the cable. We'll create the heat by pushing high amps through it instead."

Ian's harsh frown should have hurt his face.

Grace patted his arm. "It's complicated, Ian. Simply put, we're going to move energy through the cable very slowly and eventually stop it dead, causing an accident that will create heat."

Ian shook his head and shot her a crooked glare. "Ya said something earlier about causing a fire," he said gruffly.

Grace nodded. "We're going to convert this line to two-twenty in order to get the amps we need. And that can be dangerous. The plastic casing could melt and start a fire."

Or the generator could blow up, but Grace was not willing to voice that possibility aloud. "Jonathan should have been back by now," she said instead, glancing out the shed door toward the end of the hotel where the generator was. "It doesn't take that long to splice a couple of wires."

Ian walked to the door and looked out. "Maybe the bastard's gone to look for those disks by himself," he said, turning to smile at Grace, looking for all the world as if he hoped Jonathan had. "And I wouldn't cry none if he gets lost and freezes to death."

Grace ignored Ian's gruesome hope and carried the wire she'd prepared over to the lift cable. She studied the entire system, trying to decide the best—and safest—way to create her dead short. She needed for this to work without involving herself in the accident.

Grace rubbed her throbbing forehead. Lord, she was starting to think in terms of trucks and accidents, not scientific equations. Either she'd been away from her lab too long, or her mind was not on her work because it was focused on Grey.

She was worried about him. Fighting a fire was dangerous. All sorts of complications could arise. Water heaters could blow up, glass could explode and come flying out, or the grange could collapse on top of them.

What a sheltered life she'd been leading these last fourteen years, locked away with her work, pushing numbers around until they fit into whatever puzzle she was building. How safe she had been. How self-consumed.

And how trivial compared with baby giggles and smiles, flint green eyes boring into her soul, kisses that made her heart melt, and waking up with a man of steel draped over her body. Now, that was danger. Risk. And the very fabric of existence that she intended to experience every day for the rest of her life.

"Are ya thinking it's going to blow up right now?" Ian asked from right beside her.

Grace looked over to find him also staring at the wire in her hand. She stood on tiptoe and quickly wrapped the naked wire around the cable.

"No. Nothing will happen yet," she assured him, taking the other piece of wire and wrapping it around the frame of the huge wheel anchored in concrete that turned the cable back up the mountain.

She darted a quick glance at Ian. "Have you ever been electrocuted?" she asked. "Touched a bare wire or been close to a lightning strike?"

He eyed her suspiciously. "What does lightning have to do with this?" he asked, waving at the lift.

Grace shrugged. "Nothing. You just wanted to know if touching this cable would burn you. And lightning bolts are shafts of electricity without the protection of wire casing. Lightning can kill a man, or sometimes it just knocks him senseless."

"I know that," he said, taking a step back. "Is that what we're doing?" he whispered, his face suddenly paling. "Are ya making lightning, lass?"

Grace turned away to hide her frown. "No," she said. "The voltage will be too low. Lightning strikes are much more powerful and impossible to predict."

He took another step back. "I . . . I'm thinking I should go have a look for that Jonathan fellow," he said. "To see if he needs my help."

He was out the door before she could protest. Grace moved to watch Ian's limping but sure-footed retreat toward the hotel. She absently looked down at her own feet, turning an ankle to see the spare set of creepers Ian had brought her and insisted she put on. What had she said to upset him? The man had all but run away, looking as if he had just seen a ghost.

Actually, Ian looked much the same way Michael had when he'd told her his story of traveling through time.

Grace turned back to her work, thinking about Ian's reaction and why she had felt compelled to bring up the subject of lightning in the first place.

Perhaps it was because she was unable to get Michael's story out of her head. He had been so sure of what had happened to him. So believable in the telling, the attention to detail, from the lack of buttons all the way to noticing the difference in calendars. Granted, she didn't know much about ancient Scottish warriors, but Greylen Mac-Keage owned a sword, Ian acted as if electricity were more magic than science, and all of them lived in a castle.

Four years, Michael had said. If for some phenomenal reason time travel was indeed possible, was four years long enough for medieval men to be assimilated into modern society?

Grace started to tremble at the realization of what she was thinking. It wasn't possible. She knew it wasn't possible. The scientist in her knew that no one had ever been able to prove that manipulation of the fourth dimension was possible.

But then again, neither had anyone been able to prove it *wasn't* possible.

A desperate shout suddenly came from the direction of the hotel, and Grace quickly ran to the door. She peered through the rain, saw movement just inside the generator shed, and started running toward it.

As she got closer, she could see more clearly that Ian was struggling with another man. Ian was holding the man's wrist over their heads. Then she saw that the other guy was holding a gun. As she approached the shed, Grace frantically scanned the area for a weapon—a stick or a shovel or anything other than her bare hands. She saw nothing and decided that if she could just get close enough, she could kick Ian's assailant in the shins with her ice creepers, which would distract him enough for Ian to overpower him.

But as she stepped into the shed, an arm came around her waist and lifted her off the ground. A hand covered her mouth at the same time, muffling her scream of surprise.

Chaos erupted as the small area filled with men, all of them scrambling in every direction. Grace flinched when a gunshot suddenly cracked through the shed, reverberating off the granite stones in deafening echoes. Grace screamed again into the hand over her mouth and lashed out with both feet as she watched Ian fall to the floor.

She was whirled around and slammed into the wall, the breath knocked out of her. Her assailant grabbed her hands, turned her to face him, and roughly wrapped duct tape around her wrists.

"Jesus Christ, Frank," the man who'd fought Ian said, wiping his mouth with the back of his hand. "You could have helped. The bastard is stronger than he looks," he added, kicking Ian, who lay crumpled on the floor.

Grace could see blood seeping from Ian's forehead and the corner of his mouth. She threw herself at him, but the man named Frank caught her and shoved her back against the wall. He roughly slapped a piece of duct tape over her mouth before she could protest. Grace kicked him as hard as she could in the shin.

With an angry curse, Frank drove his shoulder into her stomach and lifted her over his back. He turned, whirling her yet again, and Grace feared she would throw up and choke to death on her gag.

"Wayne, grab Stanhope, and let's get the hell out of here," Frank said, walking around the large generator in the middle of the shed and heading out the back door. "Tom, did you get that snowcat running? Where the hell is it?"

Grace lifted her head and saw Jonathan being hauled to his feet, bound and gagged. Jonathan's assailant, Wayne, picked him up by the shoulder and shoved him toward the woods in Grace's wake. The other man, Tom, held the gun that was still smoking from the heat of being fired.

Tom was the man who had shot Ian.

But Ian wasn't dead. She knew he wasn't. He had opened one eye just a slit and nodded his head slightly just before Frank had carried her out the back door.

Bless Ian. He knew he was no match for three men, two of whom had guns. He was playing possum and would go for help if he had to crawl to the hotel on his hands and knees.

Grace heard the snowcat's idling engine before she saw it. Frank had carried her a ways through the woods up the mountain behind the hotel. Tom had jogged ahead and was already waiting at the snowcat, holding the door open while Frank unceremoniously shoved her into the backseat. Jonathan came barreling in beside her and was shoved up against her. Wayne followed him inside and finished filling the backseat, crushing Grace against the far wall with enough force to make breathing through only her nose nearly impossible.

Frank sat on the passenger side, and Tom climbed into the driver's seat and sent the snowcat growling forward before his door was shut. Frank reached into his jacket, pulled out a map, and studied it.

Grace lifted her bound hands and carefully pulled the

duct tape off her mouth, working her jaw and running her tongue over her lips to feel for missing skin. She looked at Jonathan. He was staring at her over his own gag of duct tape, his left eye swollen nearly shut, his nose bleeding, and his one undamaged eye leaking tears as he fought for breath.

Grace gently worked the duct tape from his mouth. Wayne tried to push her hands away with the barrel of his gun, but Grace refused to let go of the tape and ended up ripping it from Jonathan's lips.

Grace batted at Wayne's hands when he tried to replace it. "He's suffocating," she hissed, glaring at Wayne.

"Leave them alone," Frank said. He turned in his seat and shot Grace a nasty grin. "You throw a mean kick," he said, rubbing his leg. "You as smart with computers and rockets as they say you are?"

Grace didn't know whether to nod or spit in his face, so she did neither. Frank's grin widened. "Just as long as you're smart enough to behave yourself, Ms. Sutter, we'll get along fine," he finished, turning back to study his map.

He squinted at the ski trail they were climbing. "According to the FAA, the crash site is on North Finger Ridge," he said to Tom, pointing to the left.

Grace looked out the fog-covered window beside her toward TarStone's summit. The rain had abated yet again, but the low-hanging clouds obscured the view of the peak. She turned and stared at Jonathan.

If Frank was headed for the crash site, that meant he knew about the disks. And that meant Jonathan had been in contact with either AeroSaqii or these men.

"What did you tell them?" she whispered to Jonathan.

He shook his head. "I was only trying to buy us some time, Grace," he rasped. "I told them we needed the disks to fix Podly's transmission and that they were up on the mountain. When we talked, Frank promised to give me some time."

"Yeah, well, time's up, Stanhope," Frank said, obviously hearing their conversation. He turned and looked back again. "This storm's not going away, and the roads out of Pine Creek are closed. I'm on a schedule and not giving you any more time."

"Then how are you planning to leave?" Grace asked. "What's the point of going after the disks if you're trapped here just like we are?"

He lifted the map for her to see. "Interconnected Trail System," he said in explanation. "According to this, there's a main ITS snowmobile trail leading down the south side of the mountain. We go get your disks, and then the snow-mobile trail takes us to Greenville. I've got men waiting there to take us to Bangor," he finished, turning back to face front.

"The trails will be blocked by fallen trees just like the roads are," Grace countered.

Frank shot her a glare over his shoulder. "Better hope not," he growled. "Or it'll be a long walk to Greenville if they are."

Grace fell silent and watched out the window beside her, ignoring Jonathan and the three men who didn't seem at all concerned that kidnaping was a federal crime. She wiggled her hands, putting pressure on the tape, attempting to loosen it before her fingers went completely numb.

She wasn't dressed to walk over the mountain, no more so than she had been four days ago. At least she had ice creepers this time, and the other men also wore creepers. But Jonathan didn't even have boots. He was wearing Virginia's version of winter shoes, and Grace knew they weren't waterproof and only lightly treaded. Jonathan would never make it off the mountain if they ended up walking.

But truth be told, Grace hoped the trails really were blocked. Time is what she needed now, time for Grey to come after her.

And he would. That wasn't even a question in her mind. Just as soon as Ian was able to get himself to the hotel, someone would go after Grey and Morgan and Callum and tell them what had happened. And then look out, Grace thought with a secret smile to herself. Superman would come to her rescue.

She only hoped he would bring a gun and not his sword.

Chapter Twenty

Grey adjusted his sword on his back as he crossed the bridge from Gu Bràth and headed toward the equipment garage. Morgan walked beside him, securing his own sword to his pack and slinging it over his shoulders. Morgan also carried a rifle.

"Dammit, Grey, I'm coming with you. The snowmobile will carry both of us," Morgan said. "Ian told us there were three men who took Grace."

"Three moderns," Grey clarified.

"Moderns with guns," Morgan countered, stopping just outside the open garage door. "I should be with you."

Grey shook his head as he worked his fingers into his gloves. "I can travel quicker by myself." He looked up at the mountain, then back at Morgan. "They stole one of our snowcats because the only way out of this valley is over West Shoulder Ridge. They'll head for the snowmobile trail once they retrieve Grace's disks from the crash site. And that's exactly where I want you and Callum to go now. Take the snowcat, and head directly for West Shoulder Pass."

Morgan held out the rifle he was carrying. "At least take this," he said, trying to hand it to Grey.

Grey turned without taking the gun and climbed onto the snowmobile. "I donna want it," he said, starting the engine. "I've no intention of getting into a gunfight with these men. Not with Grace in harm's way," he finished loudly over the growl of the snowmobile's powerful engine.

He gave the machine some gas and edged it out of the garage and onto the ice-covered snow. He stopped when he saw Callum and Ian coming from the hotel. Ian, his head wrapped in a bandage, was holding on to Callum's arm. He limped toward Grey like a man determined to help rescue the woman he'd let down.

Grey wiped the rain from his face with his glove. More than four hours had passed since Grace had been taken. It had taken only minutes for Ian to stagger to the hotel and explain what had happened, but it had taken John Bigelow nearly two hours to travel the six miles from TarStone Resort into Pine Creek to give Grey the news. More trees had fallen across the road, and John had somehow managed to walk the last mile without breaking his neck, to tell Grey that Grace and Jonathan had been kidnapped.

Grey turned his gaze back to TarStone Mountain. The only reason he wasn't out of his mind with worry was the fact that these men needed Grace for her knowledge.

They wouldn't harm her. Not intentionally. But all manner of problems could arise, this accursed storm being the greatest threat. If the snowcat broke down or became damaged or was unable to continue through the trail, Grace would find herself walking the mountain again, this time with men who would care little for her welfare if their own survival came into question.

"I'm going with ya," Ian hollered over the sound of the engine.

Grey shook his head. "You'll slow us down."

"I can drive the snowcat," Ian insisted, determined not to be left behind. "I failed in my duty to protect your woman," he said in a harsh whisper. "I ran like a worried child because Grace started talking about lightning. I'm sorry to ya, Laird MacKeage, that my cowardice caused our Grace to be in danger. And I'm wanting to right my mistake."

He stepped closer to the snowmobile, his hands clasped at his waist to cover their trembling. "The lass feels I'm mad at her for asking us to help MacBain," he continued, his voice shaking. "It's . . . it's important that she knows I'm not. Let me go with Callum and Morgan. I promise not to get in the way. If I do, ya can leave me up on the mountain."

Grey wiped at his face again and slowly took a settling breath. He could not leave his man behind. He looked at Ian and nodded, then turned his gaze to encompass Morgan and Callum.

"The four of us and Grace need only return," he growled, tension lacing his words with anger. "The others, including Stanhope, can rot on the mountain for all I care. No mercy," he finished, nodding curtly and then punching the throttle on the snowmobile.

Grey moved quickly up the mountain, turning the nimble machine onto the steeply rising ski slope to follow the tracks his stolen snowcat had made.

The men who had taken Grace had a four-hour lead over him, but that was their only advantage. Grey knew the mountain, and his snowmobile was quicker and easier to maneuver than the snowcat. He could travel around fallen trees, over stumps, and up steeper inclines.

Grey turned the snowmobile into the forest toward North Finger Ridge and the crash site, ducking low-hanging branches and ignoring the ice slapping his face. For the third time in only four days, Grey found himself repeating his litany of prayers that asked for God's intervention.

Grace was surprised at how the sight of the plane crash affected her. Memories rose unbidden—the screeching sound of ripping metal, the smell of fuel stinging her nose, the terror of tumbling through chaos, the sudden silence.

And the strange blue glow that had lingered in the air.

She remembered Grey's arms of steel holding her securely. His gentle breath bringing Baby back to life. And his passionate kiss.

Grace wiped the moisture away from the window of the snowcat to see better and stared at the silent, abandoned remains of the airplane. It was barely recognizable, completely entombed in ice. She watched as Frank and Tom walked around the wreckage, beams from their flashlights reflecting like gemstones over the ground.

It was completely dark now, late into the bleak and drizzling February night. It had taken them hours of rugged and haphazard travel to make it this far, and Grace was worried that getting over West Shoulder Pass was going to be impossible.

Frank had foolishly endangered them all. And if Grey didn't come after her soon, it looked as if she'd come full circle to die. She was back on the mountain, and for the second time in just four days, Greylen MacKeage was her only hope for survival.

Apparently unsuccessful in his hunt for the disks, Frank came striding back to the snowcat, opened the driver's door, and grabbed her roughly by the chin.

"Where are they?" he growled. "Where are the disks?"

Grace pulled her chin free and gave him a negligent shrug. "I don't know exactly," she said, too tired to enter a battle of wills. "I remember taking them out of my bag when I was sitting just outside the plane. They may have slipped under the fuselage."

Frank plodded back to the plane without bothering to close the door, which caused the interior light of the snow-cat to stay on, making it impossible for Grace to see outside anymore. Grace looked over at Wayne sitting beside a defeated and possibly concussed Jonathan. Wayne lifted his gun slightly and gave her a warning glare.

Tom and Frank suddenly came striding back. Tom climbed into the driver's seat and reached down to connect two exposed wires, which he must have stripped earlier to hot-wire the snowcat.

"Wait," Frank said, still standing outside, his head turned away. "Listen," he commanded, waving a hand at Tom.

Tom opened his door and stood on the track, straining his head above the roof of the snowcat. Grace listened, too. All she could hear was the sound of the forest cracking under the strain of the ice.

"That's a snowmobile," Tom said. He ducked down and looked through the cab at Frank. "It's coming this way."

Frank climbed inside and slammed his door shut. Tom took his seat again and grabbed the wires, but he looked at Frank before he started the engine. Frank stared silently out the windshield.

"We keep going," Frank said finally. "We just need to get up on West Shoulder. I should be able to get a signal from there to call Greenville. I'll have our men come in by snowmobile and meet us on the trail."

Grace lifted her bound hands to her chest, attempting to keep her suddenly racing heart from exploding. Grey was coming after her on a snowmobile, and he was closing in on them.

"It sounded like only one sled," Tom said as he touched the wires together and started the engine. "And it was still far away. Sound travels funny in these mountains." He put the snowcat into gear and sent it rumbling away from the crash site. "If it's carrying two men, it will be traveling slow," he added.

Grace saw Frank's head turn toward Tom. "We're leaving a trail a blind man could follow," he growled. He reached inside his jacket and held up a small black case under the beam of his flashlight. "These your disks?" he asked, turning to see her answer.

Grace nodded. Frank tucked the case back in his jacket, then reached into another pocket and pulled out a small, strange-looking radio. He turned it on and scanned the face for a signal, holding it up and extending the antenna.

The red light suddenly turned green, and Frank immediately depressed the talk button. He spoke into the transmitter and was quickly rewarded with a faint but distinct voice from Greenville.

Frank and the mystery voice conversed for several minutes before Frank shut off the radio and picked up his map again.

"What about the snowmobile?" Tom asked. "You want to drop Wayne off and let him take care of the problem?"

Grace held her breath waiting for Frank's answer. Grey would be an easy target for Wayne.

"Not yet," Frank said. "We're almost there. We'll make our stand at the trail while we wait for the others."

Grace started breathing again.

Frank suddenly chuckled. "Not that anyone from this boondock town will be much of a challenge." He twisted in his seat to look back at her, his face an abstract of sinister lines and shadows in the beam of his light. "You got a local sheriff in Pine Creek, sweet buns?" he asked. "One with more brawn than brains?"

"No," Grace answered calmly. "But we occasionally get a visit from Superman."

Grey stopped his snowmobile several hundred yards down from the crash site and walked the rest of the way. He circled first, making sure no one was waiting to surprise him, then finally approached the plane. He dug his flashlight out of his pocket and shone it over the ground. It was pitch-black now, with the moon hidden by cloud cover and fog, and without the light he couldn't see his hand in front of his face.

What the light did show him were tracks, two distinct sets of creeper-covered boots that had churned up the ice and kicked it away from the gaping hole in the fuselage. Grey noticed where someone had dug a burrow under the plane, and he guessed that Grace's missing disks had slipped under it four days ago.

He trailed his flashlight beam along the forest floor until he found where his stolen snowcat had stopped long enough for the engine heat to melt the ice. He sent the beam upward, letting the light follow the track the snowcat had made and decided that he was right. They were now headed toward West Shoulder Pass and would try to pick up the snowmobile trail on the other side.

Grey walked back to his own snowmobile, turned the machine northwest, straight toward the summit of Tar-Stone Mountain. He could make better time despite the steeper terrain and be over West Shoulder Pass before Grace and her kidnappers. Ian and Callum and Morgan were approaching the pass from the south and should have arrived there by now. Grey knew he was betting Grace's life on his gut instinct, but eight hundred years ago it was his gut that had most often kept him and his men alive. He'd been sure of very few things in these last four years, but tonight every drop of sweat pouring from his body screamed that he was right.

And his instinct would have been perfect if he had remembered the long, deep, high mountain pond carved into the southern slope of West Shoulder Pass.

Grace balked when Frank tried to pull her onto the frozen pond. It was still the dead of winter, but she knew these high ponds were usually spring-fed. The ice could be three feet thick in one place and two inches in another.

"Wait. It isn't safe," she said, finally getting him to stop. "There are springs."

"It will hold us on foot," Frank said.

He had taken the duct tape off her hands so walking wouldn't be so awkward, but his grip on her wrist was unbreakable. And his sense of urgency was palpable. He looked down the ridge at their back trail through the weak dawn light, then turned and glared at her. "And I'm not going back empty-handed," he finished, scanning the opposite shore.

"It won't do you any good if we all drown," she said, trying to reason with him. She used her free hand to tug on his sleeve and get his attention again. "The disks are all you really need. Your scientists can unscramble the transmission. Leave Jonathan and me here. You'll travel quicker without us."

Frank stared down at her, his eyes narrowed as he thought about her offer. He slowly smiled. "I'm getting an extra half million for you, sweet buns." He shrugged. "Make me an offer I can't refuse, and I'll think about it."

Frank started to pull her onto the ice then, but Jonathan, whom Tom was holding at gunpoint, finally spoke. "She has a five-week-old son, Frank. What if you take the disks to AeroSaqii and I pay you for Grace?"

Frank turned to face Jonathan. "How much?"

Jonathan straightened and stepped forward. "One million," he said.

Frank laughed. "How about two?"

Jonathan paled but nodded. "Two," he agreed. He reached out for Grace's hand, but Frank pulled her away.

"No. You're both going with us," he said. "We get off this mountain and back to civilization, then we work out the details. You get the money, Stanhope, and then I'll turn Grace over."

That decided, Frank pulled her forward again, ignoring her now frantic struggles. "We'll go with you," Grace said, "but at least go around. It's not safe to walk across the pond."

"There they are," Frank said, not paying attention to her. "I can see the snowmobiles."

Grace squinted through the increasing daylight and scanned the opposite shore. A good quarter-mile away she could just make out three snowmobiles with sleds attached to them, parked on the edge of the forest by the pond. But she didn't see anyone standing beside them.

Grace sat down. Frank wouldn't shoot her; she was worth too much money to him. He skidded to a halt and nearly fell backward because he wouldn't let go of her wrist.

"Dammit. Get up."

"No."

He pulled a gun from his pocket and set the barrel in front of her nose.

She sneered at him. "Two million bucks, Frank."

"Dammit to hell." He shoved his gun in his pocket and grabbed her by both arms, lifting her up and tossing her over his shoulder.

They made it almost to the middle of the pond before the ice cracked. Frank suddenly stilled, slowly setting

Grace on her feet and then moving several steps away. She immediately lay down on her back, hoping to distribute her weight over as large an area as she could.

"Shit," Jonathan whispered on an indrawn breath, also stilling at the realization they'd overtaxed the ice.

Tom, still holding his gun trained on Jonathan, moved several steps away, his eyes wide with terror. Wayne, who had run ahead only a few yards, also stopped and whirled to face them, then suddenly started inching his way backward to the opposite shore.

Grace turned and looked back in the direction they'd come from. Where was Grey? He was not being a very good Superman. She caught sight of a movement just off to the right about a hundred yards away. Father Daar stepped out of the woods and onto a boulder by the edge of the pond.

Grace blinked. Twice. It was the priest, all right, but he wasn't wearing his usual black wool cassock. He was dressed in a long, billowing green robe, and his crooked cherrywood cane was now taller than he was.

Where had he come from?

"You lie still, girl," the priest said to her, his voice carrying over the surface of the pond with gentle strength. "Don't you move so much as a muscle," he added, lifting his cane and pointing it at the five of them.

There was another sudden pop, sending a wave of vibrations through the ice. The entire pond shook. Grace snapped her head around and saw Wayne inching his way to shore. "Stand still," she said, spreading her arms and legs wider.

"Holy shit," Frank said, backing up another step.

"Hold still!" Jonathan hissed at him.

"Grace!"

Grace lifted her head at the sound of her name being

bellowed with a force that vibrated the air around them. It had come from someplace past her feet. She squinted through the drizzle and saw Grey, a good two hundred yards further down the shore from Father Daar, step onto the ice.

"Go back!" she yelled at him. "You're going to drown us!"

Grey wasn't paying attention to her, though. He was pointing his sword at Daar.

His sword? Superman hadn't brought a sensible weapon to fight off the villains; the man was charging to the rescue with an antique sword. Grace didn't know whether to scream or cry.

"Back off, old man," Grey shouted, walking over the ice toward Father Daar. "Don't do it."

The priest either couldn't hear him or didn't care. Daar chanted loudly, his eyes closed and his stick pointed at Grace and the four men with her.

The mantle of ice under her back suddenly shuddered, and Grace watched in horror as Grey fell into the freezing water. He disappeared for a few seconds before he shot back to the surface and stood in water only as deep as his waist. The ice beneath her rippled again in undulating shock waves, and Grace took a large gulp of air and held her breath, gritting her teeth to prepare for a dunking that didn't come. Miraculously, the ice beneath her held.

She looked back at Grey. He just stood there as if he couldn't feel the freezing water, staring at the priest, his sword raised as if he intended to throw it like a lance.

The heavy, humid air around them suddenly crackled with electricity, humming so sharply it hurt her ears. The sky began to sparkle with such brilliance Grace had to cover her eyes with her hand. Lightning snapped over the surface of the pond, sending tingles of awareness through Grace's body that stopped just short of being painful.

Grace peeked through her fingers at Grey. He was frantically breaking the ice with the hilt of his sword while shouting something at Daar in a language she didn't recognize.

"No!" she heard him yell as he climbed onto land and began running again, ignoring the swirling, electrically charged air that surrounded the priest. Grey swung his sword in a long, sweeping arc and sliced Daar's stick cleanly in half.

If she lived to be a hundred, Grace would never be able to explain what happened next.

Daar's stick, now two distinct pieces, floated in the air as if held up by strings. The two pieces of wood twisted and twitched, bolts of lightning shooting from them in every direction. Sparks rained through the air like fireworks, spraying upward and out in flashes of sizzling white energy.

A stream of brilliant blue light suddenly appeared from the clouds over TarStone, capturing one of the sticks as it danced in the air. Grace watched, fascinated, as that stick vibrated the merest of seconds, then suddenly flew out over the pond and landed on her. She stared, unmoving, as it hummed with the resonance of a purring cat against her chest, enveloping her in crystal-clear blue light.

The other stick fell back to the ground with a loud thud, striking a rock and shooting out a blast of laser-sharp energy toward the five of them that was so bright Grace was sure she would be blinded for life.

The percussion of the explosion beside her finished the job of shattering the ice they were lying on. She grabbed the stick on her chest as she fell into the freezing water.

Only it wasn't cold.

Or dark.

As the water closed in over her head and Grace sank

toward the bottom of the pond, the stick she clung to enveloped her in a warm blue light so bright it shone through her eyelids. Slowly, and without effort on her part, she rose back to the surface until her head was above water.

A pair of strong hands suddenly grabbed her and began pulling her through the water. She couldn't see or hear a thing. Spots danced in her eyes, and her ears still rang with dulled thunder from the explosion.

Grey had finally come to her rescue. She was going to let him know just how much his timing stank, just as soon as she came to terms with what had just happened.

Grace was lifted onto the shore. She looked over through the spots still flashing in her eyes to glare at Grey, only to find herself face to face with Michael MacBain.

Now, where had he come from?

And where was Grey?

Grace heard her name bellowed again, this time from the north end of the pond. She squinted and saw Grey making his way along the edge of the now open pond, his stride angry and determined, water dripping off his hair and shoulders—and that damn sword still in his hand.

She looked at Michael. "I—I think you should leave now."

But he wasn't paying her any attention. He was staring across the pond. Grace heard him whisper the word *drùidh* under his breath.

Drùidh? Wasn't that a wizard or something?

She looked in the same direction as Michael. Daar was now sitting on the rock he'd been standing on earlier, his hands dangling over his knees, his head shaking slowly back and forth as he stared out at the floating slabs of ice littering the pond.

"Wh-where's Jonathan? And the other men?" she asked in her own strangled voice.

"Gone," was all Michael said, unable to look away from Daar.

"G-gone where?"

He finally turned his haunted gray eyes on her. "Back to my time, I think," he murmured faintly, his face draining of color. In unison, they both looked back at the spot where Jonathan, Frank, Tom, and Wayne had been standing.

"Get away from her, MacBain," Grey said, now standing on a rock next to them, his sword pointed at Michael.

Grace let go of the stick and scrambled up to stand between Grey and Michael. The cold suddenly struck her like a violent slap to the face. She looked down and saw that the stick was humming quietly on the rock, still glowing with shimmering blue light. She reached down, picked it up, and clasped it to her chest. The cold retreated as fast as it had come.

"Move out of the way, Grace," Grey said, his stare never leaving Michael.

"He saved my life," she reminded him. "While you were busy attacking a priest, I might add," she said, if for no other reason than to get his mind off his obsessive anger at Michael.

Grey finally looked at her. "I saw him like that before, four years ago. I thought he was going to . . . that he was . . ."

"He was going to what?"

He shook his head, unable to explain his actions any better than she could.

"I want to go home now," she told him. "I want to see Baby."

Callum, Ian, and Morgan silently stepped out of the woods and moved to surround Grace and Michael. She pointed her stick at them threateningly. It wasn't a sword like the one Grey had, but she was ready to smack them with it if they so much as scowled at Michael.

"Be careful with that thing, girl!" Daar shouted from across the pond, where he stood wringing his hands. "Don't be pointing that at anyone!"

She stared at the stick in her hand. "Where—where's the other half?" she asked in a quivering whisper.

"It disintegrated when it . . . well, it's ash now, floating in the pond," Grey said, also staring at the stick in her hand.

"What in hell happened here?" Callum asked, having no clue of the danger the stick presented. "We saw lightning."

"It's a long story," Grey said, turning his gaze to her. "Will ya set that thing down, lass?" he asked, his voice coaxing and a little distraught.

She hugged it back to her chest. "It keeps me warm."

"Then at least don't point it at anyone, like the old man said." Grey looked at Morgan. "What happened to the men on the snowmobiles?" he asked, his voice now sounding more like the Superman he was supposed to be.

Morgan darted a look at her, then at Grey, and slowly shook his head. "They'll not be missed," was all he said, grinning a bit. "Nor will they ever be found."

Michael, who had been sitting on the rock with his arms wrapped around his knees, finally stood up. Grey raised his sword. Grace lifted her stick away from her chest, but she didn't quite dare point it at Grey.

"He didn't know anything about these men," she said, lifting her chin.

Michael agreed with her. "That's right," Michael said, moving to stand beside her. Grace guessed his pride wouldn't let him hide behind a woman.

"I heard their machine laboring toward the pass, and I hid at this end of the pond to see what they were doing," he explained, facing Grey. "I saw them leading Grace onto the ice against her will, and I was waiting to ambush them."

"Something you're fond of doing," Grey said in a low growl. "What are you doing up here?"

Grace saw Michael gaze out at the pond before he turned a narrowed look back on Grey. "There were men in town yesterday asking questions about where Grace's plane had crashed. I thought they might be from StarShip Spaceline, but something about them made me suspicious. I came up here to see what it was they seemed to be looking for."

Michael let out a tired sigh and wiped his wet hair back from his face. "I found nothing but the empty plane, but I remembered these men had been asking the store owner if he had maps of the snowmobile trails. So I decided to keep climbing up here to the trail to see what they were doing."

"Wait a minute," Grace piped up, staring wide-eyed at Michael. "You know the name of the company I work for?"

"Yes. StarShip Spaceline. Mary told me."

Grace's jaw dropped. She turned to face Michael. "You knew where I worked? And lived?"

"Yes."

"Well, you must have realized when Mary left that she would run to me. Why didn't you come after her? Or call?"

Michael looked down at her, his eyes pained. "And say what?" he asked, shaking his head. "Mary needed to come to terms with all of . . . all of this," he said, his voice trailing off to a whisper as he looked at the slabs of ice floating in the still churning water of the pond.

Grace hugged the stick back to her chest, wanting to

weep. This entire tragedy never should have happened. Mary shouldn't be dead. She should be here with Michael and Baby, living happily ever after.

She turned to Grey. "Will you take me home now? To Baby?"

Grey stared hard at Michael a bit longer, then slowly looked at her and nodded.

"You can take my snowmobile, MacBain," Grey said, still looking at her.

Grace turned to Michael and touched his arm before he could leave. "Ellen and John are at TarStone Resort," she told him. "Stop there first, and let them know you're okay. They're worried about you."

He nodded curtly and turned and walked away, brushing past Ian and Callum and Morgan without saying a word.

Grace sighed and turned to Ian, stepping to the edge of the rock she was standing on so she could touch his arm. "I'm glad you're okay," she whispered. "Thank you for coming to save me."

Ian's old face turned a dull red, and his gaze shot to her feet. "I didn't save ya, lass. I nearly got ya killed."

Grace reached out and enveloped him in a heartfelt hug, wrapping her arms around his shoulders, the stick in her hand touching his back.

Ian jumped as if she had pinched him, his eyes wide and incredulous as he stumbled away, staring at the stick in her hand. It wasn't glowing blue anymore, but it still hummed with gentle vibrations. Grace hugged it to her chest again and stepped back to look at Grey.

"I want to go home now," she repeated.

"Morgan," Grey said. "You and Callum get that damn priest and take him back to his cabin. Ian, bring the other snowcat around the pond and pick us up."

Without comment, the three MacKeages suddenly disappeared as silently as they had arrived.

"And what are my orders, Laird Greylen MacKeage?" Grace asked once they were alone, staring at his still angry posture, his wet freezing clothes, and the sword that looked so at home in his hand.

"You can lay yourself over my knee while I whale the living daylights out of you," he said, sitting on a rock and spreading his arms, his free hand pointing at his lap. "You scared ten years off my life, woman."

He didn't sound as if he was kidding. "I—I still have the stick," she said, holding it up for him to see.

He held up his sword. "I've cut it in half once already. Shall we see if I can do it again?"

She hugged it to her chest. "No. But if you set down that sword and stop threatening me, I'll let you touch it."

"Why would I want to touch that accursed thing?" he asked, looking incredulous and horrified.

"It's warm," she told him. "See? I'm not even shivering, and I'm half dry already. If you touch it, those icicles will melt off your hair."

He set his sword on the rock beside him and slowly held out his hand to her. Reluctantly, hoping she was doing the right thing, Grace carefully gave him the stick. The cold immediately assaulted her again.

Grey closed his fist around the burled cherrywood stick and stared, his eyes widening as he felt the hum of energy move through him. Grace smiled at his expression.

He suddenly swung it in an arc, slashing at the air as he would with his sword. He hefted it several times as if feeling its balance.

"It's not a toy," she scolded. "Remember Daar's warning. You're going to set these woods on fire or something. Give it back."

He stilled his hand and gave her an incredulous look. And then he slowly moved his arm back and put all of his strength behind his swing, arcing the stick down and then back up before releasing it to sail through the air and land in the center of the mountain pond.

"What did you do that for?" she said with a gasp, staring at the angry fizzle of steam that erupted on impact. Blue light shot from the center of the pond in a blinding thunderbolt of pure energy back toward the summit of TarStone Mountain, shaking the air with booming vibrations that echoed over the ridge.

"Why?" she asked in a whisper, gaping at Grey.

He grabbed her by the waist and pulled her down against his chest, holding her so that her eyes were level with his. "Because I don't intend for that priest ever to get his hands on it again," he said, just before covering her mouth with his own.

Grace wrapped her arms around his neck and kissed him back. She'd lecture him on his lack of respect for other people's property later. And on his lack of timing when it came to rescuing her.

And on bringing his sword instead of a gun.

Grace quickly forgot all about being cold. There was enough heat coming from their kiss to melt the snow off TarStone.

Who needed a silly old stick, anyway?

Chapter Twenty-one

The ride down the mountain in the snowcat was made in silence, none of them willing to speak about what had happened at the pond. Ian was especially silent, concentrating instead on steering his machine through the sad-looking forest straining under a siege of ice that was now a good two inches thick. If it didn't look so devastating, it would be absolutely stunning.

Grace was softly crying. Not that she let the two men in front know that. She was curled up on the backseat, wrapped in a blanket, her face buried in her arms.

It was too much for her to comprehend: Daar's mysterious appearance, Jonathan's disappearance, the fireworks, the impossible aspect of it all.

The most distressing part was Michael's whispered speculation that those four men had been somehow transported backward through time.

Somehow the old man—*drùidh*, Michael had called him—and his long, crooked, glowing stick had conducted enough energy to breech the fourth dimension.

Just as Michael had seen four years ago.

Just as Grey also admitted seeing before, and the reason he had attacked the priest at the pond.

But all of that, no matter how unexplainable, was nothing compared with the realization that if Michael MacBain was crazy, then so were Grey and Callum and Morgan and Ian and Father Daar.

And so was she.

Grace heard Grey tell Ian to drive directly to the hotel, and she scrubbed her face clean of tears and sat up.

They were back. She was safely off the mountain for the second time in four days, only this time Grace knew that the journey to keep her promise to Mary was over.

She saw the snowmobile Michael had used to come down the mountain parked in front of the lobby entrance. Before the snowcat was shut off, and before she had to face Grey again and he realized her intent, Grace jumped out of the snowcat and ran toward the lobby doors.

Ellen and John and Michael were there, just stepping outside under the carport that protected the entryway from the weather. Baby was in Ellen's arms. Grace walked up and plucked the child from Ellen and hugged him to her chest, kissing every inch of his sweet-smelling face.

"Oh, you feel so good," she whispered to Baby. "Give me a smile."

He did better than that. He giggled out loud, shivering from the kisses she'd given him. Grace hugged him tighter for several heart-pounding seconds, then lifted her gaze to Michael MacBain, who was watching her silently.

Grey and Ian walked under the carport to get out of the relentless drizzle. Ian turned his back on Michael to look out over the resort. Morgan and Callum came out of the hotel and silently joined Ian.

"He's been such a good boy," Ellen said, tucking Baby's blanket up onto his shoulders as Grace held him. "Any time you need a sitter, Grace, you call me. It's been a pleasure."

"I will. Thank you."

A low, rumbling moan suddenly trembled the ground beneath their feet, traveling toward them from the direction of TarStone Mountain. The moan slowly rose in pitch and volume until it sounded like the hum of a tuning fork moving closer.

"Dammit. The ski lift!" Grey shouted, grabbing Grace and pushing her and Baby to one of the carport pillars, wrapping himself around them in a protective embrace. Grace only had time to see Michael hug Ellen and John together and use his body to shield them from the direction of the lift before Grey pushed her face onto his chest, over Baby, and covered their heads with his arms.

A sudden detonation, like a sonic boom, shook the ground and rattled the windows of the hotel. Grace lifted her head just enough to see past Grey's shoulder. She watched, horrified, as the cable of the ski lift finally snapped and whipped angrily through the air, backlashing against the lift shed. The shed collapsed under the force of the blow.

The tower arms broke then, each one sounding like a succession of gunshots that trailed off in beating echoes up the mountain. Gondolas smashed to the ground in a hail of shattering ice and glass. Trees near the lift trail bowed and broke from the indiscriminate whip of the cable.

Grey moved to his right, protecting them from the spectacle. Grace squeezed Baby's ears between her chest and Grey's to protect him from the percussion of the unbelievably loud cannonade that rumbled on and on, slowly decreasing in volume as the destruction traveled up the mountain.

The sudden silence was almost as shocking as the noise had been. It was broken only by occasional thumps and cracks high up on TarStone. Grey stepped back and turned, looking into the mist toward the remains of his ski lift, his expression awed.

It came then, the sound Grace had been waiting for and dreading. High up, far out of sight, the thunder of the summit house collapsing slowly rumbled back down the mountain toward them. The top tower had snapped under the strain of two miles of cable breaking free, and everything in the cable's path was destroyed. All that was left were naked towers, still vibrating with an energy that had finally stripped them clean of the ice entombing them.

"Holy Mother of God," Ian whispered, his eyes huge and his face pale.

And that, Grace thought as she looked down to check on Baby, was about all that needed saying.

She noticed a drop of water on Baby's hat and wiped it away. Another one immediately replaced it. She wiped it away also. A large finger suddenly lifted her chin, and a warm thumb brushed across her damp cheek. She looked up through blurry eyes at Grey.

"It's only metal and cable, Grace. Don't weep for the loss of something as unimportant as a ski lift."

"I promised to save it for you."

"Nay, lass. You promised only to try. And you were going to win. The destruction is on my shoulders, Grace, not yours."

The people of Pine Creek came pouring out of the hotel then, milling around and staring at the destroyed ski lift. Michael stood with Ellen and John, one of his big hands on each of their shoulders. Grace didn't know if he was steadying them or holding himself up.

She wiped her eyes clean of tears and stared up at Grey. She took a deep, painful breath, steeling herself for what she was about to do. She cupped Baby's head with her hand, then stood on her tiptoes and kissed Grey on the chin. "I love you," she whispered just before she turned and walked away from him.

Every step she took hurt. Her breathing became labored. The blood rushing through her body pumped with the violence of an erupting volcano, and her vision narrowed until everything—the resort, the people standing in stunned silence, the stark remains of the chair lift— all of it faded into the background and ceased to exist.

Clutching Baby against her chest, Grace fought to keep herself focused on the man in front of her now, fought to keep herself from giving into the voice screaming in her head, telling her to run as fast and as far as she could before she opened her mouth and broke her own heart.

She stood there in front of Michael MacBain and fought back the tidal wave of emotion that threatened her courage as nothing else ever had.

"Michael," she said in a shuddering whisper, drawing his attention. He turned away from Ellen and John, his face showing concern for what he must have seen in her eyes.

"I'd . . . I'd like to introduce you to your son." She turned Baby to face him. "Mary gave birth to him just a day before she died. He's yours and Mary's, Michael," she told him, holding Baby out for him to take.

A myriad of emotions crossed Michael's face in rapid succession—confusion, disbelief, pain, and finally wonder—as he turned his gaze from her to the child she was handing to him.

He slowly, carefully, took Baby and held him up until they were face to face, staring into young eyes the mirror image of his own. Baby shot him a sudden, spontaneous smile.

Michael looked stunned. He brought Baby to his chest and pulled off his cap and covered his head with his large hand, smoothing down the length of spiky, dark auburn hair. He looked back at Grace in silent question.

"He—he doesn't have a real name yet," she told him, wiping another tear from her cheek. "Mary said that was your duty."

Pain clouded his expression, and his hand trembled as he looked back at his son and ran one large finger over his face, much the same way Mary had done on her deathbed.

Both of Grace's eyes flooded then, and there was no stopping the flow of tears she finally allowed to run freely down her cheeks. She was shaking with the force of her mixed emotions.

"Sh-she said you would love him as no one else on this earth can," she continued hoarsely, determined to say her piece before she broke down completely. "I promised Mary I would bring him to you, and I have. Now I want your promise that you'll love him and raise him to manhood in a way Mary would want for her son."

"Aye," he said fiercely, nodding at her, then looking back at his child with a new glint of passion lighting his eyes. Baby shot him another smile, and Michael MacBain held the infant's cheek against his.

"Good," Grace said, a sob catching in her throat. She turned in the direction of the driveway and began walking home.

"Grace."

She stopped at the sound of Grey's voice and turned and lifted her chin, more to keep her tears from spilling down her face than to challenge him.

"Home is that way," Grey said, pointing toward Gu Bràth.

"Not today it isn't," she whispered. "Not yet."

She turned again, holding her breath as she once more began walking home. No one stopped her this time. No one said another word. Grace concentrated on setting one creeper-covered boot in front of the other, careful not to trip over her broken heart.

Chapter Twenty-two

Daar sat in front of the fire of his cozy little cabin and whittled on the new cherrywood cane. He carefully stripped the bark off it in long pieces of curling string, the aroma of cherry oil wafting pleasantly through the air. The young sapling felt awkward in his age-bent hands, its smooth, straight, unflawed surface hard to hold on to. It was much more delicate than his old cane and smaller. But then, it was meant for a much smaller hand.

This new staff would belong to a woman.

To Winter, Grey and Grace's seventh daughter.

He'd been dragging out this chore for too long, and now that his own staff was sitting in pieces at the bottom of the mountain pond, it was necessary that he begin carving and training this new one immediately.

It would have only one or two burls on it by the time he presented it to Winter, and she and it would grow old together once he placed it in her hands. He would train them both, and as Winter's power increased with knowledge, the staff would twist with burls and strengthen. It was the way things worked in his wizard's world.

Daar ran his hand along the smooth surface of newly exposed wood. He couldn't believe his warrior had had the audacity, or the foresight, to throw his staff into the pond. Grey knew the danger Daar's cane presented. He had seen its energy firsthand. Yes, Greylen MacKeage had known, when he'd held the remaining piece of that still humming wood in his hand, that he was holding the power to send him and his men back to their natural time.

And when he had banished it to the depths of that high mountain pond, Greylen had quite deliberately given up any chance that such a thing would ever happen.

Grey didn't bother to knock. He silently let himself into Grace's kitchen, kicking off his boots and setting his jacket and Mary's tin of ashes on the kitchen table. The house was eerily silent except for the occasional snap of a log on the fire in the living room and the faint sound of a sniffle every so often coming from the same room.

He walked sock-footed into the living room, and his heart fell down to his knees.

Grace was sitting cross-legged on the couch, a box of tissues beside her, another box's worth of used tissues balled up and thrown on the floor in front of the hearth. He watched as she sniffled, blew her nose, and threw another tissue at the fire. She was in so much pain, and for the life of him he didn't know how to help her.

She'd given up the child of her heart today. She had united a son with his father because it had been the right thing to do, and now she was paying the price.

Grey admired her strength. And he hurt for her now.

"Grace," he said softly, moving to stand in front of her.

She turned wide eyes to him, a gasp catching in her throat. Her face was freckled with pink blotches, and her swollen, red-rimmed eyes were devoid of life. He wanted to hold her in his arms and squeeze the pain right out of her.

She got down on her knees and started gathering the evidence of her grief, tossing all the balls of wet tissue into the fire.

Grey let her get used to the fact that he was there. He walked out to the attached shed and filled his arms with wood, then brought it inside and dumped it in the box by the hearth. He made two more trips before it was full, stopping the last time in the doorway to watch Grace silently.

She had come into the kitchen and put the kettle on to boil on the range, but he noticed she forgot to turn on the burner. He didn't correct her. He went back into the living room and dropped his load in the woodbox, then used the poker to resettle the logs on the fire.

Grey walked back into the kitchen and stood in the doorway, leaning against the frame. Grace was now sitting at the table, staring at the cookie tin in her hands as she fingered the dents on it.

"Do you know why Michael moved to Pine Creek last year?" she asked, not looking up.

"I hadn't given it much thought," he told her honestly.

"Because he needed to be near the only other people on earth who knew what he'd been through four years ago."

She looked up then, and Grey's breath caught in his throat at the sad and understanding look she gave him.

"It didn't matter if you were enemies or not. You and Callum and Morgan and Ian were all he had left."

So she now knew what he'd sworn never to tell her. She understood that Michael wasn't insane, because she was in love with a man from another time.

She probably couldn't comprehend what she had seen today, no more than any of them could. But she was smart enough to put things together, to realize that he lived in a castle and carried a sword for a reason.

This beautiful, intelligent, twenty-first-century woman knew he was ancient. And she had said, just before she'd given away the child of her heart, that she loved him.

"And so you gave MacBain his son so he wouldn't be alone anymore," he said.

"Yes," she said softly. "I kept my promise to Mary because my own selfishness was not an excuse to keep Baby." She ran her thumbs along the rim of the cookie tin as she stared sightlessly at it. "It wasn't my decision to make. It never was. Baby's mother wanted him with his father, and I have to respect that."

"Tell me how to fix it, Grace," he said, coming to crouch beside her. "Tell me how to help you now."

"Tell me you love me," Grace answered softly.

"Dammit, woman. I love you!" Grey stood and swept her into his arms, clutching her to his chest as he walked back to the living room. He sat down on the couch in front of the fire, settling Grace on his lap.

She looked at him while she thought about that, then laughed out loud as she swiped away more tears. "Of course I knew that," she said, waving his declaration away with her hand. She rolled her eyes. "I'd have to be an idiot not to. You've all but shouted it at me all week."

"When?" he snapped, disgruntled that she was so highly amused.

"Oh, let's see," she said, her tear-swollen face awash with a disarming smile. She held up one finger. "I believe your actions said so when you came back and pulled me out of the snow cave after the plane crash."

"I didn't love you then. I didn't even know you."

"Two," she said, ignoring his protest and holding up a second finger. "You stripped me naked and crawled into bed with me at Daar's cabin." She gave him a mischievous grin. "You had to love me then."

"That was lust."

"Three," she said, holding up another finger. "You had no intention of leaving the summit house until we made love the other day."

"That was lust, too."

She gave him a narrow-eyed glare.

"Continue," he said, squeezing her again. "When else did I say I loved you?"

She had to think for a minute, and that irked. He was just about to shake an answer out of her when she held up her fourth and fifth fingers and smiled sadly.

"Today. Twice. When you attacked Father Daar, worried that he was the real threat. Although I think he was trying to save me, not get me blown . . . blown someplace."

Grey wasn't ready to go there yet. "And when else?" he asked, giving her a more gentle squeeze.

She looked at him, her deep blue eyes rimmed with unshed tears again. "When you stood silently behind me and let me give Baby to Michael."

He smothered her against his chest so she couldn't see the moisture threatening to cloud his own vision. "I'm sorry for your hurt," he whispered into her hair. "I'd take it away if I could."

"I know," she said into his shirt, hugging him back.

He held her in silence for almost an hour, watching the fire consume the logs in the hearth. If he could only hold her long enough, he could lift some of the pain from her shoulders. He wanted to share it with her. He wanted to share everything with her for the rest of their lives.

The fire finally waned to a glowing bed of red coals. Grey tilted Grace's chin so he could see her face. A warm, sleepy-eyed, endearing smile greeted his gaze. She stretched against him and lifted her mouth to his, giving him a gentle kiss on the lips.

The fire that had been banked inside his own body suddenly roared to life. Lord, he wanted her madly. And Grey knew that when he was ninety, he would still want her with a fierceness that would astound him. He resettled her in his arms to kiss her back more easily—just as gently, just as endearingly—brushing his fingers through her hair as he stroked his hand over her hip.

"I want to feel you inside me again," she said as she looked up at him with eyes bright with desire. "Now. Here. Make love to me, Grey."

She ran her fingers under the hair at the back of his neck, fisted her hand in it, and forcibly pulled his mouth back down to hers. She made a sound at the moment of contact, a rich, husky purr of pure pleasure.

With a surge of molten energy humming through every muscle in his body, he stretched full length on the couch and settled Grace on top of him. She didn't let go of her grip throughout the entire process. She used her tongue to tease his mouth, slipping it inside with another mew of pleasure. She used her hands, awkwardly, creatively, and desperately, to drive him insane. And then she wiggled her hips more fully over his until he was shaking with need.

He had to slow her down. This was getting explosive. *He* was getting explosive. He wanted her beneath him now, to drive into her with the force of his passion.

Grace moved from his mouth to trail kisses over his chin, down his neck, to the base of his throat. Grey closed his eyes and locked his jaw. Two of the buttons on his shirt popped off and clattered against the walls in opposite directions.

She licked his nipple. He shouted then, nearly throwing them both off the couch. It was definitely time he took the lead, before he lost his control.

In one fluid motion he reversed their positions, tucking

her beneath him, trapping her fevered hands over her head. She stilled, blinking up at him.

Her face, puffed from hours of crying, was flushed with passion now and framed dark blue eyes swimming with lust. Her breathing was irregular. Her scent was alluring. He could still taste her, warm and delicious, on his mouth.

"Oh, God, Grey. Please don't stop," she pleaded, moving restlessly beneath him.

Trying to steady his own irregular breathing, Grey lowered his forehead to hers. "I'm not. I'm not stopping, lass. But you've got to slow down. You're burning me up, and I won't last long enough to get inside you."

She tilted her head back and lifted her lips, kissing him again, completely ignoring his petition for patience. He growled into her mouth and captured her lower lip in his teeth, relishing her indrawn breath of surprise.

The surprise didn't last long. She darted her tongue over his teeth and dug her nails into his back, pulling him even closer, firing his lust back into a bonfire.

He could see he was going to have to get sneaky if he wanted to survive this day. She wasn't listening to him; she was too far gone with passion. He untangled himself from her arms and lifted them over her head again so that he could lean back and give her his warmest smile.

"Hold your hands there a minute, lass," he told her, slowly releasing them to see if she obeyed.

Frustration and curiosity warred in her expression, but she did as he asked. "Good girl," he said, quickly undoing what buttons remained on his shirt. He pulled it off and tossed it on the floor, relishing the waft of air that ran over the sweat on his back, cooling him off enough to let him think straight again.

Grace's gaze widened, and her curiosity quickly turned to admiration as she stared at him with eyes as dark and as deep as Pine Lake in the midst of a storm. She stretched, purring like a cat about to devour a mouse, and folded her hands behind her head in contentment.

Well, this mouse intended to get in a few good licks of his own before he was eaten.

Grey made short work of his socks and his heavy belt, his hands automatically going next to the snap on his pants. He stopped suddenly, thinking better of it. Not yet. Not until he could trust himself.

Her lower lip came out when she realized he wasn't taking off any more clothes. Her hands came from behind her head, reaching for his chest.

"Oh, no," he said, grabbing her wrists again just as her nails lightly raked over his skin. He closed his eyes, clenched his teeth, and prayed for strength.

He was a ball of sweat now, actually shaking with the need to possess her. Lord, but he wanted to sink into the softness she was offering.

"You're next," he said, letting her go and quickly grabbing the hem of her sweater. He didn't know if she was squirming to help him or if she just couldn't lie still. He pulled the sweater over her head, at the same time lying over her again, bringing their chests together.

As soon as her face was exposed, he kissed her, capturing her gasp of pleasure. He continued to work the sweater up her arms—but not all the way off. Grace continued to kiss him demandingly, rubbing her pebble-hard nipples against his chest, wrapping her legs around him, and digging her heels into his thighs, using her tongue to lay a scent of her taste all through his mouth.

Sweat broke out on his forehead.

Blindly, and quite desperately now, Grey moved the body of her sweater over the arm of the couch, pushing until it locked firmly into place.

He lifted himself up on his elbows and brushed the hair from her face. "Do you remember what happened yesterday at the summit house?" he asked, his voice heavy with need.

Her eyes clouded with confusion and a bit of impatience. "We made love," she said in a husky voice, lifting her face to kiss him again.

He leaned further back and shook his head. "Nay, lass, we didn't. That was not lovemaking we shared. That was a claiming."

Her confusion grew, her face darkened.

"It wasn't even sex, Grace," he continued, after giving her a quick kiss on her nose. "When I broke through your maidenhead and then gave you my seed, I was claiming you as mine." And, he continued quickly when she started to speak, "when you gave yourself up to me and placed that red badge of your innocence on my thigh, you claimed me as yours."

She suddenly had nothing to say to him. He kissed her again, on the cheek this time, letting his mouth linger as he felt a shudder go through her.

"Tonight we make love, Grace," he said into her ear, keeping his cheek on hers. "This time you'll find your woman's pleasure."

Her entire body shivered beneath him, sending a ripple of electricity firing through his muscles, making the blood rush to his groin.

He began by kissing her forehead, her eyebrows, then her eyes as she closed them on a moan of pleasure. He worked his mouth in a path down her face, stopping at her lips for a deeper taste of her sweetness. He moved on to her chin, her throat, the base of her neck.

"Wait. My hands are caught," she said, tugging to lower her arms. "I can't get them out of my sleeves."

He looked up and gave her a feral grin. "Aye. You are caught, Grace. And you'll be staying caught," he said, grinning at her dumbfounded expression.

She tugged harder, her face getting red with outrage. "You did this on purpose?"

He nodded again. "Aye."

"Untie me."

He shook his head. "I'm sorry if you're offended, Grace. But honest to God, woman, I won't even get inside you if I feel your hands on me right now. Stop fighting," he said, continuing his mouth's journey down her body. "Stop thinking. Just feel what our bodies do to each other."

Her reply turned into a moan of surprise when his hands unclasped the front of her bra and he kissed the exposed skin between her breasts. He assaulted much more than her body then; he battered her senses with his lips, his hands, with words meant to inflame her heart. She forgot her fight for freedom, giving herself over to the passion he awakened on every inch of her body. He stripped off her pants, socks, and panties, slowly exposing her beauty, telling her just what he thought of her, what he wanted to do to her.

And then he backed up his words with action. Grey started where he'd left off, kissing her breasts again before moving further down her body, dipping his tongue into her feminine, dimpled belly button, raking his teeth lightly over her hipbone. She nearly bucked them both off the couch when he settled a kiss on the inside of her thigh, her gasp of excited wonder echoing through the silent house.

With his head lifted only enough to see the expression on her face, Grey kissed her more intimately then, his tongue darting out to caress her womanhood. She keened from deep in her throat, throwing her head back and arching her hips to meet his mouth, a shudder of pleasure raking her body, sending a hum of energy coursing through his own body.

Her thighs fiercely hugged his shoulders, her muscles slowly coiled, straining for release. He felt it then, her woman's pleasure, arching through her body in waves of rippling awareness.

She screamed his name.

Grey was shaking with impatient desire when he settled himself between her thighs and finally gave into his need to feel her wrapped around him.

"Now, Grace," he said, freeing her arms from her sweater. "Put your hands on me now. Touch me."

He needn't have asked. She was reaching up to him, pulling him down to her, lifting her hips to his. The wildfire in her eyes was burning out of control, every inch of her skin flushed with excitement. Now free, she touched him everywhere she could reach.

Grey moved into her until he filled her completely. She shouted again, bucking against him as she stared into his eyes and continued to repeat his name in husky whispers.

He felt her tighten around him, and then suddenly Grace convulsed in a second pattern of resonating pleasure. She triggered his own tidal wave, and with his gaze locked with hers, her name caught in his throat, Grey held Grace by the hips as he traveled over the edge with her into the world of passion fulfilled.

And he stayed there with her, suspended until he was empty of everything—except for one lingering thought.

He hadn't moved once he was inside her.

Grey collapsed on top of Grace with all the elegance of a beaten dog. He hadn't moved. Not even so much as one gentle stroke, one lengthy caress, one simple push of his hips. He had felt her heat, the ripple of her woman's pleasure, and he'd lost his grip on reality.

Like a lad on his first time out.

Grey lifted himself to his elbows and watched, fascinated, as Grace took in a sudden gasp of air and started coughing. Her movements nearly sent him sliding off her sweat-drenched body. He adjusted their positions so that Grace lay on top of him, so she could continue to breathe and he could continue to hold her.

"Don't ever do that again, MacKeage," she told him raggedly, her eyes closed and her head tucked up against his throat.

"Don't do what? Nearly crush you to death? Spill myself the moment I enter you? Or tie you down?"

"Yeah," she drowsily muttered into his chest. "Don't do that."

He lifted her head away from his shoulder to look at her, fearing she might fall asleep. "So are you ready to come home now?" he asked, brushing her hair back.

She suddenly scrambled off the couch as if he had pinched her. She blinked at him like an owl, until she realized she was beautifully naked. With a gasp she turned and bolted into the bedroom. Grey was left staring at the dying fire.

Now, what had he said? They'd established the fact that she loved him and that he loved her. What more was there? She belonged at Gu Bràth. In his bed. Preferably tonight.

He rubbed his forehead and blew out a tired sigh. He was never going to understand Grace Sutter. He looked back at the fire and suddenly smiled. He hoped not. That was half the fun of loving her.

Grey finally got up and found his own clothes. As he slowly dressed, he tried to think of an argument that would convince Grace she belonged at Gu Bràth. He added some kindling and a few logs to the nearly dead fire, then walked into the kitchen.

He found a now fully dressed Grace glaring at the cold kettle on the stove. She twisted the switch as if she were expecting a fight and looked surprised when the flame suddenly came on with a gentle whoosh.

"We're back to where we started yesterday," he said, leaning against the door frame. "You still don't have any electricity, running water, or sufficient heat. You'll be more comfortable at Gu Bràth."

"It's not decent. We're not married. I can't just move in with you." She looked at him from the corner of her eye. "I'd keep waking up in your bed, wouldn't I? And Father Daar would make me kneel in a corner someplace and say a novena for nine days straight."

"Then we'll get married tonight. The old priest can perform the ceremony." He took a deep breath and let it out slowly. "And you can invite MacBain and Baby, if it pleases you."

She straightened from watching the burner and gaped at him, so she didn't see the flame under the kettle go out. "You want us to get married tonight?"

He nodded. At Grace's horrified look, a thought suddenly struck him, and he pulled away from the door.

"You're not afraid, are you, Grace? Of us. Of Callum and Morgan and Ian and me?"

She continued to gape. "Afraid of what?"

"That we . . ." Damn. What to say? He didn't want to go where this conversation was heading. But it needed to be said. "That we came from another time," he said in a near shout, more because of his own anxiety than anger.

"You were never going to tell me, were you?"

He knew as soon as he said the words *another time* that he was bringing up a subject he wasn't ready to discuss.

"No," he told her truthfully, crossing his arms over his chest and glaring back. He was standing firm on this.

His honesty startled her. "Why not?"

"Because none of it matters. If I was born thirty-five or eight hundred and thirty-five years ago, it doesn't change who I am."

"You live in a castle, MacKeage. And you carry a sword."

"There are plenty of eccentrics running around in this world today. I could just be one of them for all anyone knows."

"But you're not."

He closed his eyes and wiped his face with his hands, then rubbed the back of his neck as he looked at her. Damn. Her lower lip was quivering again, and she was blinking her eyes as if to hold back tears.

He sighed and walked over to take hold of her shoulders. "Grace. I want you to use that intelligent brain of yours. Think, lass. Think hard about this from my perspective. If you were the one to have such a secret, would you be willing to chance losing what we've found together?"

She stared up into his eyes for the longest time. "You thought I would leave you if I knew."

"Mary ran from MacBain."

She stared at him again, her expression thoughtful. "You don't think much of me, do you?" she whispered.

He pulled her to his chest so forcefully he heard the wind rush out of her. He didn't care that he was probably squeezing her so hard she couldn't breathe. By God, he had to make her understand.

"I will not allow this to come between us," he growled into her hair. "You will not run away."

She muttered something against his chest just as her little fist suddenly poked him in the ribs with surprising force. He let her go and stepped back. He was expecting another scorching glare for manhandling her, but what he got was another thoughtful look instead.

"How many times have I given you my blind trust this last week?" she asked, resting her hands on his chest. "How often did I do as you asked, without question, and put my welfare in your hands?"

He closed his fingers over hers to stop her from drawing distracting circles on his chest. "That's different," he snapped, knowing where this was leading and not liking it. He could feel his hard-won resistance beginning to crumble, and he didn't like that, either.

"Blind trust, MacKeage," she said, her mouth curling into a grin. "I think I've earned it."

"It's a moot point. You already know."

"And I'm still here."

Aye. She was still here. And she had said that she loved him after the incident at the pond. And she had also just made love to him like a woman possessed. He smoothed down her hair with an unsteady hand, taking a calming breath as he pulled her, very gently this time, against him. She cuddled into his embrace and wrapped her arms around his waist.

"I don't suppose you've ever given anyone your trust before, have you?" she asked with a sigh against his chest. "It probably would have gotten you killed eight hundred years ago."

He was silent to that, surprised that she could even comprehend such a thing, much less be willing to accept it. He rubbed her back in slow, gentle circles, savoring the feel of her in his arms, her warmth, her smell, her softness.

"I trust you," he said, and realized that he did. It was a very liberating truth.

He especially trusted her to trust him, and that was probably the greatest gift two people could give each other. He set her away enough to look her in the eye. She was grinning like the village idiot.

"You're going to have to be patient with me, lass. I might forget sometimes that I trust you."

She patted his chest and left her hands there, drawing those distracting circles again. "I'll try and remember that the next time I'm tempted to brain you with your sword."

Grey decided it was time to get back to his original question. "So you don't have a problem with marrying an eight-hundred-year-old man?" he asked.

"I don't understand any of this," she said, digging her nails playfully into his chest. "But I will by the time we get married."

"And when will that be?" he asked, releasing the breath he'd unconsciously been holding.

"Summer Solstice."

He stepped back so fast he bumped into a chair. "That's four months away!"

"Do you know I have six brothers?" she asked softly, not even flinching at his shout.

"Six? I knew you and Mary had half brothers. Six?" he repeated. He wondered what kind of gauntlet he'd have to run to get their approvals. And where her questions were leading now.

She nodded. "Do you have any brothers or sisters?"

His gut tightened. "Just Morgan now," he told her.

Her mouth fell open. "Morgan is your brother?" she asked in a squeaky voice.

"My half brother. Different mothers."

Her mouth still hanging open, she shook her head at him. "You two don't act like brothers."

"That's because I'm his laird first, his brother last."

"I can't believe you're brothers," she kept repeating.

The woman was beginning to sound like a parrot, and

he was not getting any closer to getting her out of this house.

"Well, now you know. Let's go home, and you can scold Morgan for not telling you."

She snapped her mouth shut and crossed her arms under her breasts, pushing them up in a way that made Grey even more eager to get her into his bed tonight.

"We've known each other for six days," she said then, looking as if she was planted in place. "And all we've learned in that time is that we love each other. And also that we trust each other. But there's more. We need these next four months to learn the little things, the details, the simple things."

"And if you learn you don't like me?"

"That won't happen."

"I don't want to wait. We can spend the rest of our lives learning these details."

"I won't stop loving you, Greylen MacKeage. I promise, on the twentieth of June, at sunrise, I'll marry you."

He looked at the tin on the table, then back at her. "Grace," he said softly. "Your sister's funeral and your wedding day will be the same. That's not a memory you want to live with the rest of your life."

"It's not a funeral. It's a celebration of our love for Mary. There's nothing sad about it. It's a release of our sorrow," she told him, walking up and touching his arm again.

"It will be like having my sister at my wedding. You have no idea the great memories my family share of TarStone Mountain at sunrise on Summer Solstice. Every year that Mom and Dad were alive, we all went up there. All my brothers came home, and we had a huge birthday party on West Shoulder. We spent the entire day picnicking and playing and laughing. And that's what I want my wedding to be."

Grey covered her hand on his arm with his own hand. "It's a woman thing, isn't it, this wanting a nice wedding with everyone there?" he said, resigned to being a bachelor for four more months.

That sure as hell didn't mean he had to be celibate.

She nodded and leaned up and kissed his chin. "I'm not getting married without my brothers. They'll be here then. They already promised to come for Mary. You can fix your ski lift for the wedding, and we can all ride up to the top on it."

That reminded him. "Ah, about that," he said, taking her by the shoulders so she couldn't run away. "I think I promised the people of Pine Creek a little party." He shifted his weight to his other foot. "And I sort of had you in mind to plan the thing."

"Well," she said, thinking about that. "We could combine the two if you want. I was going to have to invite half the town anyway."

He closed his eyes and hugged her. "Thank you. I don't know what I was thinking when I mentioned having a grand opening."

"I do. You've discovered that you don't live in this town all alone, haven't you?"

"Aye. With the ice storm throwing us all together the way it has, it was like back in the old . . . well, it's nice."

She squeezed him hard. "Please don't let go of the 'old days.' I'm curious about what your life was like." She pulled away and smiled up at him. "And now we've got something to do for the next four months. I can ask you a million questions, and you can tell me everything. The time will go by before you know it."

She smoothed down the front of his shirt. "We'll have a real old-fashioned courtship, with us getting to know each other and going on dates." She gave him a mischievous, nasty grin, patting his chest. "And I might let you kiss me good night at my door and send me flowers the next day," she added, just to get even for his snide remark about the modern men she had dated.

"I'm not keeping my hands off you for four months," he told her, deciding he'd better set her straight right now.

And that he'd better get out of there before she came up with another hare-brained idea. He kissed her quickly on her lips and headed for the door.

She ran up and grabbed him by the back of the shirt, and he obligingly let her pull him around to face her. She gave him a stern look and actually pointed her finger at him.

"You will," she said to his declaration. "It's bad enough I won't be a virgin on my wedding night, as I always intended. I don't want to be pregnant as well."

"There are things we can do, lass, so that doesn't happen."

She waved that away. "Like we did just now?" she hissed through her teeth. "Three times we haven't used anything, because whenever our lips make contact, there isn't one single functioning brain cell between us. So it's pecks on the cheek when we say good night at the door," she said, poking him in the chest with her finger, "or I'll see you on Summer Solstice. I will not be pregnant when I get married."

Chapter Twenty-three

She was going to be four months pregnant when she got married, Father Daar told her. Grace hadn't been able to work up the nerve to visit the priest, so instead the old man had decided to come see her just seven days after their little adventure on the mountain. And the first things he'd asked when he walked through her door were how was she feeling and how was that babe in her belly coming along.

Grace had burst into tears.

Now she was sitting at the kitchen table across from him, going through her last box of tissues.

"Now, now, girl. It's not as bad as all that," he said, looking at her uncomfortably, the way most men did when they were around a crying woman. "Having the Mac-Keage's bairn is a wondrous thing."

"I don't want a baby. I haven't gotten over the last one yet."

And she hadn't. For two days she'd forced herself to stay away from Michael's home, giving him time to bond with his son. They had been the longest two days of her life, and she had spent both of them crying her eyes out. By the third day she couldn't stand it any longer and had knocked on the Bigelows' door at six in the morning.

Michael must have seen her from his upstairs window, because he came down with Baby in his arms and handed him to her without saying a word. He'd gone back to bed and left her alone to feed and change Baby and coax a few smiles out of him.

She'd been back another six times in the four days since. At each visit she'd used the excuse of bringing some of Baby's things over for him. She was down to only one pair of socks and a hat now, though, and she was thinking she'd have to bring the socks over one at a time, saying she'd found each in the crack of the couch or stuck in the hamper.

"I'm surprised you haven't been up to see me," Daar said, stirring his marshmallows around in his cup of hot cocoa.

Grace blew her nose and tossed the tissue at the wastepaper basket, missing it yet again. "You were waiting for me to visit you?" she asked, wrapping her hands around her own cup of cocoa, watching the marshmallows melt.

"I expected a person with your mind wouldn't have been able to stay away."

She looked up at him. "My mind?"

"You're a scientist, girl. Or have you forgotten that fact?"

"I haven't felt very scientific lately," she said with a sigh. "I've been running on the right side of my brain since I arrived in Pine Creek."

"It was a good and proper thing you did, Grace," he said tenderly, giving her a warm, sincere smile. "Mary's child belongs with his da."

"It doesn't feel very good."

"Time will help. And so will your new daughter."

Grace sat up a little straighter and fixed her gaze on

Daar's twinkling eyes. Her hand went to her belly. "My daughter?" she repeated.

"Aye," he said, nodding. "The first of many."

She eyed him with skeptical regard. "Exactly how many?"

"At least seven. After that, it's up to you," he said, shrugging his shoulders and taking a sip of his cocoa.

"Seven," she repeated, not caring that she sounded like a parrot. "Why seven?"

He lifted a brow at her as he set down his cup, a satisfied smile wrinkling his face even more. "Ahh. Your left brain emerges," he said.

The old priest pierced her with a crystal-clear blue gaze that looked as patient as the earth and far too perceptive for her liking. "Have you heard the tale, Grace, of the seventh son of the seventh son being gifted?"

She sat back in her chair, crossed her arms under her breasts, and stared at him. "Yes," she said, wondering where this conversation was headed. "I've heard it all my life. My dad was a seventh son, and I was supposed to be *his* seventh son. But I came out a girl. And so did Mary, which smartly put an end to that little fantasy for this family."

"No, it didn't. Your birth simply began the change in ownership of that gift."

She leaned forward, intrigued despite herself. "What are you saying?"

"I am the seventh son of a seventh son," he told her, turning his cup around as he watched the steam waft into the air. "And it's been written that there's going to be a change of the guard in the next millennium."

"Written where?"

He suddenly looked startled. And then he frowned and waved his hand in the air. "It's just written. I don't know where they keep the damn book."

"Who are they?"

"I don't know that, either, girl. That's not the point."

"Then what's the point?"

"Winter."

She stared at him.

"Your seventh daughter, Grace. Her name will be Winter, and she'll be my heir, the one I gift with the knowledge of life. She's going to be born on the Winter Solstice." He pointed toward her stomach. "All of them are, starting with this one."

Grace covered her belly again, sitting back in her chair, trying to comprehend what he was saying. And the more she thought, the more confused she grew.

She was going to have seven daughters.

And they'd all be born on the Winter Solstice.

And she was supposed to name her seventh daughter Winter.

So that she could become a . . . a wizard?

"Why?" she snapped.

"Because it's written," he snapped back.

Grace rolled her eyes and stood up. "You're drunk."

"I am not," he said, glaring at her. "If I am, then explain to me what happened at the pond last week."

"I can't," she whispered, sitting back down, shaking her head. "I've tried, but I can't."

"I must say, you're taking this a bit better than MacKeage did," he said then, picking up his cocoa and taking another sip, watching her over the rim of the cup.

"You *told* Grey this?" she choked out, grabbing the table with both hands for balance.

"Of course not. Not all of it. I just told him that he's here because of you."

"What?"

"He didn't act quite so surprised," he said with a

frown creasing his brow. "As a matter of fact, I think he already knew." He suddenly smiled. "He's a damn astute warrior."

"Okay," Grace said with waning patience. "Let's start over. Are you saying that you brought Grey eight hundred years forward in time because of me? So we could give you a daughter, whom you can gift with your . . . your knowledge?" she whispered, trying to comprehend the magnitude of what he was implying.

"You're pretty damn astute, too."

She had the good grace not to point out the fact that Daar was a priest and he was swearing. "Why?" she asked again, closing her eyes for fear of starting another round robin of foolish questions and even more foolish answers.

"I'm needing an heir, girl. And you and Grey are going to give her to me."

"I will not."

"That's what Grey said," he said, nodding his approval. He held up his hand to forestall her next question. "It's not what you think, Grace. I'm not wanting your baby. I don't know anything about the tiny creatures. Winter will come to me a grown woman in her seventies. Before that, she'll be a good, dutiful daughter to the both of you."

"No."

"You won't even be alive, Grace, when this happens."

"What if I don't have a seventh daughter? What if I have my tubes tied or take birth control?"

He looked horrified. "Ya can't."

"I can."

"Why would you be wanting to deny your own flesh and blood this gift?"

"What if she doesn't want this . . . this gift?"

"But she will."

"How do you even know that?"

"Because she's the product of the two of you." He rubbed his forehead and closed his eyes with a sigh of frustration. He finally looked back at her with steady, solemn eyes.

"Grace. Winter will be a wonderful woman. She'll be an inquisitive child, excited about the joys and mysteries of this world, much like yourself. Now, tell me truthfully," he said, laying his hand on the table, palm up, toward her. "If you could know even one-millionth of those mysteries, wouldn't you want to see them unlocked in your mind? Take my hand, Grace, and I'll give you a peek at what powers lie ahead for your daughter."

She stared at his long-fingered, age-bent hand. Oh, she wanted to touch it. She wanted a peek. Just one little peek.

Slowly, carefully, Grace laid her hand in his, palm down. A warm, tingling vibration traveled through her arm and into her head as Daar gently closed his fingers over hers.

Energy suddenly flashed in her mind's eye, and she was traveling at the speed of light through space—backward.

No. Wait. She wanted to go forward in time, not back. She wanted to see people living on Mars, flying to the moon and back again for vacation. And she wanted to see ion propulsion taking them there.

Instead, she saw emotions, not physical things. She could almost touch the pride of a mother when she held her new child for the very first time. She could see the excitement an infant felt when he discovered that smiling got him another smile in return, and maybe a kiss and a cuddle. She could see the sorrow of a mother not wanting to leave her new son in this world without the promise he'd be with his father. And she saw death as the beginning of something new.

She saw them as colors in her mind's eye, rather than

emotions—bright, vivid, detailed, and four-dimensional. They were energy turned into matter, traveling at a velocity that made them timeless. Constant, without beginning or end—just always present, everywhere.

Grace opened her eyes when Daar released her hand and sat back in his chair, staring at her. "She's still with you, Grace," he told her. "Mary's been your guardian since you were born, and she'll walk in your heart for the rest of your life."

She couldn't speak. She looked at the tin on the table beside them, then back at Daar.

"Give this gift to Winter, Grace. Allow your daughter the chance to fulfill her destiny. Give her life, and then let her come to me when she's ready."

"Will she want to come to you?"

"Yes."

Grace lowered her lashes, trying to decide if she believed him or not. The man was an ordained priest, for crying out loud. He might swear a bit, but surely he couldn't lie to her.

"Ask me something," he told her, as if he could read her thoughts. "Exercise that left brain of yours."

Grace decided to take him up on his offer. Or call his bluff. She had a million questions she wanted answered—about what exactly had happened at the pond, how Grey and the others had been able to travel through time, and why the priest couldn't have found her someone who wasn't eight hundred years old.

She decided to take things one step at a time and asked about something that had been worrying her all week. "What happened to Jonathan? And the other men? Are they dead?"

"No," he said, shaking his head. "But they are finding themselves in a bit of a mess." He suddenly chuckled.

"Don't worry about them, girl. With their modern knowledge, they're probably ruling some twelfth-century nation by now."

"When you pointed your stick at them, what were you intending?"

"It's a staff, girl, not a stick. And I was intending only to propel them into space for a quick little trip around the world, maybe drop them in the Sahara Desert for a vacation." He suddenly scowled. "MacKeage damn near did us all in."

"Can you tell me if ion propulsion works?" she asked, getting them off the subject of Grey's little indiscretion.

"No."

"No, it doesn't work, or no, you won't tell me?"

He shot her a warm grin. "It works, Grace. Eventually. As a matter of fact," he said, leaning toward her and whispering, "your fourth daughter will see that it does."

Grace covered her mouth with her hands. "She will?"

"But don't tell Grey," he said, still leaning forward and still whispering.

"Why?" she whispered past her hands.

"Because he's wanting a parcel of boys to rebuild his clan back to the greatness it once was. And it will go much easier on all of us if he doesn't realize he's not getting them until it's too late."

"You didn't tell Grey he was having daughters?"

"I'm old, girl, not stupid," he said, leaning back in his chair again, his voice overloud.

"So you had a talk with Grey? When?"

"The day after he threw my staff into the pond."

"I'm sorry he did that, Father," she said sincerely, wishing she could get her hands on it again herself.

"Not half as sorry as I am." He suddenly stood up. "It's getting late, and I've a long walk ahead of me."

"You're not walking all the way back to your cabin, are you?" she asked, standing also.

"Well, I can't get there any other way. Your husband saw to that right enough."

"He's not my husband yet."

He turned and looked at her. "Aye, Grace, he is. You just haven't realized that fact yet. You think you're needing a ceremony to make it legal. I do wish you'd stop with this foolishness, though, about not sleeping with the man. He's a veritable bear to be around."

Grace felt herself blush all the way down to her toes. She was standing in the middle of her kitchen with a priest, and he was all but telling her to have sex with Grey.

"It's not a sin, you know," he told her, looking somewhat perturbed. "You're married in all eyes but your own. But it is a sin against nature for a woman not to lie with her husband."

She wanted to melt into the floor from embarrassment. "You—you're from a time much earlier than Grey, aren't you?"

"Aye." He straightened his shoulders and puffed out his chest. "I'll be fourteen hundred and ninety-two come March."

She blinked at him. Good lord, the man was ancient.

"Well, this is the twenty-first century," she told him, just in case he hadn't realized that fact. "And women are good for more than warming a man's bed. And men are a bit more civilized about not demanding such things."

"I suppose they did away with spanking, too," he muttered just as he left, leaving Grace to stare at the open door of her kitchen that led out onto the porch. She walked over and slammed it shut behind the audacious old priest, and half a ton of ice came sliding down off the roof like thunder. Grace opened the door back up to see if she had just been condemned to hell for killing a priest.

He was standing in the middle of her driveway, glaring at her. She smiled and waved and closed the door again, softly this time. There were spots swimming in front of her eyes for a good two minutes from the brightness of the sunshine outside.

The ice storm had lasted nine days, and the ice was still melting off the trees. The electricity hadn't come back on yet, but she had seen the line trucks working their way up her road just this morning.

"Well, Mare," she said to the cookie tin as she went to clean up the cocoa cups. "I guess I should thank you for saving my life the other day up at the pond." She stopped her chore and picked up the tin, turning it around to face her. "It felt like you," she told her. "When I saw that warm blue light coming down from TarStone and into that stick, it was as if . . . as if I could feel *you* there. And suddenly I wasn't afraid."

She waited a bit longer this time before she put the tin back on the table, just in case Mary had something she wanted to say. The Oreo cookie tin suddenly hummed with warmth, and the air in the kitchen gently glowed with blue light. Grace stared around herself in awe, then clutched Mary's tin to her chest. Grey hadn't been lying. It was the tin she'd hugged in the snow cave. Mary had been saving her again.

Just as she had during the plane crash and after, while she'd waited for Grey to find out where they were. And in the snow cave, keeping her warm, keeping her alive until Grey returned. All this time . . . Mary had been with her, watching over her and Baby.

Patiently waiting for Grace to keep her promise.

Grace thought back to their childhood and all the times

Mary had pulled her out of messes she'd made from experiments her brothers kept bringing home to her. Like the time Mary had pulled her out of Pine Lake, when Grace had fallen in trying to reach her weather balloon, which had come crashing back to earth prematurely.

And all the nights Mary had climbed into bed with her because Grace had been overwrought. Like when the *Challenger* had blown up or whenever something had happened in the news that told her the world had lost another pioneering hero. Mary had been younger by three years, but she had been Grace's rock to cling to whenever the world overwhelmed her.

And Grace knew that Grey was her new rock. He'd proven himself more than once already to be a fine guardian angel, worthy of the name Superman most of the time.

All she had to do now was coax that sword away from him, get electricity wired to his bedroom, and convince him that daughters could be the future of his clan. Basically, all she had to do was take a not so modern man, polish the roughened edges of his ancient soul, and cover him with a more modern, more civilized veneer.

Chapter Twenty-four

The grand opening of TarStone Mountain Resort was slated to begin tomorrow at noon at the base of the mountain in the ski lodge. Tonight's gathering wasn't part of that celebration, although Grey thought there were still a hell of a lot of people present for a party that was supposed to be private.

They were camped out on the floor of the new summit house, despite the fact that there were no walls or roof yet. There was just a huge deck that they'd used to set several tents on and a mantle of stars for a roof.

It was eleven o'clock on Summer Solstice Eve, and his woman showed no signs of wanting to turn in and get some rest for the big day tomorrow. He didn't blame her, though. She was too busy laughing and crying and visiting with all six of her brothers.

Grey stood on the rocky summit of TarStone and leaned against the deck of the summit house, his arms crossed over his chest, Morgan and Callum and Ian beside him. They were watching Grace sitting next to the bonfire, catching up on the lives of her family.

"The woman's going to wear out her tongue," Ian said,

smiling at the seven Sutters. "She hasn't shut up since the first one arrived."

"I haven't seen her this happy since I met her," Callum added, also grinning at the picture before them. "She's actually glowing."

"She wasn't glowing yesterday," Morgan said. "Not when she found out her oldest brother's plane was delayed. What's his name?"

"I think she said Samuel was the oldest," Ian told him, scratching his beard. "He's the one with the crooked nose."

"You suppose he got that in a fight?" Callum asked.

"Could be," Morgan agreed, his esteem for the man obviously high. A broken nose was as good as a badge of honor in the warrior's eyes.

"None of them looks like Grace," Ian observed. "They're bigger and much rougher around the edges. And one of them, what was his name? Brian, I think she called him. He looks as if he eats babies for breakfast."

Grey noted the inflection of praise in Ian's voice for that possibility. "He lives in Alaska," he told Ian. "Brian works on an oil rig. It's a demanding job."

The four of them looked at the tall, boisterous, powerful-looking man Grace had introduced them to yesterday as Brian.

"Do ya think they noticed she's with child?" Callum asked. "None of them has mentioned it."

Grace was just starting to show. She had come to Grey frantic last week when her pants weren't fitting, wailing that her brothers were going to kill her—right after they killed him for getting her pregnant without a wedding first. He had refrained from laughing at her and had taken her shopping instead. She had bought pants with elastic waists and oversized sweaters and shirts.

He didn't know who she thought she was fooling. It wasn't her belly that showed she was pregnant, it was her face. Grace Sutter positively glowed with the promise of new life.

Grey thought back to his heated talk with Daar after their adventure at the lake. Grey had told Daar that he didn't care who he was or what he was doing messing with their lives, only that it stopped. There would be no more magical storms, no more interference, and no more talk of heirs not yet born.

Grey knew his decree had lasted all of six days, when the old priest had gone to Grace's for a visit. But he hadn't said anything to Daar because Grace's spirit had lifted after her talk with the old man.

She had actually come to Gu Bràth for a visit the next day, unsure at first of the welcome she'd get from Ian and the others. Grey had had another little talk with his men, about a father's right to have his son and a woman's courage to see that he did.

Ian had been contrite, and when Grace arrived, the old warrior had nearly tripped over himself promising he held no ill will to her for being somewhat related to MacBain. Ian and Grace had actually become fast friends since then, working together on building the new ski lift and planning the grand opening.

"Don't tell me you four big powerful men are afraid of my brothers," Grace said, all but skipping over to them.

"We're not wanting to intrude on your reunion," Ian said.

She waved that away with a smile and walked up to Grey. "They're asking about you," she told him, a mischievous twinkle in her eye. "They want to know about the man who dared make me break a promise."

"What promise?" he asked, thinking hard on what she

could be talking about. Near as he knew, she'd kept every damn promise, even the heartbreaking ones.

"The promise we browbeat her into making when she was twelve," Samuel Sutter said as he approached.

He wasn't smiling.

And his brothers were following him over.

"It's a known fact that Grace was saving herself for marriage," Paul Sutter interjected, now standing beside Samuel and frowning at Grace.

"It's cold over here," Grace said, grabbing Grey's hand and pulling him toward the fire. "Let's make some cocoa."

Grey let her lead him away, smiling at her glaring brothers as he walked past them. The six Sutter men turned in unison and followed, and the three MacKeages, not to be left out of what might possibly turn into a rousing fight, followed them.

As soon as they reached the fire, Grey sat down and pulled Grace onto his lap, ignoring her faint little gasp, wrapping his arms around her to trap her in place.

"Are you nuts?" she whispered to him, trying to wiggle free. "They're already mad that I'm pregnant. You're going to upset them more."

He tightened his hold on her and effectively stopped her struggles. "I'm Superman, remember?" he whispered back, pleased to feel her shiver sensuously against him when his breath teased her ear. "It'll take a bit more than these six to intimidate me, lass."

She turned a frown on him, and just because she looked so cute in the glow of firelight, he kissed her on the end of her nose.

"She actually told you she was saving herself for marriage?" Morgan asked, unable to comprehend a woman being so bold with her brothers.

"Well, she didn't exactly tell us," the youngest Sutter

brother said. Grey thought his name was Timmy. "We more or less wrung the promise from her."

"Did you make Mary give this same promise?" Callum asked.

Grey guessed Callum's esteem for the men had just gone up another notch. There wasn't a big brother alive who would not wish the same thing for his sister.

"We did," David Sutter said.

Morgan snorted. "Fat lot of good it did either of them. They both got pregnant."

The woman on his lap was getting restless, and Grey felt an ultimatum coming on in hopes to get them to change the subject.

They were saved when Michael MacBain appeared out of the darkness, walking up the moonlit trail from the resort.

"Michael," Grace said, jumping up to greet him.

Grey let her go. She ran to Michael and unzipped the pack he had on his chest, pulling little Robbie MacBain into her arms.

"Thank you so much for coming, Michael," she said, reaching up and kissing his cheek. She turned to her brothers, who were now standing again.

"This is Robbie, your nephew," she told them, walking over to the fire to show them the babe. "He's five months old next week. And he can already sit up by himself."

Five Sutter men crowded around to see Robbie, who was staring wide-eyed at all the faces staring at him. He clung to Grace's shirt with his fist, then suddenly turned and buried his face in her hair.

Samuel Sutter was not watching him but was looking at Michael MacBain instead.

"So you're the man who got our baby sister pregnant," Samuel said in a low, guttural voice.

The five other Sutter men turned to join their brother. With a snort of disbelief at what he was about to do, Grey found himself going over and standing beside Michael MacBain. Even more unbelievable was that Morgan and Callum and even Ian joined him, until the five men formed a united front against the six Sutter men.

Grace had to blink several times to believe what she was seeing. She had just been about to step in front of Michael to defend her sister's love for him to her brothers, but every one of the MacKeages was already doing it for her.

The fact that Ian was there warmed Grace's heart the most. She and Ian had run into Michael and Robbie in town one day a month ago, and when Ian had turned to leave, Michael had stopped him. Grace had held her breath, expecting a fight. But Michael had said, in a quiet, gentle voice, that he had something he wanted Ian to know. Stern-faced and rigid, the older man had waited with his hands balled into fists at his side.

"Maura didn't kill herself," Michael told him then. "We were running away to get married. She was coming to meet me when she wandered off the path and onto the rotten ice of the loc. It was an accident, Ian. And a tragedy that I have regretted all my life. I should have come to you and openly asked for her hand."

Ian had only stared at him then, stone-still and silent.

"I loved your daughter, old man," Michael had said, his hand lovingly supporting Robbie in the pack of his chest. "And I'm sorry for you. For both of us."

Michael had turned and walked away then, not looking back. As apologies between men went, Grace had thought that was about as good as it got. She had seen Ian's shoulders tremble slightly as Michael walked away. And so she had walked away, too, into the store to finish her shopping, leaving the still grieving father the privacy to come to terms with what he'd been told.

And now Ian was actually standing beside the man he had hated for seven long years, supporting him.

"If your question is did I love your sister," Michael said calmly to Samuel, "then yes, we had a child together. However, Robbie would have been born in wedlock had Mary lived."

That simple reminder that Mary was not here to defend herself seemed to take the anger right out of her oldest brother. Timmy, though, who was the youngest and had lived at home with Mary and Grace the longest, was still not willing to let Michael off so easily.

"The wedding usually comes before the pregnancy, not before the birth," he said, taking a step closer to Michael.

Grace rolled her eyes. They were all such *men*.

"Oh, look!" she exclaimed as excitedly as she could. "A falling star. Quick everyone, make a wish."

All eleven men turned and glared at her. "Watch," she said, pointing up at the heavens. "There'll be another one."

"Go to bed, Grace," Timmy said. "You've only got maybe five hours before sunrise."

"I can't sleep."

Samuel, who knew her well enough to know she was lying, walked over and took Robbie from her arms and pulled his little cap over his ears.

"Pregnant women can always sleep," he told her, having the experience of watching his wife bear five children to back up his words. He reached out and tapped the end of her nose. "We just want to have a little talk with your fiancé, sis. We'll try and keep it quiet."

"You leave Grey and Michael alone," she told him in a whisper. "They both love both your sisters."

"I know," he agreed, looking at Robbie with a warming smile. "Mary did well, didn't she? He's a cute little tyke."

Grace wasn't about to point out that his hat was hiding the fact that Robbie had big ears and uncontrollable hair that made him look like a troll. Besides, he was the most beautiful troll she had ever laid eyes on.

"I'm not going to bed until the rest of you do. I don't want you telling Grey about my childhood antics."

Samuel laughed out loud, shaking Robbie to the point that he laughed aloud, too, and clapped his hands. "That would take more than the rest of this night," Samuel said.

He took her by the shoulder and physically turned her toward the tents pitched on the summit house floor. He gave her a gentle shove to get her moving and then a stern pat on the rear to make sure she kept going.

She turned around and glared at him, rubbing her bum. "The next person to swat my backside," she said through clenched teeth, looking at Grey as she spoke, making sure he got her message, "had better learn to sleep with one eye open."

"I wouldn't dare do it any other way, lass," Grey said with a chuckle. "Now, go to bed, Grace. We promise not to roll your brothers off the mountain."

With one last skeptical look at the eleven of them, she finally gave into her fatigue and climbed into the small tent that Grey had set up for her.

He'd set up three more for her brothers, but that was all. She'd asked him where the other tents were, and Grey had laughed. He said they had never slept in a tent in their lives, not even in the rain. God provided all the shelter they needed, and why would they want to surround themselves with cloth on such a beautiful night?

She'd wanted a tent for Michael, at least, because of Robbie. Grey had looked appalled at that thought and asked if she wanted him to make peace with the man or insult him. Robbie was a Scot, and a warrior's son to boot. The babe would be fine wrapped up in the warmth of his father's arms for the night.

Grace crawled into her sleeping bag, not even bothering to undress. They were all warriors, she'd discovered. Ian had been her greatest source of information. While they had worked together, she had gently plied him with questions about life eight hundred years ago, and Ian had opened up, telling her about the family he'd lost and about their duties as men in that hard yet wonderful age.

He explained Grey's duties and what being a laird meant. He also explained that stealing a neighbor's cattle—reeving, he had called it—was more a sport than an act of war. True wars rarely happened between clans, but disputes over land or resources or insults were more common.

He told her that women were chattel eight hundred years ago and needed guidance from men. He had quickly added, his face a dull red at the time, that he knew better now, that women were equal partners in life and able to think for themselves.

"Are you sleeping, lass?" came Grey's voice through the side of her tent, sounding as if he was no more than ten inches away from her head.

"No." She smiled up at the ridge pole. "Is everyone gone to bed?"

"Aye. Your brothers have had their fill of beer, and their beds seemed more appealing than a good fight. They've turned in for the night."

"Why haven't you?"

"I have."

"Outside my tent?"

"Less than a foot away, lass. Does that bother you?"

It did, but not in the way he was thinking. She rolled

over so she was facing him through the cloth. "Thank you for letting Michael come tonight."

"Ah, Grace. Never give thanks for something that's not needing it. MacBain's not here as any favor to you on my part. He came because he and Robbie belong here. It's his woman we're all saying goodbye to in the morning. Not one of us can deny him that right."

Grace unzipped the tent and wiggled her head out until she could look up at the stars.

"You'll freeze," he said, trying to push her back in.

"You haven't enough heat for both of us?" She turned to look at him. "I remember when you did once before."

He stopped pushing and pulled instead, until she was curled up beside him. Grace snuggled against him like a spoon and took his arm and wrapped it around her waist, sealing herself in his heat.

"About this spanking thing," she said, deciding to set things straight between them. She was about to say "I do" in just a few hours, and if this little discussion didn't go the way she wanted, she might be saying "I don't" instead.

He nuzzled her ear with his lips. "What about it, lass?" he asked, sending a shiver down the length of her spine, right into the pit of her stomach.

Grace lost her train of thought.

"What about it?" he repeated, sliding his hand between her breasts and pulling her against him.

"Have you ever actually spanked a woman?" she asked, trying to wiggle away from him so her brain would keep functioning.

He let go of her breasts and slid his hand over her slightly protruding belly, pulling her against him and thrusting his hips forward.

"No," he said, his voice lazy, his lips brushing her ear.

She turned to see the glint in his dark, heavy-lidded eyes. "So it's all been bluster?"

"No," he repeated, kissing her lips.

She turned completely around until she was facing him and gave him a good scowl to let him know she wasn't going to be distracted. "You can't spank a woman today," she told him. "You can't even threaten to."

He lifted his head to look down on her. "Not even if she's needing it?"

Her throat tightened. But she was careful not to shout at him. Not with her brothers within earshot. "Needing it?" she repeated.

"Aye," he said, the slash of his grin showing his teeth. "Sometimes it's the only way to end the argument."

Grace forced herself to take a calming breath. He was teasing her. He had to be. "Did your father spank your mother?"

Her question surprised him, and his grin vanished. "No," he said, shaking his head. He suddenly smiled again. "I remember he tried to once."

He rolled onto his back and laced his fingers behind his head, staring up at the sky. Finding herself deprived of his heat, Grace cuddled against him, laid her head on his chest, and wrapped her arms around him.

"She hid his sword," Grey told her, his chest rising with a chuckle. "She didn't want him to go out reeving that night, saying she'd had a premonition that he might not come back."

Grace lifted her head to look at him. "Did he go?"

"Honest to God," he said, shaking his head at the memory. "Mama stood firm and wouldn't give up her hiding place. And Da wasn't about to leave without his sword."

"So he spanked her?" she asked, indignant. The woman had been trying to save her husband's life, and he had spanked her for it?

"He tried." Grey turned to look at her. "He actually sat down and told Mama to lay herself across his knees."

"And did she?"

"Aye," he said, looking back up at the stars, his white teeth gleaming in the moonlight as he grinned. "She walked over and lay on his lap and just stayed there, not saying a word. And Da lifted his hand in the air."

Grace closed her eyes. She could see it all in her mind, a giant warlord with a paw as big as a bear's, about to hit a defenseless woman in anger. "Did she cry?" she asked in a whisper.

Grey suddenly rolled over and pinned her beneath him, brushing the hair from her face, lacing his fingers through her curls, and anchoring her in place.

"Da lowered his arm," he continued, "but gently, until he was cupping her bottom. Without saying a word, he picked Mama up and carried her upstairs. They didn't come down the rest of the night."

"He didn't do it," she said. "And neither will you."

"I'll never hurt you, Grace," he whispered, his lips mere inches from hers. "I'd cut my arm off first."

"Good answer, MacKeage," she said, trying to lift her face up to kiss him.

He wouldn't let go of her hair. "That doesn't give you license to be reckless with my temper, lass," he warned, his eyes glinting with the promise of some other form of retribution.

Grace sighed as deeply as she could, considering she had two hundred pounds of hot, sexy forged steel sprawled on top of her. She had resigned herself to the fact, months ago, that she had fallen in love with a man who saw the world through the eyes of an ancient. She would never change him; you can't change the soul of a warrior.

She could, however, at least enjoy trying.

Grace stretched her arms over her head and wiggled beneath him, hugging him with her knees and lifting her hips against his. His eyes darkened, and his breath caught in the back of his throat.

"Don't do that," he hissed, rolling to the side, his breathing suddenly labored. "If you don't want a bloody brawl to break out, you'll remember your brothers are not ten feet away."

Grace sighed again, more freely now that he wasn't on top of her, keeping her smile to herself. She had a weapon much more effective than his hollow threat to spank her. She mimicked Grey's posture by placing her hands behind her head and looked up at the stars.

"We'll bring our children up here every summer," she said.

"Aye. I'll build us a cabin on West Shoulder," he told her, his voice sounding strained as he fought the passion she had awakened in his body.

"No. I want them to learn to live in God's shelter, not man's. Will you teach them to hunt and fish and run through the forests like you do? And handle a sword? A smaller one," she added, remembering the weight of his.

"Damn right I will."

She wondered what his answer would be if he knew he was having daughters. Grace was unable to keep the question to herself any longer. She needed to know he wouldn't be disappointed.

"Would you be upset if this baby's a girl?" she asked.

"You're wanting a daughter?"

"Of course I do. Every mother wants a daughter. I'm not living in an all-male household for the rest of my life. I have six brothers," she reminded him.

"Okay," he murmured. He laid his hand on her rounding belly. "If you need this one to be a girl, that's fine, lass."

Well, that was also the right answer, for now. But she would wait a few more years yet before telling Grey that none of his children would ever be able to lift his sword.

Chapter Twenty-five

🦌 *even Sutters, four MacKeages,* two MacBains, and Father Daar were all standing on the edge of the meadow high up on TarStone Mountain at daybreak.

Grace couldn't stop smiling, partly because she was so happy to be surrounded by family and friends and to be marrying a Superman, but also because that Superman couldn't stop staring at Father Daar's new cane long enough to repeat his vows.

"Where did that come from?" were the first words out of Grey's mouth when the priest had arrived with the aid of a new, smaller cherrywood cane.

"I made it," Father Daar had said, his wrinkled face lit with amusement.

"I bought you a new cane four months ago," Grey had snapped at the grinning priest. "Where is it?"

"I used it for kindling. It was uncomfortable in my hand."

Grace had gone up and touched Daar's new cane, admiring it. It hadn't hummed or felt warm, it had only felt smooth and delicate. "It's very pretty," she had told him. She'd darted Grey a reassuring smile. "It's not as large as your old one."

The old priest had held it up and fingered the one lonely burl in the wood at the top of the cane. "No, it's not. But then, it's so new, you see," he'd told her, a twinkle in his clear blue eyes, "that it hasn't been properly broken in yet."

She'd been satisfied with his answer, but apparently her almost-husband was not. It was his turn to declare his love and pledge himself to her, but he wasn't paying attention.

"You've changed your mind, then?" she asked, tugging on his sleeve.

"About what?"

"Marrying me."

He looked startled. "Of course not."

"Then say 'I do.'"

"Do what?" he asked, glancing back at Daar's cane.

She walked away, heading down the mountain.

That got his attention.

Grey ran after her. "Wait. Where are you going? I thought we were getting married."

"I've been trying to marry you for the last ten minutes."

"We've started?" he asked, whipping his head around to look back at the assembly of people staring at them.

"It's not a staff, Grey. It's just a new cane. It probably can't even heat a can of soup."

"I don't want anyone having the power to separate us," he told her, his gaze filled with desperate anxiety.

Grace was damn close to crying, she loved this man so much. She reached up and ran her finger down the side of his worried face. "Nothing can ever separate us now, my love. You and I are going to grow old together."

"Have I ever told you that I love you?" he asked, his entire body suddenly relaxing as he realized he believed her.

"Aye," she said, mimicking his brogue, which was more pronounced these days. "Several times a day, without saying a word."

"Are we getting married or not?" Ian asked in a shout of impatience. "The sun's not waiting, people."

They walked back to Father Daar hand in hand, and Grace repeated her vows to Grey. And this time he looked directly at her, his evergreen eyes fierce with possession, and said the words she had been waiting eight hundred years to hear.

Then he kissed her to seal their bond.

"It's time," she whispered to Grey before turning to Samuel. "Mary attended my wedding, and now it's time to give her to TarStone."

Samuel picked up the Oreo cookie tin and traded it to Michael MacBain for Robbie. With unsteady hands, Michael pried off the lid and held it out to each of the brothers, then to each MacKeage and Grace and Grey, and even Father Daar. In turn, each of them pulled a palm full of ash from the tin and waited until everyone carried a part of Mary in his or her hand.

Michael took Robbie back in his arms and smudged a bit of ash on his son's fingers before he took his own handful. They turned in unison, lifted their hands over their heads, and opened their fingers.

The first gentle breeze of summer carried Mary into the meadow with whimsical playfulness, scattering her over the face of TarStone Mountain, taking her home.

Grace watched the ash slowly settle in the ebb of the breeze, now scattered over the meadow like wafted snowflakes. She turned to her brothers. Every one of them had tears in his eyes and a wide grin on his face.

"Happy birthday," she told them.

"We're not doing this for another sixty years," Brian

said, wiping at his face with his sleeve. He pointed at her. "You damn well better take good care of yourself, little sister. Because I'm not doing this again."

She went up and hugged the huge, powerful oil-rig worker. "I promise," she told him.

"Happy birthday," he muttered, hugging her back so fiercely she squeaked.

"It's time for the pancakes," Timmy said, failing miserably at trying to sound cheerful.

"I brought party hats," she told them all, smiling at their groans of dismay. "I found them in the attic last month. Mom never threw anything out."

And that was when the Sutter family taught the MacKeages, Michael MacBain, and their nephew how to celebrate birthdays. They spent the morning eating strawberry pancakes and playing touch football.

The football match became more like a weaponless war of strong-bodied and even stronger-minded men. Not one of them headed down the mountain to continue the celebration with the people of Pine Creek without sporting at least one bruise and a torn piece of clothes. Timmy had a black eye, and Paul sprained his thumb. Morgan was limping, and Ian supported his back with his hands. Callum kept tonguing the cut on his lip until it was so swollen he couldn't speak without slurring his words. Michael didn't have one piece of clothing without a rip in it.

And Grey? Well, Superman had managed to dodge most of the tackles her brothers had tried to land on him, but he probably wouldn't be swinging his sword for the next couple of weeks. Big boy Brian had stepped on Grey's right hand, apologized, and then stepped on his shoulder.

Grace had laughed until tears came to her eyes. You don't grow up in a house with six older brothers without having learned that good-natured violence is a way of life, especially when more testosterone than blood ran in their veins.

And Grace was very glad that some things never changed. That through timeless worlds without end, modern or ancient, men would forever be men.

Epilogue

Grey bent down and kissed his wife on the cheek, then quietly lifted his daughter from her sleeping arms. With her cradled safely in the crook of his elbow, he stared in awe at the tiny six-and-a-half-pound bundle. Barely hour-old crystal-blue eyes stared back at him as he ran his finger gently over her wrinkled pink cheek.

Carefully holding the greatest treasure a man could wish for, Grey carried his daughter over to the crowd of anxious young ladies patiently waiting by the hearth. He sat down in the chair and laid this precious new addition to his family out on his knees for them to see.

"This is Winter," he told them. "Your new sister."

"She's wrinkled," eight-year-old Heather said, carefully pulling back the blankets to see better. "And her eyes are blue, not green like ours."

"She has your mother's eyes."

"She's small," six-year-old Sarah said through her missing front teeth.

"She's been living in a very small place the last nine months," he explained.

"When can we play with her?" Sarah's twin sister, Camry, asked. Camry had only one tooth missing as yet.

The other one was barely hanging on, though, wiggling back and forth when she spoke.

Grey smiled at her expectant look. "Soon. Once she's strong enough to sit up and crawl around."

"Can she talk, Papa?" four-year-old Chelsea asked, pushing her sisters out of the way to see better.

"Not yet," Grey told her with a sigh of relief for that small blessing. There was plenty of nonstop chatter echoing through the halls of Gu Bràth now. "But I'm sure all of you will be teaching her that trick soon enough."

"Can she fwim?" Chelsea's twin sister, Megan, wanted to know, proud of her own newly acquired skill. Grey had been forced to build an indoor pool for his daughters, who complained every autumn when the cold weather arrived and rudely put an end to their swimming for another year.

"We'll teach her in a couple of years," he told Megan. "And then she can join the rest of you in the high pond when you hunt for Daar's cane."

Three-year-old Elizabeth touched Winter's cheek and giggled when the infant turned to root at her finger. Grey leaned back in his chair and watched as his daughters examined and welcomed their newest sister.

Seven girls in eight years. Two set of twins. And every blessed one of the precious, exhausting darlings had been born at Gu Bràth on Winter Solstice, in the same bed where all but Heather had been conceived. Grace had insisted on that trick, much to Grey's dismay. He had argued mightily against it, but his petitions had fallen on deaf ears. They were MacKeages, she had reminded him throughout each pregnancy. They would be born on MacKeage soil.

And they had all learned to swim at an unusually young age, also thanks to his wife's determination. Every summer for the last eight years, they had spent several days camped out at the high mountain meadow, when it was covered in a mantle of blooming forget-me-nots, which shouldn't be growing at all that far up the mountain. Grace insisted it was Mary's doing, since the flowers only grew in that one place where her ashes had been spread.

So every summer Grey had made his growing family of females a camp amongst the forget-me-nots and had taken his daughters over to the high pond where they learned to swim, appreciate nature, and hunt for Daar's magical cane.

That was another strange thing none of them dared comment on. That pond had never frozen over with ice since the day Grey had thrown the old priest's cherrywood staff into it.

Winter stirred on his lap, awkwardly moving her head to see the many young eyes staring back at her. Grey's hands warmed with a vibrant energy, reminding him of the feel of Daar's cane when he'd held it for that brief moment before he banished it forever—he hoped—to the depths of the pond.

He was a rich man, he decided as he looked at all seven of his children, not one blessed son in the lot. Now all he had to do was find them husbands—modern, intelligent, gentle, but strong men who would cherish his daughters without dominating them.

Men also willing to change their names to MacKeage.

Pocket Books
Proudly Presents

Loving the Highlander

Janet Chapman

AVAILABLE IN PAPERBACK
MAY 2003
FROM POCKET BOOKS

Turn the page for a preview of
Loving the Highlander . . .

$\mathcal{S}$*adie Quill was still in awe of her luck.* She was actually being paid to do what she loved most—hike and kayak through the beautiful forest of Maine. She'd gladly given up her job as a meteorologist in Boston to return to Pine Creek and the mountains she'd grown up in to map out landmarks for a proposal for a park. These last ten weeks had been a pleasant dream she never wanted to wake up from.

Well, most of the job had been a dream, except that some of her work was being sabotaged. But having her trail markers stolen was more of a nuisance than a setback. The orange ribbons were nothing more than a visible tool for her project. She had the coordinates written on the large wall map back at her cabin, and she could map them into her GPS to find the trails whenever she wanted.

Now she was cataloging the flora and fauna of the valley, noting in her journal points of interest and areas of animal activity that future hikers would want to see.

Sadie stifled a chuckle and raised her camera, pointing the long lens through the honeysuckle bush where she hid on the shore of a small lake. The scene unfolding before her was priceless, and exactly why she loved her job so much.

At the urging of its mother, a young moose stepped into the shallow water of the protected cove. Sadie depressed the shutter on her camera, captured the shot, and advanced the film. No noise betrayed her position, thanks to her father's ingenious skill in making the mechanics of the camera silent.

She and her dad had walked these woods for years, taking pictures as she was now, and Sadie's heart ached with sadness that he was not here with her today. It had been Frank Quill who taught Sadie the fine art of moving silently among the animals, and had instilled in her not only an appreciation of nature, but a respect for it as well. And now she was thanking him by the only means she could find, by helping to build a park in his memory.

The mother moose suddenly lifted her head and looked toward the open water of the lake. Sadie used the telephoto lens of her camera to scan across the calm lake surface. And there, on the opposite shore, she saw the movement.

Something was swimming toward them.

Sadie leaned forward to get a better view. The mother moose heard her, whipped her head around and stared directly at Sadie. For a moment, their eyes locked.

There wasn't much in these woods that worried a full-grown moose, but a mother had to be more cautious of the vulnerability of her calf. Sadie's presence and whatever was swimming toward them was apparently more than the mother moose was willing to deal with. She gave a low grunt of warning and stepped out of the lake, pushing her baby ahead of her.

With a sigh of regret for scaring the moose, Sadie turned her attention back to the lake. Whatever was swimming towards her was too small to be another moose and too large to be a muskrat or otter. Sadie sharpened the focus on her lens and watched, until finally she saw the rise and fall of arms cutting a path through the water.

Arms? There was a person swimming across the lake?

Sadie settled herself deeper into the bushes, making sure she was well-hidden as he moved ever closer. Yes, she could see now that the swimmer was male. And that he had broad shoulders, long, powerful arms, and a stroke that cut through the water with amazing ease. The swimmer moved with lazy, rhythmic grace, right up to one of the boulders in the cove Sadie was hiding in. He placed two large hands on the rock and pulled himself out of the water in one powerful, seamless motion.

Sadie blinked.

She tore her eye away from the viewfinder. She didn't need the vivid clarity of the telephoto lens to see that the man was naked.

She looked through her camera again and adjusted the focus. Yup, as naked as the day he was born. He sat on the boulder, brushing the hair from his face and wringing the shoulder-length mane out in a ponytail at his back.

Well, heck. The guy's hair was almost as long as hers. Sadie pushed the zoom on her lens closer, aiming it at the top half of the man. She almost dropped the camera when he came into focus. He was huge, and it wasn't an illusion of the lens, either. His brawny shoulders filled the viewfinder, and when he lifted both hands to push the water away from his forehead again, his chest expanded to Herculean proportions.

Sadie noticed then that the guy wasn't even winded from his swim. His broad and powerfully muscled chest—which was covered with a luxurious mat of slick, dark blond hair—rose and fell with the steady rhythm of someone who had merely walked up a short flight of stairs.

Who was this demigod of the woods?

Sadie zoomed the lens of her camera even closer, on his face. She didn't recognize him from town. She'd only been back in the Pine Creek area for a few months now, and had only gone into town six or seven times for supplies since returning, but she would have remembered such a ruggedly handsome face on a man his size. She definitely would have remembered such startling green eyes framed by such a drop-dead gorgeous face. His jaw, darkened with a couple-day's growth of beard, was square, stern, and stubborn looking. His neck was thick, with a leather cord around it that dangled an odd-shaped ball of some sort over his chest.

Sadie zoomed the lens out again until his entire body filled her viewfinder. His stomach was flat and contoured with muscle. He had long, powerful looking thighs, bulging calves, and even his feet looked strong. He was turned away just enough that his modesty was barely intact.

It wasn't every day she was treated to such an exhibit of pure unadulterated maleness. And despite her own sense of shame for being a blatant voyeur, Sadie wished he would turn just a bit more toward her. She was curious, dammit, and made no apology for it.

She liked men. Especially big ones like this guy. Sadie was six-foot-one in her stocking feet, and she usually spent most of her time talking to the receding hairline of the men she knew. Since she had hit puberty and shot up like a weed, Sadie wished she were short. Like the heroines in the romance novels she loved to read, she wanted to be spunky, beautiful, and petite. And she was tired of falling short of the three by at least two of those traits.

About all Sadie could say for herself was that she did possess a healthy dose of spunk. She may have come close to beauty once, but a deadly house-fire eight years ago had ended that promise. And no matter how much she had willed it, she hadn't stopped growing until her twenty-third birthday.

She was taller than most men she met, and every bit of her height was in the over-long inseam of her jeans.

She'd bet her boots that the guy on the rock had at least a thirty-six inseam, and that he wore a triple-extra-large shirt he had to buy from the tall rack.

The vision in her viewfinder suddenly began to fade, and Sadie had a moment's regret that it had all been a dream.

Until she realized that the viewfinder had fogged up.

Well, she did feel unusually warm. And she was breathing a bit harder than normal.

Wow. Either she was having a guilt attack for being a Peeping Tom, or she was experiencing a fine little case of lust.

Sadie didn't care which it was, she wasn't stopping. She used the back of her gloved right hand to wipe the viewfinder dry before she looked through it again.

The man was now laid out on the boulder, his arms folded under his head and his eyes closed to the sun as he basked in its warmth like an overfed bear.

Sadie suddenly remembered that she was looking through the lens of a camera. If this guy was willing to parade around the forest naked why should she feel guilty about a couple of pictures? She just wondered where in her journal of fauna she should place his photo.

Probably at the top of the food chain.

Feeling pretty sure that the man had fallen asleep, Sadie snapped the shutter on her camera and quickly advanced the film. She zoomed in the lens and snapped it again.

But just as she advanced the film for another picture the man leapt to his feet in an unbelievable blur of motion. And suddenly he was looking directly at the bushes where she hid.

Dammit. He couldn't have heard that. Animals couldn't hear the damn thing, and their lives depended on their ears.

Sadie sucked in her breath and held it; she wasn't sure if she was doing so from fright, or from the fact that she now had a full frontal view of the man.

She snapped the shutter down one last time and scurried backward to free herself from the bush. She foolishly stood up, then immediately realized her mistake when she found herself face to face with the giant, with only a hundred yards of water between them.

She couldn't move. He was magnificent, standing there like a demigod, his penetrating stare rooting her feet into place.

"Come on, Quill," she whispered, her gaze still locked with his. "Move while you still have the advantage."

He must have heard that, too, because he went into action before she did. He dove into the water and began swimming toward her.

Freed from his flint-green stare, Sadie snatched up her backpack and headed into the forest. She broke into a run as soon as she hit the overgrown trail and set a fast, steady pace toward home.

She grinned as the forest blurred past.

The swimmer didn't stand a chance of catching her. He had to get to shore first and then find the trail as well as the direction she had taken. Sadie's long legs ate up the ground with effortless ease, and she actually laughed out loud at the rush of adrenaline pumping through her veins.

This was her strength; there were very few people she couldn't outrun. Especially a barefooted streaker that looked like he outweighed her by a good sixty pounds. It took a lot of energy to move that much weight through the winding trail, ducking and darting around branches and over fallen logs.

Yes, her long legs would give her the edge this time, rescuing her from the folly of trespassing on a stranger's right to privacy.

Sadie slowed down after a while, but she didn't quite have the courage to stop yet. Only a maniac would have followed her, but then only a maniac would be swimming naked in a cold-water lake.

So Sadie kept running, easing her pace to a jog.

Until she heard a branch snap behind her.

She looked over her shoulder and would have screamed if she could have. The man from the lake was fifty feet behind her. Sadie turned back to watch where she was going, the adrenaline spiking back into her bloodstream.

There was nothing like seeing a fully naked, wild-haired, wild-eyed madman on her heels to make a girl wish she had stayed in bed that morning. Sadie ran as if the devil himself was chasing her. She could actually hear the pounding of his feet behind her now; could practically feel his breath on the back of her neck.

She grabbed a small cedar tree to pivot around a corner, and that was when he caught her, hitting her broadside in a full body tackle. Sadie wanted to scream then too, but he knocked what little air she had left out of her body. They rolled several times, and Sadie swung her camera at his head. He grunted in surprise from the blow, and grabbed her flailing arms as they continued to roll.

When they finally stopped he was on top of her . . . and her wrists were being held over her head . . . and her back was being crushed into the ground . . . and she had never been so scared in her life.

Sadie thought about really screaming now, but her throat closed tight. She pushed at the ground and tried to buck the man off of her. At the same time she lashed out with her feet.

That was when he shifted from sitting on her to laying on her, trapping her legs with his own.

Sadie instantly stilled. This was going from bad to worse; she now had a naked madman on top of her— and she was wearing shorts.

Oh, God. Now that she had such a close and personal look at him, he was no longer a demigod. He was a full-blown god, Adonis or Atlas, maybe. Heck. His broad shoulders and amazingly wide chest blocked out the light. His warm breath feathered over her face. Sadie could feel every inch of his long, muscled legs running the length of hers. And she could feel something . . . something else touching her bare thigh. He was excited, either from the thrill of the chase, their suggestive position, or the anticipation of what he was planning to do. Sadie didn't want to scream anymore. She wanted to faint.

She did close her eyes, so she wouldn't have to look at his triumphant, lethal looking, very male face.

Why didn't he say something?

Sadie opened her eyes to find him staring at her hands, which he still held firmly over her head. Sadie immediately opened her bare left hand and let the camera fall onto the ground.

Still, he kept staring over her head.

He reached up and tugged at the glove on her right hand. Sadie closed it into a fist. Momentarily deterred from his task, he turned his attention back to her face.

She turned her head away.

He pulled her chin back to face him, then gently ran his thumb along her bottom lip, watching it as if fascinated.

Lord save her. This gorgeous, naked man was going to kiss her.

His finger trailed down her face, over her chin, to her neck, and Sadie felt him touch the opening of her blouse. She twisted frantically and tried to bite the arm holding her hands over her head.

He lowered the full force of his weight onto her then, and Sadie fought to breathe. Well, heck. She hadn't realized he'd been holding himself off her before. She stilled, and he lifted himself slightly, allowing her to gasp for air.

Their gazes locked.

His long blond hair dripped lake water on her chin and throat. The heavy object dangling from his neck nestled against her breasts, causing a disturbing sensation to course all the way down to the pit of her stomach. Sadie could feel her clothes slowly sopping up his sweat, his hairy legs abrasive against hers, his chest pushing into her with every breath he took. The heat from his body scorched her to the point that she couldn't work up enough moisture in her mouth to speak.

Not that she could think of anything to say.

The silent brute leaned forward and Sadie froze in anticipation of his kiss, but he only picked up her camera. He obviously knew how it worked, because he carefully lifted the rewind and popped it open. He was not so gentle however, when he ripped the film from it. He tossed the exposed film and the camera on the ground beside them.

He opened her pack next, spilling the contents on

the ground. He poked around in the mess he'd made and found her GPS. He turned it over, pushed several buttons, and tossed it back on the ground. He picked up her cell phone, flipped it open, then discarded it like trash to the ground.

And then he picked up the small roll of duct tape she used for emergency repairs.

Now Sadie had heard that victims were often killed with their own guns. She suddenly understood that concept when the man freed a length of her own tape and grabbed her wrists to tape them together. He then slid down her body and started to take hold of her legs.

Sadie kicked him hard enough in the stomach that he grunted, then she rolled and scrambled up to run. She didn't even make it past her camera before he grabbed her by the ankles and pushed her back to the ground, on her stomach this time. Sadie looked over her shoulder as he wrapped duct tape around her legs.

The damn crazy man was grinning again.

She kicked out at him again with her bound feet.

Sadie flinched when the brute gave a sharp whistle. She snapped her head around to see what he was doing.

Was he calling a friend?

Sadie looked at the scattered contents of her pack. Where was her knife? She needed something, a weapon, to defend herself. She checked to see that he was still looking off into the forest, watching for someone, while she rolled toward a group of young pine trees. She found a lower limb devoid of bark and wiggled to sit up beside it. She looked up at the man again, only to find him looking over his shoulder at her, still grinning, not at all worried she would get far being trussed up like a turkey ready for cooking.

But this turkey was not going into the pot without a fight.

Visit the
Simon & Schuster Web site:
www.SimonSays.com

and sign up for our
mystery e-mail updates!

Keep up on the latest
new releases, author appearances,
news, chats, special offers, and more!
We'll deliver the information
right to your inbox — if it's new,
you'll know about it.